The Training House

The Training House

Eden Bradley

The Training House

Copyright © 2016 by Eden Bradley
Cover by: Scott Carpenter
Edited by: D.S. Editing

All rights reserved. Without limiting the rights under copyright reserved above, no part of this publication may be reproduced, stored in or introduced into a retrieval system, or transmitted, in any form, or by any means (electronic, mechanical, photocopying, recording, or otherwise) without the prior written permission of both the copyright owner and the above publisher of this book.

This is a work of fiction. Names, characters, places, brands, media, and incidents are either the product of the author's imagination or are used fictitiously. The author acknowledges the trademarked status and trademark owners of various products referenced in this work of fiction, which have been used without permission. The publication/use of these trademarks is not authorized, associated with, or sponsored by the trademark owners.

ISBN-13: 978-1537309255
ISBN-10: 1-537309250

www.EdenBradley.com
Email: eden-bradley@yahoo.com
Follow Eden on Facebook or Twitter!

Printed in U.S.A

DEDICATION

These stories are truly the books of my heart—even more so because of the amazing people who supported and inspired me through this process.

First, I must thank the incredible Robin L. Rotham, author and critique partner extraordinaire. You held my hand through these stories, encouraging me to go deeper, particularly with MASTER, which absolutely could not have been written without you. Thank you for your endless patience, your wise guidance, and your own writing talent, which helped me to grow and blossom as an author in the process. You are the bomb!

I also have to thank my dear friend Dawn Vaeoso. Your enthusiastic (or should we say giddy?) encouragement to push boundaries, to explore those dark, nearly unspeakable places, made these books what they were meant to be—and it wasn't only the pony play scenes, although I did write those just for you!

Lastly, but never least, are my wonderful readers, who dared to take a chance on these very hard-core stories, allowing me to challenge them, and myself. I adore you all!

THE TRAINING HOUSE Series is Eden's hardest-core BDSM yet! More 'erotica' than 'erotic romance', there will nevertheless be a love story woven throughout these *very* kinky pages.

WARNING:

These books contain material that may be difficult to read about and/or cause triggers for some readers. Do NOT try this at home!

TABLE OF CONTENTS

THE TRAINING HOUSE CONTRACT.................. 7

GIRL.. 11

BOY.. 95

MASTER.. 185

ABOUT EDEN.................... 288

THE TRAINING HOUSE

Contract and Terms of Agreement for Servitude

I, _____, being of sound mind and body, do hereby agree and pledge myself in entirety as personal slave and property to The Training House as the Master of the House sees fit to use for a period of one year, to commence on _____ and to end on _____. I do this without reservations or stipulations, and without recourse or right of revocation. I have been informed and understand that I will not be harmed or have any permanent damage done to my body or mental well-being, nor shall any of my personal property be subject to ownership or use by The Training House, its Master, or any associates. I pledge under the terms of this contract my body, my obedience and my deep desire to serve.

I understand and agree to all terms within this contract. Terms are as follows:

1) I will remain naked while within The Training House or other outside facilities the Master of the House may visit or send me to.

2) I may be sent to outside locations and/or lent to other Masters, Mistresses or Trainers at the Master's

discretion. I pledge the same obedience to them as I do to The Training House under the terms of this contract.

3) I will be collared, cuffed, shackled or bound by any variety of means as the Master of the House or his associates see fit. Restraints will always be used in a safe manner.

4) I may be subject to piercings of the nipples and/or genitalia, to be performed only by a licensed piercer, including the Master himself.

5) I will be subject to branding with the house crest only if it is agreed upon by both parties at the term of this contract or any future existing contract that I remain in permanent service to The Training House.

6) I will be subject to sadomasochistic activities at the discretion of the Master and his associates, including various types of impact, impalement and use of any orifice for pain or pleasure, electrical stimulation, canes, whips, and implements which may scratch and/or open the skin. Any bleeding, open wounds or heavy bruising will receive appropriate medical attention by the House nurse or attending EMT.

7) I will be subject to humiliation, degradation, loss of personal identity.

8) I will have no rights as an individual, or freedom to make decisions.

9) I will remain silent unless commanded to speak.

10) I will accept without question or resistance any and all punishments or discipline the Master of the House or his associates deems necessary or desirable.

11) I am charged to learn all the ways in which I may please the Master of the House and his associates.

12) I will have no control over my orgasms, which will be given or denied at the whim of the Master of the House or his associates. I agree to never pleasure myself, saving my pleasure for the Master's use.

I hereby certify that I am in excellent health, and had my last medical exam on _____. Paperwork to verify the state of my health will be supplied upon signing this contract. I furthermore agree that I may be subject to medical examination and treatment for my safety and for the safety of those I come into contact with, or purely for the Master's pleasure. I also have supplied information regarding possible personal triggers any of the above activities might prompt. The Master agrees to ensure my body is kept in good health by means of diet, rest and exercise.

If at any time before the end of the contracted period the Master of The Training House is not pleased with my performance, obedience, ability to give pleasure or to endure his preferred treatment of me, he may decide to revoke this agreement, at which time I am released from the terms of this contract.

I affix my signature willingly and without any duress or under any threat of harm.

_____   _____

Slave's legal name   Slave's signature

_____
Date

_____   _____

Master's legal name   Master's signature

_____
Date

_____   _____

Witness   Witness signature

_____
Date

Girl

CHAPTER ONE

He walks into the room and I don't know where to look, what to do with my hands, what to say. Of course, I'm not supposed to say anything, am I? But even if I could—even if I dared—he is simply too overwhelmingly beautiful.

I didn't expect it—didn't expect *him*. My bare feet shift on the soft Persian rug, the wood floor beneath creaking like a quiet sigh of pleasure. Taking in a quick, gasping breath, I inhale the scents of aged wood and plaster, the papery smell these old San Francisco Victorians have. Scent and sound were all I knew until a moment ago, when someone removed the blindfold from my eyes. I know the city I'm in, but not where, exactly. I am not supposed to know. And now I know what the man I have been sold to looks like. My new Master. The man I would have served with deep devotion simply because he owns me, because this servitude is what I want—what I need—but who now is making me dizzy with indescribable lust and expectation.

He must be six-foot-four, with broad shoulders under a dark blue button-down shirt. European tailoring—the shirt fits his shoulders and his narrow waist too perfectly to be anything else, which I recognize right away from my time in Italy, Spain and London with my previous owner. A small stabbing ache in my chest at that thought, but I focus on the shirt, on the man before me, and the pain drifts, fades away.

His sleeves are rolled up, revealing strong forearms. There is a tattoo of a Japanese style dragon curling around his right arm—a symbol of power, which suddenly, inexplicably, seems funny to me, if only because this man's power seeps from every pore and needs no sign of proof. I let out a small, stupid giggle. Unable to help it. Helpless. Perhaps that's why the giggle.

Helpless. Yes.

Or perhaps because the giggle is more from relief, the knowledge that my desire for pain, for punishment, will soon be sated.

He raises one dark brow over eyes that gleam like pure, blue fire in the dim light of the room. His voice is a low threat. Upper class American accent. "You find me amusing, girl?"

Girl. Is that to be my name in this place? Not Aimée? Why does that frighten me so when this is everything I've asked for? To be rendered invisible in a way *I* choose.

A flash of my father, his back turned to me. How many times did that actually happen, and how much of it is purely symbolic, when in fact, I hardly ever saw him? But I don't want to think of all that now. I am here to forget. To forget my past. To forget myself. To immerse myself in this powerlessness that is of my choosing.

Still, it occurs to me for one moment, sharp with the edge of panic, that maybe I should have read the contract more carefully before I signed it.

"Speak up," he demands.

"No, Sir."

"Nerves?" There's a long pause—long enough to make me feel the truth of what he's suggested down to my toes, in my belly, in those dark, dark recesses of my mind that brought me here to begin with.

"Of course you're nervous," he goes on. "If you weren't I'd send you back. I don't take foolish girls. I don't take a lot of things, but you'll find out about that soon enough." He steps closer and even his earthy, spicy, elegant scent frightens me, partly because he smells so good I want to drop to my knees before him—*need* to—which scares me half to death. "What I will take…is you. Whenever I want. I will do whatever I want to you. And any time you doubt why you're here I will find a way to remind you. I will remind you through pain. Through denial. Through darkness. I will remind you by giving you exactly what you asked for when you agreed to come to my house. The Training House never fails its…victims."

I'm shaking now, my legs trembling so hard they're about to go out from under me, and then I will be on my knees, like it or not. I *will* like it, which I already know. I am also drenched with desire, my pussy slick and pulsing, which should not be surprising, but it is. Every single detail about this moment is shocking to me.

He steps closer and I look up at his face, knowing this may be the last opportunity I'm allowed. And God, his eyes are so, so blue—midnight blue, eyes like I've never seen before. His hair is dark and the slightest bit unruly. His jaw and cheekbones are sharply cut, as if from stone, and his mouth is both lush and cruel. I want to touch it, with just my fingertip. I don't dare even think of kissing him. Oh, but I am a liar; I *do* think of kissing him. I think of that mouth between my thighs.

Neither of those things is likely to happen in this place.

Torture.

Torture already, and I've just gotten here.

He strokes one fingertip along my jaw and I swear I could almost come. He slides that fingertip down, across my throat, which he grabs with his big hand and squeezes until I gasp as he takes me down to the floor. I am on my hands and knees, then elbows and knees as he slides his hand to the back of my neck, allowing me to breathe but pressing my face into the carpet. It smells like wool and despair. It smells like long-forgotten perfume and my fondest fantasies fulfilled. I don't know what to think.

He will tell you what to think.

Yes. My body goes loose, giving itself over to him. To submission in the purest form I have ever experienced. All of the Dominants I've played with at the kink clubs, all of the lovers who have tied me up, spanked me, fucked me too hard, even my Master who decided to let me go, to offer me up to this place, disappear in the wake of this man who gets power play in a way I've never felt before.

Oh yes. This is where I need to be. At his feet. In his house.

Under his hands. He has reminded me.

He kicks my thighs apart and I feel completely exposed. I know I am, that he can see everything—every small, pink curve and valley of swollen flesh. It makes me feel beautiful. It makes me afraid. But before I have even two breaths to think about it, he thrusts his fingers into me and I'm biting down hard on my lip not to writhe, not to cry out. He does something with his hand inside me—I can't even begin to describe what it is—but desire is like a knife, cutting into my cunt… No. It's inside me, everywhere at once. Pleasure and pleasure and some pain too, but I welcome it. Suddenly he adds another finger—a third or a fourth…I don't know—and pumps me so hard it rocks my entire body, and I feel pressure building, building, then I scream as liquid gushes from me. Oh God, someone please tell me I didn't just urinate all over the man who is to be my Master here!

He starts again, his fingers making that odd motion, that strange sort of snapping thing inside me, against my g-spot. This time I focus on the pressure as it builds. He fucks me hard and fast with his hand, hard and hurting, except that it's so good… excruciating, and I am screaming again, and oh God…

"Again," he demands.

Once more he strokes and snaps at my g-spot, and I really am hurting now, but I can't stop as I gush again, even more this time, and it's like coming, yet it's different and I am already addicted.

He doesn't say a word as he starts again. The breath absolutely leaves my body as I scream as hard as I come, or whatever it is that's happening to me. I crumple, panting, onto the floor.

With hard hands he yanks me back up onto my knees, drags me across the rug until I am kneeling in front of him, between his knees as he sits in a chair. He grabs the back of my long, red hair in a tight fist, pulling my face toward his, and instead of yelling as I expect, he pauses, looking at me, and I am lost in the blue of his eyes, in trying to memorize his every feature. Then, to my utter surprise, he kisses my cheek, my jawline, then my cheek again. He pulls back, his gaze on mine, burning suddenly, then shadowed, and whatever was going on with him is gone, and he is closed and harsh again. He pulls my hair so hard I nearly scream from that alone. I love having my hair pulled, but this is brutal. I love it — and him, for doing this to me — even more. For the pulling. For the kisses. For whatever I saw in his eyes.

"Squirt for me again," he demands, his voice low and dangerous as he impales me once more with his lovely, punishing fingers.

I whimper as he fucks me savagely, and it is mere seconds before I gush all over his shoes, the beautiful rug, my own thighs. He doesn't even pause this time before doing it again once more. And God, it feels better than anything ever has in my life, and I don't think I can take it anymore.

Tears pool in my eyes, pour down my cheeks as he makes me do it over and over again. Over and over until my screams turn to guttural groans and whimpers. Finally I slip onto the wet floor, crying in earnest, unable to move. He sits quietly, watching me, I think. Then he gets up and moves away from me. I hear sounds I can't identify at first, but which I come to recognize as ice tinkling in a crystal glass. He is to have a nice drink while watching me cry on the floor. Oh yes, he knows exactly what he's doing.

The crying has mostly stopped, but I'm still hiccupping. Exhausted. He moves closer, until he's bent over me. I don't know what to expect, which is clearly the idea, of course, and I have to order myself not to flinch as he reaches for me. When he touches a finger to my lips, I know to open for him. He thrusts into my mouth and I suck, wishing it were his cock, knowing I may never be fortunate enough to service him, this man I want so badly, want so much to serve it's like an ache in my stomach.

He slides his finger in, then out, slowly, sensually, and I lose myself in sucking him, sucking exactly as I would if I had his cock in my mouth, tasting my tears that are apparently still falling.

Oh yes...

His finger slips out, leaving me empty as his hand goes to my hair again and he yanks me to my feet.

The door opens. Blinking, I try to clear my vision, but everything is a blur of tears and whatever it was he just did to me.

Two women stand in the doorway. Both are as naked as I

am except for the shining steel collars around their necks. They are a matched pair of tall brunettes, both shaved clean and with pierced nipples. Both wear a small brand of a fleur-de-lis over their left breasts I recognize as the house crest, which makes me shiver, but whether with desire or fear I don't know.

"Intake," he tells the girls. "You know what to do."

"Yes, Master," they answer in unison, like pretty little robots. Pretty little robots that I want to become.

I am so filled with envy I can hardly stand it. And in fact, I can hardly stand. But the matched brunette slaves take one arm each and half drag, half carry me down a series of narrow hallways until we reach what I think is the back of the big Victorian house. We go through a door into a small room.

Even in my dazed state I see that it's spare, with nothing but a lovely, old-fashioned porcelain tub in the middle of the room, a pallet done up in white sheets on the hardwood floor in one corner and a bucket—a bucket!—in another.

They lay me down on the pallet, and the tears have started again. One of them holds out a bottle of water.

"Drink this," she says. "All of it."

I prop myself up on an elbow and drink half the bottle down. The water is cool. I didn't realize how thirsty I was, how sore my throat is from screaming.

"Finish it," the same girl says.

I nod, wipe my mouth with the back of my arm, take a few more sips, wipe my mouth again, then my eyes.

"What's your name?" I ask the one closest.

"Girl," they both answer, the robots again.

I shake my head. "Girl?"

"Just drink your water. This one too." She pushes another bottle toward me. "You'll know what to do with the bucket. Otherwise, rest. You're going to need it. Someone will bring some food to you eventually."

My head is spinning as they leave, shutting the lights off before they go. I am in complete darkness other than the very dim light coming through the heavy damask curtains over the single window. But there is also an enormous amount of relief at her words. Instructions. This I can do—give myself over to this place where I don't have to make decisions. Where someone else will tell me even when to drink, when to eat. When to come.

This is exactly what I asked for, to such a degree I may never have asked if I'd known this were even possible. To be rendered so completely invisible, even as I am seen, touched, hurt. To experience those extremes of sensation, both pleasure and pain, in a way that makes it safe for me to *feel*, because I'm no good at doing that on my own. I never have been. No, it's the restrictions and rules and expectations in being a slave that allow me to. It's the only safety I have ever truly had. I'm shaking again, but it's need coursing through my body — need and the relief making me go weak all over.

I cannot believe I get to do this. I cannot believe I have to do this. There is nothing I can do to get out of this.

I breathe a sigh and repeat those lovely, luscious words, whispering them quietly in the dark.

"There is nothing I can do to get out of this."

I slept. I only know this because suddenly I am awakened by rough hands on me, pulling me upright, then shoving me down onto the mattress and flipping me onto my stomach. A big hand on the small of my back holds me down hard.

I hear a voice — a male voice. Him! He says, "Hold her still."

Smaller female hands on my body: on the back of my head shoving my face into my white pallet, on my ankles, pulling my legs wide. I want to scream but I swallow it down. I'm sure he'll give me more reason to scream if I only wait. And I do. Helplessly. I can hear them breathing in the still air. Waiting.

The waiting goes on for such a long time I begin to wonder if this is all he will do to me. And the longer it continues the more I have to struggle to hold still, until I'm shaking with the effort.

Finally one finger strokes down my spine, slowly, gently.

"Do you want this, Girl?" he asks me.

My last Master would often ask me the same thing, and the answer was always yes, because it was never enough with him. He could never play me hard enough, even when his beatings drew blood, leaving me bruised for weeks. He could never be quite strict enough — not in the harsh way I yearned for. And the answer is still yes, even in this frightening place. But I don't know if am to answer at all, so I stay quiet. Shaking. I can barely feel the other girl's hands on me any longer.

"It doesn't matter, you know," he says quietly.

His fingers impale me so quickly my teeth rattle, and the pain spears through my body like a knife, I am so sore from before. But it doesn't matter, none of it does. Only the pain and the desire and his hand fucking me hard and fast. Harder as he adds fingers, filling me up. I am so wet, needing to come, but there is no relief—only this rapid fucking, his evil fingers so deep in my pussy I think he may have gone in up to his wrist.

When he spreads the cheeks of my ass and presses a finger into my anus I exhale, a long breath that is perhaps more a sighing gasp. He doesn't wait for me to try to relax, which is impossible in any case, before he pushes the finger in, ramming it deep.

I cry out, but it doesn't matter. God, how often will I be reminded of that? It doesn't matter that he is hurting me, except that I crave it. Love it. Love him already in the way I do anyone who takes my power from me as his wicked hands fuck me harder, as he adds another finger to my ass, opens both fingers them wide in order to fill my ass as much as my cunt.

I am burning. Need and fear and surrender washing over me in intoxicating waves. When his hand deep in my pussy stills and he thrusts viciously into my ass, I come, a sobbing cry on my lips, my body twisting in ecstasy, the girls holding me tight. And I need it. I need them to hold me down. To keep me safe in their grip so I won't lose myself. Or so that I will. I don't know anymore.

His hands slip from me before I'm done coming, leaving me not quite sated. Bereft. The girls let me go and they all leave the room. I hear the door close, the *snick* of the lock. Not that they need to lock me in. I am a good girl, mostly. But knowing I'm locked up in here really does something to my head.

Rolling onto my back on my pallet on the floor, I pull in one sharp breath after another. I whisper into the dark, "This is really happening."

I stare up toward the ceiling, and maybe my eyes have adjusted, because I think I can make out the light fixture up there. But there is nothing else to discover in this room, other than what I will discover about myself.

I lie there for some time, thinking sleep will take me at any moment, but it eludes me. Instead my mind is filled with reflection. Memory.

"The Training House is where you need to be, Aimée. It will be good for you. I can never hope to achieve what I want for you if I keep you with me."

"Please, Graham, Sir. Don't let me go."

I bury my face in his lap, kneeling on the floor in front of him in his cold London flat, tears running down my face.

He lifts my chin, forcing me to look up at him. "You have been with me for a year, pet. You know I never expected to keep you. I never expected to want to. But I must let you go because I want you for myself. Too much. I will not be so selfish with you when I can't give you what you need. This is simply beyond my scope. My resources. You need to be under harsher hands. You need a Master who excels in mind fuck perhaps more than you require anything else. This is the only way you will be able to truly let go."

I continue to cry but my tears do no good. His hand on my chin grips a bit harder.

"You yourself have asked me to send you someplace where you would be worked very hard. Relentlessly."

"That was months ago," I argue.

"You never stopped needing it," he says quietly. He lets my face go and gets to his feet. "It's all arranged. There is paperwork in my study. Go upstairs. Read it. Sign it if you will. But even if you decide not to go, you can't stay here with me any longer. I've taught you everything I can and your time with me must be done. You know this is the right thing for you, Aimée."

My heart shatters as he walks toward the door. But even as it does, I know he speaks the truth. I do want more – my body, my very being, yearns for the stark, brutal training in a way that has made me feel fragile lately, as if my skin has stretched too much to accommodate the need. I have to go.

A small pain forms in my stomach when I think of Master

Graham, like a tiny knot made of barbed wire. I *had* loved him, in my own way. I always loved — at least a little bit — those who dominated me and did it well, but I'd never spent that kind of concentrated time with any of the others. And now there is *him*. The new Master. I know already I'll fall hard for him, as hard as he will work me.

Oh yes.

This is part of what I crave — to love my Masters so heedlessly, so completely, that it frees me to give myself permission to do these perverted, forbidden things. Dangerous things, as my poor, hurting cunt and ass can attest to. And I know it's only beginning, that today has been nothing but a small taste of what is to come. And I rather love that I have absolutely no idea of what might happen to me. I've signed myself over, body and soul, like a pact with the Devil himself.

The thought makes me smile as I turn onto my side, curling into a ball.

I am in the Devil's house. I am exactly where I want to be.

I curl my fingers into the sheets beneath me, the only thing I have to hold onto. And happier than I've been in a long time — maybe ever — I close my eyes and drift into sleep once more.

CHAPTER TWO

When the door bangs open and I'm startled awake, there is light coming through the curtains. I must have slept through the night. One of the brunette slaves comes in with a tray. She sets it on the floor beside me, but as I reach for the steaming cup of tea she smacks my hand away.

"Bucket first, then food."

"Oh, I..." I don't know what to say about the damn bucket, even though my bladder is full.

"You didn't use it last night?" Her voice is harsh. "Get up. Pee. Now."

"But how?"

She purses her lips, then goes to the bucket and demonstrates, squatting over the bucket, facing the wall, her hands braced there. Then she stands and turns to me. "You'll get used to it. You'll get used to everything. Well...maybe not everything."

I straddle the bucket the way she's shown me, but my body seizes up. "I don't think I can."

"You'd better figure it out. He'll make you do it in front of him, you know."

"Oh God."

She laughs. "If peeing in front of the Master is the thing you're worried about, your priorities are in the wrong place. You have a lot more to worry about, trust me. Just go. And hurry it up. I only have so much time before they'll expect me to take your breakfast tray downstairs."

I sigh, but close my eyes and concentrate, my fingers scrabbling at the wall for balance. Finally my body lets go.

There's a small, wicked smile on her face as she watches me struggle to hold myself up, to pee into the bucket and not onto the shining hardwood floor. I can't imagine what they'd do to me if I peed on the floor. But it's such a relief, and I can't stop. It feels as if it goes on forever, my bladder emptying, the splash as it hits the bucket. When I'm done I go to stand up, then look wildly around.

"Toilet paper is next to your foot, Girl."

"Oh."

I wipe myself carefully. I'm still sore and raw, but even touching myself to wipe makes me shiver with desire. It's something about being here, in the Training House. And maybe even more about having seen what the Master looks like. *Smells* like. The way he abuses me with his big, beautifully made hands.

"Come and eat before it gets cold," the Girl says. "It doesn't do to insult Cook's efforts."

She holds out a bottle as I move back toward my rumpled white pallet. When I raise my brows in question, she says, "Hand sanitizer. Keep it next to the bucket."

I nod. "Thank you. Is it…am I supposed to talk to you? I don't want to be rude. I don't want to break the rules."

"You can talk to me or my sister when we're alone. Well, to me, mostly. I'm sure you know to speak to the Master only when spoken to. The same for any of his guests, or staff like Cook and Robert, the valet. If you didn't understand that, you would never have been referred here."

"Yes, of course. Your sister?"

Picking up the steaming cup, I hold it between my hands for a moment, then make myself wait to feel its heat on my tongue while I add milk. I sip carefully and it scalds a little, but it's wonderful.

"Yes, my sister. She's older by a year. She brought me into the life. We came here together four years ago." She sits on the floor next to me, curling effortlessly into lotus, and I notice for the first time that her eyes are a lovely, pale gray. "Tell me something about yourself."

I have a piece of real buttered sourdough toast halfway to my mouth, but I pause, my mouth watering for it. I love this little ritual of making myself wait. It's something I've been doing my whole life, even before I knew what it meant—but I have always loved the discipline of it, the enforced denial of both needs and pleasure. I've known this sensation since I was as young as five or six years old. I remember sitting in the swing at the park, my nanny—whichever one it was that year— staring at me questioningly while I held perfectly still, not even allowing my feet to sway while my body filled to overflowing

The Training House

with anticipation of that lovely falling and flying, then falling back to earth again. How it felt the same even when I would hold my full bladder. I used to make myself silently count to one hundred before I would take a bite of food. It was all part of it, like making my bath water too hot—oh yes, even at six, after the nanny had left the room and I could turn on the tap without anyone noticing. Everything in secret until I found the kink life. It made this sort of situation, having signed myself over in a full slave contract, so beautiful to me I could barely stand it. I'd cried in joy when I signed the papers.

But what was she saying to me? Oh yes.

"Tell you something? Like what?" I ask.

"Like anything. Anything but what your name was before you arrived. That's not important anymore."

I finally take a bite of the toast, the butter melting on my tongue. Pure heaven as I swallow it, then wash it down with a sip of hot tea.

"Well…I was born in Paris, but raised mostly here. Well, not here in San Francisco, but in Manhattan."

"Ah, I thought I detected an odd accent."

"My mother was French, my father is…an American." And a complete and utter bastard, but I don't want to think about him now. I never want to think of him.

"How did you get into kink?" the Girl asks as I pause to sip my tea once more, then to spoon some lovely, garnet-colored raspberries into my mouth.

"It sort of started when a friend of my father's seduced me. I was nineteen, and such a rebellious teenager. I slept around. Drank too much. Dabbled in drugs. Max—Mr. Merrick—offered to set me up in an apartment if I'd stop the partying. And if I slept with him, although I wanted to, so that wasn't a problem. He was handsome. Exuded authority. Irresistible bait for a girl like me. The sex was rough from the start, and I loved it. He had to be nearly fifty, which seemed so much older at the time, but he was the first man who gave me a taste of what I wanted. I didn't even have to ask. It was like a revelation, to be fucked so hard it left me bruised. And eventually he began to spank me, to tie me up. I had to beg him to bind me and leave me there in his house while he went to work. To allow me to sleep on the floor at the foot of his bed. He liked his sex rough, but he didn't quite understand the extent of my yearnings. Well, neither did I."

"It often happens that way, for a lot of us," she says.

I nod. "So I've heard over the years."

"How old are you? How long have you been doing kink?"

"I'm twenty-seven, so eight years. But it really started when I was a kid, which I've only realized in the last year or two—I mean that the stuff I was doing and thinking about was related to my kink desires. I remember being eight or nine, and there was another girl who lived in my neighborhood in New York. She was a year older than me, and lived in a beautiful house with one of those precious courtyard gardens. Our nannies would sit in the kitchen and drink coffee, and we'd have the run of the house and the garden, free to do whatever we wanted. We'd play this game where she would be the wicked queen from *Snow White*. She would make me take my clothes off and she'd scratch me with her nails, pretending there was poison on the tips. I would lie on the floor, writhing, pretending I was dying. She always wanted to play the same game. I didn't mind. There was something about it I loved. Not being poisoned, but... having someone take my power away like that, even if it was all pretend. A part of me wished she really would poison me."

"Heady stuff, for a kid. A kid with a propensity for kink."

"Yes."

An image of the neighbor girl's young face flashes in my mind, the wicked grin lighting up her big brown eyes, the flush on her round cheeks as I pretended to die.

"Tell me more about Mr. Merrick," the Girl prompts me.

"Oh, well...I think he really did love me, you know? In his way. He wanted to guide me and it was something I wanted desperately. Something I *required* in a way that goes far way beyond merely needing. Something I'd never gotten from my own father." I pause, biting down on my lip. How much had I never gotten from my father? Not even before my lovely, sad Maman died. But the slave girl is watching me, waiting for me to go on. "I have classic daddy issues. I'm such a cliché. But it worked for me. Beautifully. As it turned out he never got me that apartment—I stayed with him at his flat in London for close to a year. And then he...he died. Heart attack. And of course he'd made no provisions for me, and his grown children took the flat and I was on my own again."

She looks interested in what I'm saying, leaning toward me a bit. "And then what did you do?"

"Went to Paris. I couldn't lick my wounds in London, you know? The experience of loss was...pretty rough for me. So I packed some of my clothes and just took off. I met some girls my age and we shared an apartment, four of us stuffed into two tiny bedrooms, but it was fine." I sip my milky tea. "And then I stumbled into the BDSM club circuit and everything changed almost overnight."

She nods, picks up my toast and takes a bite, then sets it back down on the delicate china plate. It's white with the blue crest of the House in the center, edged in gold leaf. So pretty. Like the brand over her breast.

"Am I allowed to ask about you?"

"You can," she says. "But I probably won't answer."

"What about... What do I call you? I know, I know. Girl. I don't even know how to tell you apart from your sister, how to think of you."

Her thick lashes come down for a moment, batting at her high cheekbones. "Do you *want* to think of me?" she asks.

My body goes hot all over as I take in her pretty gray eyes, her long fluttering lashes, her even prettier breasts, the nipples dark and suddenly hard. I am always taken by full breasts, wishing they were mine. Wanting to suckle them. To feel the heaviness in my hands. "Yes," I whisper, afraid this might not be the right answer.

She leans toward me, her hand slipping behind my neck. I close my eyes and shiver with pleasure. I can feel her breath warm on my cheek as she whispers, "If you're a very good Girl, maybe I'll allow it."

She slides her hand down and pinches the tender skin at my waist very hard, then lets me go so suddenly I have to catch myself. Standing, she picks up the tray. "Breakfast is over," she says, all business suddenly. "My sister will be back to bathe you. And by the way, you really shouldn't try to get her to talk unless you want to be punished. She doesn't like it, and we're allowed to punish you. And she's a little mad that the Master is so pleased with you."

Is he? I file that away to savor later.

I nod. "Thank you for breakfast. And for talking to me."

Pausing in the doorway, she watches me for a moment, then turns without another word, shutting the door behind her. I listen for the lock and it comes a moment later, making me sigh with relief.

Safe once more.

I am more than a little fucked up, I know. But these long silences, locked alone in a room, are a sort of retreat for me, the way it must be for nuns, or for those Buddhists who go to the Green Gulch Center in the hills overlooking the San Francisco Bay across the Golden Gate Bridge. Kink is my religion. And I am awed at the holiness of this place I've come to. I need the time alone to meditate, to absorb it.

As I said, I'm fucked up.

I'm also nervous and completely blissed out at being among my fellow freaks, at being dedicated to them, my year-long contract a covenant to me.

Lying back on my hard pallet, I stare up at the ceiling, at the dust motes dancing in the dim ray of sunlight coming through the damask curtains. I take in a breath, hold it for a beat, exhale slowly, then do it again. I try to let my mind empty, but the only time it's not spinning in some mad mind fuck is when I am in service. When I'm being beaten or restrained. That's when I can let my ego go, when I become nothing to the point where my silly little worries or endless loops from my childhood stop whirling through my brain and I can just be.

I am thinking of Master Graham. Does he miss me? I like to think so, which feels a bit childish, since I'm the one who ultimately chose to leave. I inhale, imagine his scent: lemongrass soap and a touch of cherry smoke from the pipeful of tobacco he allowed himself once a week. It is the smell of comfort. Of kink, yes, but not enough protocol for me. I am safe only when I know I am trapped. He kept me safe for a while, but I needed so much more. To be taken to these frightening heights in order to feel utterly powerless—to know that I am. It is a place out of his reach, and therefore out of mine if I'd stayed with him. But I miss him. I miss him, and yet...

I take in another breath, breathing through the butterflies that have been beating their wings in my stomach every waking moment since I saw him yesterday. The Master. My Master.

My Master.

Oh yes.

Lust floods me: nipples and pussy, stomach and limbs. Every soft, fleshly part of my body is full and plush suddenly, swollen with the need for his touch. I know better than to touch myself—that is absolutely forbidden and one of the first things a slave learns. No, we are meant to suffer in our desires, and our suffering is beautiful. It's this place getting inside my head, into my body, as much as it is him, I think. The restrictions, the inflexible rules. The contract. So darkly threatening, all of it, which is exactly what I've dreamed of, exactly what a slave training house is for. But there is no way to prepare for this, even if you think you know what you're getting yourself into. And then the Master has to be so beautiful! I suffer for his handsome face, his enigmatic, powerful presence. His big black boots.

I am suffering now, and I have no idea how much longer this will go on, when he'll call for me again. It could be in five minutes. This evening. A week. I know nothing. But that's part of it—knowing nothing, deciding nothing, ultimately being nothing. I am here to be completely broken down, and I know it. I want it. Which is perhaps the biggest mind fuck of all.

Several days go by in which I am fed, taken to another room and run on a treadmill, bathed in a cool shower by the silent Girl, and in between I'm left alone in my room to dream about my beautiful, mysterious Master. I do my best not to touch myself, and am ashamed at how often I find myself pressing my thighs together, which are damp with my juices. At night I dream of him—of him beating me, touching me, even kissing me. On the second night I woke on the verge of orgasm, and it was a long struggle to get my body and my tortured mind to calm.

By my fifth morning here I'm really beginning to panic. Does he not want to see me? To even order that I be worked? There is nothing but this terrible isolation in which I suppose I am to discipline myself into some sort of meditation, which is what I've learned to do and have done in the past. But perhaps I am not such a good Girl, after all, since all I can do in between my meals, my exercise and my showers is dream on my hard, white pallet, my body in a lazy trance.

The sun hasn't been up for more than a couple of hours when the door to my room opens, and I have a brief, joyous glimpse of him. He's dressed in dark slacks, a crisp white shirt, the sleeves rolled again to reveal his tattoo work. His dark hair is a little wavy, a little too long, like some hero in a Jane Austen novel. Too perfect.

I begin to sit up but he pushes me back with his rough boot on my chest, and the air goes out of me as my body floods with lust. Those boots! And *him*. I bite back a moan, trying to resist the urge to press my thighs together to ease the wet, aching want there. He gives a wave and one of the Girls—I still don't know which one—and an elegant older man with close-cropped gray hair I know from my arrival to be Robert the valet, kneel on either side of me. While the Master holds me down with his booted foot, they slip a leather blindfold over my eyes and fear is like a siren shrieking in my mind—I hate to be blindfolded. My heart races, making me want to scream. But they seem to have thought of everything. Someone holds my cheeks firmly, then a ball gag is shoved into my mouth and strapped at the back of my head.

The boot is removed from my chest and I'm flipped over onto my stomach, my arms pulled behind my back. I can smell the leather of the cuffs before they're buckled firmly around my wrists. And my head is emptying out in a way my silly little meditations could never accomplish, as I'm lifted then thrown over the Master's shoulders. Oh yes, it is definitely him, and it's pure heaven to feel the muscles working in his shoulder, my breasts resting against the solid wall of his broad back. My nipples are so hard they hurt. I'm so wet I worry about mussing his lovely shirt, but there's nothing I can do about it.

Nothing you can do.

And so, when I begin to drool a little around the gag I give myself over to it. No tears as there usually are when I'm gagged or blindfolded. Because I can do absolutely nothing. And because it's for *him*.

He carries me down a flight of stairs, his boot heels echoing on the wooden risers, then we turn to the right. It's only a few moments before he makes another turn and I am dumped facedown onto a smooth wooden table, or a counter, maybe. I inhale the scents of coffee and food cooking. The kitchen?

Then his voice—his beautifully modulated voice, so devoid of any accent he must be from California. "Cook. Prepare this one for me."

"Yes, Sir." A deep female voice, and I imagine a tall, handsome woman, with large hands. I also imagine her tenderizing my flesh with one of those mallets used for steak. The reality is not far off the mark.

I hear her moving about the room and what sounds like utensils being shuffled, and almost right away she smacks my ass with something that feels like a very large, flat wooden spoon. When I squirm she places a firm and surprisingly small, strong hand on the back of my neck and smacks me harder and harder, my tender ass stinging, burning as blood rises to the surface of my skin. She pauses for half a breath, allowing me to swallow a gulp of air before she starts in again with something much heavier this time. And oh God, it hurts as she lands one solid blow after another, hammering deep into the muscles so that sensation goes from sting to a deep bruising thud, yet it still stings somehow. She works the heavy, wooden implement—a rolling pin?—down over the backs of my thighs, silent until she utters a simple, stern order.

"Spread your thighs. Wider."

I do as she asks—of course I do—and she pinches my pussy lips so hard a tear seeps from the corner of my eye and drool pools in my mouth behind the gag. She holds onto that delicate flesh with one hand while she spanks me with the other, her palm on my flesh almost sweet in comparison to the hard wooden tool she'd used before. Pain builds, and what begins as something I welcome quickly turns into more than I can process—there is such a rapid build with no warm-up at all. Harder and impossibly harder until I am crying out around the gag, the noise a raw contraction of the muscles in my throat, drool spilling onto my chin.

I am helpless.

Thinking the words soothes me as much as it frightens me. It has always been like this.

Suddenly the spanking stops, although her hard, hurting fingers are still twisting my poor tortured labia. My breath comes in short, gasping pants as I try not to choke on my own salty tears.

I sense her moving nearer, then her breath is hot against my cheek. She says in a low tone, "You'd better learn to take it more quietly, Girl. The Master won't like all this fussing. Didn't your previous owner teach you any better? Or are you too hard-headed to learn?"

My heart drops into my stomach. I try so hard to be good. To please. To aim for perfection. But this place is too new and I haven't been told all the rules.

And suddenly it comes to me that maybe they *want* me to fail. I'm hoping it's only to have more reason to punish me and not because they simply don't want me. That *he* doesn't want me. I need so much to belong…somewhere. And if not here, where?

Memories flash through my head, spurred by my panic, a million thoughts rushing by like a film in fast-forward: My arrival at Millbrook Academy, the boarding school that was my father's answer to having an invisible child who was still somehow in the way, when I was only eleven. How alien the place seemed at first—the long, vaulted hallways, the towering trees on the grounds, the headmistress, Mrs. Brerens, who frankly scared the hell out of me. But then there were my series of crushes—Mr. Curtis who taught math and looked like something out of an Abercrombie and Fitch ad. My dance teacher Ms. Lordham, who was the perfect blonde English rose, and whom I'd caught fucking Mr. Curtis in the stables like something out of a classic porn film. She was naked, her gorgeous, lithe body bent over a bale of hay while he took her from behind, and her shouting, "Fuck me harder!" Oh yes, even though I'd only been thirteen years old, that scenario had fueled my fevered masturbatory fantasies until long after graduation from Millbrook.

And then there had been the girls… It was a school for "young ladies", after all, and we had to do something to keep our raging hormones busy. It was either that or sneak out after curfew and meet strange men in town, ask them to buy us beer in exchange for a quick hand job. If the wealthy and powerful parents of the Millbrook girls had any idea what their daughters were up to, that place would have been shut down decades ago.

Boarding school had been that terrifying and intoxicating combination of fear and yearning. Loneliness and wanting. It was those things I still sought, always feeling as if satisfaction were just beyond my grasp.

But now I'm here. In the Training House.

Cook yanks me up until I'm sitting on the long table, my ass burning against the cool wood, and I realize I am truly afraid. *Will* he reject me? Is it possible, once my contract has been signed? But of course it is. I can't bear it if I'm returned to Master Graham in shame.

Not good enough.

No.

I'm crying in earnest now, in long gulping sobs, the ball gag nearly choking me.

"Hey! Stop that now."

Cook slaps my face, leaving my cheek burning. But the shock of it calms me down right away. I swallow the next sob and do my best to contain myself.

"Better," she murmurs, not unkindly. "Here." A soft, damp cloth on my cheeks as she wipes the tears and the snot and the drool away. "Don't get me wrong," she says with a small chuckle, "he likes his Girls to cry, but he prefers to be the one to make it happen."

I sniff. I'd smile if I could, both because she's being kind to me along with being cruel, and at the idea that he's one of those who enjoy a woman's tears, which is inexplicably hot for me.

Taking a deep breath, I try to breathe out around the ball gag, then inhale again—and swear I *smell* him before I hear him. He smells of leather and sex and expensive cologne. My body turns to warm rubber, all but my nipples, which are hard as stone.

"What nonsense is this?" the Master demands. His heavy boots ring on the hard floor as he crosses the room. "I could hear you halfway down the hall, Girl. All of this over a spanking from Cook?"

I sense Cook stepping back, but it's too late to be afraid. The

Master grabs my hair—not even close to the scalp, a sensation I love—he simply winds my long strands around his fist and pulls me right off the table. Something goes crashing to the floor and I know it's my fault, but I couldn't apologize even if I weren't gagged. He's pulling me along and my feet hit the edge of a carpet and I stumble. He catches me, pulling up on my hair, and the tears want to start again because I am being so clumsy. But the Master simply keeps dragging me along, and I keep tripping over my bare feet, blind, with my arms bound behind my back and no way to catch myself should I fall. I'm a little shattered by how he's handling me. But that's his intention, I'm sure. Keeping me off-balance, physically, mentally, emotionally. People like him, the real trainers of the world, are masters of the mind fuck. They are the masters of everything, as far as I'm concerned. *My* Master, and I feel it on a new, deeper level. This is exactly what I wanted. This is exactly what I fear.

This is exactly what I have needed all my life.

Yes.

CHAPTER THREE

The carpet ends and there is hardwood beneath my feet for a moment, then another rug, this one soft and plush. Immediately I sense that someone else is there. I try to take in my surroundings through the means remaining me, to retain my balance as the Master has me stop, keeping a hand on my shoulder to steady me. I take in the earthy, sharp scent of ash and wood from a fire burning in the hearth, and behind it is the scent of perfume. It smells expensive, like jasmine and lace. My ass and my thighs still burn from my beating in the kitchen and I'm not quite over the emotion of the tears—I'm really beginning to overload. Taking a deep breath, I try to give myself over to it all. But the trick right now is to give myself over to *him*. That's what will help me.

"What do you think of my latest acquisition, my dear Mistress Alexa?" the Master asks.

"Hmm."

I hear her step toward me, then I can feel the heat of her body as she moves closer.

"Beautiful hair," she says. "I adore red hair on a woman. But hers is really more auburn, isn't it? So straight and sleek." She runs a hand through my hair, her fingers catching in a tangle. "Silky. Very nice. Beautiful small breasts. The pale nipples are perfection. Sweet." She tweaks one of them, and I try not to wince, but I do, making her laugh, a low, wicked sound. "Sensitive girl. She's tall for me, but I could put on my stilettos to fuck her with my strap-on."

He chuckles. "I suppose wanting to fuck her means you approve?"

She tweaks my nipple again, pressing hard into the flesh and I breathe into the pain, exhale as she does it again, harder this time, not letting the pressure up. I have to really focus to convert the pain, and finally get a small flood of endorphins. Lovely.

"Look how hard her nipple gets," she murmurs quietly. "How deliciously it darkens. And how naked they look, don't they, Damon?"

Damon.

I savor the sound of his name on my tongue, a name I will never, ever use. But knowing it is like a gift.

"They might be pierced soon enough," he says, making me shudder. Or shiver. I don't know which.

"Of course—you pierce all your House slaves. Except for the beautiful Christopher."

A slave called by name? Is that possible here? But I'm too immersed in what's happening to give it more thought.

"He came with the left one already pierced and I liked the way it looked. I like even more that he did it himself."

"Well, so do I. Speaking of your beautiful boy, I'd like to borrow him if you don't need him and he's not promised elsewhere."

"As long as you bring him back in one piece."

The mysterious Mistress clucks her tongue. "Come on, Damon. I would never return damaged goods to you. He can take quite a lot, that one. He needs it."

"He does, absolutely. And he's yours for the weekend."

"I can offer you Selina the next time you visit me in exchange."

"No exchange necessary. He needs to be worked anyway, and as you can see I've a new one to work with."

"I'd like to see more of her, as well."

She is one of those women who are expert at sounding bored, but I have been a submissive long enough to read the small thrill under that tone of disinterest. Of disinterested interest. I think the Dommes almost *have* to do these things, playing in this sort of old boys' club that are the male Dominants and Masters. The Mistresses have to be tougher. Hide their emotions. They are certainly more cruel than the men.

"I thought you might," the Master says.

Suddenly, I am shoved roughly to my knees and the blindfold is whipped off. The bright light is glaring and I blink hard, my eyes watering. My heart is hammering, my pulse going at a thousand miles an hour, as if some sort of protection was taken away along with the blindfold, even though I hate the damn things.

"Oh! You didn't tell me her eyes were green," Mistress Alexa says. "And such long, long lashes. Even a few freckles across her nose. Dusted in gold."

She walks in a circle around me, and when she's circled back around to stand in front of me she bends down, her hand sliding around behind my neck, that firm grip all of the Masters and Mistresses know how to use. It's that particular touch they subdue you with. Command you with. Such a simple thing, but it works like crazy. She squeezes harder, her hand sliding up into the base of my scalp, where her nails dig in a little as she leans closer, until her face is only inches from mine.

She's beautiful. Dark hair, almost black, and glittering ice-blue eyes. Her mouth is a cruel cupid's bow of red lipstick. She's dressed in red leather: skirt, corset, stiletto boots that come up over her knees. She wears a glass vial on a silver chain around her neck, and whatever is in it is red, as well. I only see it because it swings in my face for a moment before she absently tucks it into her cleavage.

Mistress Alexa stares into my eyes, forcing my gaze to hers. And she begins to explore my body, my responses, by pinching me here and there: at my waist, just beneath my breast, at the side of my neck, the back of my arm. Evil little pinches that don't last long, but one comes right after another and I'm overloading on pain again. But my body loves this—it's addictive, being overloaded. As addictive as it is disturbing. I'm soaking wet, my pussy clenching at nothing, wanting to be filled. My clit hard and needy. It's making me pant, the pain and the desire, and the panting makes me drool a little again—I can't help it with the damn gag on.

"Oh, poor, poor girl," Mistress Alexa croons. "Drooling is just not pretty, my pet." She uses her thumb to stroke the drool from one corner of my stretched lips. She does it again at the other corner, this time her thumb pressing hard into my flesh, her nail scraping as she pushes the moisture away. She does it over and over, and it's really hurting, but I focus on her lovely blue eyes and manage to hold fairly still.

Finally she straightens up. "Her nipples are stiff, her pupils dilated," she says, her eyes narrowing, her gaze wandering over my body. "She loves it all."

"Yes," the Master says, moving around to stand in front of me, and all I can see are the back of his legs, clad in dark trousers. And if I dare—and I do for one brief moment—I can see what a fine, shapely ass he has.

I want to lean in and rest my cheek on that muscular curve. To place a kiss there. Need runs through my system like a shock, like lightning. I try to swallow it down.

"She's fighting it. Fighting something. I don't know how far you'll be able to take her training if you can't work her past it, Damon. But she does love it. She needs it."

"She does. Look at this," he says, bending to swipe his fingers between my thighs.

I gasp, pleasure shivering over my skin.

He holds his hand out to the Mistress, and she strokes one finger over his. She smiles.

"Absolutely soaking wet. It doesn't surprise me." Holding my chin in her fingers—one of them still wet with my own juices—she says to me, "You're turned on by us discussing you, aren't you, Girl? You like to be objectified. And you love the pain, even if you hate it. But I don't think you do." She smiles, then drops my chin.

I want to answer her, but of course I am allowed to do no such thing, even if I weren't gagged. But she's right. About everything.

"She'll get plenty of that here," the Master says. "Perhaps from you, since you're staying the weekend, unless you're too busy with my boy. By the way, I'll have him sent straight to your room tonight, if you want."

"That would be wonderful. I'd play with your new toy, but I can only stay tonight, and I really would like Christopher right away."

"You shall have him."

"Thank you for your generosity, Damon."

He nods at her, catches me watching and slaps my cheek. I have to blink the tears away. "Eyes down, Girl, unless instructed otherwise."

My cheek burns, but shame at having displeased him, at having forgotten myself, burns deeper than the small slap, scalding me to the core. I must remember myself. I was so much better for Master Graham. He called me a "push-button" slave. But Master Graham never challenged my senses the way the Master does. The way the futility of any struggle against this place and the chosen powerlessness of my contract do.

I am so in love with everything about this place.

His attention has turned back to the Mistress as the valet comes into the room, which I know from the toes of his shiny black shoes. My eyes are glued to the Persian carpet.

"Robert, see that Christopher is bathed and sent to Mistress Alexa's room."

"Yes, Sir. Right away. Mistress, may I escort you to the east wing?"

"No, Robert—I prefer you see that Christopher is readied for me. Give him a good enema before you bring him."

"Yes, Mistress."

I hear her kiss the Master's cheek. "I may miss dinner tonight. And Christopher may not be able to sit down for a week."

"Of course."

"Don't sound so amused."

"Alexa, darling, we are always amused at the thought of you fucking one of my boys with your enormous, harnessed cock all night."

"I think *you* need to find some way to amuse yourself, Damon. All work and no play is making you a dull Dom."

"Hardly, Alexa. But luckily, my work *is* play."

"As is mine. And I plan to play very, very hard tonight."

"So do I."

She laughs, and I can feel it aimed at me. But I don't mind. All I can think of, all I can hope, is that he means with *me*. This makes me wet again. It also terrifies me.

I understand perfectly well that part of what I agreed to when I signed the slave contract was being broken in to a new house, to a new Master. This is going to be very, very hard, as he said. I am shivering all over. Wet. Ready. Wanting whatever cruel lessons he sees fit to dole out. I am ready to be his.

The Master stands in silence as Mistress Alexa's stiletto heels retreat down the hallway. I don't know what he's waiting for. What he plans to do. Of course I don't. My arms have already begun to ache from being bound for so long. Taking a breath, I try to sink into the ache, but my poor brain is too much all over the place. Everything is too new. I try to roll my shoulders, and there is just enough give to get one tiny roll in before the Master grabs me and shoves me to the floor, onto my side, then rolls me over on my back.

"What the hell do you think you're doing, Girl?" he asks. "Did I tell you to move?"

He doesn't need to raise his voice. Every single thing that comes out of his mouth is a threat.

I don't dare shake my head. He is so thoroughly intimidating, straddling my body. If only I could tear my gaze from his for a moment to collect myself, but he would never allow it. He stares down at me, his blue eyes burning with a dark fire that looks like banked anger and something else. Something impossible not to recognize: banked desire. He *wants* me.

My heart leaps, my body thrumming as he continues to stare at me, into me. There are long, breathless moments in which I feel as if I am held suspended in mid-air. In which I swear desire is like a sound wave just out of reach, then a buzzing in the room, then a drumbeat pounding between my thighs.

He takes a deep breath, holds it for a moment, and I can't begin to imagine what that means. Then he blinks, leans down and slaps my face—one light smack, then another. He pauses only to take the gag from my mouth, and I have perhaps a single second to press my lips together before he starts slapping my face once more, my left cheek, then the right, harder and harder.

Why do I feel joyous? Maybe it's because he hasn't taken his burning gaze from mine. He's hurting me, but I want the pain. I want to take it for him. To be nothing for him. To be everything. I want it because he is the most wicked sadist I have ever met, which makes my heart trip and tumble. Which makes me need to please him all the more. And something in my chest loosens, opens up like a black chasm lined in silver.

Terrifying.

Yes, please.

Finally he turns me over and drags me on my knees to a small sofa, but I don't have a moment to see what it looks like—the room is a blur of red velvet and gold damask and God knows what else as he bends me over the sofa, my breasts resting on the seat. I hear him remove his belt, and with the first blow I know he's doubled it, making a heavy loop of the leather. He hits my poor ass with it, hard and fast. The pain is intense right from the start, and at first I get a nice flood of endorphins, pleasure making me wet, making me need to come. But very quickly he's hitting me too hard for any of those lovely brain chemicals to help, and it's simply my unbridled desire to please that enables me to take it.

Anything for him.

I hear his ragged breathing over me as he drops the belt and his fist goes into my hair once more. He pulls me to the floor, onto my back again, and kicks my thighs apart. I watch him through a haze of wonder and pain as he drops the belt and smacks my breasts with his bare hand. My body arches into the pain, into his touch, into the lovely brutality.

Anything for you.

"Do not defy me, Girl." He places one booted foot on my right shoulder, then reaches down to give my breast another hard slap. "In time—and let's both hope you're smart enough— you'll come to find I have little patience for an unruly slave. You are mine." He slaps the other breast, the pain making my ears ring. "*Mine.* I will be sure you never have the opportunity to forget that."

Yes, please.

He stands there watching me for endless moments. Then he leans down and grabs my jaw in his strong hand. He says in a low tone, almost a murmur, "You are too damn beautiful for your own good. Or maybe for mine."

Before I can help myself, I shake my head my head the tiniest bit, and he allows me to do it.

"Yes. I don't know what this means, either." He stops for a moment, takes a deep breath, purses his lips, then squeezes my jaw harder. "If I asked you—told you—to suck my cock, you would," he says harshly.

I nod, not knowing what else to do, not knowing what's going on.

"If I beat you—and I will—you would accept it gratefully. And accept me making you come just as gratefully. But if I kissed you... What would you think of that?"

I take a moment, confused.

"You may speak," he tells me.

Still, it takes me several long seconds to find my voice. "I would accept it all with utter gratitude and desire, Master," I whisper.

"Because I am your Master," he says, rather than asks.

"No," I tell him. Then more harshly, my heart oddly full, "*No*, Master!"

Straightening up, he runs a hand through his hair, then takes a step back and sits on the edge of the little sofa, watching me still. After a full minute goes by in which my heart is a small hammer trying to beat its way out of my chest, I hear footsteps behind me. "Robert, leash her and have her taken to the basement. Let my driver work her over after you've fed and rested her for a bit. He's earned a little bonus."

"Yes, Sir."

"And have Cook send my dinner to my suite."

"Of course. Anything else, Sir?"

"Leave her in her chains down there tonight."

"Very good, Sir."

He's done with me? Tears burn behind my eyes. Robert pulls me to my feet, loops one of those choke-chain collars onto my neck, snaps a leash onto it, then he leads me back to my room. Unsnapping the carabiner which attaches my cuffs behind my back, he draws my arms to my sides, taking a few moments to massage my shoulders, to check my hands for circulation. Then the leash is removed but the choke-chain stays, like a metallic reminder of my utter submission around my neck, and it feels sacred, somehow.

My mind is whirling, creating a tempest within the floating ether of subspace. He is so, so handsome, the Master, but it goes beyond that. His very darkness draws me, calls out to my own. And what was it he said to me? What could it possibly mean? And then to send me away like that... I have to force myself not to cry. I have never cried so much in my life, and I feel certain this is only the very beginning of a storm of tears the Training House will bring.

Yes, please.

"Stay here," the valet tells me.

And I do, standing in the middle of the room, trying to breathe through the confusion. After some indeterminable time Robert returns with a tray, which he sets on the floor beside my pallet.

"You have one hour," he tells me, then he leaves, locking the door behind him.

There are so many thoughts and questions whirring through my brain I can barely stand having to eat—I'd rather lie down on my white pallet and think and dream. But I know better. If I am to withstand the beatings and God knows what else, then I have to eat and rest and stretch. And I do stretch for maybe five minutes before I eat my meal: a small portion of roasted chicken and vegetables, all of it beautifully prepared. There is tea on the tray, and I pour some, longing for milk and sugar, but there is none. I knew this about the Training House—about all such formal places—that we are afforded few luxuries, and I'd had mine with my first meal. No, here the luxuries are in being beautifully bound, harshly punished, having no sense of self or time or meaning beyond what the Masters want us to be. Slave. Girl. Without identity. With no need for it. Yes, to sink into that. To drown in it.

Bring it on.

I lie down on my hard white pallet and close my eyes, although I don't sleep. My mind is churning with images and memories I don't want to see, but which I am helpless against, as I am at times.

My mother's face, so, so pretty, with the red lipstick she always wore, and the scarf around her slender neck. She whispers to me in French. "Je t'aime, ma petite." This is almost the only thing I can remember about her, I was so young when she died. This and the lilac perfume she wore. I was so little, and yet I had the presence of mind to drag a chair into her closet, to pull one of her sweaters down and keep it in my room, where I slept with it until the scent disappeared.

The day of her funeral I overheard things I probably shouldn't have—my angry father talking to his lawyer. I was a teenager before I understood his implications that my mother had died while driving home from an assignation with a lover.

But my father being who he is, I refuse to judge her for it. We all have to look for love somewhere, don't we? The Training House is where I am looking.

I can find it here. I can find everything I've ever needed here. With him.

The gears in my head instantly switch, and I imagine my exquisite Master's hands on my body, the things he did to me that first time—the forced squirting. I've never felt anything like it, and even remembering it now, I have to squeeze my thighs together, the muscles aching with need.

Maybe the driver will fuck me tonight.

Yes, please.

I don't even care who he is or how he might do it, how difficult he will make it for me. No, I want him to make it difficult.

I sigh, and the sigh turns into a moan of deep yearning, my body on fire. I squeeze my eyes shut and pretend he is here with me—the driver. But no, it's the Master, with his finely made hands. His clever, hurting hands. And they are inside me, pumping hard, the pressure building, and oh God, I can't hold it back!

I bolt upright as the door opens and Robert steps in. He comes toward me quietly, and I am so ashamed of having worked myself up, nearly to orgasm, that I kneel up for him, head bowed, hands behind my back. The loose choke-chain collar is like a weighted sacrament around my neck. It redeems me—a little, at least.

"Very nice," he says as he pulls my arms farther back, clipping the carabiner onto the cuffs once more, and I realize how sore my shoulders are from being in that position, but I'm hardly going to complain. Then he snaps the leash on, pulls me to my feet and takes me down a narrow flight of stairs.

My head is reeling as I refocus on what is happening. The Master is giving me to someone else. He worked me, and then he was done with me. I feel a little desperate, suddenly. The Master's beating wasn't too bad—I've had much worse—and I'm a bit of a pain slut so my body can handle it. But there's something else going on with me. Why should I care that he's giving me to another man to work tonight? I'm getting more play, which is usually exactly what I want. Being given to another as if I'm merely a *thing* is one of my thrills, and I just nearly got off imagining this very scenario. But I didn't want to leave *him*. To be banished for the whole night, and who knows how much longer. It's him I really want to fuck me. But it's impossible, and I'm so worked up the driver will do. Anyone would, at this point, which is, of course, part of their wicked plan. *His* wicked plan. And it's as if he's inside my head, as if he knows exactly how it will all work on me. And oh God, does he know! Exactly.

I've just met this man. He is my Master, yes, for the duration of my contract. I don't need to like him or be attracted to him, not at this level of the kink game. At this point my desires are considered only so they can be used against me, or to please those Masters and Mistresses who play with me. But I *am* attracted. Ridiculously. And the shadows in his eyes only make him more intriguing. Perhaps that's the problem.

It *will* be a problem, because he will probably always be denied me.

Fuck.

If this were the normal world—and it's far, far from normal—I would flirt with him, try to gain his attention, do what I could to get him to talk to me. Do what I could to get him into my bed. I'm good at that in the vanilla world. I could have almost anyone I wanted, male or female, and that's not ego talking—it's simply the truth. But none of these things make any difference here. Which is one of the attractions.

It doesn't matter what you do now.

I comfort myself with this thought, the same idea of having absolutely no control that goes through my mind a dozen times a day. It doesn't matter. Nothing matters. It's not supposed to. The only problem is that for some inexplicable reason, it *does*. This is a brand of mind fuck I wasn't prepared for.

The stairs are bare wood, hard beneath my feet, and I can feel the temperature dropping as we go down and step into a narrow hallway. It's dimly lit, and at the edge of my vision I can see the framed artwork decorating the walls. We pass several closed doors on either side, and as we move past one I hear a muffled scream. But I hardly have time to think about it before we turn into one of the rooms and the door is shut behind me.

It's a simple room in terms of the lushness of the house upstairs. Bare wood floors, although they are gorgeously polished. The furnishings down here are still Victorian in style—a dark green velvet sofa flanked by two large brown leather chairs with high backs, an ottoman in front of each. But this is the Training House, so of course there is a long table against one wall covered in brown leather or vinyl, a spanking bench to one side, upholstered to match. A spreader bar hung with leather cuffs dangles from the ceiling, and there is an open armoire holding floggers, paddles, lengths of chain, other implements. I don't have time to make it all out before someone comes in behind us—the Master's driver, I imagine from the heavy, masculine footsteps.

"I just got the message. How very nice."

He has a harsh Cockney accent, which seems incredibly sinister for reasons I can't explain to myself.

The driver moves past us, and as he settles into one of the wing chairs, I can see he's a large man—tall and beefy. He looks as much like a bodyguard as he does anyone's driver. He probably is. He's wearing a dark blue suit that makes me think of a Mafia hit man. And of course, me being me, this makes me weak with both fear and desire. He's handsome in a sort of raw way—a square jaw, a cruel line of a mouth, brown stubble on his nearly shaved head. His hands are enormous.

"She's down here until morning with you, Gilby. Do let her sleep a bit, but chained and on the floor."

The big man smiles. "Master Damon's standard orders down here. I'll see that she's taken care of."

Robert takes the handle of my leash and presses it between my lips, and I know to take it in my teeth. He walks from the room and shuts the door behind him, and I am left with the Master's driver. Gilby. And although I feel certain the Master will use me more roughly than anyone else in his household, this man's size intimidates me. The fact that I have no idea what he'll want to do to me intimidates me. And we are in the basement of the house, with no one to see. Just this stranger and I, and another stranger screaming down the hall. What a madhouse this is. What kind of man would work at a place like this?

I am restless, wondering, beginning to overanalyze

everything, knowing I will never have the answers I seek. I am not supposed to know anything, to be able to really guess. That's all part of it. I know that. It's one of the things I must learn to give myself over to, but that's the hard part for me, no matter how badly I want it. I make an effort to center myself, to sink *into* the situation, rather than disassociate from it, which is the natural reaction for any human being. But we are not just "anyone", those of us who sign the slave contracts. Who agree to live in the madhouse.

For a long time—seemingly forever, but it must go on for fifteen minutes—Gilby leaves me standing in front of him, simply watching me. Crossing one ankle over his knee, he taps his fingers on the arm of the leather chair, but I know better than to glance at his hand. I've passed these tests before. And failed just as many. I keep my gaze trained on the floor, but apparently that's not good enough.

"What are you staring at, Girl?" he growls. "Hasn't anyone told you it's impolite? Especially in the Master's house. Bad Girl."

He gets to his feet, a wall of a man in front of me, and my stomach drops. I have three seconds to be scared out of my mind before he scoops me up and sits me on the edge of the padded table, where he removes my cuffs. My poor shoulders and arms are still aching, and my mouth is feeling the strain of holding the leash between my teeth, but that is not my main concern. No, it's him, this enormous man with the wicked expression and unknown desires. He places his beefy hands on my shoulders, and I pull in a gasping breath. But to my utter surprise, he begins to massage my arms, my shoulders, my hands—a lovely, deep massage that makes my sore muscles sigh in pleasure, which I don't dare do myself. It's unsettling, this little moment of kindness. I don't know what to do with it. I look up to him in gratitude. Catching his gaze, I see right away that this was a mistake, and the slap comes hard and fast, the leash flying from my mouth. My cheek burns, and my gaze goes to my lap.

"Damn right, Girl," he says. "You don't look at me, you don't talk to me, unless I tell you to. And no matter what I do to you, there's no screaming, hear me? Not a peep out of you, not even a moan of pleasure." He gathers both my breasts in his hands and squeezes hard. "There will be pleasure, if only because you're such a little pain slut, I can tell. And you'll like it when I fuck your ass. You'll like it and you'll want to scream, little slut."

Je t'aime, ma petite, my mind madly translates.

He leans in closer, until his breath is warm on my cheek. He whispers, "I have a huge cock. No lie. No bragging. It'll make you want to scream when I work it into your dainty little ass."

Oh yes. Just like my fantasy upstairs in my room.

I want to squirm on the table, his words making me shiver in lustful anticipation. In anticipation of being stretched until I tear, maybe. In anticipation of showing him how much I can take. I shouldn't be so proud, but I am. I also know this place will work the pride right out of me.

His hand darts out and he grabs my right breast in a painful grip, using it to pull me down onto the table, then his rough, hurting hands are on my waist, turning me over onto my stomach, then pulling me up onto hands and knees. By the time my ass is raised in the air I am wet with wanting and ready to sob.

His hand goes back to my breast and he pinches the nipple so hard I have to bite the inside of my cheek to keep from crying out. He is a beast of a man—I've never met anyone of his size and strength—and this doesn't bode well for my poor ass.

Yes, please.

My mind is emptying out, the analytical side gone, completely shut down. And I'm grateful for it. Grateful to him.

"You love it, don't you, little slut?" he asks.

I want to answer that I do. But his hand slips between my thighs and finds my cunt slick with need.

"Ah, yes. You fucking love it."

Pinching my clit, he pulls on it, elongating it, and pleasure whispers over my skin, my pussy clenching. Empty. Unconsciously, I arch my hips and he pulls his hand back.

He clucks his tongue. "You really should not have done that, slut." He shoves my cheek down onto the table, and I breathe in the leather along with my fear. "Stay," he orders.

My mind is tumbling into that dark place I go sometimes. A place where everything sort of fades away, even the fear and pleasure of the moment, because I'm too scared to even begin to imagine what is about to happen. But I don't have long to wait, suspended in the emptiness that has become my mind. I can feel the heat of his big body at my side, then his hands prying my pussy lips apart, holding them wide. Something solid presses against my waiting hole, and I don't know what it is, except that it's big. Automatically, I widen my thighs.

"Good slut," he murmurs as he begins to work the solid thing into me.

And God, it really is huge, whatever it is—big and smooth and I think it's made of wood. I'm soaking wet and growing wetter by the moment, but it's too big for me, I'm sure of it.

I start to cry a little, trying to swallow the tears down, squeezing my eyes shut tight. I hate to fail.

He shoves harder, and it feels like my insides are burning, the tissues stretching impossibly. And it's a huge turn-on, pleasure and pain and even the tears. Maybe more so *because* of the tears. Yes—I know it's true. I love the tears as much as the Master does.

"Come on. You can take it. Don't make him pull out the lube, or you'll pay for it later, Girl."

I open my eyes to find the Master sitting in a chair across from me, his legs crossed, his hands steepled, his dark blue eyes glittering, a cruel smile on his exquisite mouth. And it is as if my body, my mind, explode in pleasure. I'm so overcome I nearly speak to beg him to stay.

I inhale, try to let my body go loose as I exhale, then do it again. And Gilby works the damn object—whatever it is—into my dripping cunt. With his other hand he grips my hip and begins to rock me onto it, back and forth, slowly at first, then as my body becomes accustomed to the thing, harder, faster, until he really is fucking me with this enormous makeshift dildo as the Master watches, and this is probably the hottest moment of my life. Until the Master gets up and approaches me, and my pussy weeps with desire.

He grabs my jaw in his strong hand, hard enough to hurt, forces my mouth open and presses three fingers inside.

"Suck, Girl," he demands.

I do it greedily, savoring his fingers, licking the tips, sucking hard, sliding my mouth up and down until my jaw aches with the effort. Until I'm crying again, the tears washing over my cheeks, over his hand. He is fucking my mouth as Gilby fucks my aching, hungry cunt with the rigid object, and I no longer even care what it is.

Soon I need to come so badly, so badly, but I don't have permission. More tears.

"Good slut," Gilby says, the roughness of desire low in his throat. "You fucking hold it back. You don't get to come while I'm in your little cunt. Maybe when I'm in your ass. If you please me enough. You'd better hope you can take it. That you can fuck me with your tight ass the way you're fucking this billy club with your tight cunt."

My head comes up, the Master's fingers slipping from my mouth and I know right away what I've done. He shoves my face back down onto the table, my cheek slamming into the leather surface. He slaps my cheek hard, one burning strike before he reaches under me and takes one nipple in his fingers and twists it until I have to bite back a scream. Yet at the same time my sore, battered pussy opens more for the club, and I *want* it. I am grateful for it.

"Didn't know it was a billy club?" Gilby asks with a small chuckle. "But you like it, little slut. You fucking love it. Now fuck it real good for Gilby. Show your Master how much you like it."

His hands on me go still, and I begin to work my hips, working my pussy down onto the wooden shaft, sliding up, then down again. I try to take as much as I can into me, biting back my climax as the Master leans over me, his hold on my poor nipple tight and hurting, his other hand crushing my cheek to the table, controlling me utterly. And I breathe him in, and oh God, I almost come then, but I don't. I am reveling in knowing I'm doing what I'm told. That I am a good Girl.

There is something of the performer in me as I imagine the expression on his face, and Gilby's. As I think of how I must look, my body bucking and plunging onto the wooden club. The way the lips of my pussy must be plump and pink around the thick shaft, everything slick with my juices. I'm a little too in love with the idea, maybe, but I hear the Master's quiet grunt of approval as he presses my face harder into the leather-covered table. Pleasure ripples through my system at this tacit approval, driving me on. But soon it seems like an impossible task to hold myself back from coming, and I am afraid. About to come. *Afraid*.

Gilby's big hand grips my hip, stopping my motion, and he pulls the billy club from my body.

"Still," the Master commands me.

I hear Gilby moving around as my heart thunders, my poor, abused, too-empty cunt. Wanting. It's only a few moments before he returns. The Master releases my tortured nipple and takes a step back before Gilby shoves me down onto the table, then pulls me so my legs hang off the edge. Very quickly he binds me to the table with rope, the slick little knots holding my legs spread wide, bound to the table legs. He does the same to my arms, the ropes tight around my wrists. My legs are shaking, but the ropes and the table take care of my unsteadiness. The choke-chain helps in its own, strange way too.

I love this about being restrained—it's as if I am being held safely in the arms of the ropes or the chains or the cuffs. Or saran wrap or bondage tape, or whatever it is anyone binds me with. It calms me. I take in a breath, try to relax as I push it out, as Master Graham taught me. It seems like a thousand years ago, even though it's only been a little over a year since he began training me.

Is it terrible that I can barely think of him already? That his memory is fading in the wake of the unusual and extreme conditions of the Training House, and my fascination with the beautiful Master? As I wait for whatever the cruel Gilby will do to me next?

Cruel. And crude. Yet elegantly so, in this fantastical setting. Yes, elegantly crude. I can still hardly believe it's all real.

But Gilby's voice brings me back to the moment.

"My fat dick is going into your ass soon enough, little slut. Into that sweet pink hole. It's waiting for me to fill it. To fuck you until you can't help but scream, despite the fact that I've told you not to. Think about *that*, Girl."

And I do, even though the Master grabs my face in both his hands and squats down to look into my eyes, which is mesmerizing and beautiful and nearly unbearable. It makes my throat hurt to swallow the sobs—sobs that build and swell simply because his gaze is locked on mine, because even in this state of heavy subspace and rawness, I see something just as raw in his blue eyes, and it makes my heart ache.

Gilby begins to cane me, and it fucking hurts. I can tell it's Lucite or some other man-made material. I feel the welts coming right up on my skin, the sting unbelievably sharp. He goes at the tender flesh of my ass cheeks, down the backs of my thighs, my calves, which would make me dance in my bonds if there were any give to them. But there's not. There is no escape from the pain.

There's no escape.

The thought makes me smile through the pain—a pain so vicious I'm not sure I can stand it. Yet at the same time my brain is pumping out endorphins and dopamine and God knows what else—and all the more because the Master is there with me, holding me, looking into my eyes as it's happening, which is some beautiful mind fuck in itself. I'm dizzy and my traitorous pussy is weeping with desire. And all I want is for Gilby to keep caning me, to fuck my ass, no matter how huge he might be. To tear me apart while the Master watches.

When I hear the faint *snick* of a zipper I know it's time.

CHAPTER FOUR

There is no preamble. No warning. Just his thick fingers sliding into my cunt, then swiping the moisture back and onto my anus, pushing briefly inside. Then his huge hands part my ass cheeks and his condom-clad cock is at the entrance, the swollen head enormous against that small, pink pucker.

Oh God.

But God can't help me now. No one can.

No one can help you.

My body goes loose and warm, and I tumble into those words.

Yes.

The Master smoothes his palms over my cheeks, and his touch is unbelievably gentle, which only makes me expect something far worse. From him. From Gilby. But for several moments in which I feel as if time is suspended, nothing more happens. Just Gilby's big cock resting against my ass, and the Master's hands stroking my face in a way that makes me begin to cry again very softly.

Gilby pushes in, slowly at first, which surprises me, until he's past that first tight ring of muscle. I do my breathing, but he's so damn big I know ultimately it will be no use.

I cry a little more when the Master releases my face. If I blink I can see that he is still standing close by, which makes my heart soar. It's Gilby fucking my ass, but it's the Master's presence that commands me. It's the Master I am falling in love with.

"Oh, yeah," Gilby mutters. "The little slut is tight as a virgin. I like it tight. It means it'll hurt all the more. It means it'll make you want to scream, slut. My fat cock will make you need to. Let's take care of that."

He clamps a hand over my mouth and shoves his huge cock into my ass, driving it in all at once. I make some rough noise deep in my throat as my insides burn, but it only makes him push deeper, harder, until it's like a heavy drumbeat pounding my body from the inside out. He starts a jabbing, punishing stroke, and as soon he gets his rhythm, he begins caning my thighs again. There's too much going on and I can't process it all—pain and pain and the pleasure of being abused this way and the even greater pleasure in being watched by the Master, who I worship already. The pleasure of having my ass fucked by the biggest cock I've ever felt in my life, and Jesus, I'm going to come, or maybe pass out, or maybe both.

His hand over my mouth is cutting off my air a bit, but I love it, my head light as he fucks me, as he hits my poor, tender flesh with the cane, creating welts upon welts. And God, I love being fucked this way, in my sore ass, sore inside and out. I'm overloading like mad, my head spinning, my cunt contracting, pleasure deep inside me, shimmering outward, like some arc of electricity, like light itself. I feel sensation shining through my body, as if I am translucent. As if I could light up the sky. And my orgasm is some screaming animal, loosed from its cage, as my ass tightens on his plunging flesh. I scream beneath his hand, then everything goes black.

When I come to, he's untied me and I'm on my back on the table. My insides hurt. So does my skin. But my brain is floating, weak with pleasure and that strange, almost detached love I feel for anyone who plays me well, who can make me lose myself like this.

Blinking, I slowly realize a fire has been built in the hearth—I can hear its crackle, feel its heat. I dare to glance around, and see the Master's wide back, and I realize there is nothing detached about the love I feel for him at this moment. Nothing.

Save me.

Punish me.

Love me.

I bite the inside of my lip hard, needing the pain to carry me away, but it doesn't work.

Fuck.

The Master is on the phone. Gilby is nowhere in sight.

"Send the two Girls," he says into his cell phone. "We're done with her for the moment."

For the moment? Does that mean there will be more later? I don't think I can take more, but I want it, anyway. I want it all, whatever he wants to give me. Gifts of pleasure. Gifts of pain. I am so selfish.

Lying on the table, I am luxuriating in the aftershocks of orgasm and pain and his presence in the room. I want to keep my eyes on his strong back, the fabric of his linen dress shirt stretching over the hard muscle and broad shoulders, but I'm starting to dream a little. Or is it a memory?

I never really had a boyfriend. Not really. The first "relationship" was with Mr. Merrick. After him, when I went to Paris, one of my roommates, a Belgian girl named Arianne, invited me to a kink club. She didn't really understand what it was, but it didn't matter. The moment we got there, I did. She left an hour later. I stayed and didn't come home for two days. I played with some guy — I don't even remember his name — but it was nothing. A flogging. Nothing, yet *everything*. After him was Madame Cerrine. I played with her for four months. She tied me up. Flogged me. Caned me. Fucked me with a strap-on. She used a violet wand on me, my first foray into electrical play, which I loved right away.

Her little apartment on the Left Bank is too warm in the summer, but a small breeze comes through the open window, caressing my naked skin as I kneel on the floor. She loves me being on my knees — I've hardly stood upright the entire time we've been together.

"Again, cherie," she commands breathlessly.

Bending to do her bidding, I lick her slick cunt, one slow stroke up, then slowly down, pushing my tongue inside her, just the way she likes it. She grasps my hair, pressing my face harder into her fragrant sex, and I love it, love being forced.

I lick fervently, until she shatters, cries out, her pussy convulsing around my seeking tongue. I love the taste of come, male or female, but I swear hers always tastes like perfume smells. I look up, and as always, she looks perfectly put together, her blonde hair in its tight bun, her red Chanel lipstick not even smeared.

She smoothes a palm over her perfect updo, then tells me, "Get my wooden paddle and I will give you your reward."

I fetch it eagerly from its cupboard and bring it to her, my knees rubbing on the carpet. Sitting up, I present the paddle to her as if it's a gift, and perhaps it is. My gift.

"*Come here.*"

I lay over her lap, my hands on the floor, my toes bracing my lower body. She is warm against me, her corset stiff in contrast to her soft lap.

"*Count now, my darling,*" *she purrs, and hits me.*

"*Un!*" *I cry out in French as she has ordered me to do, the pain making me yell.*

She hits me again, and this time I move into it, into the swing of the heavy wood. The impact rumbles through me, pleasure swarming me even as my ass stings. And as she paddles me, harder and harder, she pushes her clever fingers into me, making me come. I am coming and coming, screaming the count.

"*Trois! Quatre! Cinq! Six! Sept! Huit! Neuf!*" *And finally, breathlessly,* "*Dix!*"

She made me love her. They all do. But she wanted to own me, and I wanted to *experience*. She cried when I left her, but I had to go. And she is nothing now compared to the Master. No one is. My mysterious Master who ignores me for days, and sends me to be abused by someone else.

I wipe the tears as they slip onto my cheeks. All the damn crying! But I can't help it. It's one of my favorite and most loathed humiliations.

I hear footsteps, and I watch from the corner of my eye as he leaves the room—I can't stand to really look. I am empty and filled at the same time. The Master touched me, watched as Gilby fucked me, beat me. I saw the excitement and what I could swear was some sort of adoration in his sapphire gaze. And this idea feeds me—that he is pleased with me. Wants me. But now he's leaving me once more. I am not so foolish as to expect anything else from this gorgeous, alluring, utterly dominant man with a house full of beautiful slaves.

I want more, and it is a deep, rabid craving that cuts into my insides. But as I said, I'm selfish.

A few minutes later the sisters enter and one of them has gentle hands and the other's are rough on me, even pinching me here and there and pulling on the chain around my neck as they help me down from the table, steadying me as my head rushes in my post-orgasmic haze, and with the punishment my body has received.

They take me into a bathroom, remove my chain collar and put me into a hot shower, both of them getting in with me and washing me quite thoroughly. I am beyond spent, and still their smooth little hands feel sensual on my skin—that and the warm water as it spills over my sore flesh. Then one of them rubs a bar of soap between my thighs, and it feels so good. She squats down and parts my ass cheeks, washing me there, and my clit begins to pulse once more. I am insatiable. Selfish, as I said. I should be happy with the working over Gilby gave me, with the Master being a part of it, putting his hands on me. And I am.

But she is rubbing me with the soap again, ass and pussy, then she presses two well-soaped fingers into my ass and begins to pump and turn them, and I am somehow hanging onto the other sister's neck, my head on her shoulder, my body shaking all over. And that sister pinches my nipples very hard, making me yelp, then rock into her cruel hands. I spread my legs a little wider to steady myself as my hurting ass gets worked again. But my body is frankly loving it, needing it. I lower my head, not even caring which sister it is in front of me—the one who will talk to me or the silent one—and I nuzzle her plump breast, feel the nipple come up hard beneath my cheek. Turning my head, I take her succulent, swollen nipple into my mouth, and swirl my tongue over the distended tip. She moans quietly, which tells me this is probably the one who talks to me. And the other girl—the other *Girl*—is still silently working my ass like mad with her fingers. And with her other hand she invades my cunt, her fingers sinking in deep. I'm soaked again. I can never get enough. I want to come all over her hands. I want to give her my orgasm.

But no, this one I want all for myself.

I arch against her, grinding down onto her fingers, and she stops so suddenly I am rocked off my feet, and the other Girl catches me. She says, "Rinse her off."

I bite my lip to keep from crying in outrage.

They use the shower sprayer to rinse the soap, being careful to aim the sharp spray at my tortured asshole, then I'm hustled from the big shower stall and roughly dried before they take me into another room—Gilby's bedroom, from the look of it.

There, the sisters fasten my wrists and ankles into pairs of heavy, unforgiving steel cuffs. One holds my hair, giving it a wicked tug, and the other latches a matching steel collar around my neck. It feels so rigid. I feel as if I belong. The sisters quickly clip my cuffs, shackles and collar to short chains attached to some bolts at the foot of his high, wooden bed. I'm on the hard, bare wood floor, and not even a sheet is given me. But it's warm enough in the room, and I resign myself to my uncomfortable night. I am maybe too tired and worn to care. And still thrumming with the need to come from what the Girls did to me. From what this place is doing to me.

I lean against the footboard, since the chains don't have enough give for me to lie down, and in moments my head drops to my chest, and I am lost in the hazy realm of dreams.

I think I expected Gilby to wake me and use me again, to beat me, but suddenly it's morning and he's nudging me awake with one slippered foot.

"What? You think you get to sleep all damn day, slut?"

Of course no answer is expected and I keep my mouth shut, blinking hard, trying to focus, to wrap my head around the current situation: slumped on the hard wood floor, naked, bruised inside and out. I flex my toes, stretch one leg experimentally. Everything seems to be working, if sore, but the soreness I take great pleasure in. And in thoughts of the Master, of his scent in my nostrils as Gilby fucked my ass.

Need him.

"Smiling?" Gilby says, and I blanch that he saw it. "Don't worry, there'll be little enough to smile about later on. Today's a school day."

He lets out a harsh chuckle while I wonder what this could possibly mean. The only thing I'm certain about is that any lessons I learn here will be harsh ones. I am terrified. Enchanted. I can hardly wait.

Soft footsteps on the floor and one of the Girls is back. Gilby gives a nod of his chin and she kneels to take me out of the cuffs and shackles and snaps a leash onto my steel collar. She gets to her feet and when I don't rise quickly enough, she kicks my leg, and I get up and follow her as she tugs on the leash. We go upstairs and into my room, where she hands me toothbrush and toothpaste, signaling for me to brush my teeth, using a bottle of water and spitting into the now-clean bucket, which she also motions for me to use to relieve myself. Since all I get are hand gestures I know this is the silent Girl, so I don't ask any of the thousand questions that wait at the tip of my tongue, baiting me.

When she turns to start the bath, I notice a second bucket on the floor next to the bathtub, and suddenly I know exactly what is about to happen, even before she bends over to screw the long nozzle onto the faucet. And I blush for some inexplicable reason, as if I have anything left to be embarrassed about. As if this has not been done to me before.

She waves a hand and I step over the side of the bathtub and squat in it, the porcelain cool under my bare feet. Bending to retrieve the empty bucket, she places it in the bottom of the tub, then she parts my ass cheeks and inserts the slim nozzle into my sore anus.

The water is pleasantly warm as it begins to fill me up, then uncomfortable as the pressure builds. I do not want this to happen. I do not want this to happen. But it's too damn late, and too damn bad. I am here of my own accord, because a larger part of me wants exactly this. Requires it. Yes, even this ultimate humiliation!

I take long, deep breaths, remind myself that everything the Girl is doing to me is at the Master's direction. But that helps only until she pushes the bucket under me and removes the nozzle. Then there is a single breathless moment where I try to hold it in before my bowels empty into the bucket, and I start to cry. This is no gentle seeping of a tear down my cheek, but horrible, hard sobs. The Girl is unsympathetic. She uses the nozzle to rinse me off, then re-inserts it and begins to fill me up once more. And I hate it, and I hate her, and some completely unreasonable part of me is grateful at the same time. For doing what will please the Master. For purifying me for him. For the degradation, which I claim to hate but which I also secretly love. Maybe because it opens me up in this way. Because I am utterly helpless against it—the humiliation and the tears and shitting into a goddamn bucket. But I don't fight it. Why would I? I am exactly where I want to be. Some part of me stands back and screams that I've lost my mind, yet at the same time I feel more sane and centered than I have in my entire life.

Three more times she fills me up and I empty into the bucket. After, I'm exhausted. She runs the bath, then quickly and thoroughly bathes me, hands me a towel, and I dry myself. She shoves me toward my pallet, and I lie down and close my eyes as I hear her pad from the room. I want to sleep. But too soon she is back with a tray and I have to sit up.

"You must be hungry," she says, making my heart leap.

It's the other Girl!

I look at her carefully, making a quick but thorough visual inspection, and I see she has a small mole over her left breast, just beneath the brand. I don't think her sister has one.

"Yes, starving," I say, realizing only then that it's true.

"Better hurry. It's a school day," she says, as if everyone knows about this but me.

"What is it, the school?" I ask, pouring a little of the rare milk I've been given for the first time in days into the bowl of oatmeal sprinkled with gold raisins.

"Uh-uh. You didn't think it would be that easy, did you?" She frowns at me. "Ah, I see you did. Silly Girl."

"Am I going right after breakfast?"

"Isn't that always when we go to school?"

She smiles a little, but I know I'm not in on the joke.

I take a few sips of hot tea, and it feels lovely. Soothing. I am too nervous to ask her more about school. Maybe I don't want to know.

"Have you ever been worked by Gilby?" I ask instead, wondering if she will answer.

"Of course. He was the one who brought us here."

"What?" I don't know why I feel shocked by this—maybe it's simply my fragile state after the working I've had—but I do.

"He was my lover. My Dom. But he likes to share his submissives. When he found out I had a kinky sister, well, we were his fondest wet dream." Her brows draw together for a moment as she takes a blueberry from the fruit bowl on my tray. She pops it into her mouth. "He was hard on me. He was the one who made me see I need it. He's very good. But he's not the Master."

She looks up at me, and her gray eyes are gleaming with what I recognize as that hint of subspace we all carry when we are well-played. It's then I notice the bruises on her thighs. Am I so in my own head, my own experience, that I failed to see her beautiful marks?

She catches me looking and smiles a small, Mona Lisa smile as she runs her hands over her bruises and welts, but she doesn't mention them. There's no need to. We both understand. It's happiness for people like us. And I smile back, my own mysterious smile, because we are both freaks, and we know it. We glory in it. We are all of us freaks here. A lovely shiver of belonging runs through me, like a song in my veins.

Yes.

"This is ultimately a very small world we exist in," she continues. "I've been given to Masters and Mistresses from all over the world, they've taken me places, to other houses in Europe, one in Bali, one just outside of Tokyo. It makes me know my small place in it all."

"I think I know what you mean."

She shakes her head. "This is your first time in this sort of environment. You don't even know the half of it."

Some small part of my ego wants to argue the point, but I don't do it. How would I know? Nothing can truly prepare you for this kind of formal place. For being a slave in the deepest sense. I understand I am at the very beginning of this journey. And isn't a big part of it about learning to let ego go and simply *be*? Isn't that what I'm looking for? To be forced out of my busy, busy brain, to be *made* to be present?

I nod. "I think I've only touched the tiniest tip of experience. I know that as much as I *can*."

Her smile lights up her face. She is so lovely, and my body aches for her touch again. "You're a philosopher, like me. It gets us in trouble, you know. But we like that." Pausing, she bites her lip for a moment before releasing the plush, pink flesh. "It won't serve you well in the schoolroom."

I nod. "Will the Master be there?" And suddenly my heart is hammering with hope, my sex pounding with need for him.

She picks up the tray and stands, leaving me disappointed, anxious. "Brush your teeth and empty your bladder again. Someone will be back for you."

I watch her long, brown hair swaying around the curve of her hips as she leaves the room, holding my breath until I hear the lock turn, allowing me to exhale.

The schoolroom.

Gorgeously threatening words, simply because the idea has been presented to me that way all morning. If only I knew he would be there. I need to feel his demanding hands on my flesh, to hear his voice. To breathe him in. But that will happen only when *he* decides, and right now I hate that aspect of my powerlessness.

I take a breath of acceptance and do as I'm told—of course I do. But the whole time I am wondering what this school will be like, what might happen to me there. I flash back to the last days of summer before starting kindergarten. I felt so entirely alone, a sad thing for a five-year-old. But my beautiful French mother had died the year before, and my father, an American, had moved me from my early childhood home in Paris to his grand home in New York. There was no one but the new nanny to take me to my first day at school. It had felt a bit like being thrown from a ledge. Perhaps that's why I now seek the relative safety of being bound, being made to do things that are beyond my control. I need to go back to those feelings of powerlessness in the world in a way in which I feel protected. In which *I* make that choice.

I make that choice.

Yes. Everything is different now. I choose even the fear and the isolation. My pulse calms a bit as I breathe in that idea, as I try to banish thoughts of kindergarten and my father from my mind.

A few minutes later a man I've never seen before—another slave wearing nothing but a shining collar and a halo of long, curling blond hair—comes in and grins at me.

"I'm here to take you to school."

The words themselves make me shiver with dread, and I find myself clenching and unclenching my fisted hands. Enough anticipation has been built up to make me sink into subspace—

into *slave* space—and my mind is emptying out so fast I barely have time to be alarmed. The fear is all in my body, a purely physical response.

Go.

Don't go.

But of course I am going.

Eden Bradley

CHAPTER FIVE

The male slave holds out a leash and I go to him, stand quietly as he clips the leash to my collar, staring down at his half-hard cock. It must be so much more difficult to be a male slave, with your excitement worn on the outside. I've always thought so. But my own nipples are hard as two stones, and I'm sure anyone could see a blush on my cheeks and my chest. It's the curse of being a natural redhead. The Masters and Mistresses all love it. Of course, they always slip their searching fingers into my cunt, finding it wet. I am wet more often than not, my body always seeking out pleasure, and finding it in the tiniest detail: my Mistress's perfume, my Master's voice, a quiet command, a rough beating, another beautiful slave. It will all set me off. I spend much of my time fighting my orgasms.

My pussy clenches hard now as the slave boy leads me from my room and into the hall. Across from the Master's study a door is open, and we turn there and enter.

The room is arranged as a schoolroom, much like the ones I sat in as a child, even with chalkboards and maps on the walls. Except in the long rows of desks, there is a phallus carved from wood in the center of every seat. My gaze roves over these lovely, wicked seats, noting that the farther toward the front of the room, the larger the dildos become. I am suddenly so shaky it takes me a few moments, as the slave boy leads me to a desk in the back row, to notice that most of the dildos in the very front row are double-headed, and in the single seats are huge butt plugs, cones of graduated beads. A wave of desire and fear washes over me. But then the slave boy has a hand at the small of my back and another on my shoulder, forcing me to bend over. He kicks my legs apart a little wider, and I feel his fingers between my thighs.

"Good. No need for lube. The Master will be pleased."

The Master?

My heart stutters in my chest. I want to look around, to see if anyone is seated behind the large wooden teacher's desk at the front of the room, but I don't dare. Instead I let the blond boy help me straddle my seat, using the desktop to hold some of the weight as he lowers my already-clenching cunt onto the protruding phallus. Sighing as it enters my body, I have to bite back my climax. He pulls my body up, then lowers me again, smiling a little at me as he does it a few times, fucking me with the phallus in my seat. Finally he settles me onto it, but it's not terribly large, and my lustful body accepts it easily. I make an effort not to squirm, not to rub my g-spot against the smooth wooden surface. Not to come — oh no, not to come. What might the punishment for that be? A rebellious part of me — a daring part of me — wants to know.

"Stay still," the slave boy warns me before he snaps the handle end of my leash to a metal loop on one side of the desk, and walks from the room.

I do look around then. It's a classic schoolroom, with the desks perfectly lined up. There are others in the seats in front of me: a girl with long, blonde hair woven into a single braid, a delicately built boy with fair skin and dark hair, another girl who's bobbed, chin-length hair is bright pink — she has a pair of red roses tattooed on the back of each shoulder. And in the front of the room is a boy — no, clearly a man, despite his predicament — who is so spectacularly beautiful he takes my breath away. He has smooth, golden skin, a hard-packed muscular body with strong thighs and shoulders and a broad chest. But it's his face that makes me feel as if I might melt into a pool of pure liquid fire. A finely sculpted jaw and chin, high, high cheekbones and almond-shaped eyes that look even more golden than his skin from where I sit. His mouth is strong and incredibly lush at the same time, a hard pout on it, and I can hardly blame him. He is mounted on a cross beside the teacher's desk, arms spread, wrists cuffed by heavy metal shackles. His knees are drawn up and bent so that his feet are flat against the crossbar of the big wooden cross, ankles heavily shackled. And despite the tall, pointed dunce cap on his head, he is glaring angrily at the room, which may be the most enticing thing about him.

I have never seen a slave with such fire in his eyes. With such tension in every beautiful muscle while he is made to hang there as if crucified, and I suddenly understand that he is as impaled as I am, hanging from the cross. He is like some kind of caged beast up there, a primal rage just barely contained, and I'm fascinated.

Oh, to touch him... My fingers itch with the need to feel that fine, golden skin. My mouth burns with the yearning to press kisses on his dusky nipples, one of which is pierced. To wrap my lips around his thick, golden-headed cock, which is every bit as beautiful as the rest of him, and just as hard, the head so swollen, his lust barely contained. I wonder what a terror he would be if he weren't chastised, bound, his ass skewered. A shiver runs through my entire body.

To have that beautiful beast on me. In me.

Suddenly the door slams open and I jump, my pussy jarring against the hard wooden shaft inside me. It hurts, but I welcome it. Want it. Want the Master, who has just entered the room, to see what a good Girl I am, impaled and still in my seat. But I have *not* been a good Girl, lusting after this new slave at the front of the room. The bad slave.

Oh yes. Even better.

I bite my lip and try to calm down.

The Master walks in and sits down at the desk, paging through a notebook, ignoring us so completely he might have been alone in the room. He is stunning, as always, with his slightly mussed hair, his fine bone structure, his large hands. Even the crispness of his shirt seems erotic to me, revealing his tattoos almost carelessly—although I am sure this man does nothing carelessly.

I want to fidget, for reasons I can't explain. Why do I feel a need for him to notice me, when I am no one in this House? I glance back at the bad slave and see his expression hasn't changed. But no, I'm wrong about that. He is silently fuming more than ever, his nostrils flaring. I squirm the tiniest bit simply to feel the dildo inside my squeezing, wet cunt. To imagine it is this slave's rigid cock.

The slave, and not the Master?

What is wrong with me? I am half in love with my lovely new Master already—more than half—and yet this slave boy has so easily distracted me. My gaze flicks back to the Master, who, as if he senses my disobedience, looks back at me, then rises to his feet. Keeping his gaze on mine, he moves toward the bad slave, one of those long, wooden pointer sticks in his hand.

He asks me, "Does this slave's predicament amuse you, Girl?"

I flinch, but don't dare to answer.

"Or are you thinking, perhaps, that you'd love to be in his position? It can certainly be arranged."

He turns to the bad slave and smacks his chest with the pointer stick, hard enough to leave a long, pink welt. The slave doesn't move a muscle.

"This is what happens, Boys and Girls, to bad students. To slaves who have a smart mouth. And this is only the beginning of the punishment he will receive today. You see, Christopher here lacks the appropriate respect for myself and my staff. And he is *very* bad at answering the test questions. Aren't you, Christopher?"

I am shocked to hear this slave called by name! But I remember the name from the Master's conversation with Mistress Alexa yesterday. I am just as shocked when the bad slave spits on the floor.

The Master grabs his chin in a hard, vicious hand and squeezes, holding Christopher's angry gaze to his own as he beats his thighs with the pointer stick. When it breaks, the wood splintering with a jolting crack, he drops it, releases Christopher's face and walks away. At his desk, he opens a drawer, takes a white handkerchief from it and wipes his hands carefully.

He says, "Shall we?" as if nothing has happened.

Christopher, for his part, wears the same angry glare, his cock harder than ever, his mouth more set. My body surges with heated desire. Who is this slave that he can take a beating like that without moving, without flinching? His thighs are striped with pink welts, and I want to kiss them away. I want to kiss his beautiful hard-on away too.

Who is this slave that he still has a name in this place?

The Master pulls another pointer stick from behind the desk, where I imagine he has a good supply of them, goes to the blonde and grabs her long braid, yanking her head back. "Girl, tell our newcomer what to expect here in my classroom."

"Yes, Master," she says in a soft, timid voice. "We will be asked questions by the Master, or by the schoolmaster, Mr. Clare. If we are correct, we may be allowed to kiss the Master's hand.

If we are unable to answer correctly, we will be advanced one row, until we reach the front of the room. If, in the front row, we get a wrong answer, we will earn a beating with a ruler, or… something worse. Is that right, Master?"

"Very good, darling Girl," he says, leaning down to brush a kiss across her cheek, and I am filled with jealousy.

If only he would kiss *my* cheek, call me "darling". Or if only Christopher would.

I silently berate myself as I try to focus only on the Master. He moves toward the Boy with the dark hair.

"Boy, first series of questions. Define a light year."

"Yes, Master. A light year is the distance light can travel in vacuum in one year's time."

"Very good."

He extends his hand, and the slave turns so that I see his face in profile. He is beautiful, as we all are here in our own way, with sharp features, like a faun. He places a soft kiss on the back of the Master's hand.

"Now answer this: name the nearest spiral galaxy from the Milky Way, and its distance in light years."

"Yes, Master. The nearest galaxy to ours is the Andromeda Galaxy, and it is…over two million light years away…?"

"You sound uncertain," he says, tapping the pointer against the toe of his polished shoe.

His dark hair is a little more mussed than usual after his small struggle with Christopher, and he is so stunningly handsome I find it difficult to look at him. Yet at the same time the only thing that can really tear my gaze from him is the sullen Christopher and his beautiful erection. I force myself to keep watching the Master, as I'm fairly certain he'll catch me if I don't, and I have no idea how bad the punishments are in the schoolroom. This thrills me a bit—more than a bit—but not enough to risk it. As I said, I am mostly a good Girl.

The Master taps the Boy's calf with the pointer stick. "Is that the best you can do?"

The Boy bites his lip. "Master, Andromeda Galaxy is two point five million light years from the Milky Way."

"Ah, very good." He lets the Boy place another kiss on his hand. "And what is the most commonly used measure of distance in astrometry, the branch of astronomy that deals with measurements and positions of celestial bodies?"

"That is the parsec, Master."

Again the slave is allowed to press his lips to the back of the Master's hand, while I panic in my seat. I couldn't possibly answer these questions. But as much as I crave the Master's hand beneath my hungry lips, I am still eager for the punishment. I want to move up the rows until my cunt and my ass are penetrated in the front of the room. To please the Master in this way, which, I am certain, is more satisfying to him than our ability to answer the questions. This idea makes me relax a bit. But only a bit. There is still the narrow pointer stick and the Master is creative in his use of us.

"Girl," he says suddenly, making my head jerk up, and I realize I've been daydreaming. But he's addressing the Girl with the pink hair. "Which of the Greek philosophers said 'No intelligent man believes that anybody ever willingly errs or willingly does base and evil deeds; they are well aware that all who do base and evil things do them unwillingly'?"

She sits perfectly still, but I can see the tension in her shoulders — until the Master, out of patience, slams her desk with the stick.

"Answer," he demands sharply, making me shiver.

I want that harsh voice aimed at me. And I don't want it. I fear it. Oh, but fear can be such a delicious thing.

"Master, I think it was Diogenes."

"Wrong," he says as he smacks her thigh with the pointer stick.

Her body goes loose, and I understand this reaction so perfectly, the release that comes with an anticipated punishment. Then he marches to his desk at the front of the room, presses a button on a device I hadn't noticed before that looks like an old-fashioned intercom.

"Advancement," he says.

A moment later the door opens and two men come in, both of them burly in build, and I recognize one of them as Gilby. They unhook the pink-haired girl's leash and lift her, moving her up one row and lowering her onto the phallus so quickly I barely have time to take in what's happening. It's then I see that all of

The Training House

the dildos in that row are carved with intricate patterns, and I can only imagine how they feel. My cunt squeezes the hard shaft inside me, which is suddenly far too small. How I want to be that Girl! I tremble with need at my school desk. Even more so when Christopher raises his chin and his urgent, angry gaze finds me. His golden eyes lance through me like flame and smoke and the keen edge of a knife. He is sublimely savage, this bad slave. The longer he stares at me, the more deeply I feel it. Feel *him*.

I cannot believe he is looking at me. I feel my mouth fall open a little, and a small smirk appears at one corner of his wicked lips, a dimple flashing for a moment in his cheek.

Ah God. I could die now. Come now.

Come. Now.

My cunt squeezes.

No!

I take in a breath. I hate to do it but I have to look away.

And suddenly the Master advances, his gaze on mine. He presses the tip of the pointer between my breasts. Lovely little pain.

"Girl, your first question. Who painted the infamous *Garden of Earthly Delights*?"

I almost want to get the answer wrong, but this I know. Art has long been an obsession of mine.

"Hieronymus Bosch, Master."

"Ah, the new Girl answers correctly. You may kiss my hand."

He extends it and it is all I can do to control myself, to place a quiet kiss there rather than licking it, sucking on his fingers.

"And now tell me, what element on the periodic table included in those below the atomic number ninety-two is not naturally occurring?"

My mind scrambles for information it doesn't have, then freezes, my tongue going numb.

I don't know, I don't know, I don't know!

I cannot say this. But I must.

"Master…is it uranium?" I say, trembling all over, knowing I'm wrong.

"Incorrect." His voice rings in the room before he slams the pointer stick down on my thigh.

I squirm — I can't help it.

"Try again," he commands.

I make an effort to focus, but my thigh stings, and my body wants *more*.

"Colbalt, Master?"

"Incorrect! The correct answer is technetium."

He smacks my thigh with the pointer once more, then again and again in the same hurting spot. My hands are balled into tight fists as I struggle not to cry out.

He pauses. "Advancement," he announces. "Front row for her."

Even before the two enormous henchmen arrive to unleash me and carry me up the rows, my body is melting, aching with desire. They bring me to the very front of the room and the breath goes out of me as I spy the two-headed dildo in the seat. Fear and desire are like fire and water in my system, my clit pulsing, my cunt contracting. Then they are lowering me onto it, the beaded shaft burning as it presses into my ass. The larger phallus slips easily into my wet pussy. I can feel them both inside me. And through the haze of needing to come I feel both ashamed and glorious, as well as shocked that I ended up here in the front row. I don't know how this has happened to me, and yet it has, and I can do nothing. *Nothing*. Beautifully humiliating.

The Master ignores the entire process, turning his attentions to Christopher once more. He presses the end of the pointer beneath Christopher's chin, forcing his head up. Those golden eyes are still glittering with rage. I am still wet and wanting him. Wanting them both—my beautiful Master and this beautiful slave, whose naked flesh and naked anger drive the yearning for him to inexplicable heights.

"Christopher, I would advise that you answer correctly," the Master says in a low, threatening tone.

Christopher's only answer is a flaring of his nostrils, his golden eyes flashing. But his cock jumps.

The Master gives a low chuckle and slaps at the cock with his hand, then does it again. The head is going darker, and I can only imagine the need for release burning through the bad slave's veins, his balls, that gorgeous, succulent cock. I swallow hard.

"We begin," the Master says. "Christopher, here is your

question. Jane is walking her dog, Spot. She sees her friend, Dick, walking toward her along the same long, straight road. Both Dick and Jane are walking at three miles per hour. When Dick and Jane are six-hundred feet apart, Spot runs from Dick to Jane, turns and runs back to Dick, and then back and forth between them at a constant speed of eight miles per hour. Dick and Jane both continue walking toward each other at a constant three miles per hour. Neglecting the time lost each time Spot reverses direction, how far has Spot run in the time it takes Dick and Jane to meet?"

"Are you fucking kidding me?" Christopher spits out, the dunce cap falling to the floor, revealing a short, platinum Mohawk.

There is one moment of silence as tension fills the room, then the Master grabs Christopher's swollen cock and squeezes until the slave's face turns beet red. But his jaw is clenched tight and he doesn't make a sound. His face grows even darker, that simmering rage boiling over and beaming from his eyes. The Master lets go so suddenly I think Christopher would have collapsed to the floor had he not been so tightly bound, his head falling forward for a few moments. He's breathing hard. And my own body is steaming, lust a wild searing in my tortured cunt, my throbbing clit. The Master goes to his desk, opening a drawer, and calmly pulls out a pair of thin metal rulers. Calmly, I believe, until he turns slightly and I see the bulge beneath the expensive fabric of his trousers. And oh my God, what this does to me! To know they are both so turned on by this exchange.

The Master hits Christopher's chest and sides and thighs with the evil metal rulers, which are long enough to be flexible, and I can hear the snapping of them against the beautiful slave's flesh. They leave dark welts on his golden skin, and I start to pump my hips, fucking myself with the wooden dildo in my seat, biting the inside of my cheek not to moan, not to come.

Excruciating.

When blood begins to seep from the wounds the Master drops the rulers, grabs Christopher by his short, spiky hair and kisses him. I nearly come, then. Only my training allows me to bite it back, to make myself take a few deep breaths. But I have never seen anything this thrilling in my life. And the solid shafts in my ass and my cunt feel as if they have expanded, or perhaps my body has contracted around them. I don't dare move or I'll shatter.

The Master pulls back, and he's panting almost as hard as Christopher. He gives a nod toward the back of the room, and the two large men come up and take Christopher off the cross, half carrying, half dragging him out the door. The Master runs a hand through his hair before he wipes his hands once more with the handkerchief. Then his gaze rests on each of the other Girls, then the Boy, and finally on me. My heart hammers in my chest, my pulse hammering in my clit.

Please notice me.

Don't notice me.

He gets up and stalks toward me, and I'd shrink in my seat if that were physically possible with these wooden dildos so lusciously buried in my body. He leans over me, his sapphire eyes boring into me.

"That little scene excited you," he says. It's a statement, not a question.

I nod the tiniest bit, bite my lip.

He leans closer and I can smell him again, that elegant scent filling my head. He strokes my cheek, his fingertips brush my lips and it takes every ounce of discipline I have not to kiss his fingertips.

He whispers against my hair through gritted teeth, "*You.* There's something about you watching me do these things. Knowing you *want* to watch, that it thrills you, that makes it… Be careful, little Girl. Be careful what you wish for."

He gives me a small shove as he straightens and moves back to the front of the room, keeping his back to us.

"Class dismissed," he says, then walks out.

I am left with my mouth hanging open in shock. Something about me? *Me*? And how does he know what I wish for? But of course he knows. It's his job to know. And I am crushed and frightened and so hopeful my heart is soaring all at once. I stare at the front of the room, my gaze searching madly for… something. I don't even know what. Some trace of him, perhaps? But what I find are traces of the beautiful Christopher: several tiny drops of blood on the floor. And I want to touch them, to lick them up, to absorb them, somehow.

He is not for you. You are the Master's.

But I can't help the craving that is driving me mad. The craving for them both! I am not supposed to feel this way. Not to this degree—for either one of them, not even the Master so soon.

It's nothing. It's lust.

But I've felt lust before, many times, and it didn't feel like this.

By the time the blond slave Boy comes for me I'm shaking all over, and when he puts his hands on me, simply to lift me off the wooden dildo, I am so close to coming again—or still—that I resist him for a moment.

He laughs. "What's this? Don't want to leave your seat?"

I shake my head mutely and let him snap the leash back onto my collar. As we move down the hallway I keep my gaze on the floor, the patterns of the wood grain making me a little dizzy.

"Boy."

I look up at the sound of the Master's voice, my heart racing.

"Give her to me," he demands, putting his strong, beautiful hand out for the leash, which the Boy gives over to him with a small bow.

"Yes, Master."

My heart races. Is he angry with me? Did he see me looking at Christopher? Did I do something else wrong?

He pulls me along behind him without another word, and I can barely keep up, he's moving so quickly. We reach the end of the hall at the front of the house and he marches me up a flight of wide, carpeted stairs to the third floor. At the top of the flight he turns and presses on the back of my neck.

"On your knees, Girl."

I go right down, the idea of being on my knees and crawling for him making my limbs go warm and loose. The ivory carpet is soft and scratchy at the same time as I follow his polished black boots. I love that he wears these big, bad-ass boots with his European-tailored slacks. It's divinely decadent to me, reminding me of the contrast that is kink at this level—an alluring combination of pure luxury and dirty wickedness.

I have no idea where he's taking me, but I don't care as long as I can be with him. Unless he plans to lock me up somewhere in an attic room, alone to suffer.

Please, no.

But in a moment we move through a pair of double doors into what can only be his private rooms, the space is so enormous and luxurious. The floor is a dark wood with lovely Persian rugs in deep red, black and gold. I don't dare look up to see what the rest of the room looks like, but it *smells* expensive. It smells like him. When the Master stops and turns to me, I immediately bow down, my forearms resting on the floor, my ass in the air.

He's silent for several long moments, then he says, "Very nice. Where did you learn that little trick? It pleases me, that you do this without me having to ask. It shows a certain level of devotion. To submission, if not to me. *Are* you devoted to me? No, don't answer that." I feel him moving around me, the slight pull on the leash as he paces, then I hear him blow out a long breath. "Do you know why I brought you to my rooms?" he asks, his voice a quiet murmur. "Well, neither do I. Fuck."

What is this? I don't understand what he's saying to me.

"Come here."

He tugs on the leash and I follow him on my knees to a seating area with a long sofa and two large chairs on either side, all done in masculine brown leather, diamond-tucked with brass studs. He sits on the sofa.

"Kneel, Girl."

I do so, in classic slave pose: head bowed, palms upturned on my spread thighs. I love this position. It reminds me that I have given myself to him, handed over my power completely.

"Very pretty." He tucks a few fingers beneath my chin. "But I want you to look at me," he orders.

When I do, his eyes are like a shock as they meet mine. They are so impossibly blue, and there is such intensity there. I don't know what to think of it.

"Tell me your name," he orders.

It takes me a moment to find my voice. "Girl."

"No, I mean your *name*."

My name in this place *is* Girl. What else could he possibly want? Then it hits me. He actually wants to know *my* name. Who I am. And I panic.

CHAPTER SIX

"I…" I stop, shake my head. "Master…?"

He runs a hand through his dark hair, tension in every line of his body. "I know it's on the contract. I knew it when I paid for you, when I reviewed your medical records. But I want you to say it."

"Is it…is it not Girl, Master?"

"Not right now. Tell me."

Shaking my head once more, my hands clenching, I have to force the words out. "It's Aimée." It feels strange on my tongue. It feels as if I've done something terrible.

"Aimée," he repeats, his shoulders dropping a little. He pats the sofa next to him. "Sit with me."

I climb up slowly, warily, sitting very stiffly, my eyes on the floor. He unsnaps my leash, then my collar, and I want to cry. Is he so displeased with me? I turn frightened eyes to him.

"Don't worry, I'm not releasing you."

A tear escapes then, making him smile a little, just one corner of his lush mouth, and for the first time all day I feel as if I've done something right, even if it's only crying for him. And this man's smile is every bit as stunning as the rest of him.

"Aimée, I want you to talk to me. That's why I took your collar off. You are still mine." He pauses, watching me, his gaze searching my face, but I don't know what he's looking for. "Do you want to be?"

I hadn't realized it was up to me. And perhaps it's still not.

"Yes, Master! Please." I am trembling all over.

"Then talk to me. I know this is…unprecedented under the circumstances. But this is *my* House, and I make my own rules. Understood?"

"Yes, Master."

"Good girl. Are you cold? Here." He takes an angora blanket, woven in shades of maroon and gold, from the arm of the sofa and wraps its softness around me, his fingers pausing on the bare skin of my shoulder.

It occurs to me that he understands how difficult it is for me to talk with him while I am still a naked slave, after the terms of this place have been ingrained in me for the last week, or however long I've been here. Deeply ingrained, which is his clever intent, and my mind is having a terrible time wrapping itself around this sudden shift.

Suddenly he leans in, his face very close to mine. "I must tell you this—that I don't know exactly why I brought you here, why I feel the need for you to talk to me as if you weren't simply another one of my slaves. But you aren't." He sits back and drags tense fingers through his hair. "Goddamn it, you aren't. And I'm as confounded by this as you appear to be."

I'm really shaking now. I don't know what to think, where to look, except at him. He is too handsome to be believed. So utterly masculine. Still exuding dominance like a pheromone. When he takes my hand I nearly yank it back. But I would never do such a thing.

"Aimée, don't be afraid. I need to know you. Tell me something…"

"Tell you what, Master?"

"I don't know. Anything. You were born in Paris, weren't you?"

"Yes, Master."

"Where in Paris?"

"Saint Germain-des-Prés."

"Ah. A child of privilege. Your family is wealthy? That always makes for a very particular kind of slave. Maybe that explains your perfect posture, the grace of your movements."

He runs a fingertip along my collarbone, up the side of my neck slowly, and I want to lean into him. I want to purr. Except that I'm still too shaken up by this turn of events.

"Or maybe that's simply *you*," he says. "Tell me how many Master's you've had, what your kink life has been like."

"I have been owned twice before. Once, briefly, by a Mistress in Paris, once by Master Graham, who sent me to you."

"And in the time between?"

"I've played at the clubs. I've bottomed for many people. But it never fulfilled me."

"Why not?"

"I have a need to be owned, Master."

"What else?" he demands, and I know I can't be so brief with him. He truly wants to *know*.

I fold and unfold the edge of the blanket between my fingers, but when I see him noticing I stop. "I'm...not sure I've ever thought it all the way through. When I was with my Mistress in Paris, I was too young to appreciate it."

"Sometimes when we're very young, we need to get out and try different things, experience life. Experience submission on a variety of levels."

"Yes, that was exactly how I felt."

"You look surprised that I would understand. But I was once in the same position, you know."

"You were a slave?" I cannot keep the shock from my voice.

He glances away, runs his hand over the high arm of the sofa, and I see the muscles in his forearm flex, making the dragon tattooed ripple over the bone and sinew. The black and gray detail and shading is exquisite. "Yes. A long time ago. In this very House."

He remains quiet, pensive, and I don't dare disturb him. I want to know this story too badly, and I'm afraid if I speak, if I move, it will break the mood, and he won't tell me anything more.

Finally, his gaze still turned away from me, he says, "The Training House has been owned by several generations of Masters and Mistresses. It was run by Master Stephan when I came here. He was a remarkable man. Tall, with long, blond hair he wore slicked back. Very European. He was Austrian. And I was only nineteen years old, so I understand being too young for such confinement. I came and went a few times, and he allowed me back every time. By the time I was twenty-two we were lovers. I don't know that I was ever a proper slave—not in the way the others were. I don't know that I truly had it in me. Well." He turns back to me, and I'm not certain why he's trusting me with all of this, or with the rawness in his expression, the shadows in his eyes. "We were together for six years when he became ill. Cancer. For the next two years I took care of him, as well as the House. During that time I expanded my skill set and my knowledge of domination, although he'd had me Top other slaves for his entertainment many times over the years. He'd had me fuck them, Girls and Boys, in front of him for his pleasure. Sometimes we'd take another slave to bed, sometimes entire orgies. But I'm not interested in that any longer. I haven't been for some time."

His gaze is burning into me. And I find I'm holding my breath, trying desperately to take in this information while he is mere inches from me, distracting me, my body on fire, my emotions cycling through so fast I can't grab onto any one thing and make sense of it: yearning, fear, sympathy, hope, despair.

"Aimée. I don't know what it is I'm looking for, but I felt the moment you arrived in my House I'd found…*something*. And it's driving me mad."

He stands and the panic takes over once more as I watch him pace the floor, his hand buried in his curling black hair.

"The thing is, I don't know that I ever really loved the man. How terrible is that? How unfortunate for us both. Surely he knew." He comes to me, kneels down in front of me. "I can't stand if that were to be the case with you. If you were never to serve me because you loved me in some way and not simply because of a contract you'd signed. If it served only your need to submit, and not some true desire for…."

I can feel my jaw dropping. My heart tumbles in my chest and the only thing I can get out is a harsh whisper. "Master, I serve you *because* I need to. I came here because I needed to serve, but after that first day, I think only of you."

And I have just lied to my Master. Because after today I am also thinking of Christopher. But at this moment, it is the Master in front of me, and I want…everything. I want him to touch me, to hold me, to hurt me. I want to do anything he asks of me, demands of me. I do have love in my heart for him. And I realize this connection was forged the moment our eyes met in his study downstairs, when I was simply a nameless Girl. Can I ever be that for him again?

He reaches for me and cups my cheek. Tears sting my eyes.

"Why do you cry, when I'm not punishing you?"

"Because I don't know how to cope with this tenderness from you."

He watches me, and murmurs, "Perhaps you'll simply have to learn how, my Aimée."

Oh! I do my best not to burst into tears, but it happens, anyway. And then more tears as he pulls me from the sofa onto the floor with him, into his lap, and the blanket slips away as he kisses me. And oh, his kisses are delicious, his lips tender, then his teeth biting hard enough to hurt. And I understand that I will be able to take the tenderness because with him, it will always be countered with pain. I stop struggling as my heart surrenders.

He draws both wrists behind my back as he continues to kiss me: my lips, my neck, where he bites me harder, and it hurts enough to make me pant in pain and pleasure. Lovely. Excruciating. Then he's using the pressure points just under my collarbones to hold me still, and he lets my wrists go while he runs the other hand over my body. And this is so completely different from any way he's touched me before, from any way I would have ever expected him to after the rigid harshness of his command that I've known since the first moment I saw him.

Is this some dream? Am I alone on my white pallet, eyes closed against the moonlight, imagining the Master wants me? *Me*, not a nameless, faceless slave—the slave I came here to be, but which I don't want to be at this moment.

His hand caresses my side, slips down to the curve of my hip, and it's like being touched by a lover. There is still command there, but oh, his kisses are soft and sweet in between the hurting little nips of his sharp teeth.

He forces my thighs open a bit, his hand demanding, yet sensual. And it's like some kind of mad mind fuck, being caught in this strange in-between state. Am I the slave girl? Am I myself? Maybe I don't even know who that is anymore. Which was what I thought I wanted. But now…

Tentatively, I bring my hands up and lace them behind his neck, feel the heat of the tender skin there, burying my palms under the curling hairline. And my heart twists in my chest because he feels so utterly human. *Vulnerable*.

I can't stand it. It is everything I never knew I wanted.

He presses his lips harder to mine, as if he silently understands exactly what I'm thinking. His tongue is hot and sweet, tasting the tiniest bit of mint beneath a flavor that is simply him—like leather and strength. Intoxicating. As intoxicating as his hands, which are really exploring me now, sliding over my flesh: my stomach, the small of my back, then up my spine, leaving chills in the wake of his touch. I am covered in goose bumps. Soaking wet. I want to spread my thighs wide for him, welcome him in. Beg him for it. But I am still mostly a good Girl, so I remain quiet, passively accepting his kisses, his touch, except for the little gasping breaths I can't help.

Soon he's pressing me down on my back on the soft rug, the weight of his body over mine, the buttons of his shirt pressing into the soft flesh of my breasts. We're making out like teenagers, except that there is nothing innocent about it—about him as his panting breath fills my mouth, as I breathe it in. He uses his knees to kick my thighs apart and I want to scream at him to fuck me.

Please, please, please...

Shaking all over, my clit is pulsing with a desire that is stunningly sharp. A small sigh escapes me when he lowers his head and takes my aching nipple into his mouth, drawing it in, sucking hard, swirling his tongue over the sensitive tip. Then biting down hard enough to make me cry out.

"Ah!"

"Did that hurt you? You must know I meant it to," he murmurs, his voice a low, rough rumble I can feel in his chest. "You know we both wanted it to. Needed it to. There are certain things we understand about each other, even with so much still to discover."

He turns his face and rubs his soft hair over my breasts, and it feels unbelievable. So, so good I have to hold my breath in fear that he'll stop. Finally I dare to take his face in my hands, running my fingers through that thick, lovely hair. But he immediately takes control from me, pinning my wrists over my head with one hand, kissing and sucking at my throat, using his lips and teeth to press, to constrict my breath, which always renders me helpless—it's the hard surge of desire as much as it is surrendering to his control. It's everything at once.

Everything.

Him. Me. This House. My surrender to someone not only as a slave, but as something—someone—*more*, and the two ideas seem to be completely antithetical, to crash together, making a little explosion inside my brain. And as if that isn't enough, he suddenly raises his head, stormy blue gaze locked on mine, shadows passing like clouds across the sun. There is something tortured in there. But he gives a little shake of his head, and it clears—some of it, anyway. Then his brows draw together as he takes my jaw in one powerful hand. He bends to nip at my lip, his tongue darting out until I open for him. Then pulling back, he gives a sharp nod of his chin.

"Open, Aimée."

My lips part, my pussy slick and wet for him, open already.

He bends and catches my lower lip between his teeth, bites down until I begin to squirm and pant from the pain. Until I taste blood. He releases the tortured flesh and licks it. And as my mouth opens on a moan, he licks again, then again, then he kisses me, and for a few moments we're making out once more. He slows things down, his tongue darting between my lips, then again, wetter this time, and I realize he is pushing his saliva into my mouth. And this is one of the hottest things that's ever happened to me.

He pulls back just enough to look at me.

"Yes, Master. Please. More," I dare to beg, if only because the rules have changed and I don't know what they are anymore, and maybe he doesn't, either.

He leans closer, holds my jaw in his hand, squeezes, his fingers prying my lips open, holding my face with a firm grip. And I can feel as he lets his saliva drip into my mouth. I drink it in, swallow, as I would his come. Desire is like a flash of heat lightning in my body, and I am twisting beneath him, but I think we both understand I have no desire to get away.

He ends with another sharp nip, releases my jaw and sits up, straddling me. "Unbutton my shirt," he orders.

My hands are shaking as I work the buttons, hardly able to believe I get to do this. Not that I never undressed Master Graham or Madame Cerrine. But everything is so much stricter in the Training House. He is so much stricter than anyone I have ever come across. Until right now, when the strictness is mixed with his own raw desire and emotions I have yet to understand.

As his shirt falls open, it reveals fair skin, a little dark hair on his chest and a narrow line of it below his navel. He slips the shirt off, and I can't take my eyes from the muscles working in his shoulders and arms, from the tattoo which I can see now goes all the way up to his shoulder—more Japanese work, but I'm far too distracted to make it out, or even to care. All I know is that he's unbuckling the slim belt at his waist, and I don't even care if he's going to beat me with it. Or, I *do* care—I want it, yearn for it as much as I ever have—but what I want even more is for him to be naked with me, inside me. I have no idea what will happen. I am still powerless. Helpless.

Helpless. You can't do anything about it.

For the first time in many years, this thought is of no comfort to me at all.

No, suddenly everything is terrifying. The unknown, because even though each day, each moment since coming here has been unexpected, and keeping me in a state of continuous surprise is part of the plan of such places, even *that* has been something I can count on. But now, it is the inability to fall into that state of utter powerlessness that scares me, because it's been my comfort zone for a long, long time. And I realize in a blinding flash that I truly have nothing and nowhere to escape to.

The Master stops, belt in hand, and wipes a tear from my cheek with his thumb. "What is it?"

"I just…had an epiphany, I guess, Master."

"Master *Damon*. Tell me," he demands, and I wouldn't even think of disobeying.

"I just…I didn't realize until this moment that kink has been my escape."

"Explain."

"I knew it was my *retreat*. That I loved sinking into submission, that it makes the world fall away. I thought, because I'm a masochist, that what I needed was to feel more acutely. But I was wrong. What I needed was to be rendered numb in the face of overwhelming sensation. To go numb in being faceless. And it's…a shock."

He continues to stroke my cheek, his tone low while the weight of his body as he straddles me reassures me as much as his voice. "We all need something, Aimée. That's why we do this. It doesn't matter what it is, as long as there is no intent to damage anyone. Fetish is a coping mechanism as much as it is sexual. It's the fulfillment of needs. Are anyone else's needs any worse? Any better? These are things I had to come to terms with when the sadist in my soul was crying to get out. Roaring. Screeching. For me the world becomes both more and less real when I am here in the House, when I am disciplining my slaves. Are you afraid this makes you wrong, somehow? Sick?"

"Oh, I accepted that about myself a long time ago."

He smiles a little. "So did I. Why the tears, then? If you can accept that you're a masochist, your desire to serve, to be enslaved, then how has anything really changed?"

I shake my head. "I don't know, exactly. I only know it has."

"Because I'm here with you like this?"

"Maybe."

"Then I will ask you again. Do you want this, Aimée?"

"Yes. I do. I want anything and everything you are willing to give me, to make me do, to be for you, Master."

"Master Damon," he says again, so quietly I can barely hear him.

"Master Damon," I repeat, not certain if this makes things better or worse.

"Tell me again," he commands.

"I want it. I want you. I want you to do *everything* to me, Master Damon, Sir. Please."

He reaches down and swipes my soaking pussy lips with his hand, smiles. His teeth are perfect rows of white. "Your lovely cunt speaks the same truth. And I want to eat it, to shove my tongue inside you and drink you up. To suck so hard on your tender little clit that you scream in pain and delight. But I can't."

"I...what? I mean, pardon me, Sir." My heart is beating so fast I think it might explode.

"Because, my perfect Aimée, if I don't fuck you right this moment, I feel like I might die."

"Oh..."

Somehow he kicks his way out of his big boots and his fine Italian slacks and he is beautifully naked, kneeling over me. His thighs are so strong, with the same fine, dark hair. His cock is magnificent. Tall and proud, as commanding as he is. The head is swollen. Succulent. *Pierced.*

God.
My pussy clenches.
Need him. Need to feel him inside me.

I open my thighs wider, and he pulls my ankles up, resting them on his broad shoulders. Then he presses with his body until he's resting his weight on top of me, my knees folded against my breasts. He presses harder, until the pressure hurts my crushed breasts. But I want it. Need it.

"Anything," I whisper. "Everything."

He uses his fingers to spread my labia, then his steel-tipped cock rests at the entrance to my wet cunt, and I have to make myself hold perfectly still.

He waits, the head of his cock thundering in a pulse beat like a killing hunger against my slick flesh. He waits, my cunt dripping with liquid desire that pours from me as if I've already come. He waits, my mouth straining with the need to suck his beautiful cock, drink in his sweat, kiss his mouth.

How very vanilla of me.

But this thought has barely entered my brain when he rams his lovely, long cock into me, deep and hard and hurting in a way that makes me swoon. He gasps as he pulls back, as he rises up to stare into my face, and there is something like wonder, like awe, on his. And his expression sort of crumbles above me as he begins to move, in and out, yet there is nothing mundane about this lovely, sinuous motion that is his body moving in mine. It is elemental. Transcendent. Connection.

"Connection," I whisper. Or perhaps the word doesn't even come out.

This is the one thing I have been missing my entire life. And the truth hits me like a brick to the chest. I feel for several long moments as if I might actually have a heart attack. As if my heart really could burst from my chest, splattering the walls with emotion. So, so strange, I don't even know what to do with it.

Love. The real thing. I never knew.

I'm crying again—yet again!—but he does nothing more than dip his head and lick up one of my tears. And I focus then on the exquisite pleasure surging through me as desire builds, spirals, and I imagine it like a long, satin ribbon, twisting and looping through my pussy, wrapping around his balls, threading through the heavy steel barbell in the head of his cock, twisting tightly across my clit until I know I *must* come. Must. Come. Must…

"Ah, God!"

My body bucks, out of control, and the only thing holding me down is his fine, fine flesh, one strong hand on my wrists, the other digging into my hip. He is fucking me so hard I know I will be bruised, inside and out.

Yes.

He plunges into me, one rough, piercing jab after another, and the beauty of his face is a fierce thing to behold as he begins a low, threatening growl that turns into a howl that turns into voiceless panting, teeth bared as he looks into my eyes. And I'm coming again with him. I can't help myself. His beautiful face is making me come, his harsh cries, his pleasure transferring into my system as if it were my own times a thousand.

I know I'm not making sense.

He falls onto me, and I inhale, taking in the scent of his come and my own. Our sweat mingled. The faint trace of shampoo in his dark hair. I have never felt happier in my life.

I have never felt happy in my life.

My stomach twists, but he is there—right there—holding me down. Keeping me safe.

Yes. It's all right.

I want to twine my hands behind his neck once more, to feel the reassuring warmth of him letting me. But I can't do it. Instead I raise my chin and hope for him to kiss me. And when he does it feels like a benediction. Permission to *feel*. Because he has made me feel this.

I don't know what will happen to me now. But for this one moment, I can simply be.

Eden Bradley

CHAPTER SEVEN

Morning sun finds its way through the heavy brocade drapes in Master Damon's room. I wake in the softness of his big bed, and have to blink in confusion.

In his bed.

Then I remember last night. How he fucked me on the floor, then pulled me up onto the bed and spanked me until I screamed, then fucked me again before we had dinner brought to us on a silver tray by the calm Robert.

It occurs to me if I don't turn my head to see if he is there, this can still be real. I ball my hands into fists, wanting to fight the urge to find out.

Do it. Don't do it.

"What are you concentrating on so hard, lovely Aimée?"

Biting my lip, I open my eyes, let my lashes flutter while I take in the fact that I am truly here, that this is happening.

"Aimée. Tell me."

Blinking up at him, I whisper, "I wasn't sure…if this all existed. I thought it was simply one of my pretty dreams."

He laughs. "Is your sore ass and your sore little cunt pretty too? Yes, your cunt is perhaps the prettiest thing I've ever seen. And you know I love the marks on your ass—my own handprints. Unfair question."

I smile, then. "Master Damon, you are the master of unfair questions, Sir. Or so I've been led to believe, given my brief time in your schoolroom."

His smile widens. His teeth are so sharp and white. Makes me itch to be bitten. Again.

"Well said. Now, shall we have breakfast? I find I'm hungry."

"As you wish, Sir."

"Ah, in that case…"

He pulls me with him as he sits up, dragging me across his lap, and I feel his erection pressing into my belly. If I squirm a bit I can press my mound against his muscled thigh.

He smacks my exposed ass, one wickedly hard slap.

I bite my lip, focus on keeping quiet.

"Are you trying to be a good girl for me? Yes? Well, today you will be good for me by moaning and screaming without holding back. I want to hear it. All your sighs of pleasure. All your cries of distress. You give those sounds *to me*. Understood?"

I smile only because I am certain he can't see me. "Yes, Sir."

He shifts my body until most of my torso rests on the bed, on the sheets that are the finest Egyptian cotton soaked with our sweat and come. I breathe in, then exhale, my lungs emptying in a loud bark that burns my throat as he bites my ass with his evil teeth.

"Ah, fucking God!"

"Not I," he says. "The Devil might be closer."

"Yes, Master Damon," I answer through teeth gritted in pain.

"Say it to me," he commands.

"You are closer to the Devil," I tell him obediently, smiling.

"And how do you finish that sentence?"

I can hear the humor in his tone.

"You are closer to the Devil, Master Damon, Sir." I'm careful to cover all bases, even though I know he will bite me again, or worse.

Oh yes, he might do something worse.

I am luxuriating in that idea.

"Better," he says.

But he bites into my poor flesh anyway, then over and over again, layering teethmarks upon teethmarks until I can smell the blood seeping from my skin. I want him to make me bleed. Anything and everything, as I've thought to myself, as I've told him. I want him to kiss the blood from my wounded flesh, and he does, kissing and licking, luring me into the lovely heights of subspace, where the world is all sweet sensation and the brain chemicals I'm addicted to. But in a flash everything changes as he spreads my thighs and starts the hard stroking motion inside my cunt that made me squirt over and over that first day.

I try to prepare myself for that sense of abject helplessness I felt the first time — only eight days ago, but it feels like a month — but now it's tempered by the connection I know I felt with him last night, that seems so apparent even this morning.

My body goes loose inside as I give myself over to it.

"Good girl, Aimée," he murmurs, and I can hear the sharp lust in his voice, feel it in his swelling cock. "Not that resisting would be of any help to you."

I let out the smallest laugh, and he pauses to press a thumb into the most tender pressure point in my groin.

"Oh!"

"Let me hear it. Did you forget so easily?"

He presses harder, that evil thumb, until I'm panting and squirming, unable to stop myself from trying to escape from the pain. But he stops me with the hand he has inside me, using all his fingers to fill me up. I hold still, hold my breath.

"No, Aimée. Are you going to be bad, suddenly? No, I don't think so."

He starts the hard stroking against my g-spot once more, and I know better than to fight it. He strokes and strokes, harder, faster, then his hand pumps up and down, fast and cruel, hurting me, although I love it. And I'm squirting all over the place, soaking his hand and the bed and my naked thighs as I scream. He begins again, and it takes only seconds before it happens once more, and this time my calves get wet, my ankles.

"Again," he says, as if I could possibly argue.

My head is spinning, light, as he forces me to squirt again, then twice more before I collapse onto the bed. He turns me over with rough hands, straddles my face and tells me, "Suck me."

I open my obedient, greedy mouth, my body buzzing with sensation, my mind misty but full of need. Full of wonder that I am allowed to take him into my mouth. He shoves his cock down my throat, choking me, and my eyes tear up. I try to breathe through my nose, but he's fucking my face so hard there's no time to breathe. The steel piercing hits the back of my throat and I fight not to gag too hard, glad my stomach is empty. He snakes a hand around the back of my head, grasping my hair in a punishing fist, holding my head up off the bed while he keeps ramming his lovely cock down my throat. My face is full of tears and snot and I can't pull any air into my lungs, but I *want* this. I want to please him. I want to swallow his flesh whole. To take all of him into my mouth, down my throat, into my body any way I can.

He arches above me—I can feel it rather than see through my tear-glazed eyes—and he cries out, plunging into me, and I taste his hot come as it shoots down the back of my throat.

Yes. And now some small part of him is mine. *In* me. Belonging to me, and no one else.

He draws his softening cock out, smacks my lips with it, then my cheek. Then he's using his hand to slap my face, making my cheeks sting, making me feel like *his*.

"Where are you, Aimée?" he demands.

"Right here, Master Damon. Sir."

He grabs my face in a crushing grip, forcing me to focus on his face, on his blazing blue eyes. I see so much in there, something I don't know how to describe. Something is happening here that feels…different. With him. For me. And so, it comes as no surprise somehow that he keeps me in his rooms and all to himself for the next two weeks.

It's a Sunday, which I only know because I've come to realize the weekly bells I hear in the distance are church bells. Fifteen days I've been in the Master's chambers, taken out only to be exercised in his private gym next to his suite. Sometimes it's Robert who takes me, and sometimes it's one of the brunette slave girls, who now cast me resentful looks, and even the one who talks remains silent. But I am too giddy to care.

Although…when I am left alone, I still find myself wondering about the beautiful, bad Christopher. What must he be doing now? Is he as resentful as the Girls that I am monopolizing the Master's time? Does he think of me? And is any of this some sort of mind fuck for him, the way it is for me that I am thinking of anyone but my Master?

My beloved Master. He works me mercilessly, still, which I need. Crave. He has instructed me to wake him with his cock in my mouth, which I do happily every morning. And just as happily I give him massages, serve him meals on my knees. He has taken to using leather, laced arm binders to hold my arms tightly behind my back, placing a piece of toast or a small berry between my teeth and making me feed him, which thrills me, makes me wet for him. Everything makes me wet for him. Everything makes me love him.

We've talked more. All the time. He's asked me so many questions about my past, but I've managed to mostly find a way around answering when it comes to my horrible father, my lovely, dead mother. We talk instead about my time in Paris, the trouble I got into at school, which amuses him. He never truly laughs, but tiny creases appear around his eyes when he smiles, or chuckles a little. So sexy I can barely stand it.

The sex and the kink are so intertwined now I can hardly remember how I've ever done it any other way. Not that he allows me to come all the time. Often it's only the squirting, which is still sort of like coming, and yet it's not. He loves to do that, and to leave me needing to come so acutely sometimes my stomach actually aches with the need. But I cherish it, that sign of his absolute authority over me, even when it wakes me in the middle of the night.

And the nights... I am always collared now, and I sleep chained to his headboard most nights, yet there is enough slack that I can move around, and he keeps me close enough that he can touch me. He does touch me. Before I am allowed to sleep. At three in the morning. Some days he must attend to the House or other duties, and he leaves me chained for hours at a time. I love those quiet moments alone too, when I'm left to meditate on the soft cotton sheets, on the weight of my chains, on the scent of him left lingering in the room like some ghost of his presence. When I allow my thoughts to dwell for brief moments on Christopher. But even in those moments I understand he is nothing but fantasy material, and what is real is the Master, what is happening now between us, what I feel for him.

When my Master returns to me he is always more aggressive than ever, and that's often the times he really hurts me. I am covered in his marks, from the cane, the metal claws he uses to scratch my flesh, the whip, which makes me swoon in some lovely and awful way. I have teeth marks on my breasts, on the insides of my thighs, in my armpits, which he delights in torturing. He has hung me in complicated torture rope work from the ceiling, the knots carefully placed to make me scream in dizzying pain. I love the helplessness in being suspended, the sensation of being decorated in his rope. But I love the chains even more. The cold steel. The primeval clank and rattle. I love it all. I love him. And as he suggested—as I knew would happen—the love has only grown, until it's like a balloon overfilled with air, needing to burst. Until it's like the building pressure just behind my g-spot before he makes me gush all over him.

I have swallowed those fearful moments in which I'm uncertain how this will end. The pain and my deep submission help me do this. I have little else to hang onto.

He's been away all day, and I know to expect some harsh treatment when he returns. I've been in my chains for only a few hours. One of the sullen Girls took me for exercise, then bathed me in the Master's bath. She won't even look at me, and her hands on me were cruel, but I find it hard to mind. I have not, after all, been asked to stay permanently. If only they knew that I'm as tortured by seeing them and their proud House brands as they appear to be seeing me kept in his rooms.

I'm dreaming in my chains when he is suddenly on me—I've failed to hear him come into the room—and he unfastens my leather cuffs from the chain and yanks me off the bed with one fist around the cuffs. I stumble to my feet, and he catches me just before I fall. He loves doing this sort of manhandling with me, keeping me literally off-balance. And it does the job beautifully, my head sinking down and down into subspace. Into confusion. He yanks me around by my long hair, kicks my legs apart, then again until they are spread as wide as they can go, and I can barely keep my balance.

"Hands behind your neck," he orders.

I bring my hands up and over my head, then behind my neck, and clasp them there.

He goes to work right away with his hand, fucking my cunt, still sore from his attention last night.

"Don't you dare come, Aimée. You squirt for me, but don't come."

And I do. I soak his hand, his arm, my thighs.

"Ah, look what you've done to my rug. You must be punished."

"Yes, Master Damon," I say, filled with agonizing need and shimmering joy.

This was what I was made for. For *him*.

He moves around behind me and shoves me toward the bed, and I catch myself on the side of it with the front of one shoulder. My hands are still clasped behind my neck. Then he's behind me, and I can feel his bare thighs against mine. He parts my ass cheeks and plows into me, which hurts like hell without the benefit of lube. But he does this often, and I've learned to take it. To take great pride in it.

"Beautiful, tight little ass," he says from between clenched teeth. "But you insult me, Aimée. Your marks are too faded."

"My apologies, Master," I manage to gasp as pleasure moves through me.

"As you should be," he says before he hits the side of my thigh with a sharp blow—sharp because the wooden paddle he's using is covered in razor-edged metal spikes.

The pain is exquisite, even more so when he starts to fuck my ass once more, the strikes of the spiked paddle keeping time, until I feel the blood trickle down my leg. But I will gladly bleed for this man. My Master. My love. I am so, so grateful for all that he gives me.

He pumps hard into me, his hot come filling me up, his hand dragging the metal spikes up my thigh as he convulses in pleasure.

"Ah!"

"Ah!"

We cry out together. Pleasure and pain. Love and wonder. Perfection.

Everything goes a little dark for me after that, until he lays me on his big bed and cleans my bloodied thigh with his own hands. My bindings are gone, and I am naked other than my collar. Letting my gaze explore his beautifully muscled body, I sink into the softness of the mattress and the fine sheets. Into his oddly gentle touch as he tends to my wounds.

He looks down at me. "My good girl, Aimée," he says, stroking my hair from my cheek, that mysterious smile on his beautiful lips. "I am so pleased with you."

There is nothing I want to hear from him more than these words. Except...

"I love you, Master," I tell him, the words issuing from my

lips before I can stop them.

But he only smiles, moving onto the bed, pulling me with him until my head rests on his chest.

We lie quietly for a long time, and I begin to wonder if he's fallen asleep when he says very quietly, "I lied before."

"About what, Sir?"

"About my Master—Master Stephan. I did love him." A long pause, and then, "I did. I hate that I told you I didn't. I feel as if I've dishonored his memory. But even after all these years…this is the first time I've said either of those things out loud—that I didn't love him, that I did. And since I'm being so honest with you, I have to tell you, it left me unable to ever love again. Watching him die for two years…I was so young. It was a terrible, terrible thing. At some point I made a conscious vow never to love anyone the way I loved him."

"Never?"

"Not until you, Aimée."

I pull in a sharp, gasping breath. "Surely not me," I say.

"What do you mean? Why not you? You are imminently loveable. If I can see it, the rest of the world must see you the same way."

"No, Sir," I have to whisper. I don't want to think of my cold, cold father. Not now, when I am in the arms of a man I have come to love. "And Sir, I haven't been here very long."

"And yet you say you love me."

"I do."

"Then how is it impossible for me to feel the same?"

I chew on my sore lip for several moments. "Forgive me, Sir, but I am not sure you do."

He strokes a hand over my hair. "You're probably right. Everyone feels these things differently. You may love me only as a slave loves her Master, which is only right. And I may love you only as a Master loves his lovely, obedient slave, who strives so very hard to please me, and I do. But it's more a starting point than I've experienced in years. That in itself means something to me. I want it to come to mean much more. Do you, Aimée? Do you want to stay with me, learn to love me as I learn to love you? Do you understand what I'm saying? Asking of you?"

"I think I do, Master. You make sense. I've always loved

those who commanded me a little bit, but it's different with you. I love you, Sir. Enough to make my heart ache with it. But I know I'm only dancing around the edges of what might be. So yes, I understand you, Master Damon. Yes, I want what you're asking of me."

He turns and lifts my chin with his fingers, looking into my eyes. "I *am* asking. I never ask anything of anyone, I simply tell. I've been doing that for a very long time. But this I have to ask. Because love can only be given freely."

He leans in to kiss me, and it is so sweet, this strange, utterly unexpected moment. I drink him in, wondering how I can want this along with the harshness? But I do. I want it all from him.

Everything. Anything.

He pulls back, and I feel him retreating, but I understand that too. This will take us both some time to get used to. I don't want to think about the fact that we may never be able to, freaks that we are. But why can't freaks love? Why not?

It hits me that the Master may love Christopher too, and the idea makes my heart leap and fall in the same breath. Is that why he has a name in the same way I do now? I haven't dared to ask, to utter his name. I'm too afraid it will reveal how drawn to him I am. And suddenly I'm afraid I may be some passing fancy for the Master, and my chest aches with the thought.

Don't lose your love for me, Master.

Don't lose your love for Christopher.

I can't bear to think of the bad, beautiful Christopher going unloved, he seems to need it so badly.

Don't think of him.

Finally, we sleep, and I dream I am in a boat on turbulent waves — they crash around me, tearing the boat to pieces, until I'm floating in the cold water, hanging onto one piece of wood. Alone.

I wake with a start to find my Master standing naked at the window, his back to me. Realizing I've been left unchained, I think perhaps the dream is nothing more than a result of sleeping unbound.

I have become very good at lying to myself.

When he returns to the bed I pretend I'm asleep, and after a few minutes of him lying stiffly beside me, he curls into me, taking me into his arms, burying his face in my hair. And I cry myself silently back to sleep, careful not to shed too many tears, while he holds me in a way he never has before. Desperately. So tightly I can barely breathe, his legs wound around mine.

I don't know how much later it is when I'm startled awake. Something is slipped over my head and it's pitch dark in a way the room never has been before. Rough hands binding my ankles together with rope, then I'm dragged from the bed and thrown on the floor, rolled onto my stomach and my wrists are bound in the same manner.

These are not the Master's hands on me, and I'm panicking. The panic turns to full-blown terror when I'm lifted by two sets of hands and carried from the room.

Down the stairs and outside—I can feel the cold air on my skin, smell the salt of San Francisco even through the bag covering my head and fastened around my neck.

Where am I going and who is taking me? Taking me away from the Master's House! But I'm too scared to even cry. I am afraid someone has broken into the House and kidnapped the Master's slaves. That it has been raided by the police, which can happen at these places where kink is practiced to such an extreme. Or—even worse—that the Master is sending me away.

No!

A small sob catches in my throat as I'm thrown down onto what feels like carpet over metal, and I know I'm in some sort of vehicle. A van? The door is slammed shut and I'm left alone.

I want my Master, my beloved Master, to rescue me from this. To come and take me back into the House, into his rooms, to tell me it's all a mistake. But I know already it's not. Except maybe *my* mistake, for telling him I love him.

Master!

The tears pour down my cheeks unheeded. This is a form of torture I really cannot endure.

The door opens with a creak and I cringe, wondering what they will do to me. But no one touches me. Instead there's a grunt, a loud thud, then a voice.

"Are you people fucking kidding me?"

I know that voice. It's him. *Him*! The bad, beautiful slave. *Christopher.*

The engine starts with a rumble as my heart turns over in my chest, and we drive off into the night.

Eden Bradley

The Training House
BOY

CHAPTER ONE

"Are you fucking kidding me, people?"

I kick hard and connect with a body—Gilby's chest, I think. I know it's him from how hard he's breathing, the rasp more from the excitement of abducting me than from carrying me down the stairs with one of his henchman to help.

They're taking me away again, to the Pet Ranch in Carmel Valley. I've been there before. It's not that I don't like it there. I do. I'm just fucking pissed that the Master is sending me away again. I love and hate the way they do it—grabbing me in the middle of the night, sliding a bag over my head, throwing me into the van. And now I know what's coming even before I feel their hands grab me roughly and close the metal shackles around my ankles. I kick again, chains rattling, but all I hit is air—it whistles as he strikes my thigh with a leather strap. I barely feel it, but I kick again and he hits me again—it's our same old dance. We both enjoy it.

"Fuck you, Gilby! You and whoever else is with you!"

"Oh, you'll be fucked all right," he says with a low chuckle. "Unless you can catch 'em and fuck 'em first, but I hear they have some new stock down there. Wish I was going to be there to see it—you being taken down by some slave Boy and pegged good and hard up the ass."

"You wish, Gilby," I mutter.

"Yeah, I do. I'd fuck you myself if the Master would allow it. I'd fuck that mouthiness right out of you. Enjoy the ride,

Christopher."

He hits me one more time across the chest before I hear the door to the van slam shut. And as soon as he does I become aware that someone else is in the back of the van with me. This is new. I inhale, and the minute I do I know it's her. *Her.* The beautiful new slave Girl I saw a few weeks ago in the school room. The Girl with the long red hair and the innocent face, and the lush, pink mouth that makes me think of nothing but sex. I think about it a lot—those lips wrapped around my hard cock, green eyes looking up at me. I've been a little obsessed with her since the moment I saw her, that mouth making a perfect "o"— perfect to suck my cock with—when the Master was punishing me. And I know her scent because when Gilby and Patrick were dragging me out of the room after my beating, I pulled in a long breath as we passed her seat. She smells like clean, female skin and female desire. Even her skin smells like innocence. My pheromones went fucking crazy. They're doing it again now.

I wish I'd been the one to slip the black bag over her head and throw her over my shoulder. My dick is doing a mad, twitching dance just thinking about it.

I inhale again and this time I smell fear. My cock stiffens even more.

I wait for the van to start before saying anything, enjoying my little mental scenario and the smell of her flesh and her fear.

"Hey," I say quietly. No answer. I try again. "You can talk to me, you know. They won't hear you."

"I… You're sure it's okay?"

"You're her, aren't you? The Master's new favorite?"

There's a long pause. "I'm sorry," she says.

"No need to be. Not with me. I'm a favorite, too. Or, I was. Apparently I'm out of favor since he's sending me off again."

Sometimes I love the Master. And sometimes I hate him. And sometimes it sucks to be me. But maybe this isn't one of those moments.

I hear her sniff.

"Hey, you crying?" I ask.

"I just… Does this mean I'm out of favor, too?" I can hear the desperation in her voice.

"Nah. Not necessarily. Sometimes it means you're too much

in his favor and he needs to distance himself."

She lets out a sob. "That's just as bad," she says quietly, her voice small in the echoing metal chamber of the van.

"Look, I've been there—out of favor, too much on his mind. But I'm still here, in The Training House." I grimace, despite myself, despite my attempt at reassuring this Girl. This Girl who makes my blood run hot. Who makes me want to sink my teeth into her flesh, just to taste her. "Or, I was. But he always brings me back again. Always."

"For how long? I mean, how long have you been at the Training House?"

"Four years, give or take. And off and on, because sometimes I just have to leave. He always takes me back. He always will. We have a sort of understanding. He'll take me back until he gets fed up with me, and then he won't."

I can hear the implied shrug in my own voice. Fucking too much ego, still, no matter how many people have tried to beat it out of me. But despite my casual tone, it matters. It always has. My beautiful Master. He's mattered since I first met him.

"How did you..." She pauses. "Is it okay if I ask you some questions? Is it okay if I... I'm sorry."

"I told you, you can talk to me. It'll make the time go by faster for both of us."

I hear her exhale, long and slow. I wish I could see her. Wish I could see her pupils wide with nerves, the shock on her face from being treated so harshly. Oh yeah—I get off on that the way any Master or Mistress might. But there are reasons why. Reasons I think about only when I'm on one of my self-imposed breaks from the Training House.

"What do you want to know?" I ask her.

"How did you meet him—Master Damon?"

"It was at a kink club. A very high-level club in Los Angeles at a private home. Hollywood Hills. A few celebrities, but mostly the high-powered people with money. Pretty sure you know about those places."

"Yes."

"I was topping, at the time."

"Topping? I don't know why, but I can see that. I mean...I'm sorry. Am I offending you?"

"Girl. Let's get one thing straight. It's almost fucking impossible to offend me. And I did say you could talk to me. I'm an open book. Why wouldn't I be?"

There's a long silence before she says, "Because we all have our secrets."

Hmm. Yeah. Maybe so. I think about my mother. About the things I did when I was younger. About how I turned out to be exactly like her for a while. How much I fucking hate that fact.

"Well, I'll tell you this. When I'm not here? When I decide I need to take off for a while and get my head on straight again? I go to the clubs in San Francisco, and L.A. and sometimes Phoenix, San Antonio—wherever—and I am no one's bottom boy. *That's* when I lose myself."

"But here? The Training House?"

I know exactly what she's asking. It's the question they would all ask me, if they could.

"It's why the Master calls me by name. Because I need to stay in the moment. I need to feel every stroke of the whip, every moment of the worst goddamn humiliation, or I can just surf through it. I can make it so it doesn't affect me at all. But that's what we're all doing here, right? We *need* it to affect us, or there's no point. So he makes me be me. It's the worst mind-fuck of all, and the best, you know? But of course you do. We all understand this shit about each other."

"I do understand," she says, her voice soft with recognition and that meeting of minds only the hardest-core slaves can have.

We are the real weirdos of the world. Creatures of a strange mindset. And what most people don't know is that we're the some of the most intelligent of the kinky people. There's something about having a high IQ that makes us dissect the innermost workings of our own minds, and it kind of drives us crazy. It makes us seek out the most extreme forms of stimulation, because it's nearly impossible to meet that need any other way. I know this sounds egotistical, but it's really nothing more than a discovery I've made over the years that helps me explain it to myself. It makes a lot of fucking sense. And this Girl—she's as smart as I am, I can feel it. She's as much a weirdo as I am, if not as much a monster.

While I've been caught in the mad spinning of my own brain

she's started to sniff again.

"Hey. Are you crying again?" Why does this hurt me? Something about this Girl... "Tell me your name."

"Does it even matter? It doesn't in The Training House."

"Yeah. Yeah, it does."

"Why?"

I reach out with my chained foot, and after a moment I come into contact with silky skin, an even row of bare toes. I hear her gasp, but she doesn't pull away.

"I don't know. Maybe so that us talking matters, you know?"

Another silence. She's been trained not to talk. It's the same with all of them. All of them but me. I can talk easily enough, which gets me into trouble. But then, I like trouble.

"It's Aimée."

"Pretty. Like you."

I feel her toes curl against my foot.

"And you're Christopher?" she asks.

I laugh. "This all seems so polite, like we're at some fucking tea dance. Absurd, given the circumstances."

"I...I'm sorry. I don't mean to—"

"Hey. It's all right. It's just a weird sort of contrast, you know? Us here in our blackout hoods, chained in the back of a van on our way to the Primal Ranch, and we're graciously exchanging names and backgrounds, like we're on a first date. But I guess for people like us, this is a first date." I laugh at how ludicrous this situation is.

"Primal Ranch?" she asks, her voice trembling.

Ah, I love to hear that, her voice shaking, and to feel the shivering in her smooth, flexing toes. If I could get out of the damn chains, I could really do something about it. Like throw her down on the hard metal floor of the van and choke her and fuck her until she's too damn dizzy and coming too hard to be afraid of anything but me. But like I said, I'm an animal and I know it. Which is why the Ranch is perfect for me.

"Yeah. It's where he always sends me, and some of the others. They all use the place—the Masters and Mistresses who run in this circle. It's pretty fucking spectacular in its own way."

"But what will happen to me there?"

"Are you sure you really want to know?" I ask her.

There's a long moment of silence, then she sighs. "Maybe not."

"Change of subject, then?" I suggest, as if I am capable of some real sympathy. But it's all a sham, isn't it? Has to be. Except with her...

There's something about her, something about that first moment I saw her, that made my insides feel like glass shattering. It wasn't a bad thing, although in retrospect I realize it hurt a little in some way I'm not used to. Some part of me just kind of came apart. And like glass, I saw myself reflected in the pieces lying on the floor. I put myself back together afterward, but just like broken glass, seams remained. I feel like I'll never be the same again, from seeing her that once. Her face has haunted me, her inherent innocence maybe even more. And of course I know damn well she's not innocent. No one who is truly innocent is ever brought to the Training House. They're very careful. It's more in the way she carries herself, in the freshness of her skin. Babyskin. In some piece of herself she holds apart from the things we do in this life of taboo secrets and forbidden shadows. Maybe it's the same piece I hold apart, except that hers is clean, while mine is black with soot and guilt and sins that can never be forgiven. We are the same, yet utterly different. And sometimes I think too goddamn much.

"Yes, please," she says, and I have to take a moment to remember what the question was. Change of subject. Right. I ask her to tell me about coming to the Training House.

"It's been a few weeks," she says. "A month? No, less than that. I seem to have lost track. My last Master—Master Graham—sent me there because I needed more, which I feel terrible about. I feel as if I couldn't make him happy, because I was always craving something he couldn't quite give me. I have to ask myself...am I a bad slave? Did I fail him? Did I fail the dynamic of Master and slave? But I couldn't help it. And coming here...well, *there*, to the Training House... I had no idea what I was missing. I had no idea how much more thoroughly my needs could be met, how much more I could lose myself. How badly I needed what they have to offer me there." She stops and I can almost hear her thinking, then she says very quietly, "No one has ever hurt me like that. Or degraded me to that extent. I feel as if I've truly discovered myself for the first time. And now I'm being sent away. I can't stand it."

"But you will. That's the beauty in all this. You will be hurt and humiliated where they're taking us. And if I play this right, it could be *me* who gets to do some of that, lovely little Aimée."

"Oh!"

I stretch my leg out, caress her foot with mine, then her delicate ankle, bare skin against bare skin, which makes me hard as hell, the blood leaving my brain in a mad rush.

"Does that turn you on?" I ask. "The idea of me hurting you? Using you? Because there will be such an opportunity. And I plan to make the most of it. Do you like that idea?"

"Yes," she whispers.

"Excellent. Oh, you have no idea how good that'll be. I can hear that you have more questions for me, but you should rest now. Can you do that? Lay your head down and think about what lies ahead."

"I don't know what to think," she admits. "Not really. Except that I'm still in shock, and it's all so abstract to me."

"That's the idea, little Aimée. But lay your head down. I'll be right here."

There's the muffled sound of movement, of her shifting, and it brings her scent to my nostrils. I inhale deeply. Female skin. Excitement. Fear. If someone could make a perfume of it, they'd make a fucking fortune. But right now it's all for me. Fucking beautiful. I settle into my own hard spot on the van floor and close my eyes, thinking of her, my foot against hers. Warm flesh to warm flesh. And my cock aches for her. But so does some part of my dark, cold heart.

Eden Bradley

The Training House
CHAPTER TWO

For once the trip has gone by too fast, and soon the van is crunching over the long gravel drive to the ranch that's secreted away between the hills a few miles inland from the small coastal town of Carmel. I can't help the rush of excitement that makes my muscles tighten in anticipation, made all the more acute by the quiet presence of Aimée in the van with me. I haven't slept at all—I'm too painfully hard, too aware of her luscious body so close to mine. I've spent the last few hours imagining if they'd left me loose in the van, with her chained and hooded. How I would have used the weight of my body to hold her down while I fucked her senseless. How I would have lifted the edge of the hood and forced her to suck my ever-hard dick until she choked on it, tears pouring down her cheeks, the salt of them mixing with my come all over her lovely face.

Jesus. And now, again, I have the hard-on of a lifetime. Even *my* lifetime, which is saying a lot.

The Masters and Mistresses and handlers at the Ranch will fucking love me arriving with a raging erection. It's probably a good thing my hands are cuffed behind my back or I would have jacked off a half dozen times by now, if I hadn't been able to get my hands on her. But they know what they're doing. I get it. Because there are times when I am one of them.

Sometimes I think that's why the Master is so fascinated by me. Could it be called love? Who the hell knows? But it doesn't matter. Or, it does but I don't like to let it matter. Especially not now, when I hear the first creak of the doors being opened, then feel the rush of cool morning air hitting my skin as I blink in the relative darkness of the black hood over my head. Still, I can tell the sun is coming up. I can hear it in the rustling of leaves in the big oak trees as the birds and the squirrels start their morning routine. I can smell the morning, sunshine on dew. Yeah, I notice this stuff. I notice everything. I hear Aimée's small gasp, the rattling of her chains, which is hot as fuck to me—to imagine what she looks like in chains. I'm a poet and a perv this morning, which makes me grin. But then, when am I not? The Master tells me I am "a spectacular dichotomy". I kinda like that title.

Rough hands pull me from the van, but I'm too tuned in to *her*, to her quickening breath, to fight it much, and I know damn well she's as turned on by the manhandling as I am. I bet her juices are running down her sleek little thighs, making me want to lick them clean.

Fuck.

When I finally do get to have her, I'm gonna come in three seconds flat, like some eight-year-old with his dick in his hand for the first time. Or maybe that was just me?

"We heard you were being sent back to us, Christopher."

I recognize the voice — it's Jonathon, one of the handlers here, and not one I like. But liking them is not the point. No one gives a shit if I like the handlers. Not even me.

Another hand wraps around the back of my neck, and I'm forced to my knees. I know right away from the way he's handling me that it's Victor. Oh, I like Victor. Huge guy. Huge dick. And he knows what to do with it, knows how to fuck like a demon, knows how to handle the slaves. Knows how to put me in my place, which I will tell you is no easy thing.

There is something really beautiful in being a slave, and being handed over to someone who knows exactly what to do with you. It's fucking exhilarating, and in my case, it also pisses me off a little. I mean, I can't get away with too much shit with Victor. Even less than I can with the Master, because while Master Damon loves me, Victor is maybe no more than amused — and it's all at my expense. He is a true sadist. Jolly as hell about it, no regrets, never gets attached, and so his treatment of the slaves is completely remorseless. Which makes him a very dangerous animal — and I do mean animal. This is the Primal Ranch, and all the handlers identify as primals, the same as I do. They all have that animalistic attitude, the desire to bite, to scratch, to wrestle you to the ground, and Victor is the one man who can take me down every time.

I fucking love it.

There's a hard slap on my dick, and shit, it hurts! Victor's hand, no doubt. He does it again, laughing at me.

"Are you blushing under there, Christopher?" he asks.

Demands.

I growl in reply.

"Playing hard to get, are we? The only problem—for you, anyway—is that I can get you any time I want." He gives my aching cock another hard slap, and I feel the reverberation of pain all the way into my balls. In my belly. "Don't you forget it. I don't plan to let you, you know."

He shoves me to the ground and presses on the back of my neck with one booted foot, yanking the hood from my head, leaving me blinking hard in the misty morning light. He angles the foot to press my face against the hard ground, into the gravel, which bites into my cheek. And I love it and hate it—and him—at the same time. My life is full of these contradictions. But my cock is never confused.

Victor leans down and murmurs, "What if I jack you off right here? Make you come into the dirt? That's where your come belongs—in the dirt, Christopher. Because you are one dirty, dirty boy. And you will be *my* boy if I want you to be, won't you?"

I only growl again, a small rage burning in my throat, clawing to get out.

He grinds his booted foot against my cheek. I clench my jaw and refuse to howl.

"*Won't. You?*" he repeats.

"Yeah, sure. Whatever you want, *Victor*, as long as you'll fuck me good and hard after."

His hand dives into my short Mohawk and he drags me to my feet so fast I lose my footing, and between my hair and my wrists chained behind my back, he's yanking me around, laughing, and I catch a small glimpse of his dark, polished skin, his beautifully sharp white teeth. I fucking love it—I love it all. This little show of his superiority. The humiliation, which isn't really humiliation, since I enjoy the hell out of it. I'm sure I'll pay for it later. I hope I will.

"Little bastard," he says. "I'll fuck you with a broom handle if I want."

"Promises, promises," I mutter.

He slaps me hard across the face, leaving his big handprint burning on my cheek. I grin.

"Do it again for me, baby?" I taunt him.

Maybe I'm showing off a bit for Aimée, but I can't resist. And being punished doesn't bother me. That's why I'm here. That's why I signed up to be a slave, and the longer I live this life, the more I understand on some deep, almost cellular level how much I crave this shit. I want someone to make me...*do* something. Anything. Everything. I don't fucking care. Except that I do. I *need* it. I need it more than air sometimes. And I don't give a shit what I have to do to get that need met. So I fuck with Victor, and he fucks with me, then he fucks me until I'm so damn sore I can barely walk, and we all leave happy. Well, as happy as I ever get.

There's a small gasp, which I realize is Aimée, and I make the mistake of turning toward her.

"Really, Christopher? Falling for the Master's property? You know better."

"I don't fucking fall for anyone," I protest, but the lie sits like acid on my tongue.

"We'll see about that."

Victor shoves me down on the ground again, standing on my chains so I'll stay down while he pulls Aimée's hood off.

"A real beauty, this Girl. I can see why you're into her. You know what they say about redheads. Full of fire, a little crazy. Right, Jonathon?"

Fucking Jonathon answers, "Yeah. I'd sure like to get a piece of her myself. I could fuck this bitch into tomorrow."

I lunge at Jonathon so fast, it takes Victor by surprise, and his weight shifts off my chains. Managing to grab the weasel Jonathon by the leg, I flip him onto the ground. Then I'm on him, roaring like the beast I am, ready to tear him apart. But Victor pulls me off him, shoving me face down in the gravel again, his booted foot in the middle of my back.

"That's enough. Christopher. Enough!"

Aimée lets out a sob, and I glance at her from the corner of my eye and see she's really crying. God damn it.

"You're spending the day cleaning the stables in chains, and tonight in solitary," Victor says calmly. "Alone. Which, as we all know, is your favorite thing."

Fuck. Fuck, fuck, fuck.

My stupidity reigns supreme. Again. Of course, I could try to escape—hell, I *could* escape, if I wanted to. But I don't want to leave her behind. I don't know why the fuck not. All I know is, that is *not* happening. I'll wait out my damn punishment. Without an audience, which, as Victor damn well knows, I hate with a passion that exceeds even my hate for fucking Jonathon right now.

But Victor is talking again.

"Jonathon, chain her to the back of the van, then help me get this self-fancied libertine into the stables." Pulling me to my feet once more, he leans in until I feel the heat of his breath on my face, as he speaks quietly to me. "Think you can fuck with me, Christopher? I won't put up with your bullshit, even if it was amusing to see you tackle Jonathon. You're on work duty until the Foreman decides what else to do with you—or I do. It could be an hour. It could be a month."

That's part of Victor's allure. No matter what I do, even when he's punishing me, he's never ruffled. Never really pissed. I don't even have to wonder why I love his aloofness. He's my absentee father all over again, but with a handsome face and a big dick. All right—I don't know what the fuck my English father looks like, but whatever. And yeah, I know that's some sick shit. Freud would have loved me. Freud would have loved kinky folk, period. We're his every wet dream come to life, working out our issues through twisted sex. Don't think it doesn't actually work for us, because it does.

But I have to pay attention to what's happening.

Aimée is on her knees on the graveled ground, head bent, wrists still cuffed behind her back. And it's not that I don't find her incredibly hot, but I also feel...protective. She shouldn't have had to see this. Of course, if she's anything like me—and I suspect she is, or she wouldn't be here—then some part of her is also probably getting off on my little performance, and even the price she's having to pay for it.

My mind spins with the thousand possibilities, as ever.

Victor drags me to my feet and begins pulling me along. When I try to turn to look at this beautiful girl I've come to think of as *mine*, for reasons that would undoubtedly have me punished at the least and barred from this elite fetish circle at most, he grabs my face in a crushing grip.

"Eyes ahead, Christopher, or I'll have to blindfold you."

"God damn it, Victor," I spit out. He knows how much I hate that loss of control. As if I have any here.

"If you can't be quiet and behave for five minutes, it'll be the blindfold and the gag for you, my beautiful boy. All I need is the smallest reason."

I grind my jaw all the way to the stables—the one where actual animals are kept, and not where the slaves are quartered.

"This place smells like shit," I mutter.

Victor sighs before grabbing me by the back of my neck and propelling me into the big barn, down the center walkway, between the rows of horses, then shoving me hard into the last stall, where I land on hands and knees on the dirt floor. And he's on me so fast I barely have time to think about it as he straddles me from behind and forces my lips and teeth apart, shoving a wooden gag in the shape of a small phallus into my mouth. I choke on it for a few moments, trying desperately to reject it, my body seething with anger and humiliation as he buckles the leather strap at the back of my head. I fucking hate this. I fucking love it.

Victor kicks my knees out from under me, and I sprawl in the dirt, small rocks biting into the front of my thighs, my chest, my ever-hard cock. My hips immediately press into the ground, but I only manage a few thrusts before Victor turns me onto my back. With one heavy boot on my chest, holding me down, he quickly ropes my ankles even as I kick at him, struggling on the damn ground, screams of rage muffled by the gag down my throat. And no matter how fucking pissed I am, I want to suck that phallic piece of wood, want to choke on it until tears run down my face. I want him to hurt me. To fuck me. To make me *nothing*.

He swings the end of the rope tied to one ankle over a hook on one wall, pulling the end tight, forcing my leg wide, then does the same with the other side. I am left spread-eagle on the floor of the stall, gagged and furious and hard as stone, the head of my cock already leaking pre-come.

Victor leans down and runs his thumb over that sensitive tip, and I close my eyes and moan as his thumb slides all over the head of my rigid dick.

"Makes me want to lick it off you," he tells me. "Except I think you require something more…" he pauses, chuckling, "…*stimulating.*"

I watch as he straightens, a tower of bulging muscle and fucking gorgeous chocolate flesh. He gives my chest a good kick before stepping back.

"Don't go anywhere, Christopher," he says, taunting me.

I tell myself I'd spit on the ground if I didn't have the damn gag in my mouth. That I'd fight him off, take him down to the ground and plow his fine ass. But it's all bullshit, and even I know it. Not with Victor.

He returns a moment later with a buggy whip in one hand and a long leather strap in the other and my cock jumps. He smacks the front of my thighs with the heavy strap, first one, then the other, back and forth. It doesn't even hurt much at first, until it does. Then I can feel the welts coming up on my skin, the burn as he hits the welts. I'm fighting it at first, my torso twisting, a growl coming from deep in my throat. Then he starts with the whip.

Being hit with a buggy whip is like being stung by a hornet. He lands it on my chest, making a crisscross pattern with it while my system fills up with pleasure and rage. When he snaps the whip on my nipple, my body arcs, rising up off the ground, but in a breath it shifts, until it's just my hips pumping the air.

"Ah, your pretty dick knows what it likes. It knows better than you do what it needs."

There's not a second to tense up before he snaps the head of my dick with the fucking whip, and pain like a thousand stinging, biting insects shatters me, inside and out. And somehow I do howl around the goddamn gag as pain trembles through me, then pleasure in a fiery wave, and come spurts from my poor, beautifully tortured dick. Except it hurts too much for me to really come, and I'm left panting and wanting and choking so hard I can barely see. God fucking damn him!

Then he's on his knees, his enormous cock in his hand, and he shoves it into my ass so hard I almost pass out. This is always how it happens with Victor. How is it he knows exactly what I need — maybe even more than the Master? As he fucks me, one deep, punishing stroke after another, all I can think of is Aimée's pouting pink mouth, her gorgeously hard nipples. I want to bite her until I draw blood. I want to fuck her as hard as Victor is fucking me. Thinking of her makes me start to come again, but Victor pulls me out of it with a ringing slap to the face.

He's laughing at me, at my predicament, as he always does. I love him and hate him. Pleasure itself is something I have to fight against, because I know if I really come I'll be locked in solitary for a month. They don't make idle threats here.

I bite the inside of my lip, tasting blood, but it keeps me centered as I focus on Victor's grinning face above me. On him pinching the welts covering my thighs, then the skin just beneath the head of my cock, his nails digging into my flesh. He slaps my face again, just for good measure, maybe.

"I'm going to come in your ass, Christopher," he tells me, his tone low and threatening as he grabs my jaw in a hard, hurting grip.

I want it—want his come. But I also know it means an enema after.

God damn it.

But it's inevitable. It all is—every single thing that happens here. Which is why I'm here.

I don't even have to understand it. As long as they do.

CHAPTER THREE

I wake up sore all over. Stretching, I test my muscles to see where the ache is, and mostly it's good — it's fucking awesome, really — all except for the small sensation left over after the enema, and the burning shame of it.

I know. Even after all this time serving as a slave, this one thing still fucking gets to me, which is ridiculous. You can shove pretty much anything up my ass, and I'll love you for it. Anything but the enema nozzle. There's something too degrading about being forced to shit in front of someone. Too degrading to me, anyway. I'd love to make Aimée do it. My morning wood tenses at the thought.

But I'm chained, ankles and wrists, in the empty horse stall where Victor left me after fucking me, then the enema, then fucking me again and another damn enema. I feel emptied out — my bowels, anyway. I'm always full of come. I could come all day long.

Aimée.

Those gorgeous green eyes, the flawless curve of her breasts. The pain in her voice yesterday. All of it is unbelievably alluring to me. She's so damn *real*. I don't even know what I mean by that. Real and fucking beautiful in way no one has ever been to me before.

I *will* conquer her in the pens here. I will beat every other slave they have in this place, will fuck my way from one to the other, but I won't come until it's *her* I plow my way into, hanging onto all that red hair so damn tight, one hand wrapped around her fragile throat. Because I *have* to. Oh yeah, have to find my way into that sweet little body, into the Girl who makes me harder than I've ever been in my life.

Aimée.

My sore cock twitches, making my balls pull up tight, but I know I'll get no relief today, and maybe not for a long while. It's all up to Victor, unless one of the Masters or Mistresses calls for me.

Small pang in my chest when I think of the Master and why he sent me away this time. Is he finally tired of me? Or is it nothing more than part of his ritual of punishment for me? But I focus on my aching dick, and the pang goes away. Sex and kink help me to dissociate—not that there's any difference between the two for me—and there's no one around right now to force me back into my body, into my fucking *feelings*, is there?

While I'm lying on the hard ground contemplating my place in the kinky universe, a slave arrives with the slop bucket. He's gagged and harnessed in brown leather, nipples clamped, the flesh dark red and succulent under the evil press of the metal teeth, making me want to touch him. He's not even my type, except that right now anyone would be my type, I'm so damn hard. Glancing down at the darkening head of my cock, I silently tell it to fuck off.

I feel no better.

The slave Boy kneels prettily and ladles out a portion of slop—it's really some sort of flavorless beef stew—into one half of a small trough, pours water into the other section from a bottle tucked into a sleeve in his harness, and he leaves it on the ground close to my head. My stomach growling, I forget all about him, whoever the fuck he is, as I turn to my sorry breakfast. If I twist just right, there's enough give in my chains for me to get on my knees and bend down to eat and drink, my arms pulled back, the chain crossed between my shoulder blades. When I'm done, I need to piss like crazy, but I know better than to soil my own stall. If I'm here for a month, or even a week, I'll live to regret it. And if I don't, the handlers will make sure I do. So, I wait.

An hour goes by before anyone comes back for me, and this time it's Jonathon and two large, male slaves.

As they unhook the ends of my chains from the walls of the stall and lead me outside, I say to Jonathon, "Afraid to deal with me on your own? Is that because you know I can take you down? Or because you'd love it too much if I plowed your lily-white ass?"

He doesn't say a word, just smacks me hard across the chest with a leather strap, then again in the face when I smirk, which makes me like him the tiniest bit more.

Finally, I get to piss, and it seems to go on forever. Then they take me to the exercise pen—again, the one for the horses, not the ones they usually work the slaves in—and the slave Boys get me into harness, wide strips of brown leather that cross my chest in an 'X', and clip a lunge line onto it.

They're about to lead me into the center of the ring when Jonathon tells them, "Blindfold him."

"Fuck if they will," I spit out.

"They'll do whatever I tell them to do. And so will you."

One of them stands on my lead rope, and together they wrestle the hated blindfold over my eyes while I grunt and cuss and my dick gets hard again, at which point there's no more point in fighting it. It's done and Jonathon knows damn well I like it as much as I hate it—almost as much as I hate him.

"Run him," he commands.

They start whipping me and I start running, my lungs filling up with the clean valley air, and I try to focus on keeping my bare feet high so I won't trip and fall, on the fact that I need to work out in order to keep strong. Because someday, I'm going to whip that weasel Jonathon's ass.

I run and run, starting to focus inward, to forget the weasel Jonathon and the whip, which isn't really hitting me hard enough to do much. Instead I tune in to the smell of the trees, the birds chirping in the branches, the breeze whispering over my naked skin. I go so deep into my head, I lose track of time, and by the time they stop me and pull the blindfold off, I've lost all sense of how long I've been running. It could have been an hour. It could have been all day. I feel damn good.

Until they take me back to the stable and Jonathon stands over me while I shovel out the horse stalls. I'm fucking furious the whole time, but really only because it's him there, instead of Victor. For Victor, I'd do anything.

Finally it's done, and the slave Boys chain me up in my stall again, where I spend another night alone. The next day I'm exercised and fed, made to clean the stables again, then left alone with too much damn time to contemplate the universe. To think about Aimée. Where are they keeping her? Are they working her? Fucking her? I don't want to think about these things. I don't want to think about her, except that I *do*. I don't want to want her, God damn it. I'd rather they beat me.

I'd rather go back to my life before I saw her in the Master's classroom, all pale skin, pink nipples and that mass of silky red hair.

I go to sleep every night with her on my mind, making my dick throb with a burning need that's never relieved. It's worse than any orgasm deprivation I've ever been through, and I've been through a hell of a lot.

Over and over again, night after night, I whisper to the dark stables, to the night sky littered with stars behind the fog, "They don't even fucking know. They don't even know this torture they're putting me through."

Finally it's Victor who comes for me one morning and I know this shit is getting serious now. He'll beat me and fuck me and then he'll either leave me here, or he'll take me out of solitary. I don't know which I hope for more.

He doesn't disappoint. Without taking time to unchain me, he yanks on one ankle and I sprawl face down on the floor of the stall, and he's on me, kicking my legs apart with his heavy boots. He wraps a big hand around the back of my neck, squeezing, pulling my head up and back while he spreads my ass cheeks with the other hand. Then he's in me, hard and deep while I stretch and probably tear a little inside. But damn, it feels good, my dick pulsing and throbbing like some wild drumbeat. I don't care that he's tearing my ass apart as he pumps into me. All I know is pleasure through the pain, the grunting deep in his throat, and how much I love the merciless way he handles me, his hands snaking around to grab my jaw in a tight, bruising grip.

His nails dig into my flesh as his climax approaches—my neck, my hip—breaking the skin, and I nearly come as he does, just from his raw yell, from the way he jams his fat cock into my ass. But as soon as I'm on the edge, he pulls out.

"I do like to fuck you, Christopher," he says. "Ah, you're bleeding a little. Better give you a bath." He pulls me up on my knees, releases my ankles, then my wrists. "You're a mess. Need to pretty you up for the pens. Competition day."

"I'm wrestling today?"

He slaps my face, which pisses me off. But my still-hard cock is loving the abuse.

"No back talk, Christopher."

"God damn it, Victor, I need to—"

But before I can finish, he grabs me and shoves me down into the dirt, pressing my cheek against the ground with one booted foot. It's a show of dominance, but we both know I love this shit.

"You don't need anything, Christopher," he says calmly, almost gleefully, "except to obey and make your Masters happy. And today, what will make them happy is for you to wrestle in the arena. Now I'm going to let you up and walk you to the baths, and you will keep your smart mouth shut or you'll stay in solitary for another week. No beatings, no fucking, nothing but you alone in your own busy head. Don't think I am unclear on how to punish you."

Fuck. But I keep my mouth shut for once, and follow him as he leads me not to the horse baths, this time, but across the paddock to the other barn, the one where the slaves are kept.

Inside, it smells like good, clean soap and fresh hay, and as bad-ass as I like to think I am, I'm eager to feel hot water on my skin for the first time since they brought me here.

Victor pulls me into the baths, which are like a big shower with clean, concrete floors and maybe half a dozen shower heads, with shelves built into the walls holding soap, shampoos, oils and washcloths. Immediately two female slaves appear, both wearing the dark iron collars of the Primal Ranch, meaning they are permanent property of the owners here. They're a pretty pair, one of them dark—Middle Eastern or Mediterranean, maybe—with a lush, curved body, and the other a waif of a girl with waist-length blonde hair. They start the water, and the broken spots on my skin sting as they gently push me under the spray, but God, the water feels good. They massage the soap into my skin, and one of them washes my hair while the other shaves my face. Most of the male slaves are shaved pretty much from the eyebrows down, but the Japanese and Cherokee blood in my veins means I'm mostly hairless, anyway, so it's a quick task, with the blonde Girl kneeling to pull my ball sac up before taking a few swipes with the razor.

I almost wish she'd cut me. I'm feeling too damn much today, and it would help me. But Victor has done his usual excellent job of priming me for competition, not letting me come, getting my anger built up, and I know there will be no release today unless I do well in the pens.

I always do well in the pens.

But they don't let us come even in there until they're good and ready. My orgasms are never up to me, which, like pretty much everything else, I both love and hate.

The Girls dry me off with thick white towels, then oil me up, and the one with the dark hair and pretty brown skin gets down on her knees, blowing lightly on my cock, which has been hard for days. But I go even harder, then harder still as she flicks her hot little tongue at the swollen head.

Jesus, I can barely take it, except that I can, and I will, because that part of me which is a slave at heart is fucking proud as hell of my raging stiffness. At how pleased the Masters and Mistresses will be at my painfully acute state of arousal. Fuck them. *I'm* pleased.

Victor has been watching from just outside the showers, tapping his leg with the long leather slapper he often keeps stuffed down the side of his boot. He seems pleased with me, with my stiff and ready cock. I can tell from the way he's looking at me that he wants it—wants to suck me, as he sometimes does. But he's ultimately under the Masters' rule, and it's his job to bring the slave Boys into the ring as jacked up as possible, needing to come. Horny and angry. But no matter how many times he may have fucked my ass this morning, and who knows how many Boys before me, he's every bit as jacked up as we are. His endless sexual appetite is part of what makes him so good at his job.

He steps in when the Girls are finished with me and slips a rude bit of rope around my neck, a toothy jute that bites into my skin just enough to irritate it, to irritate me. As he moves in to tie a half-hitch, I give him a wink and he slaps me. It feels damn good.

"Come on, Victor," I whisper to him, "do it again. Do it harder. You know you want to."

He stands back, gives the rope a sharp yank, lets out a sharp laugh. "Ha!"

But he's grinning as he leads me down the wide dirt road toward the arena.

I can see it as we approach, a large wood corral with a row of small pens like the ones in a rodeo ring at each end, Girls on one side, Boys on the other. I can see their nervous, trembling flesh as we move closer, the Girls all smooth, pretty skin, their hair put up in braids, some with ribbons in the ends. Twelve of them, a lovely, even dozen pairs of plump nipples and gorgeously shaved pussies, even their bare little toes looking succulent to me in my current condition. And then I spot her.

Aimée

They've braided pale green ribbons into her red hair, making her look even more the classic little fuckable milkmaid. I almost want to snort and paw the ground. But I make sure to catch her eye as we pass, and I see her gasp, her mouth a small, lovely "o". She lifts a hand, but one of the handlers smacks it with a short whip, and she yanks her hand back, her chin dropped but her gaze still following me.

I'm taken to the Boy's pen at the other end of the ring and shoved unceremoniously into one of the tight holding pens. Victor reaches through the wooden slats to slide the rope from my neck.

"Make me proud, Christopher," he says, a wicked grin quirking one corner of his lush mouth.

I grin back at him, give a sharp nod of my chin. We both know how things will go down out there.

The Masters and Mistresses—maybe thirty or forty of them—are taking their seats under the tented stands, but these are no regular rodeo stands. No, instead of long rows of wood or metal benches are seats padded in red leather, more like small couches, with tables in between to hold beverages and their various implements of punishment. Their personal slaves kneel at their feet, some in pony garb—everything from a simple posture collar and bit to full latex pony regalia, complete with horse-head mask and hooves. Some are in classic black latex, a few in pink or purple, some in brown leather, and even one in appaloosa print, spotted in brown and white. These ponies are always beautiful to me, their heads held high. There's a certain dirty elegance to them, a regal weirdness. They make me want to stand taller. And for some stupid reason, they challenge my need to impress. But sometimes my ego knows no bounds.

There's the cracking of a whip and a scuffling sound next to me, and I turn to inspect the competition. On my right is a Boy with short, dark hair, beautiful, as we all are, but otherwise unremarkable. To my left is a Boy with the same dark, creamy skin as Victor, but not nearly as tall or heavily built. I know in an instant I can take them both. But what catches my attention is a big redhead two pens down. I duck to peer between the slats and see he's beautifully made—strong thighs, a perfect, muscled ass, and his abs are a flawless washboard. He has a well-developed chest—a wall of fair skin dusted with golden freckles. His nipples are pierced with heavy steel bars, making my cock twitch as I remember the exquisite pain of my own piercing, even better because I did it to myself. I love a good piercing, the idea of the searing moment of pain as the needle goes through the skin, and his nipples are two plump buds of dark-pink flesh, eager for the chase. Eager for my mouth, if I can take him down. And as my gaze finds his face, my mouth waters. He is fucking fantastic, his features almost too damn pretty for his linebacker body. I want to take him—not only to win, but simply because I want him. The animal in me wants—needs—to conquer him, the only real competition there is here. The small questions nagging at the back of my mind—can I take him, will he take me down?—only make me want him more. And I will need to take him down to get to Aimée, because I can see him watching her, and only her.

Motherfucker. She's mine, you gorgeous bastard.

A low growl escapes my lips just as a bell rings and a handler—a tiny but wickedly powerful woman I know as Dahlia—enters the ring and goes to stand in the center, and my heart and dick give a small leap, the beast rising within me.

"Sirs and Madams, Masters and Mistresses, the Primal Takedowns are about to begin. I'm certain most of you know what defines a primal—that they identify with the animal inside them, that it is this animal which drives their lust, inspires them, and in which their power is based. Some identify as a particular animal—dog, cat, horse, wolf, even bear. But for others, it is simply that primal, bestial energy. Not that we care, do we? As long as they have that drive.

"But let me explain how this event works. The Boys and Girls will be released from the pens simultaneously, their skin slick with oil. Some of the Girls, as you can see, have earned the privilege of wearing a stunt cock, so that they may conquer a Boy or another Girl, if they can manage it, and some of them— oh yes, ladies and gentleman—some of them will, which makes for an excellent show. Quite simply, they will go after each other. Some will put on a long chase. Some will tackle the first object of their desire. The point is to take down an opponent, and once down, they may do whatever they like to them. The opponent will often fight back for our entertainment, and no doubt their own. There will be biting. There will be scratching. Kicking." She pauses, smiles. "Fucking."

A small ripple of laughter goes up from the crowd in the stands.

"It will be vicious. It will be primal. A blood sport to rival any other, a kinky spectacular unlike anything you've seen, unless, of course, you've been here at the Primal Ranch before. Enjoy."

Dahlia walks from the ring, and my heart is hammering, blood rushing through my veins and pounding in my aching, ridiculously hard cock, which I plan to plow into *someone* in the next few minutes. I brace my hands on the gate, waiting to feel the vibration that will signal the opening of it.

I have several long moments to glance at the hot redhead two pens to my left, then across the ring to my little beauty Aimée, who looks scared as hell. She should be. Then I look up into the stands to see if I can spot the Master, but he's not there. I'm fucking pissed at the knot that forms in my chest.

Suddenly the gates swing wide and we're all out at once, running across the arena, and it's all flying fucking nerves and heat and the rage running through my veins, because I *will* have her. She is *mine*. She's running toward me, her eyes wild with fear, her green ribbons fluttering, her gorgeous breasts bouncing. The dark-haired Boy that was penned next to me tries to shoulder me out of the way, but I turn and easily take him down with one swipe at his ankle. Foolish Boy. With a growl I jump on him, straddling his body, and when he struggles I bend down and sink my teeth into the back of his shoulder. He howls, but the sound only makes my blood run hotter. Makes me more determined.

"It's your lucky day," I tell him as I jump up. "I have other targets in mind."

Things are moving quickly, and I take a brief moment to assess. One of the Girls has taken a Boy down, and is fucking him with her strap-on, holding one arm behind his back. Two of the Boys are wrestling, the oil on their skin making them slip and slide together in the dirt, and a third Boy jumps in while the crowd cheers. And beyond them, the redhead is running right at Aimée.

I am not having it.

"Motherfuckerrrrr!" I yell as I run full speed.

CHAPTER FOUR

Slamming into him, I take him down to the ground, and he kicks at me, then he wraps one long leg around mine and manages to flip me over onto my back. He's on top of me, his long cock rubbing against mine, and the hard surge of desire is a momentary part of this dance as we lock gazes. I growl again as I slam both fists up onto his chest and shove him off me. Now I'm on top of him, and I grab his sides, taking fistfuls of his tight, fine flesh in my hands, grabbing hard, clawing at him. He yells, tries to throw me off, but he can't do it, and I crow in victory, which I'm sure pisses him off. Kicking his legs apart, I almost have him, but he fights me, and those muscular thighs are damn strong. As he wraps his legs around my waist there is some endless span of time where everything is happening in slow motion—or a thousand miles an hour, I don't fucking know—when I'm uncertain about which of us will win. That's not like me, but this Boy… He's fucking something, him and his lusciously pierced nipples and huge muscles. And either I'm going to fuck him, or he's going to fuck me, and one of us will win Aimée, and it had better God fucking damn it be *me*!

Somehow, the redhead pumps up and I feel the hard length of his dick at my asshole, but I will not let him in. I won't do it. Wrapping my legs around his hips, I squeeze as hard as I can. He lets out a cry of pain and defeat, loosening his hold on me just long enough for me to throw him hard to the ground, under me, and I *will* have his ass.

He's trying to throw me off him, writhing and bucking. I lean in and sink my teeth into his throat, feeling the muscles there working, tightening. And he's yelling as I shove my dick between his ass cheeks. Then a thought stops me cold. Leaning up, I press hard on his chest with one fisted hand to keep him down, my knuckles digging into the pressure points there. I press my other hand over his mouth, constricting his breathing a little, keeping him quiet. There's blood seeping from the wounds at his sides, and my teeth marks are deep in the skin at his neck.

Nice.

"You know I'm going to fuck you," I tell him, not giving him a chance to answer before I go on. "I can do it right now, if I want. I *do* want to—you're a big, pretty monster of a Boy. Except if I plow your ass, I can't plow the girl we both want. But she's mine, that one. Don't even fucking try it or I will take you down so hard you'll be out of commission for a month. I will break your bones if I have to. I don't fucking care about the rules here. I will do what I want. Do you understand me? You will not touch her. Go after one of the others. And if you even try it, I will come for you after I fuck her, when cross-contamination isn't an issue any longer. Do you understand me?"

I can tell from his expression that he's still full of the animal we are meant to be in this place, his hazel eyes gleaming with fire and lust. His big dick is hard as ever, his nipples erect, the steel bars glinting evilly in the sun. But he gives a small nod of his head, letting me know he won't mess with me on this.

As I start to get up he says, "I'll have your ass another day, and you'll like it, *Christopher*. Oh yes, I know exactly who you are."

I give him a cocky grin. "Doesn't everyone?"

I don't even bother to look at him again as I scan the ring for Aimée. And God damn it, one of the Boys is on her, trying to wrestle her to the ground, but I'm off like a shot, crossing to the other side of the ring in mere seconds. She's putting up a hell of a fight, and I'm damn proud of her. Going in for a flying side-kick that is guaranteed to take this asshole out—this asshole who dares to approach the girl I think of as my property, even given the absurdity of our situation—I feel the air empty from his lungs beneath the impact of my foot. I don't even have to look to know he's on the ground, doubled over in pain, maybe a rib cracked. No, my entire focus is *her*—her wild green eyes, the flush in her cheeks as she falls into my arms. I have half a second to wonder what the Masters and Mistresses think of that before I simply wrap her up in my body, easing her down onto the ground as gently as I can, given how jacked up I am still—even more now, after wrestling a few of the Boys. And there's heated, female flesh squirming in my hands, and somehow her relieved tears make it even hotter.

"I've got you," I tell her in a harsh whisper. "I'm going to fuck you into the ground. Tell me you want me. Or fuck it—don't. It's gonna happen either way."

"Oh, God yes," she says, making me smile. Or maybe it's more a baring of teeth as I flip her legs up onto my shoulders, and without another moments' hesitation, I thrust into her tight, wet cunt.

"Ah!"

Her green eyes go wide, shock and desire there, and something else that makes my own legs go weak. And she feels like fucking heaven inside—even the poet in me can't begin to describe it, not with the words it requires. Velvet and clasping. Like my cock is being choked in satin. When I sling my hips back, then sink into her again, her hands go to my shoulders, her nails digging into my flesh, and already a small yell forms in her long, lovely throat. It begins as a sort of mewling, kitten-like, then turns into a growl, and I know she is truly one of *us*. Animal. Primal. Then her nails rake my shoulders as I really begin to fuck her in long, punishing strokes, then shorter, sharper jabs. She starts to come and I clamp a hand over her mouth. Her eyes go glassy as she comes, her lungs starved for air. I know exactly how being choked out makes climaxing immeasurably more intense. I love watching it happen to her.

She's still coming when I flip her over, putting her on hands and knees, then pushing down hard on her back until she's on elbows and knees, and I thrust into her sweet little cunt once more. I don't even know how I've held it back, except that I need to do things to her... I need to fuck her and mark her and *claim* her, God damn it.

Leaning in, I sink my teeth into the back of her neck and hang on as I plunge into her, over and over, harder and harder, and she's sliding in the dirt, coughing at the dust, but I don't care, except that I do, because it's fucking hot as hell. I taste her blood under my tongue, and slide my mouth around to the side of her neck, whispering "Give it to me. Give me your flesh." And she does, and I bite harder, knowing she will wear my bruises for weeks.

She's gasping, sobbing as I fuck her as hard as I can, shoving my cock deep, then deeper, my balls slapping her swollen mound. Then she's coming again and I reach around to pinch her clit, making her scream in pain, in pleasure. Finally, I let loose, coming into her hot little body. Into her hot little cunt. Nothing has ever felt so damn good to me. Better and better, my orgasm going on forever as my come dumps into her. Fucking hell, but it's good—so good I can hardly take it, the spasms like whips of fire snapping deep in my gut, in my balls as they draw up tight.

When it's over my legs go out from under me and I collapse on top of her, both of us covered in sweat and dirt and sticky with come.

We're both panting. I'm filled with a bursting joy at my victory. At the intensity of being in her body. At being the one to take her down, to command her. And I'm fucking tired of being the slave, and this shit is going to have to be over soon. But for now, my dick is still buried inside her, my body humming with one of the best orgasms I've ever had, so I really can't complain. Well, except that it's me. It's more out of habit than anything. Not one of my more charming qualities, but I feel too damn good to care. And my mind is already churning with what will happen next. If they separate us, this slave shit *will* be over, contract or not, because I'm not fucking standing for it.

Faceless handlers arrive, and I'm only vaguely aware of the wrestling and fucking and flying dirt going on around us. The only thing I can focus on is Aimée. Two women have her, and it pleases me that they have to steady her, that she looks dazed and glassy-eyed. My teeth marks all over her neck please me even more.

We're taken back to the enormous shower stall in the slave barn, along with a handful of other slaves. The handlers run the warm water, clean us up, tend to our wounds while we stand, quiet and worn out, on the concrete floor. My eyes are on her the entire time—I couldn't care less what's happening to me right now. She takes it all with her head slightly bowed, her body in a state of utter yielding. She is fucking made for this—being a slave. Except for that spark I see in her, which I can't quite figure out. But I intend to. I don't know why, but I need to.

The handlers hustle me out while Aimée's injuries are still being tended to, and I growl and try to kick them away. One of them takes a strap to me, beating my chest and my thighs, but I hardly feel it.

Turning to one of them, I murmur seductively, "Why don't you slap my dick with that thing? Then we might be getting somewhere."

He looks taken aback, but from somewhere else in the shower area is a deep chuckle.

Victor.

"Ignore him," he tells my handlers. "Let him piss and moan, if he has to. The Masters are exceptionally pleased with his performance today."

I look over at him, and he's leaning against the doorway, arms crossed over his massive chest, grinning, which pisses me off a little. I lurch toward him, but in two long strides he's on me almost before I know what's going on, and he grabs me and takes me down to the ground, Goddamn him. He has me on one knee, forcing my head lower, until my forehead touches the smooth floor.

"Don't do it, Christopher," he tells me. "Today could be a good day for you. Don't fuck it up for once."

He holds me there until my muscles relax, then he pulls me roughly to my feet. I look up at him, and he's staring me down, but not in the way he usually does. He's trying to tell me something. And after a few moments, I get it.

Okay. So maybe now is not the time to start any trouble—I have to keep track of Aimée. And Victor has let me know that's possible if I can just keep my shit together and my bratty-ass mouth shut.

I grind my jaw tight. Victor steps away and the handlers hustle me out of there and down the barn's long center hallway.

Here everything is clean and polished, unlike the livestock barn, where I've spent most of this visit. A team of slaves is mopping the floors on their knees, all of them fitted with pig snouts, short, curling tails protruding from between their buttocks. Sometimes I wonder why no one has ever thought to punish me in this way, in this style of absolute degradation. I know damn well I've deserved it on numerous occasions. But the handlers are shoving me into a stall and suddenly all I can think of, all I can see, is *her*.

She's curled up on a pile of fresh hay, and with her long hair strewn about her, still damp from the shower, she looks even more naked, which I know is insane. But that's what she does to me.

She looks up when I enter the stall, blinking, her long, long lashes coming down on her flushed cheeks. So damn fresh-faced, this girl, making me want to do every imaginable filthy thing to her, which is a lot, in my depraved mind. But I also want to see if she's okay. I want to talk to her.

I am totally losing my shit. I know it. But so the fuck what? Who better to lose it over?

The handlers push me onto my knees, and I go down easily, my gaze still locked to hers. I let them close the metal shackle around one ankle. I can see that she's chained up, too, the hard steel making her look fragile in a way that's utterly hot.

I put up with the handlers' presence while they water and feed us, not daring to talk to her until they go away. It's not because I give a damn what they'll think, or for their little punishments, but because what I have to say to her, what I want to hear from her, is our business.

Oh yeah, I can feel my slave-ness slipping away and my toppiness creeping in. Hell, it's slamming into my system like a storm. I am only still here because of her. And I'm going into Top mode because of her, too. It's like some crazed puzzle, with the pieces slipping in and out, weaving together, all perspective gone. My mind is like an Escher print, and even I can't tell what's up, and what's down.

Finally, they step out of our stall and I feel a slow grin creep over my face as Aimée blinks at me with those gorgeous green eyes.

"And so it begins," I say to her.

"I...I thought it already had. Out there in the arena."

"That was nothing. Nothing compared to what I'd like to do to you, prettiness."

"Oh..." Her lashes come down again, shadowing her high cheekbones. But when she glances back up, she's smiling. "Did you arrange for us to share a stall?"

"Not really. I may have a sympathizer."

Then she really does smile, her lovely face lighting up. "You were spectacular out there today. The way you ran everyone down, like you were on the football field."

"Or in the Primal Arena. But I had to get to you. I wasn't about to let anyone stop me."

She shakes her head, her pale brows drawing together. "Why?"

"I just had to." I shrug, but it's all an act, and a transparent one at that. I'm so full of shit. "Fuck it. I *had* to. I'm still trying to figure it out. To be honest, I don't understand what the hell is driving me so damn hard—so hard I can't resist it. Not that I'm good at resisting my urges. But are any of us, really? Any of us pervs?"

She smiles again. "I suppose not, or we wouldn't be here. As good a slave as I try to be, I get myself into trouble. And even when I'm being my best behaved, I'm wallowing in my urges, aren't I? So really, how good a slave does that make me?"

"Why do you doubt yourself?"

"Because I never feel quite good enough." She pauses, bites down on her lip. "Oh."

She glances away, but I tell her, "Aimée. Look at me."

She looks up, right into my eyes, with such nakedness I feel it like a shock.

"Because I never really have been," she says tremulously. "Not for my father, certainly. Not for myself."

"Fuck your father," I growl. "Whoever, whatever he was. It doesn't matter anymore. You're here. How does all that shit matter when we're so immersed in the kink landscape? Isn't that at least part of why we feel this need to lose ourselves so completely? Isn't this the ultimate in escapism? Why else would we be here? And I don't mean doing kink—I mean under a slave contract, for fuck's sake. Because this is some pretty extreme, twisted shit, and any decent psychologist could tell us why. And on some level, you know it. We all do."

She nods. "Yes. You're right. But when am I going to get over it?"

"Maybe we never do. Maybe all we can do is learn to cope with it. Maybe being a slave or being a Master or being beaten or made to come until we feel everything and nothing at all is the best we can do."

"Sometimes I think it is. And other times, I feel as though

I'm missing some important point. What do you think that is?"

"I think I'm probably the wrong person to ask. I'm pretty damn sure I'm more fucked up than most."

"You take a certain pride in that, don't you?" she asks quietly.

"Ha! I take a certain pride in everything. So, tell me what they did with you while I was locked up in the horse barn, serving out my punishment."

"They ran me in a ring on a lunge line every day. And the handlers worked me over a little, but nothing like I've had before—with my Master or my Mistress, or even in the kitchen in the Training House. I was sort of surprised. I think I expected more. But maybe they know what they're doing here, because I had enough time to sit and think, to imagine what might happen. And the end result was that my head was overflowing by the time they put me in the arena today. It was a total mind-fuck. As if I were over-prepared coming into this place, then they lulled me into a calm that was a total illusion, ultimately."

"Did anyone fuck you? Get you off?"

"No. I was in a stall by myself at night. No one touched me. I half expected someone to visit me in the night, the way the Master did at the Training House, but it never happened."

"Good," I grunt. Then I notice the goosebumps on her skin, a small twitch in her shoulders. "Hey, you're shivering."

"I'm a little cold. Or maybe shocking out a bit. I don't know."

"Hang on, I'm going to get next to you."

"But we're both chained."

I look around, trying to remember which stall we're in. "Reach up to the cross board above your head. No, don't ask, just do it. Good. Now slide your hand along until you feel a metal hinge, and see if you can get the edge of your fingers in there...yeah, that's it. Pull the board out—it's like a small door. You'll find a key behind it."

Her eyes go wide. "I...what is this? How did you know it was there?"

"Because I put it there myself. I have keys hidden all over this place, all over the Training House. I make sure I visit every kink facility I go to as a slave when I'm in Top mode. When I decide I'm done, I'm *done*. I prefer to be prepared."

"You're done now? No, I can see that you are, if you're even thinking of using this key. Are you going away?"

I can hear a small sob breaking her voice, and it kills me a little even as it makes me hard, makes my heart lurch.

"I'm not going anywhere but over there, pretty. Give me the key."

She does, and I unlock my leg shackle and crawl over to her, the predator in me wanting to rise up and cuddle-rape her. But mostly I want to curl around her and talk to her. It's so stupidly unlike me, I can't even bother to ask what the fuck is wrong with me. I just do it.

Taking her trembling body in my arms feels like fucking heaven, and for I don't know how many minutes, I simply hold her until she relaxes against me. Her skin is so damn soft I can barely feel it beneath my fingertips as I stroke her arms, her face, and finally she leans her silky head on my chest, making my gut twist in some unfamiliar, delicious way.

I don't know what to think about this. I can't even begin to comprehend what is happening here, because it's all new territory. And for the first time since I was a kid, I have to admit I feel…afraid. Totally alien to me because I'm not afraid of anything—not pain, certainly. Not death, even. I don't fucking like it. But nothing is going to make me leave this girl—this girl who, for the first time in my sorry life, is making me really feel something. Something I can't escape—and don't want to.

Eden Bradley

CHAPTER FIVE

"You want to tell me about this asshole father of yours?" I ask her.

"Not really. I don't like to talk about him, but I'll tell you a little because...because I want you to know, for some reason."

"Okay."

She takes a long, sighing breath. "I'll give you the short version. To begin with, you're right—he is an asshole. He's rich. Powerful. That's how he gets off—power—and he abuses it in almost any way you can think of. After my *maman* passed when I was a little girl, he found ways to dispose of me. Perhaps I reminded him of her, or maybe that's simply me romanticizing things. All I know is that I was raised by nannies, then sent to boarding school. I don't think he cared, as long as I was out of his sight, which doesn't exactly make for good self-esteem for a kid, you know? I've been thinking about that a lot lately—that kink is what's made me feel good about myself, so even when I say I'm not certain I'm a good enough slave, it's still better than what I thought of myself growing up. Kink has made me feel... useful. Valued. Even cherished, sometimes. Maybe it's gone to my head a few times, and I've gotten ahead of myself. I've left perfectly good Mistresses and Masters, because I thought I deserved more."

"Maybe you left because you did deserve more."

"I don't know. But I do know that being with the Master—with Master Damon—is the first time I've felt I had everything I needed. Everything I wanted. Well, almost."

"Almost?"

"Except for you," she says so quietly I can barely make the words out.

I'm afraid to squeeze her, which is what I want to do. But I allow myself a smile.

"I'm glad to hear it."

She snuggles in a little closer, her breast pushing against my side. I reach down and stroke the curve of it. I want to do a lot more than that. I want to push her down on her back in the hay and bite her again, and spank her and pinch her and claw her and fuck her. And I will. But we're not done. Maybe a bit of self-control on my part, after all? How novel of me.

"You love him," I say.

"Yes."

"So do I, in my own limited way. In the only way I've ever loved anyone."

"Can you tell me why you think it's limited?" she asks.

"I don't 'think' it is. I know it is."

"But where does that come from? Because the way in which we limit ourselves always come from somewhere, some incident, some person. Our parents. Do you have an asshole father, too?"

"I couldn't tell you—I never knew him. All I know is he went back to the U.K. before I was born, and his is the only white blood I have, as far as I know."

"What about your mother?"

"Half Japanese, half Cherokee. Beautiful and fucking sad as shit."

She trails one finger along my skin—over the curve of my left pec, then fluttering around my nipple piercing. Butterfly kisses on the steel bar there, making my nipple rise to her touch. Making me ache for her touch all over, inside and out, whether it's sex or kink or just…this. Selfish bastard that I am, I want it all.

"But did you know your mother?" she asks.

I draw in a breath, smelling the scents of clean girl and fresh hay. "Yeah…I knew my mother. I knew too damn much about her. She was a junkie as far back as I can remember."

"I'm sorry," Aimée says, raw emotion in her voice.

This shocks me. I don't get why this amazing girl would feel so much for me—*me*, of all people. Maybe I don't get why anyone would. But I can't *not* talk to her about this—this thing I talk to no one about. I've given even Master Damon only the barest outline.

"So was I," I answer finally, "but not too sorry to leave home at fourteen. It felt like survival at the time, and I still think it was the best choice. There were some good things about it—I don't know if you can understand. No, I take that back. Given your own background, maybe you can."

"Tell me," she says, but it's more a request than a demand. She is ever-sweet.

I take a minute, stroking her skin with my thumb, trying to regain some sense of balance, torn as I am between this strange need to talk with her and my cock's raging demands to bury myself to the hilt in her soft body.

"I was this weird kid, living on the streets in San Francisco, hanging out on Haight Street with the other urchins, except that I was reading Shakespeare in between hustling in the Castro for food money. There was this guy who used to come find me every Wednesday afternoon around three—no idea why that day, that time—and he'd take me to his house on Russian Hill. He'd fuck me good and hard, just the way I like it. Then he'd let me stay with him for a while. We'd sit at the table in his marble kitchen and he'd talk to me. Really talk to me. Ask me what I wanted out of life, stuff like that. But smart-mouthed little bitch that I am, I always told him I only wanted his dick in my young, sweet ass. But he never got angry. He'd make omelets for me, feed me with a fork from his own hand. And he was the one who gave me Shakespeare to read. And Dickens and Moby Dick. He wanted to set me up in an apartment, to keep me for himself. And honestly, something about that appealed to me—the bird in a gilded cage shit. Except I've always thought of myself more as the wolf. I knew if I did it, I'd rip into him sooner or later. And anyway, a part of me loved life on the street. A part of me still craves it. The dirt and the danger. I guess that's what I'm doing here."

"But here everything is so civilized, despite how extreme it all is."

"Is it? Wasn't I the wolf today?"

"Mmm, yes," she purrs.

She curls hard against my side, and my dick is hard again—or maybe still—and I have to really concentrate not to reach over and grab her by the throat and plow into her. But there's also something buzzing in my body that has to do with that strange eagerness to tell her every damn thing about me. When the fuck have I ever done that with anyone? No one knows everything about me. I like being the enigma too much.

"I get what you're saying, though," I tell her, taking a lock of her hair and rubbing it between my fingers. "It's insane how civilized they make it, which is for our benefit as much as it is to indulge their need for luxury. Not that I should talk. Because when I'm on the outside, I'm one of them."

"Will you tell me more about that?"

"I don't know how much I want to talk about it right now, because I *feel* it—fucking Dominant rising, like some bird of prey, and it needs to hunt." I let her hair go, needing to put even some minute bit of distance between us, because as I say the words, it's a physical sensation I have to grit my teeth to swallow down. "It wants to come out, take over. And to be honest, I'm having to fight it damn hard just to stay here with you." My chest goes tight as I admit this out loud—how badly I need to be with her, no matter how it's costing me to stay in the slave role when I'm so damn done with it. For now, at least. But I go on. "I *want* to. But you have to understand certain things about me. When I'm between slave contracts, or when I walk out on one, which happens most of the time—okay, whatever, every time—I live out there like they do. I go to the clubs, to the private training facilities. I work the slaves, and I'm an evil Master. But I never have my own slaves. I don't want that. My own need to be enslaved is too much at odds with agreeing to oversee someone else's care. It would never work. Except being a slave obviously never quite works, either. I'm a walking contradiction." I stop, running my free hand over my short Mohawk. "I don't fucking make sense, even to myself."

She's quiet for a moment. "Why do I feel like that's something you're very practiced at telling yourself?"

I turn and look down at her, and her sweet little face is turned up to look back at me. *Watching* me. There's a flash of fear in her pretty green eyes, but she was brave enough to put the question out there, and I realize that, other than those brief moments, she's not afraid of me. Which is unusual in itself. Most people are, which I enjoy. But I also love that she can face me down. I don't know. That's not the right way to describe what she makes me feel.

Fuck it. I don't have the right words for this. I stroke my thumb over her jawline, and she closes her eyes, a shiver going through her, and my whole body surges with need. "Aimée. I have to fuck you now."

"Oh, yes, please."

Shit. This girl is gonna kill me.

"It has to be rough. I don't know any other way, and you make me want to pull your hair and choke you out and fucking bite you until you bleed."

She opens her eyes and stares right into mine. And again, she says, "Yes, please."

I can see that she means it. Down to her bones, in every cell of her body.

"Goddamn fucking Christ, Aimée."

I slip an arm behind her and drag her down, until I have her under me, her wrists pinned at the small of her back, and I don't care that it's got to be uncomfortable for her. As I raise her free leg, the other rattles the chain attached to her shackled ankle, and I feel a grin spread over my face. Fucking beautiful, with her red hair all over the place, shining against the gold of the straw, her green eyes glossy as she slips right into subspace. Slave space. Even better knowing there is a person of real depth, one who analyzes and tears herself apart trying to get to the bottom of her kink. Of herself. Oh, yeah. Because it's *that* person turning herself over to me.

Leaning right in, I take one luscious, pink nipple into my mouth, and it hardens under my tongue. I bite into her tender flesh, and she gasps, then sighs, gasps again when I bite harder, chewing on her nipple. And in moments she's panting, her hips rising against me, pressing against my rigid cock, and I shift and slide right into her.

"Ah, fuck, you're so wet."

Her sweet little cunt is contracting around me almost instantly, and I sink my teeth into her nipple, tasting blood as she begins to come, a raw mewling issuing from her throat. I can smell her come in the air—come and desire, hers and my own. I keep at it, fucking her, fucking her, and I can't get enough, driving hard and deep. Pleasure is like a hammer, threatening to pound me apart, to shatter me. But this girl always shatters me. And too soon, I'm about to come.

Pulling out, I quiet her protesting moan with a hand over

her mouth. Her eyes go wide as I use my thumb and forefinger to squeeze her nostrils shut, and her body goes limp with yielding. I feel her throat tighten and release her nostrils, letting her take some air in, and I let go of her wrists so I can press a finger into her ass.

Ah, God, so damn tight and velvet and fuck, I need to be in her ass, too. And she can take my dick, I know she can. But I'm too fascinated with watching her face as I slide my hand to her throat and put just enough pressure on the carotids, making her swoon. But even as she begins to lose consciousness, just my finger in her ass is making her come again — she's coming even as she passes out, and it's almost more than my rabidly throbbing dick can take. And still, I need to see her, to watch her lovely face.

Too much. Too much to feel. But I can't run from it, for once. Can't run from her.

As her eyelids flutter, consciousness returning, I flip her over and pull her onto her knees, holding her with one arm around her narrow hips, and with the other I part the cheeks of her perfect, heart-shaped ass. Spitting onto my hand, I push one finger, then another, into her asshole, fucking her with my hand, harder and harder. It feels like she's about to come again, and I stop.

Leaning over her, I bury my fist in her hair and yank hard enough to pull her head up and back. "Tell me," I growl into her ear. Then, when she doesn't answer right away, I take the shell of her ear between my teeth and pull.

"Ah! Christopher... Tell you what? I'll tell you anything."

"Good girl, Aimée. That's exactly where I want you. Tell me you want me to fuck your asshole. Tell me you want my fat cock buried in your fine ass. Tell me you want to come that way."

"Please," she sobs. "Please, Christopher. Oh God, can I call you that, even now?"

"Yes. Do it. Call me by my name."

"Christopher," she says, making a shiver run through my system. "Make me come with your cock in my ass. I want it. I want *you*. I need you."

Slipping my fingers out, I spread her cheeks, her firm flesh in my hand. I pause to give it a hard pinch, then another, but I can't wait any longer. I cannot fucking wait. Pressing the tip of my cock at that tight little hole, I tell her, "You will open for me. You'll take all of me, take me deep. It's going to fucking hurt. I'm going to tear you apart—I won't be able to help myself. I *have* to hurt you."

"Yes. Tear me open. Make me bleed for you," she begs. "For *you*, Christopher."

She spreads her knees wider, granting me further access, and I spread her ass cheeks wide with my hand, until I can see the pink, puckered flesh of her asshole. So damn delicious-looking, I have to lean down, bite the lovely curve of her ass, then bite again and again, leaving teeth marks all over her ass, her lower back, her spine, her shoulders. And the whole time she's yelping, squirming in a way that makes her back twist and dance like a snake of gorgeously tempting flesh that I have to kiss, to draw my tongue over in between taking that same delicate flesh between my teeth. And soon I break the skin, the metallic scent of blood like magic to me. I have to fuck her ass now—as if I didn't before—but the smell of blood really makes my head swim, makes my body hum with a ravenous desire.

Pressing the head of my cock against that sweet little puckered hole, I thrust, sliding in with a single motion. She gasps, cries out, making me smile. I begin a hard pumping, hard and deep and fast, hammering into her. In moments I hear her really start to cry, but it only makes my smile spread into an evil grin. It only makes me fuck her harder, my lust fed by her beautiful tears, flesh for the hungry beast. And I grab her by the hair, pulling her head up, her body, until we're both on our knees. Taking her jaw in my hand, I squeeze, turn her face so I can see her crying. Her cheeks are wet. She's sobbing quietly. And still, I'm bucking into her fiercely. Savagely. And pleasure is like a tightly bound coil in my belly and my balls, in the pumping head of my iron-hard dick. I hold it back, but soon I can't fucking take it anymore, and I come, filling her ass with my jizz.

"Fuck, yeah."

Wrapping an arm around her waist, I pull her down onto the straw with me, spooning her, my softening cock still deep in her ass.

Her breath is a hard panting—I can feel it under my hand

on her stomach. Her hips are undulating the slightest bit. She's a good girl, after all. A good slave. But she's as taken away by desire as I am. Reaching around, I press onto her tight clit, the flesh swollen with need. I shift my hand until I can use the knuckle of my finger to tease her clitoris, and with the side of my thumb I press just into her sweet, slick cunt.

"Oh…Oh!"

She comes in a torrent, her cunt gushing with her juices, my beautiful, squirting girl. Nice to know she can do that. Fucking hell, more than nice.

Slipping from her ass, I quickly use a handful of the straw to wipe down my cock before tossing it aside, then roughly turning her onto her back, I force her knees up with my hands, spreading her pussy wide. Then, still holding one leg up, I push my fingers into her soaking cunt and begin to work her g-spot, rubbing at it until I feel it swell. Then, using a quick, rough, up-and-down motion, I pump her cunt until she starts to yell. Until her pussy gushes and she squirts all over the straw and her own thighs and mine as I kneel between her legs.

"Again." I command.

She whimpers—maybe that's all she's capable of at this point—and acquiesces, her body relaxing, knowing what to do in order to let herself gush for me. This time I watch her face as it builds, as she screams, as she squirts like mad, soaking us both once more.

When it's over she's panting hard, shaking all over, small spasms still wracking her body. And her very helplessness does something to me. I pull her upright, into my arms, into my lap, and hold her tight.

This girl…she *touches* me. And even though the catalyst is sex and kink, it doesn't matter. It's only a catalyst. The important thing here is that she's gotten to me, gotten inside me. Inside my heart and my fucking soulless soul. But she's too damn beautiful at this moment for me to be afraid of anything. I am filled with wanting—wanting to some raging degree. It feels like madness. It feels like everything I never knew I wanted. It makes me feel in some way like a different person.

Her head is on my shoulder as she catches her breath, her arms limp at her sides, which is the correct manner for servitude.

I take her arms and loop then around my neck, both because I know it will comfort her, and because I need to feel her holding on to me.

Finally, I feel her relax in my arms, and I lay her down in the hay. That's when I realize there's blood on my hands—her blood.

"Hey. Stay right here for me. Okay? I'm going to get the first aid kit and clean you up."

She nods, curling into a ball as I let her go and get to my feet. My head is still spinning, but I find the handlers' room, which would have been the tack room in the horse stable, and open a cabinet, pulling out the first aid kit, blankets, and a few bottles of water. After cleaning myself thoroughly, I take it all back to our stall.

When I return she blinks up at me, her green eyes glazed and sleepy and full of slavespace, a small smile on her pretty pink mouth.

"Drink this." I hand her a bottle of water and watch as she drinks it all down. "Good girl. Do you need the bucket?"

She's too dazed to answer, so I take her by the hand and lead her to the metal bucket in one corner, steady her as she squats over it and pees.

There's a certain eroticism in having your lover or your slave urinate in front of you, even if it's not necessarily done for erotic play. It's the vulnerability of it. She doesn't even flinch—she simply does it, as though it's the most natural thing in the world. And it feels natural. But even so, it's fucking hot, making my blood boil. Any other time, it would make my dick hard, but currently it's too spent to do more than twitch lazily.

She's quiet as I clean the blood from her ass first, then using a handful of wipes, I clean her stomach, her thighs, the plump, pink flesh of her pussy. Then I use the wipes, followed by the antibiotic ointment, to treat the bite wounds, which are on her breasts, her shoulders, her ass, the back of her neck. My heart is hammering the entire time—with excitement, a deep pleasure, and stark emotion I don't know what the hell to do with, other than to lie down next to her when I'm done and pull her into my arms, spooning her once more. Her lithe little body is warm, then gets warmer as I pull a blanket over us.

"How are you?" I ask her.

"Sooo good," she says, drawing out the syllables, still totally gone from sex and pain and the D/s dynamic. "Wonderful. That was…wonderful." She ends on a sigh.

"You're in dreamland, prettiness."

"Mmm…yes. I never want to wake up," she murmurs. "I always want to be here with you, in this stable, with you commanding my body. This is perfect."

I chuckle to hide the tightness in my chest. "You may change your mind about that once you've recovered, once you're thinking clearly again."

"No. This is the clearest I've ever been in my life."

I don't know what to say to that, so I say nothing. Instead, I bury my face in the back of her hair and inhale, rub my face in the satiny strands. Kiss the back of her neck over and over.

"Christopher?" she says finally. "May I… Is it okay if I turn over to face you?"

Rather than answer I turn her with my own hands, keeping my grip rough so she'll get that I'm still in command, that the dynamic never stops with the sex. That it never will.

When she's facing me, she snuggles right in, and I don't know if it's because she's lost that sense of the power dynamic, if my being nice to her has diluted my dominance, or if it's only because she feels that at ease with me, regardless. But it doesn't matter too much at the moment. It feels too damn good. It calms even the rage of the beast that lives within me, which is no easy fucking task, and I sort of melt into her soft, sweet skin, the tender flesh of her body, finding comfort myself, which is entirely new to me. But what the fuck? Why can't I be comforted? Does it have to mean I've been rendered weak? And fuck it. I don't give a shit if I have been. I'll be weak for a few minutes with her. I'll be weak for the first time. And for the first time, it doesn't fucking matter.

That's what I'm telling myself, anyway.

CHAPTER SIX

We sleep. When I wake up, the hazy amber light streaming in through the top half of the stall door, which has been left open, tells me the sun is setting. It occurs to me that there are probably other slaves in the stalls close to ours, that they heard us fucking, heard Aimée coming, sobbing, screaming. I know what it is to be in such a position, how it makes your body thrum with jealousy, with the need to come that can be so intense it feels like your skin is burning, as if you need to tear it from your body simply to get some relief. Or maybe that's just me. I've done those things to myself. There were times when I needed it.

Aimée stretches, yawns, and I hand her the water bottle. She drinks obediently. She does everything obediently. Almost. There's just enough fire in her to let me know she is no mindless sheep of a slave, which is something one often finds in this crazy, kinky world of ours. Some slaves have been in it too long, have lost themselves so completely there's nothing left of *them*. Some Masters love this, but I hate it. The sheep are boring to me, devoid of interest, devoid of the spark that makes them a challenge. Yes, I love to see them hand themselves over, and I understand we have a need to lose ourselves. But you still have to be a person under all that—an individual—or what's the fucking point? If you have nothing left of yourself, you have nothing left to give, or so it seems to me. But what do I know? I'm the one who doesn't fit in, as Dominant or slave.

I run my hand down her sleek side, and she surges into my touch. Nice. I'm hard again, instantly, but that's a condition of my life, and I can handle it, my nearly-eternal erection.

"How are you doing?" I ask her between the throbbing pulse-beats of my hardening cock.

"I'm good. A little sore, but fine. How are you doing?"

"What?"

"You sound surprised that I would ask."

"I am."

"My Master Graham threw his back out fucking me," she

says, a hint of amusement in her voice.

"Your Master Graham wasn't me."

There's a long pause, then, "No. He certainly wasn't."

I look down at her and she's biting her lip, those pretty white teeth coming down on the plush pink of her mouth, making me want to bite her, too.

"Christopher? I don't want you to be him. I don't even want you to be the Master — Master Damon. I want you to be whoever you want when you're with me. Master or slave, or this heady combination of both that makes me… I don't know, exactly. But it makes me drunk with the possibilities. Sub-drunk. Is that even a word?"

"It can be. It can be your word. Our word."

She smiles. "Will you tell me something?"

"Tell you what, pretty?"

"Anything. Something about yourself. About what you went through before becoming a slave, when you were young."

"Why do you want to hear about that?"

"Because that's when you reveal yourself to me. Is that…is that okay to ask of you?"

I roll onto my back, pulling her with me, and press her cheek down on my chest. She curls in like the kitten she is. And suddenly I have an image of her lying on her back, fluffy white ears on her head, purring at me as I dangle a toy above her.

Fucking hot.

But what was she asking? Oh yeah. My sad past.

"What do you want to know?"

"Um… What about your addiction? I mean, if you're okay telling me."

"I'll tell you anything — I don't care. Fuck. That's bullshit. I do care. I don't tell just anyone this stuff. I've kept it to myself most of my life. I don't particularly enjoy feeling like I'm burdening anyone with my crap."

"It's no burden. It's important, don't you think? To who you were, who you've become?"

"I don't know that getting hooked on smack was as important to who I am now as getting off the stuff."

"Of course," she agrees. "Because that's your strength."

"It didn't fucking feel like it at the time. Or…maybe it did."

It comes back to me, then. The fear and the thrill. The dark and the flesh. The absolute goddamn powerlessness, and me taking my fucking power back, in grand form. I exhale, long and slow.

"You know what got me to stop using heroin? One night when I was sixteen—I'd been using about a year—I was hustling at Balboa Park. This trick comes up to me, we negotiate my price to blow him, then I have him follow me to my favorite bush, and three other guys show up and fucking gang rape me. But you know what? The problem wasn't being gang-banged against my will. The problem was that I *liked* it. And I knew I had to get my shit under control to figure that out, that I had to get off the drugs—out from behind the mask—to feel that again. That's what really living is, you know? The shit with the fucking sparkle. You can't have one without the other—not anyone I ever knew. Those people who think life is one or the other? They're the ones who are missing out. Not us poor kinky fuckers. We have it *all*."

She curls hard into my side, her hands grasping at my chest, then hanging onto my shoulder, and I feel her hot tears on my skin.

"Don't, Aimée. Don't you fucking feel sorry for me," I growl, unable to keep the fury from creeping into my voice.

"I'm not. I don't. It's not pity. But it's still terrible, a terrible, hard way to grow up. And perhaps selfishly, it makes me think of my own childhood. We were both lost children, weren't we? Even if it was in very different ways. When you're a kid, it all amounts to the same thing—not having anyone to protect or care for you, not having that safety net. I suppose that's part of my need to be a slave, too—having someone care for me. Or, taking care of me, even if all they want is for me to serve their needs. But I've been lucky, for the most part. It sounds like we both have, as far as our kink lives are concerned. Well, maybe me more than you. But don't you find you get that out of it, at least at this point? No? Please don't scowl at me—I didn't mean to make any assumptions. I'm sorry." She stops, sniffling, then another tear drops onto my skin, hot and melting its way into my chest. Into my heart, whether I like to admit it or not. "But Christopher," she goes on, her voice so soft I can barely hear it,

"I can still feel sad for what you've had to go through, can't I?"

"I don't know. No one else ever has."

She lets out a breathy sigh, her fingers smoothing tentatively over my skin. "No wonder you're so angry," she says, still quiet.

But I'm fucking pissed. Pissed at my past. Pissed that I feel like a goddamn victim having to talk about it, or maybe because someone is actually sympathetic to my fucking pathetic lot in life. I don't like to feel pathetic. Anything but that.

"Yeah. Fuck it. Whatever. It doesn't matter."

She sits up suddenly, looking down at me, her green eyes gleaming softly in the twilight bathing our little stall. "Don't," she pleads. "It matters. It does. It matters to me."

"Why?" I still don't have the rage under control. It's not her. It's simply *there*, an ancient part of me, like the rings on a tree, except those rings may as well be steel cables wrapped around my body, holding the deeply fermented ire in place.

She's watching me again, her brows furrowed, her lovely face all soft, elegant lines. "I don't really understand it—why you make me feel the strange things I do. Things that are so new to me, so different, I don't even know how to process it. All I know is, this feels important, meeting you, being with you. I have to ask myself, is this what I've been missing with my Masters, with my Mistress? With the men I've tried to have relationships with outside of kink? There's always been this awful, glaring hole, and I'm constantly trying to fill it. I feel as if I've come close a few times—close, but never quite enough. Never quite right. And then you come along and…you feel right. Forgive me, but I can't *not* tell you. You rip me too wide open, and I can't allow that to happen and still have anything left to fight it with. No, that's not right. I couldn't fight it to begin with. Not with you. I have no desire to do anything but give myself to you, no matter what it does to me. It scares me to tell you, but I have to. I *have* to."

I don't know what to say, my tongue frozen in my mouth. Emotion builds, knotting my chest, my gut, threating to burst in some spectacular explosion. And when it does, that shattering sensation tearing into my skin, all I can do is fist my hand in her soft hair, push her down into the hay and kiss her and kiss her, as if my life depended on it. Maybe it does.

Her body is so damn soft, her mouth even softer, and the way this woman yields to me is powerful. Intense. She makes me want to *own* her—something I've never done before, never wanted. Sure as fuck never needed, the way I do right now, with her.

I pull back. It almost hurts to do it. "Aimée, I need to take you out of here," I tell her in a rush, and maybe I'm not even certain of what I'm saying.

"Take me out of here?"

"Yeah." I nod, the plan formulating as I talk to her. "I can get to some clothes, and I have cash stashed here. We're going away together. I don't know where we're going, not yet, but I'll figure it out by the time I have you dressed."

She's staring up at me, her eyes wide.

Laying my palm on her cheek, which is burning with a hot, lovely blush, I tell her, "I need your consent. You know that's the only way I can do this. Fuck, I shouldn't be doing this at all, violating your contract, as well as mine. I do it all the time, but I know this isn't something you'd do without my bad influence. Still..." I have to pause, chewing the inside of my lip, trying to ground myself. It's not working. All I know is a sharp-edged desperation that's going to make my guts spill all over the damn floor if I can't do this. "I need you to come with me. I can't stay here anymore, and I'm not leaving without you. But if you can't do it, I get it. I do. Just fucking tell me..."

She raises her hand and strokes my face, her gaze locked on mine, her pale little brows drawn. So serious, and so damn pretty, I can't stand it.

"Christopher. Please promise me you won't leave without me. Please. I'll go anywhere with you. I have to."

I nod, turn to kiss her sweet palm. "Wait here. I'll be back within an hour."

She nods, smiles. Her eyes are shining, brilliant.

Getting to my feet, I flex my fingers, then ball them up into fists. And there I am, naked and unchained, when I hear the stall door swing wide behind me, and the high-pitched chuckle of fucking Jonathon as the handlers grab me and throw me to the floor.

"God fucking shitting damn it!"

There are four of them on me—big, beefy guys—and they overpower me too easily, pissing me off. I kick one of them, manage to bite a hand, but there are too many of them. In seconds they have me bound in rope and gagged with the damn stuff—the spiky jute I usually love and hate simultaneously, but which I only hate right now. Not as much as I hate Jonathon.

My vision is blurred with red—the unadulterated color of raw anger—and through it I see my beautiful Aimée, hands over her eyes, tears streaming down her cheeks. And fuck, I will hate myself if she's punished on my account. I will hate *them*. I will burn the goddamn place to the fucking ground!

But they hustle me out so damn fast, I hardly have time to think, to tell Aimée I will get out of this and come back for her. I'm still struggling as they drag me down the center aisle of the slave barn, but my arms are laced tightly behind my back, my ankles shackled with rope, and I can't even fucking walk by myself. I don't mind the humiliation so much—at almost any other time, I'd love it—but I don't know where they'll put me, or how long it'll take me to escape. And fucking shit—what will they do to her? What if they send her away somewhere? Someplace where I can't find her?

But I will. I'll do whatever I have to in order to track her down. I have my connections in the kink world, and in the underbelly of the kink world—and yes, even our world, which is an underbelly of sorts in itself, has its own anarchists. I know them, of course. I'm one of them, aren't I? And I can find out anything I need to.

All of this is spinning through my head at a thousand miles an hour, and I barely noticed that the goons have hoisted me onto their shoulders. But suddenly, we're out in the cool evening air. Even now I notice the scents of rolling fog on green leaves, see the color of the sky overhead: a deep, deep blue, starless as the sun makes its final, glimmering descent over the horizon.

They're carrying me on my back, so I can't see where they're taking me. But even before I'm tossed face-down onto the boards in the back of a wagon, I hear the jangle of harnessing, then the crack of a whip as the driver starts the human ponies moving down the road. Eventually, we stop, and the goons are back, grabbing me by the shoulders and pulling me out of the cart, only two of them this time, but I need to get my bearings if I'm going to make a break for it.

Am I? They'd come right after me, set off the alarm, and the property would be crawling with handlers and obedient slaves, like a pack of hounds scenting a fox. Fuck. When they tilt me upright and set me on my feet, I can finally see where I am. My blood runs cold.

In front of me is the Victorian house the owners of this place live in, and in which they house some of their more important guests. I only know it because the Master has brought me here with him — in my life as a Master, which I think of as my "outside life", I've been put up in one of the dozen or so guest bungalows. I have no idea what it could possibly mean that I've been brought *here*. Am I being dismissed from my contract? Have I fucked up that badly this time? I've done all sorts of rotten shit, but I've never involved another slave before. Bad Christopher. If my stupid behavior hadn't put Aimée at risk, I would laugh at the absurdity of my predicament — *me*, of all people, of all slaves, being despondent at the idea of being sent away. Ha!

Except there's not a damn thing to laugh about right now. The goon squad hustles me up the front steps, through the double doors that are being held wide by a pair of latex-clad ponies, which I only catch in a dark and shining peripheral blur. They're dragging me along so damn fast, down a hall and into a large room, which, I see with a quick glance, is a parlor, of sorts. Except that there's all kinds of kink gear and furniture in here — spanking benches and examination tables are punctuated by delicately-built period furniture. At the far end of the room is a huge fireplace, but instead of a fire, a bound and gagged and blindfolded male slave is turning on a spit above a row of burning pillar candles. Of course, he's sporting a raging erection. Very nice. The sadist in me can't help but grin gleefully beneath my rope gag. And then I remember that I could damn well be next.

Fuck. Fuck this place. Fuck my damn contract.

The fury is building, and it's that crazed beast, scratching and slobbering, clawing to get out. The more I think of Aimée left alone, chained up in the barn, the more it feels like my brain will explode. I turn and growl at the handler on my left. He shakes his head at me. When I growl again he backhands me across the face, and I lunge at him—as ridiculous as that is, given that I'm bound and hobbled. He takes a step back, and I go down hard, hitting the floor with a thud that momentarily knocks the wind from my lungs, my sight dimming for a split second.

One of them toes me in the ribs, and I'd cuss the fucker out if I weren't gagged—except I still don't have enough air in my lungs to even growl at him. But a low chuckle makes me blink up, and my gaze meets Master Damon's.

Fuck.

He clucks his tongue, says in his precise tone, "Foolish even for you, Christopher, don't you think?"

I don't say anything, grinding my jaw while he turns his head and signals to the others to leave the room. It's only the Master and myself in here now. The slave "roasting" on the spit hardly counts. Master Damon waits until the parlor doors close, then he straddles my body, pulls a knife from his back pocket, and leans down, slicing the rope binding my ankles. I have a moment to glance at the blade, which is a straight razor, before he flips me over onto my stomach and drags me across the floor, pulling me along by the rope binding my arms until we reach an ottoman. He bends me over it, shoving my knees apart. I'm fucking furious and hard as a rock. Alas, my never-ending story. I know what to expect, but still, the object he shoves into my ass without preamble makes me suck a breath in between my teeth.

I'm growling and clenching my jaw, enraged spit spewing from the edges of the damn rope gag as he plows me good and hard. I hate that it feels so fucking good—that I love the pain, the tearing sensation. My ass can take a hell of a lot, so whatever he's using on me must be huge. Of course it is. The Master does not fuck around.

I feel the heat of his legs on either side of mine, then a searing pain as he runs the blade down my back, making a crisscross pattern, slashing my skin open. And no matter how pissed off I am, I want him to fuck me, to jam his cock into my ass. To shove my face into the floor. To hurt me enough that I won't ever forget him. Because I plan to leave this place, and never come back. Never see his stunning face again. It'll be fucking impossible if I steal Aimée away.

Aimée.

What in fucking hell have they done with her?

I let out a roar, but it's *him*, so all that happens is that he pulls whatever rigid object he's been pegging me with from my ass and starts to beat me with it. The blows land on my ass, the backs of my thighs, the backs of my fucking knees, even the bottoms of my feet.

From under the damn rope gag I mutter, "Yeah, harder, you bastard." He can't possibly understand my garbled cussing, but he knows me, and he gets the gist.

Immediately, it all stops, and he steps back.

"God damn it, Christopher," he says after several long, silent moments filled with nothing but his panting breath. It's the first time I've ever heard real rage in his voice, no matter what I've done. "Why *her*?" He pauses, then murmurs, "But of course it's her. It is for me. Why wouldn't it be for you? We all fall in love with this Girl."

I growl then, mad that he refuses to use her name.

Grabbing me by the sparse hair of my platinum Mohawk, he pulls my head up, making me rear up on my knees, and he comes around to look into my eyes. His are so startlingly blue—I always forget how blue they are. His dark brows are furrowed. And the expression on his face...I've never, ever seen him like this.

"You're in love with her, too, aren't you?" He gives me a rough shake. "God damn it, you love her. And she'll love you back, if she doesn't already. Everyone does. You and your exquisite beauty and your supreme brattiness, and your barely-caged anger that burns so very brightly in your eyes. Yes, everyone falls in love with you, dangerous boy. That's something the two of you have in common."

He throws me down on the rug and stalks off. I know better than to move right now, but I watch him from the corner of my eye. He's pacing the floor, and I see now he's dressed in one of his beautiful, crisp white Italian shirts, the cuffs rolled, exposing his beautiful forearms and the dragon tattoo curling around the right one. His slacks are black, as always, fitting his flawless ass in a way that makes me want to break free of my ropes and shove my unrelieved and swollen cock in there, to abuse his asshole the way he has mine. I don't get how I can be so damn emotional and still want to fuck. Always. Yeah, the fucking primal animal. That's just what I am.

He stops pacing and comes back to me.

"Christopher. Get up. We need to talk."

CHAPTER SEVEN

He's untied me, given me a glass of water and sat me down on one of the fragile-looking sofas. I don't know what this means. Am I being dismissed now? It'll be harder to get back to Aimée from outside the Ranch, and I don't know when, if ever again, they'll let me in as a Master, but I will fucking find a way to get to her. The idea that he'd separate us makes me sullen—not a far stretch for me. I'd refuse to look at him, pouty child that I am sometimes, except I'd rather stare at him, trying to unsettle him. He doesn't unsettle easily, but he's off tonight. I can see it in the tight set of his shoulders and mouth. In the way he keeps running a hand over his dark hair. If I weren't in the slave role I'd *make* him talk to me, but even I can't do that from this end of the spectrum. And naked and so recently abused by him, that's where—and what—I am, despite my recent compelling surges of dominance.

A good ten minutes goes by before he finally he says, "This isn't working, Christopher."

I raise my eyebrows at him. "Oh?" I ask, coyly, perhaps.

He strides across the room toward me, menace in his posture, in his face, but when he gets to the little sofa, he stops, running his hand over his hair again, which tells me he's distraught. Well, so am I.

"Come on, Christopher. Don't pull this with me. Not with *me*. You owe me better than that."

I roll my shoulders, sit up straighter. "All right. I'll cut the shit. But tell me what, exactly, we're talking about here. Me messing with Aimée? Fucking her? Talking to her? Topping her? What?"

"All of it. All of it, with you here as a *slave*. You undermine the system, damn it!"

"Don't I always?" I can't help the grin that quirks one corner of my mouth. "People expect it of me."

"Stop with the performance. We know each other too well."

I notice then how tired he looks. Is he really that in love with her? Am I? What are we negotiating here? Or does he just want me to spill before he bans me from this place long enough to cart her off somewhere, hide her from me? Would he really fucking do that?

I would, if I were him. Hell, I have plans to do exactly that.

He sits down next to me, taking a dainty throw pillow and tossing it at me. "Cover yourself. I can't have a serious discussion with you when you're naked."

"Telling me I'm going to take your fat, hungry cock isn't serious?" I ask him. But I cover my naked crotch with the pillow.

"You're incorrigible."

"Yes, but you love that about me."

He sighs. "I can't argue with that. But not right now. Right now I need you to talk to me." He stops, waiting. When I remain silent, he goes on. "Okay. I can see you're not going to. I'll talk to you, then. This Girl — no, *Aimée* — is special. But you already know that. And hell, I brought you here to ask you to leave her be. I saw you from the stands today, you know. I saw how you beat the other Boys to her, how you took her there in the arena. I saw the intensity of your intent, and I recognized it, because it's the same as my own. But I am asking you now to back off."

"No."

He turns to me and grabs my shoulder, but I shake him off, and he doesn't try it again. His eyes are as fevered as I imagine my own are right now.

"Christopher. Think about what will happen. You'll be fascinated for a time, then you'll leave her behind to go off and pursue the other parts of your life. Ishtar—"

"Ishtar? You know she doesn't mean to me what Aimée does. Did it ever occur to you that I might want her in my life?"

"No," he says quietly. "You never do. Not for any length of time. Don't do that to her. I am telling you, don't—"

"I won't!" I say savagely. "You have no idea…"

"No, I don't. Why don't you tell me?"

He's calmed himself, all smooth talk again, acting the Master. But I'm too much the Master myself right now, and I'm not having this shit. I get to my feet.

"Do what you will, Damon," I spit out. "You will, anyway. You have more money than I do, more power in this circle. You'll do it even though you love me, too—or, you once claimed to."

He looks down, folding his hands, then glances back up at me. He says, his voice soft, "You know I do."

I stare at him, trying to ignore the raw emotion on his face, which is always difficult for me to handle. There were times when he begged me not to go, but I always did. I always do. I'm too fucking hardened to let a man love me—that's the raw and simple truth of it. Damon is as close as I've ever come to it.

"I'm ready to go now. Wherever you're sending me."

To show him I mean it, I get down on my knees and clasp my hands behind my back. He stands, walks over to me and strokes my head. "So damn beautiful," he murmurs before moving toward the door, opening it, and giving orders to whoever is waiting outside.

The goons come back into the room, and very quickly put a heavy leather posture collar on me, lace me into leather armbinders, my arms tight behind my back. I'm blindfolded and a rubber snaffle bit is shoved between my teeth—the kind with two jointed pieces that are made of metal when they're used on horses. It's to be the ponies, then. And I will perform even more beautifully, more elegantly, because I know he'll be watching—I can't deny that, even to myself. In Master mode or not, even I, angry brat that I am, can't resist being ponied. I fucking love it, whether it's me or anyone else. Too fucking hot.

As they shuffle me out to the wagon, my mind is too full of the possibilities to even give Master Damon much thought. No, that's bullshit. I think of almost nothing but him, because he is behind every single thing that will happen to me as long as I remain at the Ranch. Will I be ridden? Paired with another pony and made to pull a wagon? Whipped along one of the trails? Or hitched to the cart they use to carry away the horseshit and straw from the stock stables? It could be any of these things. And will I see Aimée again while I'm here? I have no idea how things will go.

I will be a pony for them. It'll give me time to formulate a plan, and I'll fucking enjoy it. But as soon as I figure things out, I'm gone. *Gone*. Maybe for good this time. And Aimée is coming with me, unless they send her away first.

Fuck.

No way to find out. Maybe…

I keep my eyes on the stars peering from between the clouds overhead as the wagon bumps over the path, taking me back to the slave barn rather than the stock barn, making me realize the Master is more afraid than I'd thought. Too afraid to punish me that harshly, with the solitary confinement he knows I truly hate. I smile, but it only lasts a moment. Even I have a conscience. I don't want to break his heart. But I want to break my own even less—I've only recently discovered I really have one.

We come to a stop and the handlers pull me out of the cart. I don't bother to fight them as they begin to walk me down the center aisle of the barn. I make a mental note of the stall door that holds—or held—my beautiful Aimée before they shuffle me into the stall right next to the handlers' room. There, they remove my arm binders after they chain my ankles, then they chain my wrists, leaving me just enough give to get to the damn buckets—one for me to drink from, one for me to piss in. Whatever. The buckets are the least of my worries. My posture collar is replaced with a steel collar, and that, too, is attached to the heavy bolts in the wall of the barn by a length of chain. It's too short for me to lie down, and I'll have to sleep slumped against the wall. Again, whatever. It's no worse than sleeping on the streets, like I did as a kid.

I'm offered a dish of a flavorless beef stew, held by a slave Boy they've brought in from somewhere, and although I'm tempted to knock the plate from his hands just because I'm fucking pissed off, I know I need the nourishment.

Finally they leave me the hell alone without a single word being spoken—alone with my thoughts, with my plotting, with the fantasies of being paraded as a pony tomorrow making my traitorous dick hard as my steel shackles.

At some point I sleep, which I know because when I open my eyes I can feel the world coming alive around me. I can hear the sounds of slaves waking and yawning, the birds chirping outside, and I can see the pale colors of the rising sun filter in through the open doors at each end of the big barn.

I get up and stretch a little, testing my muscles, then do some calf raises, going up on my toes, then lowering my weight again, followed by some push-ups against the barn wall. Next, I work my abs, grabbing a cross-beam to hold my weight while I lean my back into the wall, tighten my stomach and bring both knees up to my chest over and over. Then I do it again, with both legs extended straight out, until my abs are screaming. It won't do for me to get soft now, and I haven't been exercised enough lately — unless you count fucking as exercise.

After I finish and have had a few minutes to stretch again, two handlers and another slave Boy — there's always an endless supply of them here — come to take me to the showers, where I'm bathed and dried and polished before they bring me back to my lonely stall and give me breakfast. I have to shit in the goddamn bucket in front of them, at which point I'm taken back to the showers for an enema and another thorough bath. But I've endured worse, and something in me always likes it, apparently, or I'd never keep coming back for more, would I?

Then it's back to my stall again, where I find Victor waiting for me.

He's grinning at me, the beautiful bastard. "Ah, all emptied out? Good boy, Christopher."

"You know how they are. They love to collect our shit in a bucket, these scat-loving little slave Boys. They get off on it."

"Yes, I imagine they do. But so do you — you get off on them doing it."

I just shrug.

"I'm here to dress and harness you," he says, ignoring my lack of response. "But you knew that, didn't you? You're hard already."

In two strides he's across the stall to where I've been left standing, and he slaps my dick with the flat of his big hand. I try not to flinch, but the truth is I could almost come. Son of a bitch knows how to keep me in slavespace, but I'm fighting it. I don't want to be here. Except that I do, if only long enough to play pony for them one last time.

Last time? Is it really to be the last time? Will I even have any choice in the matter?

Shut the fuck up and enjoy it.

"Victor..."

"What is it, Christopher? Speak up while you have the chance — it won't last long." He glances at his watch, a big piece on a wide black leather band. "You have exactly two minutes."

He's watching me, waiting. But the words choke me, my throat closing up as completely as if his big, black cock was shoved down there. Except this doesn't feel nearly as good. I don't know what the fuck is going on with me, until suddenly, blindingly, I do.

I am fucking afraid. This is what fear feels like. Too damn unfamiliar. I haven't let myself be afraid of anything since I left home at fourteen. That was when I decided I was done with that shit. But asking myself the question opened it up. *Is* this the last time? The last time I see Victor? The last time I can be a slave?

"One minute, Christopher," he reminds me in his ever-patient tone.

But all I can do is stare up at him.

His eyes narrow, then he slips a hand around the back of my neck, and I close my eyes as he caresses my skin.

"What is it? What's going on with you?"

"Fuck. Really don't fucking know if I can do this anymore, Victor." I open my eyes, meet his gaze. "Pony gear—fine. Fuck it. Whatever. But the rest of it? Staying here, serving them? Serving *him*? No. I can't fucking do it. And…I don't think this is going to be one of my runaway episodes."

"Okay. I get you. I do. And I'm going to tell you something, something I don't think you know about, but I think you need to now. I was pretty much the same as you, before I came to work here. I started out as a bottom boy. Oh, yeah. I did. Worked my way up, was adored by my Masters and Mistresses, because I was so strong. I could take it all, whatever they dished out. Then one Master wanted me to Top him, and I loved it a little too much. I started doing it on the side, and one day I realized bottom boy was over for me. But I gave myself some time to make sure. My advice? Don't burn any bridges you don't have to, Christopher."

I nod. "I'll give that a try." A smirk creeps over my face—can't help it. "But you know me. Burning bridges is a specialty of mine."

He laughs, claps me hard on the back. "You do your thing, then. Play nice for the crowd today, turn the charm on. Let them all fall in love with you again before you fuck them up."

I nod. "I intend to. But Victor, I may need some help."

The Training House

He's quiet for a long moment. "Understood."

The slave Boys have returned, their arms loaded down with gear. Victor gives a nod of his finely sculpted and dimpled chin, and the Boys step toward me and begin to lube up my skin, which means I'll be in latex. I look damn good in latex.

When they step away to unzip the bodysuit they've hung on a hook on the wall, Victor leans in and whispers, "Glad to have had one last good fuck, Christopher. I'll miss that."

Without turning my head, I murmur, "Maybe you won't have to. We'll see."

He chuckles as he steps back and lets the Boys go to work on me. It's a hell of a process, getting into latex. They keep adding more lube, their soft, slippery hands making me hard again, and it's a good half hour before they have me dressed. By the time they're done, it feels like I've spent the entire time edging, my cock thrumming with the reverberation of their touch. The body suit is like a second skin, in darkly shining black. They've added to that a black patent-leather harness that crosses my chest, with large silver studs set into it. I always feel a little like a Roman gladiator in a chest harness. Decorated. My damn stupid pride again, but I can't help it. I also can't help that the rest of it makes me feel elegant and beautiful, horny and fucking powerless all at the same time.

They've harnessed my head, too—one of the pinnacles in humiliation for me, but of course my dick is hard as ever. Instead of the full horse-head mask some ponies wear, this one has a square nose box that covers me from just below my nostrils to below my chin, with a mouth plug, blinders, and the ears, of course. It has three straps—two across my cheeks and one across my forehead—as well as one that runs vertically from the nose box up over the top of my head, and they all buckle in the back. I'm already standing up straighter. Pony gear always does that to me, but when they put the tall patent-leather posture collar on me, I really start to sink into pony space. I shake my head a little just to hear the jingle of the harnessing and buckles, a small thrill running hot in my veins at the sound, at the earthy scent of patent-leather and the chemical smell of latex.

Hooved leather mitts and boots are buckled into place next, and a wide belt is secured around my waist. The Boy's hands feel delicate to me now, through all the latex and leather, as if this thick skin I'm wearing makes me *stronger*. Invulnerable. Invincible. I glance at one of the Boys as he adjusts my head harness, and he pauses for a second, staring into my eyes, his long lashes coming down seductively over his baby blues, and my cock pulses. And Jesus fuck, I could almost come from his flirtatious glance.

Then Victor moves in, pushing the Boy aside to finish the adjustments himself. His hands are far rougher on me, which he knows I fucking love. I pause to breathe in the moment, because I'm pretty damn sure this is my last day in pony gear. Aren't I? It's a hell of a lot harder to be as certain with the pure pleasure of being a pony roaring through my system, like that moment of lightning-hot desire at that final point of hovering pause before you thrust your cock into a waiting hole — like that times a hundred, maybe.

I must have spaced out, because Victor grabs my harness and does some capture and control with me, yanking me off my feet, his big hands holding on tight to the chest harness and the straps at my head, his knuckles digging in painfully. Deliciously. And it does the trick — I am back in my body, in the moment. Which is either really good or kinda bad as he unzips the back of the bodysuit, and without so much as a drop of lube or fingerful of spit, he inserts the plug end of a long tail — black, I'm sure, to match my latex. Nothing is done here without a sense of style.

Why do I feel so fucking powerful like this? Powerful, powerless — it's suddenly all the same thing to me, in this garb, in this position that is the most abject humiliation for other people, and in some ways for me, too. But I glory in it, even in the confusion, when I can't tell where the bad part stops and the good begins. I flex my muscles, feel the pull of the latex like a hard caress on my flesh, and the hard knob of the plug buried in my ass just deep enough to press teasingly against my prostate, and it all feels so goddamn good. My cock is stiff as a board and ready to fuck.

I will go out there and perform my ass off for the masses who are into this shit. I will give them a show they'll never forget. And then, like Houdini, I will disappear in a flash of smoke, leaving them talking about me for years to come.

I manage to smile to myself, even with the big rubber plug gagging my mouth, then have to swallow hard so I don't drool. Can't ruin the pretty effigy of servitude I currently am. Not now. Now I plan to give them everything they want from me, before I fuck up so badly I can never come back.

Never come back.

Can I really do that? Maybe, if I have Aimée, I won't need anything else. For the first time since I discovered kink, I think this may actually be possible. But I can't really think it through right now. Now my body is burning with the sensation of latex entombing my flesh, with the jingle of the harness, the promise of my ever-inflated pride being fulfilled by my admirers. Oh yes, even Master Damon. Or maybe especially him.

Victor has the Boys lead me out by a long pair of reins while he keeps my pace going with sharp smacks of a short whip. It doesn't hurt, not through the latex—it's all symbolic at this point. But my brain cannot resist going to that pony place, and I'm sinking, sinking, into that irresistible space where the rest of the world fades away and I am allowed, at last, to lose myself. All I know at this moment is the tight embrace of the latex, the high collar holding my neck as erect as my suffering dick, and the *clip clop* of my hooved boots on the path. As we approach the arena and Victor whips me through the gate, the crowd roars, and Christopher ceases to exist.

Eden Bradley

The Training House

CHAPTER EIGHT

All I see at first is a blur of dust being kicked up in the arena, and the vague colors of the people in the stands. My focus is too much turned inward, every one of my senses on high alert, dulling my mind, making sensation blend and muddle together. I swear I can smell the dirt beneath my feet and my own sweat. Even the excitement of the crowd has its own scent—like leather and perfume, fine whiskey and sex.

Then Victor moves in close and I smell his skin, too—he always smells like coffee and sandalwood—and he whispers to me as he reaches between the straps on my head to give my cheek a cruel pinch, "This is it, my bad and beautiful steed. Do your best. Do me proud. You know you want to. You know you *have* to."

Ah, he always knows how to get inside my head. But I need it, need him to center me. He hustles me along, moving me in such a precise manner that I know instantly he is harnessing me to a cart of some sort. As soon as he backs me into place I recognize the light weight of a racing buggy. I like to race. I like to win, and I know I can. Performance is, after all, my *thing*. Nothing feeds my ego like winning in front of a crowd. I stand even straighter. I would fucking preen, if I were able to move enough. But I can prance a bit in place, and I do, my tail waving in the breeze behind me, and it feels like I'm being fucked the tiniest bit by the plug, pleasure a shiver up my spine. Oh, yeah. I do it again, stomping my hooves on the hard ground, sending shockwaves rippling through my body.

When the crowd cheers once more, I know it's not because of my shenanigans. I hear another pony and buggy lining up beside me. I inhale. *Male.* And I recognize him, although I can't turn my head to see him because of the posture collar and the blinders. But I know it's the gorgeous, hulking ginger from the arena. I would think of it as a sort of divine punishment, except I know there's nothing "divine" about it. This has to be Master

Damon's idea. His punishment. Bastard. Except when I beat this big slave Boy, I'll love the Master even more.

I wait to see if I can sense who the other competitors are, but a minute goes by, then another, and it's still just the two of us, until I hear the light footsteps as two female drivers arrive. Another round of applause, then I hear Dahlia, the evil little handler who announced the Primal Takedowns.

"Sirs and Madams, Masters and Mistresses, we have a special treat for you all today—a race with some of our strongest, most spectacular ponies! Take a look at the muscles on these two, the broad chests, the girth of their biceps and thighs. I can promise you the girth of their fine cocks matches every flexing muscle. A more promising pair you won't see at any facility on the planet. Today we pit them against each other in a three lap race, and the winner takes the other. Yes, ladies and gentlemen, this particular pony race will end up in a takedown for your viewing pleasure."

What the fuck is this? I don't know if I'm pissed or excited. Both, probably, since that's my usual response to almost everything. I paw the ground with my hooved feet, the pony surging through me. The goddamn stallion.

But Dahlia goes on. "Handlers, please prepare our steeds while the drivers mount the buggies."

Victor is in front of me, and he casts a grin at me before he begins to strike my crotch with his whip. My dick rises, pressing against the latex, nearly screaming to get out, to feel his whip on the swollen, aching head. I would go down on my knees for it about now, if I thought it would actually do any good. But I remind myself that I can have the redhead's ass if I can hold my shit together.

Victor stops the whipping and reaches down, undoing a zipper and pulling my engorged cock free. A groan escapes from behind my mouth plug as he gives it a hard squeeze.

Fuck.

I am going to die. I am going to come. Then he pinches hard at the underside of the head, squeezing the base painfully at the same time, making my body swallow some of the jizz that's demanding to burst out of me. I'm swearing silently inside my head, my mind spinning.

Victor leans in and murmurs, "Focus, Christopher. *Now.*"

The Training House

I look up at him, my gaze meeting his. His dark eyes narrow, and I understand.

Yes. Focus. Win. Fucking triumph.

"Masters and Mistresses," Dahlia continues, "today our drivers will be two slaves trained and skilled to drive this particular type of racing buggy. First we have a beautiful slave, lent to us by Mistress Clara, from London—please welcome DeLayne!"

I hear the applause, and the sound of the buggy next to me being mounted.

"And now we have a slave many of you may know—she has been training to drive the buggies, and has become one of the best in recent months. Let's welcome our own Ishtar!"

Ishtar? What. The. Fuck.

This is a Girl I myself have played many times as a Master. And God damn it, Master Damon knows exactly what the fuck he's doing, doesn't he? I'm so pissed off, if it weren't for Victor still standing in front of me, glaring me down, I'd... I don't know what the hell I'd do. Bolt? I can't do it—not now. But Jesus God, I'm motherfucking spitting mad!

Victor leans in, hitting me with his little whip to cover his quiet muttering. "Calm down, Christopher. It's not her fault. Use your anger to fuel you. You know how."

He's right—I do know. And I will do it. But later, someone is going to pay.

The buggy shifts as Ishtar—a petite blonde with large, gorgeous breasts—gets in. And as mad as I am, I'm also turned on as fuck knowing it's *her* that's about to drive me. My cock gives a hard twitch.

Then the horn sounds and I'm running—running until my legs ache, and the bottoms of my feet hurt from the impact of hard, hooved boots on the ground. With the damn blinders on, I can't see my competition, but the fact he's not up in front of me is a good sign. Then suddenly, he is, and I really pour it on, while Ishtar snaps a buggy whip at my back, catching me on the shoulders over and over. Whatever. I'll run like a fucking fiend anyway.

As I start to pass the big ginger stud, he shoulders me, nearly rocking me off my feet, and pissed, I ram into his side. It gives me a momentary lead, but in seconds he's pulling ahead again.

Just do it. Have to win.

I think of Master Damon, of what he's doing to punish me. How I need to show him up. To return the punishment a little. I'm a bastard, after all, and it wouldn't do for me to ruin my reputation.

I pull in a deep breath, taking in the scents of damp air and eucalyptus trees. It helps my lungs to open up, and I pour on the speed. I catch sight of Dahlia waving a flag as I finish the second lap. My lungs are beginning to burn, but nothing could make me give up now. The redhead slams into my right shoulder again, and again I return the hit, being careful not to overturn the buggy, which is an art in itself. Somehow, my hooves are easier to run in than they are to walk in, and I'm pounding the dirt. I'll pound *him* soon enough.

As we round the shorter curve of the arena, I stumble, and hear a startled gasp from Ishtar. I pull hard to the left, trying to pull the weight of the buggy with me, righting it, and it's fucking hard—painful—but I manage to do it. And the damn ginger is ahead again. I dig my feet into the earth and sprint forward just in time. Dahlia waves the flag madly as I cross the finish line, and the crowd goes crazy. Almost instantly, Victor and the two Boys are there, unharnessing me from the buggy.

"Good boy," Victor tells me.

I want to tell him to fuck off, but even if I wasn't gagged with the damn plug, I'm too focused on getting into the ginger's muscular ass to much care about anything else.

They're still working on releasing him from his buggy when I lunge at him, pulling him down so fast I take one of the slave Boys attending him with us. So the fuck what? I *will* have him. I slam into his big body, forcing him onto his side, and with one knee on his tail, I roll him until the plug slips out of his ass. He's figured out what's happening, finally, and he fights me—we're both back on our feet again. It's a mad wrestling match, with both of us hooved, hands and feet. One of his metal hooves slams me across the cheek, but pain only fuels my desire, my raging need to take him. My leg snakes around his, and I take him down to the ground again. I smell him—a mixture of sweat, fear, desire. Pre-cum.

Using my thighs, my knees and elbows, I get him under me, on his knees. He's trying to buck up, but the only thing this accomplishes is bringing his fine, tight ass within reach of my raging hard-on, and I jam it in as quick as I can.

I hear a muffled "oomph" despite the bit in his mouth, and pleasure is like a serpent, winding sinuously through my balls, my belly, into my ass, which is still beautifully plugged. I begin to fuck him in short, vicious strokes. Because I need to. And because it's the best way to keep him down.

The edging I felt earlier while being dressed in pony gear, as well as Victor's "fluffing" and the obvious pleasure of the crowd, makes me need to come too damn fast. I want to slow it down, to draw it out, to add to the thrill of the voyeurs watching us, but I can't fucking control myself. His ass is as tight as a virgin's, and I know I'm probably tearing him up a little, which only makes it hotter.

Yeah, bleed for me, motherfucker.

I can feel the jizz gathering in my tight balls, hot and churning with need. And with a scream from deep in my throat, I spill into him. Still fucking him, fucking him, as hard as I can, come spurts from my cock so hard it hurts. But I don't care. It's too goddamn good. So good.

I pull out of him, trying hard to catch my breath — a challenge with the rubber gag plug still firmly in place — and as I get to my feet, the crowd applauds, roars, screams. I turn and give them a little bow, which only makes them go wilder. Pleasure shimmers over my flesh like rows of goosebumps. The ginger stud starts to get up, but I shove him back down with a knee in his back. He's on elbows and knees on the ground in what looks like a pose of supplication, and I can see from the damp puddle in the dirt beside his discarded tail that the fucker came while I was pegging him.

Suddenly, I like this Boy.

But things are happening fast — Victor grabbing my reins and pulling me back a few feet while the slave Boys help the hulking redhead up and lead him away. He manages to shake them off long enough to turn and look at me, his face red beneath the straps of his headpiece, his eyes gleaming with equal parts fury and the afterglow of orgasm. Then they drag him off, and I'm left in the center of the ring with Victor hanging on to me as the Master approaches and lays a wreath of white roses around my neck. But he won't look me in the eye. I try to pull away from Victor, but he's got a good grip on the reins, controlling me. I shake my head, trying to shake him loose. Not that it does much good. Victor is strong as hell, the resident Superman, and maybe the only handler here who can really handle me if I'm ready to bolt, and I am, and I'm not. Maybe I just want to be in control. Ha!

Then the Master surprises me by leaning in and telling me quietly, "Excellent job, Christopher." He gives me a pat on the neck, then the cheek, his fingers digging in as they curl around one of the straps there, and he helps Victor lead me from the arena. Victor opens the wide gate, and we step through. On the other side the Master gives my head a hard yank, forcing me to face him, which I'm happy to do. I want to see his face, to see the pride there.

But what's burning in his handsome features isn't pride, exactly — it's some combination of emotions that's too complicated for me to take in right now. I'm still the pony, transitioning back to being myself, and my brain isn't functioning. I am too much an animal right now, and my responses are operating at a purely primal level.

"Christopher," he whispers harshly, his face inches from mine, "don't think I am unaware that you plan to leave. Remember what we spoke about. Just…see that you do, damn it."

He releases me, and walks away, leaving me feeling a little shell-shocked. Is it because I'm so unused to hearing him swear? Because of how angry he is with me?

My earlier euphoria is mixed with a sense of loss now. But I should be used to being a walking contradiction. I should be used to loss.

Victor runs a hand over my back, making me shiver even through the latex.

"Shower time for you, then rest. Do rest, Christopher. You've earned it. And you'll need it."

The Boys are back, and together they strip me down and get me into the showers. The hot water feels magnificent, and when they're drying me off, my dick goes hard again. I could stand to come again, but then, I always can.

Victor has disappeared, and I feel a little like shit that I'm relieved, but I need to disconnect. I've gotten some of my brain back after the shower, and I don't want to spend too much more time thinking about things. I'll rest, as Victor said, but then it'll be time for action.

The Boys take me to an empty stall, and I lie down in the straw, gladly closing my eyes even as they lock the shackle onto my left ankle. I have much to think about, to dream about. And it all has to do with my beautiful Aimée.

When I wake, the hazy blue-gold of twilight is drifting in through the big barn doors and the air has turned chilly. Someone has come in and laid a horse blanket over me as I slept, and left a tray of real food—a thick chicken stew and a hunk of fresh bread. I get up, take a good, long piss in the bucket, then settle down in the soft straw to eat, and when I'm done I lean into the water trough for a long drink. Then I take a look around to get my bearings.

This is stall eleven, at the opposite end from the handlers tack room, which means Aimée is at the other end of the barn. And there's a key within reach in here. I have to stretch hard enough that the metal shackle bites into my ankle, drawing a little blood, but it doesn't matter. Soon I have the key, and I release myself from my chains with only the tiniest edge of regret. Carefully, I replace the key in its hiding place, then poke my head from the stall to make sure the barn is empty of handlers before stepping quietly into the center aisle.

When I make my way to the handlers' room, I find one of my stash spots behind a cabinet and pull a tight roll of cash wrapped in a plastic bag from it—somewhere around three thousand dollars, if I remember correctly. Grabbing a feedbag from a hook on the wall, I shove the cash into it, then pull a blanket from a shelf, and head to the stall I last saw Aimée in.

But she's not fucking there! Instead it's the sleeping figure of a Boy. Luckily he doesn't stir, even as I cuss under my breath. If they've taken her away, Godless motherfucking bastards... But

I'm sure they have. *He* has. Did I really think he wouldn't fuck with me, if not make it completely impossible for me to get to her? I'm not that deluded, even blinded as I am by my need for her.

I stop swearing and pull in a long breath.

Get your shit together. Go find her.

One by one, I carefully check each stall, some empty, some with sleeping slaves. And finally, in the stall next to the one I've just escaped from, there she is—awake and lovelier than ever, blinking at me, which I can see even in the relative darkness of the barn, with only the dim wall sconces in the center aisle to offer any light

"Shh," I tell her in a whisper as I step in and kneel beside her. I take her face in my hand, feel her shiver beneath my touch. "Will you come with me?" I ask. "Come away and be with me, Aimée. I can't demand it of you, as much as I'd like to. Are you still willing?"

She lets out a small sob, and when I cover her mouth with my palm, I have my answer as she leans into me, turning her head to nuzzle my hand, to leave soft, fluttering kisses there. I pull it away before I become too distracted by my growing hard-on and the emotion flooding my system. It's too much, and I need to stay on task.

"I thought you'd left without me. I was so afraid I'd never see you again."

I hold her face in my hands, letting her tears dampen my skin, and something in me fucking loves her tears. It makes me hot, but it also makes me…what? Her tears do something that's entirely unfamiliar to me—a painful and glorious tightening of my chest that feels amazing, and at the same time, freaks me the fuck out.

I stare into her eyes, and they're more green than ever, gleaming with the tears. Beautiful. So damn vulnerable it makes me ache in places I didn't know existed. Oh, I could become the poet for this girl. I could maybe become everything for her.

"I need you to think about it," I tell her. "Once we go, there's no turning back—not for me. They'll never accept me back into this inner circle once I take you out of here. I don't know if they'd accept you again—I can't say. Do you understand what it means to go away with me?"

"I understand I will get to be with you."

"And that'll be enough?" I have to ask it. It's one of the few times in my adult life I've been unsure of myself. Will *I* be enough?

"You are *everything*," she says, keeping her soft voice low. "I know we hardly know each other in terms of time span, but the things we've said to each other...the strange kind of life we have in common, even the enormous differences in the way we were raised...it all adds up. Except it's not a mathematical equation—you can't define human experience that way. There's an undeniable connection that goes far beyond the kink or the chemistry—and you must feel the same, or you wouldn't be here right now. You'd simply be gone. You've said as much. Do I have to know more than that I want to take this risk with you? That because it's *you*, it doesn't feel so risky? Do I have to know why? Does it really matter?"

"Not when you say it like that." Stroking her hot cheek with my thumb, then my palm, I feel the fever of her sincerity burn into my hand. Into my fucking *soul*. She has to be mine. She *is* mine. I have no other option. "Let's go."

I find the key hidden in the wall and unlock her, then wrap her in the blanket I've brought. "I have clothes in an outbuilding, but nothing that'll fit you, Aimée. We'll figure it out, okay?"

"Yes. It's all okay. I know you'll take care of me."

A sense of pride unlike anything I've felt before floods my system, and as I lace an arm around her waist and we move quietly out into the cool night, I feel almost unbearably protective of her. My girl. *Mine.*

Something that belongs to me for the first time in my life.

No. *Someone.*

Eden Bradley

CHAPTER NINE

We jog up the road, then I direct her to veer off onto a side path that leads up a hill to a small tool shed. Inside, on a high shelf behind a box of rusting bailing wire, I have a bundle of clothes hidden away—dark jeans, black t-shirt, black thermal pullover, socks and boots—and a cell phone with a battery-powered charger. I plug it in before I dress her in the warm shirt, which comes down over her thighs, then dress myself in the rest. The clothes feel odd against my skin, the soft cotton much stranger than the latex I wore earlier in the day. Transferring the cash to the small leather satchel I kept the clothes in, I stash the feedbag in its place. The less traceable clues to our whereabouts, the better, for a time—until the memory of us fades away. Then I'll return the contract fees the Master paid into our bank accounts when we signed. It's what I always do, and he'll know I'm good for it. I may be the ultimate brat, the ultimate anarchist and an ex-junkie, but I'm no thief. Except that I'm stealing Aimée from him.

Don't think about it now.

Taking her hand, I lead her down another path until we get to the grand, well-lit iron gates of the ranch, and I call for a cab. The cell phone feels strange in my hand, as if I'm from some other era and unfamiliar with the technology. It's always like this, when I run. It's all a little routine to me. But Aimée has been silent this whole time, and I'm worried about how she's taking all this, escaping like refugees in the night.

"Hey. You okay, prettiness?" I ask her, stroking her silky hair from her cheek while we wait, maybe more for my benefit than hers.

"I will always be okay with you, Christopher. I promise."

"How do you know?"

"I just do."

"It's as mysterious as that, isn't it? You and I?"

"It is. But I've decided I don't have to understand it, as I told you earlier. I know this whole thing is a little crazy. I truly don't care. I've always followed what my heart needed, and this is no different, unless that it's more so. Impossibly more. And...I think you're doing the same, aren't you? Following your heart?"

I nod and pull her in closer.

The cab arrives in a small spray of gravel and dust, and we get in. The driver gives me a puzzled look in the rearview mirror, but I hand him a wad of twenties and tell him to take us to a hotel I know in Monterey, one town over. When I loop an arm around her shoulders, she lays her head on my chest in an attitude of absolute trust, and eventually she seems to sleep.

After having the driver stop at one of those all-night gas stations, where I buy my girl a pair of shorts and flip-flops, we continue on to the Monterey Hotel, an old Victorian inn just up the street from Cannery Row. Not that I plan to stay long enough to play tourist here, but we need a comfortable spot for the night. I've learned that a few hours of transition time is important.

The place is lit up, and I can tell Aimée is in shock. To be honest, so am I, but I have to take care of her, so I keep her close to my side while I get us checked in to a room. Then I half carry her up the old stairs, carpeted in a dark red floral print, to the third floor.

Our room is pretty—a suite with a fireplace and a wide, arching window with heavy white-painted shutters that remind me of New Orleans. The whole room reminds me of that old city, with its fine, carved antique furniture, the enormous bed with the intricate wood headboard, the little writing desk against one wall.

"Sit down while I take care of a few things, pretty," I tell her.

She follows my direction, setting herself on the edge of a damask-covered chair, still in slave mode, with her perfect posture, her gaze on the floor. Or maybe it's just the shock of our absurd situation. But I have to turn away from her long enough to build a fire, to call downstairs and ask them to send up extra blankets and a meal, and quietly offer them money to send someone out to get two small pieces of luggage and clothes for her. I also give them a contact number to have one of my credit cards, some of my own clothes and more cash sent to me here by courier from my home in San Francisco—I have an assistant who will know what to do. And these fine hotels, they know better than to ask any questions.

I push a glass of sparkling water into Aimée's hands, and she takes a few sips. But she looks so damn lost sitting there, I pick her up in my arms, drag the soft cashmere blanket from the foot of the bed, and sit down in front of the fire with her half in my lap.

"How are you doing?" I ask, running a hand through her hair.

"I'm good."

"Are you?"

"No. But I will be."

"Yeah, you will. Aimée, you have to know that you are my responsibility now, that I don't take this lightly. I will take damn good care of you."

She wraps her delicate fingers around my wrist, making my heart beat faster. "I know you will. I wouldn't have left with you otherwise." She pauses, then, "There's a certain safety in that world, isn't there? We sign ourselves over, and it's everything I've ever hoped for, imagined, fantasized about, masturbated to. But it's also safe. Safe in that I can lose myself. Safe in that every single thing is attended to for us. But...meeting you has made me realize that in being *that* safe, I'm losing out on something. And it's not what an outsider would think, that what I'm losing is my individuality. That's a given, although that never really goes away, or we'd do it and be done a month later. What I'm losing out on is taking risks. Being willing to walk through life and *feel* it all. I didn't know it before. I was simply doing what I thought I needed."

"And you don't need it anymore?"

"No, I do. I absolutely do, or I wouldn't have walked away with you—I would have just walked away. But I think with you I can have the safety and the fantasy, and still have those risks I've been avoiding all these years."

"I've never been able to leave the risks behind completely, to lose myself to that degree. I've always felt like it's some failure in me, some defect."

"No. I think you're more a realist than the rest of the slaves."

Grabbing her face, I look into her eyes. "Don't put me on a pedestal, Aimée. I'm sure to disappoint you," I tell her more harshly than I mean to.

She shrugs. "Then disappoint me. At least I'll know it's real. Because I don't think I can do this anymore—what I've been doing. I really was convinced it was what I wanted, craved, and maybe I did crave it, but that doesn't mean it's what I needed."

"What do you think you need now?"

"It's a little vague. I'm sure I'll feel more like I have my feet under me in the days to come. I want you. I *need* you—need to be yours—but I still need to be myself sometimes. Some kind of balance. I have no idea how to do that. Can we figure the rest out as we go? Will you help me?"

I lean down and press my lips to the tender spot at the base of her throat. Her pulse beats madly against my lips. "As long as you know you're mine."

"Yes," she whispers. "Absolutely yours. Yes, please, Christopher."

I kiss her lips, and they're so damn soft under mine, it's making me a little crazy. I push my tongue inside, her mouth unbelievably sweet. It makes me need to hurt her, to be inside her. I slip my hand under her shirt and take her warm, full breast in my palm, squeeze hard, making her sigh, then she gasps as I pinch her nipple tightly. My dick twitches, pressing against my jeans, making me flash back to the sensation of being encased in the latex.

Need to play her wearing tight leather pants…to open the fly and fuck her until she screams, my balls squeezed tight by the seam in the leather.

When I bite into her lip, she moans, and I'm fucking rigid as steel, my cock weeping pre-come already. Then there's a knock at the door, and I have to let her luscious tit go to get up and answer the door with a hard-on—not that it's anything new, and I don't fucking care if the room service guy they've sent up here sees it. In fact, when he glances down and tries to suppress his reaction to my fat cock pressing against my jeans, it amuses me.

Taking the plates from the cart, I set them on the floor, sit down and spoon-feed my girl. There will be plenty of time for her to serve me once we get settled somewhere and the shock of the day has worn off. I give her little tastes of everything: tender bits of crab meat dipped in melted butter, fresh strawberries, torn pieces of the fragrant local sourdough bread. She takes each bite carefully, like a baby bird, and her delicacy makes me want to do terrible things to her. But tonight we need to rest.

After we eat, I pick her up and set her on the bed. I pull the thermal shirt over her head, cover her carefully, and after stripping out of my clothes, I curl up beside her. I really don't intend to do more than sleep, but fuck it all, it's *me*, and in about thirty seconds I've pulled her on top of me, and my arms are wrapped around her sleek little body, tight enough to hurt, while I pinch her soft flesh — her sides, her ass, her thighs, the backs of her arms. And she's moaning and sighing against my neck. I'm hard as fuck, and her wet pussy is rubbing my dick, so I press her hips tighter against me, digging my nails in, and shove her slender frame up and down, jacking off with her whole body on my stiff cock. Her nipples are two hard points against my chest. They feel fucking great, raking over the piercing on my left side, her lush flesh so damn soft. Goddamn delicious girl.

When she starts to shake, I tell her, "Come for me," and she does, good girl that she is. And Jesus fuck, in moments I'm coming against her belly, then we're slipping and sliding in my sticky jizz.

I go hard again, and this time I roll her over, bring her knees up to her shoulders and plow into her, watching her beautiful face. So beautiful, I have to hurt her. Have to. I start to slap her, and with each slap her eyes become more glazed, her body going loose beneath me as she yields to my command, to the pain. Her cheeks are burning, bright pink with my hand prints. Leaning down, I take one of her gorgeous, succulent tits into my mouth, sinking my teeth in, finding the marks I left on her before and scraping, sucking, marking her. *Mine.*

"Fuck, yeah," I mutter, bending to kiss her hard, sucking on her lips, biting down until she whimpers, then cries out. Finding the pressure points on the back of one sleek thigh, I press, dig, until she's coming and yelling, and I have to slap a hand over her mouth. Then she's choking, still coming. I spill into her, pleasure wracking my body, spiraling into my gut, shooting up my spine and into my brain — mainlining pleasure like a fucking rocket in my veins.

Even when we're both done coming, I'm still pinching her,

twisting her nipples, biting her shoulders. I love the way she gives herself over to me, to whatever pain I want to bring her. To the pleasure. It's like an exploration for me, new territory, feeling like this. Treating a woman's body this way. Not the fucking or the pain, but the way I feel when I'm doing it. Like I have to *devour* her—her skin, her scent, her desire. I need to fill myself up with her, and I can't get enough. I can't stop until the way she smells is deeply embedded in my nostrils, until the flavor of her flesh is burned into my tongue. And even then, it's barely enough to hold me for the night.

I mean to leave the next morning, to make us less traceable, but we stay in that hotel room for another three days. The sex is fucking off the charts. Kinkier, maybe, because it's not nearly as hardcore as what we're both used to, which makes us laugh when we talk about it. I spank her—with my hands, with a hairbrush. I bend her over the little secretary and fuck her ass. I bite her until she bleeds, until I have to clap my hand across her mouth to stifle her screams. I make her squirt so much I have to call housekeeping to change the sheets three or four times a day. I order her to get down on her knees and give me head, fucking her face until she's choking and tears run down her cheeks. I make her suck my pierced nipple until I come all over her beautiful tits. But this all seems a little vanilla to us both. Still, it's unbelievable, how good it is. And in between the kink and the sex and the kinky sex, we talk about fucking *everything*.

Eventually I decide it has to be our last night, that it's time to move on. I've ordered dinner, and we're sitting on the floor in front of the fire having one of our picnics again, the scents of beef bourguignon and acrid, earthy wood smoke mixing with the scent of desire that's always a part of us. I'm feeding her again—at some point I decided this is the only way I will allow her to eat. We're both wearing the thick, soft hotel robes we've mostly lived in when we're not naked—which isn't often—and her lovely, bruised breasts show from between the folds of the open neckline.

"Prettiness, have I told you how much I love that you wear my marks?"

She smiles, batting her long lashes, tipped in gold in the amber light of the fire. "Every day."

"I plan to tell you every day forever."

Her smile broadens. "And to mark me every day?"

Reaching across our picnic to pull out her tit and pinch her gorgeous pink nipple, I tell her, "You're a very kinky girl."

"Oh! Yes, I am. I remember having these little fantasies about the priests in church…"

I laugh. "Oh, really? Maybe I'll have to get a long black robe and smack your fine ass with a ruler."

She bats those long, golden lashes again. "Yes, please."

I play with her nipple for a while, brushing and teasing it, pinching it, then brushing it again, enjoying how damn hard it is. Knowing her little cunt is slick with her juices every time I touch her. Every time I hurt her. I fucking love how responsive she is, how eternally wet. I love talking with her just as much, and over the last few days, I've learned not to question feeling that way. I want to know everything—the inside of her brain, as much as the inside of her lush body.

Letting her nipple go, I sit back and tuck a tender piece of beef into my mouth before asking, "When did you go to church? I can't imagine your father being a church man."

"No. He cares nothing about God."

"Do you?"

"Believe it or not, I do. But I don't think kink is sinful—I don't know that I really buy into the concept of sin, as long as it's consensual." She gives a small laugh. "I suppose that makes me a terrible Catholic."

"I wouldn't know. I'm a godless bastard who grew up on the streets."

She frowns, a pretty little pout. "Don't sell yourself short, Christopher."

I shrug. "Maybe I do—or maybe I'm a realist. Tell me more about church."

Her pale brows draw together. "You want to hear about church?"

Stroking her cheek, I twine a strand of her dark-red hair between my fingers, giving it a tug. "I want to hear about you."

"Well…Maman used to take me to church sometimes on

Sunday. I remember the French nuns in Paris. Even as a little girl I was fascinated by them. They were so gentle, so beautiful to me, and I couldn't wait until I was big enough to go to Sunday school. Maman taught me to say the word 'catechism'. I was so little, and yet I learned to pronounce it in French and in English."

"Belle dans les deux langues."

"Christopher— tu parles français?"

"A little. There's a Master and Mistress, a couple from Bordeaux, that I serve sometimes—or, I did. They insisted I learn their language," I tell her. "But my French isn't so good."

"Au contraire—I'm impressed. But then, everything you do, you do well, so I'm not surprised."

"Believe me, my ego doesn't need any fluffing up, my pretty girl. Tell me more about your Maman."

She bites her lip, making me want to bite it again, but I've been doing it so much, they're swollen and bruised in places, and I manage to resist. Maybe I am learning some self-control? The Master would laugh at that.

Small churning in my gut thinking of him. He's a subject we've avoided these last few days, but I'm certain he's on her mind as much as he is on mine.

"Go on, talk to me about her," I urge.

"It's difficult. I feel as if I've never recovered from her death. It altered my life so completely, at such a young age, and I've felt orphaned ever since. I know I keep saying that, but it's something I can't seem to get past. But you lost your mother, too. Don't you feel it?"

"I never had a mother—not really. Mostly I feel…anger. Shit, not just about her. That's how I feel about most things."

She pauses, glancing away, then back at me, and says quietly, "I feel it, too—angry with her for leaving me, even though that's not fair."

"Life isn't fucking fair."

"No," she says so softly it's almost a whisper. "It's not." Then crawling to me on her knees to curl up in my lap, she says, "I have this terrible feeling… I'm trying not to, but it's hard. And I have to ask you, do you think we can really have this? Because life *isn't* fair, and I know I've had it better than some. Better than most. But to think I can truly have what I want…it seems impossible sometimes."

I squeeze her tight, needing to feel her body in my arms, to feel how real she is. My heart is hammering. Can I have what I want? Can I have her? But it's my job to comfort her, not offer up my usual angsty rantings—that shit I need to keep in my own head.

"That's what we're trying to do here. I'll do the best I can for you—I promise you."

She nuzzles against my shoulder, and it's that mad brew of pure sex and raw emotion this girl brings out in me. I hold her tight, my cock rising against the soft curve of her lovely ass in my lap.

"We're getting out of here in the morning. We should leave early."

"Where are we going?"

"Palm Springs, I think. I have a place down there. I know—what the fuck is a guy like me doing with a house in the desert, with all the golf courses and polo-shirted folk? But that's exactly why. No one ever finds me there. And Aimée, we can't let them find us. Not yet. We need some time and some distance. We need to get ourselves reestablished, so they don't have any power over us."

"Do you really think there will ever be a time when they don't? Can we ever not be their slaves anymore? Even if *you* are my Master—and you are—I don't know…"

"I'd like to think so. Yeah. I think so. I can't go back to it. I'm done with that scene. I'm fucking done."

She's quiet for a long while, clinging to me, her slender arms around my neck, and then I feel tears spill onto my neck.

"What is it?"

"Do you ever miss him?"

It's my turn to be quiet. And that night, when I take my girl to bed, I'm rough as fuck with her, clamping my hand across her mouth to muffle her screams, leaving her bruised inside and out, spots of blood on the sheets. But after, I feel closer to her, in some crazy way. That's the insanity of this kink shit. She falls asleep in my arms, but I'm awake for hours, staring out through the open shutters at the clouds chasing the moon, listening to the crash of the ocean. Thinking about her question. Finally, at some point before dawn, I sleep.

Morning comes in the form of the door slamming open. I bolt out of bed, naked and peering through the half dark and the groggy haze of too little rest.

"I've come to get you," he says, locking his sapphire gaze on mine. He looks both full of fire and tortured, rage and a terrible sadness shadowing his beautiful face.

We stare at each other for several long moments, then his fevered gaze darts to Aimée, who is still sleeping quietly after our rough night, blissfully unaware of the crisis before us in the form of our Master. So damn vulnerable—I would do anything for her. *Anything*.

"Fuck you, Damon," I growl, my heart pounding like a jackhammer in my chest. I feel ready to kill. "Not this time, God damn it. This time, things are going to be different."

"Yes," he says in his calm, sophisticated tone. "Yes, they will."

The Training House

MASTER

CHAPTER ONE

My beautiful Christopher stands naked before me, glaring as if he would kill me.

Is it wrong that I'm half hoping he'll try? Nothing would give me greater pleasure at the moment than forcibly reminding him where he belongs. *With* me. *To* me.

I take a step forward. "Christopher, you need to calm down and—"

"No! Just fucking no." He's raised his hands in front of him, one curled into a tight fist.

My own hands twitch in response, but I slide them into the pockets of my slacks and run my gaze coolly over Christopher's magnificent physique. His golden skin and high cheekbones are flushed, the amber lion eyes that are a gift of his combined Japanese, Cherokee and English heritage glittering dangerously—a dangerous animal in nothing but rage and bare skin.

"*No?* After what you've done, that's all you have to say to me?"

"Oh, I have plenty more to say."

I've ignored Aimée so far, but now I focus on her with every bit of detachment I can muster. She's sitting up on the bed behind him, clutching the sheet to her perfect breasts as she watches the drama unfolding between Christopher and me. The fear in her crystalline green eyes and the tears sliding down her porcelain cheeks are gratifying—I do love a slave's tears—but they also wound me in a way that makes my chest go tight and my hands clench into fists in my pockets.

I make myself turn from her and raise a brow at Christopher. "Is that so?"

"Fuck right," he snarls. "To start with, there will not be any ordering me back—ordering *us* back. No cleverly devised punishments for my infractions, and sure as hell not for hers. I know damn well what I'm guilty of. But the thing is, Damon, I am *done*. Done with the slave bullshit." He pauses, wiping his lush mouth with the back of his hand. "Fuck. It's not bullshit. I know that. But I can't do it anymore."

"That's fortunate, because neither can I," I tell him, grinding my jaw against the anger I *must* keep under control. I am every bit as enraged as he is, for once. "Certainly not the way it's been in the past."

"Why the hell are you here, anyway?" he demands. "I've always come and gone as I pleased, contract or not. It's our little dance, isn't it? One we've been doing for four years. You've never come after me before."

"You never took her with you before."

His golden eyes gleam with dark fire as he takes a step toward me. "So this is about Aimée?"

"You know better than that," I say flatly, fighting the urge to step back. I don't like that he thinks he can intimidate me, and I like even less that he actually can. But I have to admit it's also hot as hell. He's absolutely gorgeous in all his lithe feline menace, which only infuriates me more. "Aimée is not the only different element this time. You and I both know it. But the fact that you would take another slave out of my House, that you would be party to her running out on her contract…it's beneath you, Christopher."

"God damn it, Damon. I left *because* I had to take her with me."

Turning to Aimée, I demand, "Tell me in your own words you went with him willingly."

"Fucking right she did," Christopher spits out. "We don't do it any other way—people like us—and you goddamn well know it. Jesus fuck, Damon!"

Aimée scrambles forward onto her knees and lays her hand on his arm. "Please, Christopher. He needs to hear it from me."

He stares at her for a moment, his expression stern, the muscles in his jaw clenching repeatedly. "Fine."

Sitting back on her heels, Aimée focuses her earnest gaze on mine. "Master Damon—Sir—I left of my own free will, fully aware of what the consequences could be: banishment from the formal slave training houses and more exclusive clubs all over the world. I've been around long enough to understand what we did carries very heavy consequences. But I left with him because...I couldn't bear to be without him."

"And yet," I almost choke on the words, "you were able to leave me?"

Her long, golden lashes come down on her flushed cheeks. "I wish it didn't have to be so."

"So do I."

"There," Christopher growls. "You have it straight from Aimée's pretty lips that she came with me of her own free will. Now what the fuck do you want, Damon? Just spit it out."

"All right," I say with a sardonic smile, doing my best to move past the sharp ache of her simple statement. "I am here with an offer. A generous one, I think."

His lips quirk with a smile even less sincere than mine as he takes another menacing step forward and crosses his arms. "I'm interested to hear what you think of as generous."

My pulse spikes hard and I draw a long, steadying breath.

Instantly the familiar, spicy scents of Christopher and sex nearly eviscerate me. I want to scream. I want to punish him, punish them both—fuck them both. Instead, I dig my nails into my palms, trying to keep my features arranged in such a way that I don't betray the true depths of my pain and anger. I can't let my emotions control me or I could lose him—lose them both—forever.

Fuck.

I force myself to calm—as much as I can, given the circumstances, given the strange bite of doubt woven through the anger and the driving need to really *hurt* them.

"I would never have wished for things to happen this way, but you two acted, and here we are. And *yes*, Christopher, I do think it's damn generous of me to bother coming after you, and even more for me to make you this offer." Pausing, I examine his features, taking in every tight line, the shadows on his face, his steady gaze. "Come back to the Training House with me. You will be accepted back — into my House, into our circle — however, some of the terms have changed. And again, yes, there will be punishments devised. You know that's how it works."

Christopher lets out a short, barking laugh. "Did you really think you'd drag us back to your House? Lock us in the basement with that evil bastard Gilby for a few days, make us see the error of our ways? What the *fuck*, Damon?"

"No, there will be no 'dragging'. I come with an offer, rather than a demand, although I'd much prefer to simply issue orders. If I had any illusions about that actually working, you know I'd have sent my handlers down here to throw their black bags over your heads and crate you back to my House in the van."

"And the terms of this supposedly incredible offer would be?"

"The number one term is that you don't leave again. No more skipping out on your contracts." I've had enough of begging him not to go and being ignored.

He props his fists on his hips, giving me a hard look. "You have got to be kidding me."

"Do I look as if I'm kidding?"

I hesitate for a heartbeat, knowing this could be a deal breaker but unwilling to budge on this point. It's the only way to prevent this from happening again. "The other stipulation is that the two of you will be separated while you're retrained."

Christopher's eyes narrow as he takes a step back, placing himself between me and Aimée. "Now I know you're joking. The answer is no. No goddamn way in hell! Seriously, Damon? You just fucking waltz in here trying to be 'the Master'. You used your *bourgeois* power and influence to track us down like dogs and barge into our hotel room at the ass-crack of dawn as if you owned it. As if you owned *us*. And I don't care about the fucking contracts, what they say about us granting you that ownership. You know that shit has never mattered to me other than as a symbol, a token of the game of kink."

"Do you truly think of what we do as a game? It's far too serious to be a game, Christopher."

He shrugs, his gorgeously-muscled bare shoulders

rising an inch or two. "Whatever. A fucking fancy, intense game, but still a game. The protocol only raises the stakes."

I sigh. "What am I going to do with you, Christopher?"

"Nothing. Not anymore. That's the point. You are no longer my Master."

The words send a chill up my spine, and suddenly the idea that I truly could lose them is a teetering wall of terrible possibility that could crush me. Perhaps he's right, that this is a fancy game we play. But if so, I intend to win. I can't afford not to.

"That remains to be seen." I lean to look around his broad, golden shoulder. "And you, Aimée? Will you come back with me, if I promise everything will be forgiven?"

She bites her lip, her brows drawing together, her inner turmoil clear on her face.

Christopher whirls on her. "Aimée?"

She shakes her head, her voice trembling. "Don't make me choose. Please, both of you. Christopher," she pleads, "I love you. And Master Damon," she says, turning to me, "you know I love you, as well. I want to be with you both, to serve and surrender to you both. And I think...forgive me for being presumptuous, but I believe you love each other. I don't know where that leaves us."

"Neither do I—and none of us will until Christopher gives me an answer."

He steps closer once more, until he's near enough that I can smell his skin, that lethal combination of sex and the earth. Intoxicating. Powerful. Just like him. When he reaches out and lays a firm hand on my shoulder, I have to fight not to jump.

"I have an answer for you, Damon," he says in a silky tone that puts my nerves on high alert. Christopher calm is Christopher at his most lethal. "A counter-proposal. No, that's a lie. Because this is the only way I'll have it."

"You can take my offer, or decline it. This is not a negotiation."

"Then I decline. And now you can take *my* offer or decline it."

My heartbeat throbs in my ears, an ocean roar that drowns out everything but the man in front of me. Damn Christopher! He has all the power here and he knows it. Hell, he's had it all since the moment he walked away from me and took Aimée with him.

His hand slides away as he backs off to sit on the edge of the bed with Aimée, who curls against his side, looking back and forth between us with wary eyes.

"Let's not be vague with each other," I say impatiently. "Tell me what's on your mind—not that I'll do as you ask, of course, but I will hear what you have to say."

"You still don't get it, do you?" Christopher shakes his head, sighs. "Fine, let me lay it out for you. There will be no more slave Christopher. Period. End of that fucking sorry story. I am the Master now. Of myself. Of Aimée. And of you, until I decide you've learned what you need to from the experience."

It's my turn to bark out an incredulous laugh. "What? Now who's joking? You cannot possibly think that's an option."

"Oh, but I do. It's the only option there is. Go ahead—take a minute to absorb that fact. I can be generous, too."

His grin is purely wicked. Purely sex. And purely dominant, in a way I've only ever seen from a distance, when he was in Top mode and I couldn't avoid him. I've always tried not to get too close when he's out of the slave role because not only is he not mine then, but he's even more attractive, which is annoying as fuck. I don't do Tops. And I sure as hell don't bottom, never mind being someone's slave again. That's ancient history.

So why is my traitorous cock going hard at the idea?

I skewer him with a look. "Absolutely not."

He raises a staying hand. "Ah, now, don't be hasty, Damon. Take some time. Think about it."

"This is insane. You know who I am. What I am."

"I also know you were a slave yourself once, for the previous owner of the House."

Fuck. "That was a long time ago."

"We are who we are, Damon. You had that in you. You still do. Just as I will always have varying degrees of the extreme ends of the spectrum in me. Times change. *We* change, and right now I need to be Master. I *am* Master. And you?" He grins, that irresistible grin of his, with just one corner of his lush mouth quirking. "You need to belong to me."

"Regardless of where you are on the spectrum, that is not happening. Me being a slave again? Are you out of your mind?"

"Yeah, probably. But I'm also the Master now. You can take it or leave it."

Beside him, Aimée winces. I hate seeing her so conflicted, and I hate even more knowing I'm the cause of it.

"But *why*?" I demand, trying not to sound as desperate as I'm starting to feel.

His golden eyes flash with fury. "Because you broke our trust. *You*, the Master. And I'm pretty damn certain you did it deliberately. If you want to regain that trust, you'll have to earn it back as a slave. *My* slave. I also think it'll do you a hell of a lot of good, but that's just one *Master's* opinion."

My Italian suit suddenly feels too tight—hell, my *skin* feels too tight—and I can barely breathe past the battle suddenly taking place in my lungs. I'm actually trembling.

Fuck. Faced with a choice between serving as Christopher's slave or losing him and Aimée forever, I'm panicking. I *can't* lose them.

But I can't do this either. I can't even consider it. Can I? The mere idea is…terrifying, and not because I can't take pain—my own history has already proven I can. And yet my body is rooting for the possibility, my cock fully hard beneath my fine trousers.

Still, it's too damn much. Perhaps when I was younger, more adaptable, it might have worked. But at this point in my life?

I shake my head slowly. "Christopher, I can't. Surely you must see that."

Aimée buries her face in his chest, and her distress rips me apart inside, like shards of glass cutting me open. Jesus, I hate this. I hate not being in complete control of things. Of *everything*—other than Christopher, who has always been a force unto himself. I've never expected to have total control over him. The reasons why are becoming more and more acutely apparent.

He kisses Aimée's temple and strokes her long, silky hair before setting her gently aside.

"What I see," he says as he stands again, "is a man who is about to make the biggest goddamn mistake of his life, so I'm not going to accept your answer. Get a room at some other hotel here in Monterey, Damon, and take a couple of days to consider what it is you're throwing away. Leave your contact information at the front desk. Otherwise, don't try to reach us. And don't even think about sending any of your henchmen to try to change our minds," he adds. "I'll be in touch when we're ready to talk. *If* we're ready to talk."

I stare at him, unbelieving, insulted. "What do you think I am, Christopher? Do you think I'd drag you two out of here and back to live under my roof—under my rule—when you so clearly no longer desire to be slaves in my household? That I operate with no sense of ethics? At this level?"

"No. No, you've always been a more ethical perv than I am."

He cracks a full grin then, obviously pleased with himself, and I'm relieved enough at the reprieve that it doesn't annoy me nearly as much as it should.

Straightening, I say, "Very well. But I'm not going to change my mind."

Aimée bites her lip and looks up at Christopher. When he nods, she slips from the bed and runs to me, pressing her hands and cheek to my chest.

Sliding my arms around her naked body for the briefest moment, I watch Christopher glaring at me over her shoulder, then release her and step back. There is pain on her face, and I would spare her that, if I could. I would spare my own, for that matter. But this situation is impossible, with perhaps no way to win. Not for me. And from what I gather, not for her, either.

I nod to them both, then turn and leave the room before I lose control. My knees tremble as I walk down the carpeted stairs to the lobby.

God help me, I feel like such a fool. I *was* a fool, thinking I could storm into their room and take them back without losing anything. Without giving up any part of myself. I knew Christopher had me backed into a corner to some degree, that he'd want to make me pay for my arrogance and carelessness with their feelings, but there was no way I could have foreseen that he'd go this far. That he'd demand this much as penance. I've loved him for so long, and so much more than I was ever able to admit—

Until Aimée came along and forced me to open my heart for the first time in years. Maybe the first time in my entire life. I knew I loved him, and yet I closed myself to it, pushing my feelings for him to the farthest corners of my mind, my heart.

And now I love her as fiercely as I love him, and I want desperately to be with them both. But on Christopher's terms? Unthinkable.

Isn't it?

For the first time in years, I doubt the viability of having what I want, and the idea absolutely crushes me. Then there's the complication of figuring out how I handle this new man who is now *me*, this man so filled with emotion I can barely tolerate it. Emotion I have no idea how to manage. It's what I've been struggling with since I sent them both to the Primal Ranch. I was fighting it, but I simply can't any longer and it scares the hell out of me. I don't know what I'll do if they won't accept me as Master.

Anything. I will do anything.

That's how I feel, but I don't know if it's possible. Becoming a slave again goes against everything I've come to believe about myself. Becoming Christopher's slave? I'm not even sure I'd survive. Once more, I am shivering all over, full of uncertainty as my carefully constructed world comes crashing down around me in the wake of the questions: Can I? Will I? How can I refuse, if that is truly the only option?

Eden Bradley

CHAPTER TWO

All of these thoughts rush through my tortured mind at a thousand screaming miles an hour as I make my way through the hotel lobby and out into the hazy Monterey sunshine. I don't know how to calm down.

I just breathe in the salt air and try to clear my head while I wait for the valet to bring my car around — a black F-Type R Jaguar coupe. I've always loved cars, and this one is spectacular. When I get in, I step on the gas a few times simply to feel the engine purr. Heading south, I drive directly to the Casa Palermo in Pebble Beach. It's one of my favorite hotels, but I don't think even its stunning coastal setting, lovely Mediterranean architecture and luxury suites will soothe my darkened soul today. Nothing will, until they come to me. No, that's only half the truth. I won't be soothed until and unless they come to me wanting to be with me in the only way I can imagine. And yet...

No.

I try to keep my mind as empty as possible as I go through the rituals: handing my car over to the valet at the Pebble Beach hotel, tucking the ticket into my breast pocket, moving through the front courtyard and inside to check in at the desk.

"Good morning, sir," a fresh-faced young woman says in greeting. "How may I help you?"

Sir. A nice touch that usually makes me smile. But not today. Instead I simply nod and hand her my American Express black card.

She takes it, taps the keys on her computer, then looks up at me, her cheeks flushing. "Mr. Attwood — how nice to have you with us again. Your usual room, the Palermo Suite, just happens to be available, sir. Or would you prefer something a bit cozier? I should have two other rooms open by three o'clock."

"The suite will be just fine. Thank you...Julie," I finish, glancing at her name tag.

Her cheeks burn a little brighter, and I recognize the nearly palpable whiff that might almost be perfume—a delicate mixture of desire and an unconscious tendency toward submission.

Yes, something I tend to naturally bring out in people. And yet… No.

She clears her throat. "Will you have luggage, sir?"

"There's a bag in the trunk of my car. Have them send it up."

"Of course. Is there anything else I can do for you?" she asks, blue eyes sparkling, dark lashes batting.

Not unless you want to come up to my room and let me beat you until you cry, until you come, until I manage to work some of this unbearable tension from my body.

But I only try to smile, holding back the wolf inside me that loves to eat pretty girls like this one alive. Or is it only a sheep in wolf's clothing?

No. Hell no.

Mustn't let Christopher get to me. But he does. He *has*.

"No. Thank you."

The Palermo Suite is the best this hotel has to offer, and they've skimped on nothing, from the two marble fireplaces to the French doors opening onto the private courtyard with a gleaming, blue-tiled Jacuzzi and fountain, the high, rough-beamed ceilings, the enormous four-poster bed. I've always liked it for its privacy and function. The personalized services rival any of the best hotels in New York. But I am too overcome with concern, with the sharp edges of my shattering heart, to relax into the luxury. The shards pierce me, flesh and soul. This promises to be a very long day, a long night, perhaps a long week. There's no way to know—or to know how much I can bear.

There's a tap on the door, and I let the bellman in. He sets my black overnight bag down, and offers to send a valet to unpack for me and build a fire, which I decline. It is, after all, a summer day, and even here on the coast it's fairly warm, now the fog has burned off. And I have an odd quirk—I prefer no one but my personal slaves handle the contents of my bags.

Once I remove my coat and hang it up as meticulously as I do everything, I'm unsure of what to do with myself. Is this one of those situations in which I speak with a confidante? But who would that be? Alexa? One of my other cohorts in the world of refined kink? Isn't that how we think of ourselves? We are the sexual sophisticates of the world, the deviant aristocrats. But there is also too often a certain coldness, a remoteness, in our circles, and none of these people are anyone I'm close to.

I think of my brother, Daniel. He was the one person I was ever truly close to, and he's been gone for more of my life than he was in it.

Can't think about him now.

Not now, when my mind is in such chaos. When the chaos in my life began and ended with him—or at least it had ended for a time. Then Master Stephan got sick. And now…this.

I open both sets of doors to let the sea air into the room, stretch out on the bed and close my eyes. I have no idea how long they'll make me wait—if they come to me at all. But even if it's an hour of this suffering—suffering as I've never endured, even in my years in service as a slave so long ago—it will be far too long. For the first time since I lost Master Stephan, I'm not certain how I will survive. This is a loss too grave to bear.

I will somehow, of course. I always do.

Aimée.

Christopher.

"No," I mutter through clenched teeth to the empty room, knowing how useless my fervent prayers are now.

And I know for the first time in years what it is to be utterly powerless.

It's been two days. I've made calls to see to it that my House is in order, the slaves worked, then I finally gave in and called the Ranch and asked Victor to take over the House for a while. If they do come, my two loves—and perhaps even more if they don't—I'll need to take a leave of absence. It could be a long one. The House, which has been my life all these years, is too much to think about in my current state.

I lingered in the Jacuzzi much of the day yesterday and again today. I napped in the wan sun, sat up all night with an untouched whiskey in a crystal glass, trying not to think, which has been a spectacular failure. I can think of nothing but the two of them—together, which is a comfort and a torture all at the same time, but not with me. Not. With. *Me.* And the more time that passes, the more I feel in my gut they will never come back to me, that I will have to go on without them, which is more of a mind fuck than I'd ever expected.

And so it is with great surprise that I answer my door not to a maid delivering towels, but to Christopher and Aimée. I'm nearly as shocked simply seeing them fully dressed—particularly her, whom I have only ever seen naked other than collar and chains. He's in black leather pants that fit his muscular legs like a rock star, and a loose-fitting t-shirt with a Misfits band logo on it. And Aimée...she's wearing a dark skirt that hugs her body and flares just above the knee with a beautifully tailored blouse in a shade of dusky pink that sets off the blush on her lovely cheeks and the pale red satin of her long hair. So sophisticated, except her fine stilettos are high enough that only a woman who has practice walking in "stripper heels" could manage them. I almost want to smile.

Instead I say, like some inarticulate fool, "You've come."

Christopher nods and walks past me into the room, Aimée trailing behind him, her delicate hand in his. Closing the door, I draw a breath before turning around.

"Sit," he orders her.

She settles on the edge of the sofa, spine straight, chin lifted, palms resting on her thighs. Her focus is on him, as if she's awaiting another order. She probably is. But in a moment I see the brief flick of her green gaze on me.

"Aimée." His voice is only the slightest bit stern.

He is so much the Master at this moment. He's stern and harsh, and there is as much rawness in him as there is when he's the slave. Power used to the ultimate possible zenith, yet done correctly in every way. And in some way, despite his great care in acting responsibly in that role, he is still a rebel, and always will be. It is an intrinsic part of who he is. And always utterly in control. I've never told him how it makes me shiver with some unmet longing. I've never fully admitted it to myself. What is happening to me? One small seed of utter anarchy planted, and I'm losing my mind.

I force myself to be present in the moment. They've come to see me, after all, and here I am daydreaming!

"May I offer you something to drink? I can call my personal

valet here at the hotel—"

"No," Christopher cuts me off. Then he adds, "Thank you."

He motions to Aimée—a small nod of his sculpted chin—and she goes to the sideboard, picks up the shining ice tongs, adds a few cubes to three glasses, then opens a bottle of sparkling water and fills the glasses. Every motion is full of the exquisite grace with which she does everything. I've seen this in her even while she is being punished. Will I ever see that again?

There's a small, lancing pain in my chest as she turns to hand me a glass. When our fingers brush, my body lights up with need.

Once Aimée has handed a glass to him, Christopher demands without preamble, "So, tell me where you stand."

"I came looking for you, so I believe that part is obvious. You know I want both of you back. On the terms I outlined, of course."

"The only 'of course' is that you understand the terms are the ones *I* set."

It's my turn to demand. "Do you think you can intimidate me into some sort of specific, response? Into what *you'd* like me to say?"

He locks gazes with me, pursing his lips for a moment. "Yes."

That simple answer, the look in his eyes, makes me just sort of fall apart inside. It's as though my heart has been locked in a stern and unforgiving—and largely impenetrable—cage for years. Maybe forever. And something is finally breaking through. I don't like it, damn it. I don't like the way my body is responding, everything going hard all over.

Damn it.

"Christopher," I start, then have to pause, smoothing my hair from my warm forehead. I try again, not knowing what might come out of my mouth. The words are quiet, difficult to say. "All I know is, my heart broke when you two left my House."

"You fucking forced us out!"

His words cut like a knife. "Yes. I didn't know what else could be done, and I thought it was best. For the two of you. For me. I saw what was between you from the instant you saw each other—don't think I missed it."

"You miss nothing," Aimée says softly, still keeping her gaze averted.

"It's my job to do so."

His eyes spark with anger and passion, a fire threatening to consume what's left of my sanity. "Don't give me any bullshit about you doing your damn job, Damon."

"I *had* to let you go. Even as a master of mind fuck, this was more mind fuck than I could take. I needed time to think."

"What conclusions has your well-fucked mind come to?" he asks. He's trying to appear casual, leaning against the edge of a console table, but I see the tightness in his fine jaw, in the set of his broad shoulders

"That I want to be with the two of you. Enough that I've left the House in other hands for the moment and swallowed the pride that comes with being a Master in order to come find you, to ask you to come back to me."

Christopher reaches out and lays a hand on my shoulder, and once more that barely discernable shiver at his touch runs through me — and I see it hasn't gone unnoticed.

"That's not going to fucking happen. So tell me, have you considered my proposal?

"Christ, Christopher. How can you ask me such a thing? How could I possibly do it, even if I wanted to?"

God, how the hell did I just phrase that question? *Even if I wanted to?* What is going on in my head? I *do not* want to. Absolutely not. Utter madness.

And yet the *if* is hanging in the air...

"You've been a slave," Christopher says. "You spent a number of years in that role. We both know you can handle it. We both know the desire is still there, even if it's locked down tight. But I see it. I see it as a puzzle to be solved." He leans in, until his breath is warm on my cheek. "I can solve that puzzle, Damon. Oh yeah, don't you doubt it."

My fists clench, and it's all I can do to maintain a calm demeanor. It wouldn't do to allow him to see that this conversation is making me sweat. It won't do for *me* to see it.

Fighting the urge to tug at my collar, I say, "I don't doubt your capabilities. I was a slave once, yes, and such a long time ago it seems like once upon a time. But now? Hell, no. I wouldn't even know how."

His hand slides up until it's wrapped around the back of my neck. My skin goes hot under his palm, and I hate him a little for it—but I love him for it even more, maybe.

Fuck.

"That's the beauty in this," he tells me, his tone low, gravel on velvet. "I know exactly how. I know just what to do with you, Damon—don't you worry about that."

"That is not the point."

"That is exactly the point."

I shake my head. "The point is, this request is completely insane!"

"No," he murmurs against my skin, making me flush all over, "the point is, I can see the pulse pounding in your neck. I can feel the tension in your body, the *wanting*. I can smell it on you." He brushes my cheek with his. "I'd bet my left nut you're hard as a fucking rock under your perfectly tailored Italian slacks, aren't you?"

I want to say yes. I can't do it.

"Tell me," he demands, his voice low and stern and impossible to resist, somehow.

"I... Yes. Yes, all right?" I rub a hand over my hair. "Fuck. But that doesn't change anything."

"Doesn't it?"

That shattering sensation crashes over me once more, as if I am coming apart on the inside. I think that's exactly what's happening to me. I'm breaking. But his hand at the back of my neck is reassuring. Christopher is perhaps one of the few people on the planet who could make me feel *safe*.

A rush of yearning pushes its way through the holes the breaking apart has left in its wake, becomes some palpable thing that coats my body, calms my mind, and leaves me reeling all at the same time.

Some part of me wants to do this. To serve him, be his slave. Because if this is the only way I can be with them, regain their trust, how can I refuse?

Jesus.

"Tell me," he commands. "What's going on in your head right now?"

"I'm thinking if I agree to this—and I'm not saying just yet that I will—how would you suggest I go about it? I'm not you, Christopher, with your divine flexibility in these matters, your ability to shift seamlessly between roles. I have no idea if I can do it effectively, and if not, what would be the point? There would be no real power play. It would only be to redeem myself with you, and I'm not certain that's a good enough reason, or impetus enough to get my head into the space it would need to be in. I wouldn't know how to cope with that sort of struggle, where to even begin."

"You begin," he says, exerting the slightest bit of pressure on the back of my neck, "simply by giving yourself over to me. It really is that simple. Isn't that exactly what you've told countless slaves yourself over the years?"

"Yes, but… I am no longer the slave. No, it's impossible."

"Is it?"

He slides his hand up, until his strong fingers grasp my hair at the roots, then pulls firmly. And it's like liquid fire in my legs, my stomach. But most of the heat is gathering in my cock, and in my chest, where some strange transformation is taking place. The sensation is both new and familiar at the same time. Pleasure runs rampant through my body. And pride is falling away, like bits of broken china, until I realize the shell I've built around my heart, around my own need, has been that fragile the whole time.

I haven't dared to look at Aimée during this exchange. I do so now, and find her green eyes gleaming with tears and desire. Something in me still loves to see her cry, craves it, but in that moment I discover I don't have to be the Master to enjoy it. Because I am most definitely *not* at this moment—not with Christopher challenging me in all his glorious and irresistible strength.

Jesus fuck. I am not the Master.

"Aimée," Christopher says, not taking his gaze from my face, "what would you think of Damon joining you in service to me? Of the both of you being mine?"

My entire body surges. I bite back the sensation, bite the inside of my lip until I taste blood.

No. Fuck no.

"I want what the two of you want," she answers instantly.

"I'm not being coy. You know it's the truth. I will love you both no matter what. But, Master Damon, when you sent me away, I have to tell you, it crushed me. It broke my heart, and…"

She bites her lip, and when her eyes gloss over with tears, I feel like an absolute bastard. I don't know what to say. My own pain is nothing compared to hers. God, that I *hurt* her!

She blinks hard, wipes her eyes with her fingertips, then goes on. "It broke my heart, and my trust. We've been talking about it, and this makes sense to me. I need to see your willingness, because this isn't simply about a contract anymore—it's personal. And because of that, the very formal roles required in a place like the Training House have been disrupted. Seeing you vulnerable enough to submit…well, I know how much trust that would have to entail on your part—for all of us, really."

The room is closing in on me, my head throbbing as I try to wrap my brain around what they're suggesting. "Do you? Because I don't know that I can even begin to imagine."

"I know it would require much, much more, given who and what you are, than it does for someone like myself, who is so completely a slave at heart. I also know I would have to trust you both completely in order to allow myself to participate in that dynamic. It would be so different—for me, for you, for all of us. And I wouldn't in a million years believe it was at all a reasonable thing to ask if I didn't know something of your past, that you've been in slave space before. But it seems to me that changes everything—or, it can."

Her green eyes are enormous, still shining with unshed tears and with an urgency that cuts me to the core.

She glances at Christopher, who gives a small, reassuring nod. "Master Damon, if Christopher believes it's so, then I have to believe, too. But do I want this to happen? Yes. Yes, please! I need to build that trust with you again. I want us all to be together. And I know it may not pan out that way, but I'm hoping you'll agree to try. I can't bear the thought of you being lost to me, and I can't go back."

Though my mind is still grappling with all she's said, I nod. "I understand."

"So," Christopher asks, "shall we begin our negotiations?"

The battle raging inside me is hitting a fever pitch. Complete overload. Emotion. Desire. Loss. Need.

Need.

To be with them, a part of them. Perhaps at any cost. Even if that cost is the sense of self I've so carefully and meticulously created over the years.

"You have to understand—and I think you do, and it's probably giving you a greater joy in proposing this scheme—I've kept myself laced into this very tight corner in order to function as I felt I must. You, Christopher, are one of a very rare few who have managed to flourish in both roles in the tightly-held circles we run in."

"I know it. I'm fucking proud of it. But this is the only way. And you may have lost a part of yourself, Damon, but that doesn't mean it's gone forever. The seed is in there. I can sense it in you or I wouldn't even bother to ask."

I shake my head. "I don't know. I don't think you really see—"

"You know damn well I do. I would never try to coerce anyone into serving me if they didn't have it in them. Do you trust that? Trust me?"

"I do trust you," I admit grudgingly.

"Do you trust my instincts?"

Swallowing hard, I give a small nod. For the most part it's true, and God help me, I'm feeling that far-off sinking sensation I haven't felt in…how long? Years. There is a certain comfort in it, in knowing my mind can still go to those places, even if I'm not the slave I was then. Even though much of me is convinced I can't possibly do this.

"It's never occurred to me that I might ever want to serve anyone again," I say quietly. "Or that I'd be able to have what you do. I don't think I've truly wanted to. But if this is the only way…" I swallow hard against the lump in my throat threatening to choke me on my own raging need, and the remnants of anger and betrayal that must pale in comparison to theirs. "If this is the only way back to you two, then…"

He smiles—not the snarky grin he so often wears, but a real smile, and the fact that I've pleased him shimmers through my system like a series of small, sensual shocks. Hell, it's all a shock to me. But I have to try to give myself over to whatever is happening here. My body is leading the way, but the rest of me follows — with an enormous struggle, but I'm trying to accept the fact that the things he's saying to me are beginning to make sense.

"I take it that means 'yes'," he says, "but you know you have to tell me clearly."

"I need some time."

"No."

"Christopher—"

"*No*, Damon. You decide now."

The world spins off its axis beneath my feet, making my head reel. The entire universe is whirling by too quickly for me to focus, to hang on to anything.

I say from between clenched teeth, "I have no fucking idea how to let the control go anymore."

"You just do it," he says, his tone gentler. "I'll help you. Shit, I'll *make* you."

"*Yes*," I hiss, hardly believing the single word as it leaves my lips — lips that ache for his, and for hers. My heart is hammering and my palms are damp with perspiration. "I am ready to negotiate, to discuss my being in service. To you, Christopher."

"Oh!"

I turn to find Aimée with her mouth in a pink 'o', a single tear coursing down her cheek.

"Master Damon, I am so, so glad," she says, her fingers flexing on the edge of the sofa cushion. Her cheeks are flushed, her eyes a more brilliant green than I've ever seen them.

"Just 'Damon' now," Christopher says, and I know it's true.

He takes my arm and guides me to sit at a table by one of the windows overlooking the crashing, gray sea, and takes the seat across from me. "We won't need a written contract — your verbal consent is enough for now. This will be a temporary agreement, while we both see how you take to being mine."

I nod again, my body numb, my mind on hyper-alert, listening closely to everything he says.

"But unlike Aimée," he continues, "you won't really belong to me until we get through an initial trial period. We will both have to see if you can shift everything, accept your new life, your role as my slave, before you become my property. As you said, it's been a long time, and while I see the slave inside you, how readily you'll be able to tap into it—how readily *I'll* be able to—remains to be seen. I expect a full fucking freak-out from you. The crucial element will be what happens after that." He leans toward me, his golden-hazel eyes glittering, as if they could throw sparks. So damn beautiful. "It *has* to be this way, for now."

"Yes, of course. Even I can't tell you how I'll react. I don't know that I can be broken down the way a slave must."

The slow grin is back. So wicked. He is all sexual predator. Not that he's ever been anything else, even as a slave. The idea is more unsettling than ever.

"Again," he says, "you leave that to me."

I feel a strange sense of relief…and yet it's familiar. Comforting in a way I haven't experienced since the time when I first arrived at The Training House.

I was only nineteen years old then. I wouldn't accept anyone so young into the House now, but those were different times. The parlor looked much the same then as it does now. It's always held the same scents: expensive scotch, expensive cologne, the wool of the fine carpets edged with the sharp aroma of wood smoke from the fireplace, summer or winter. He was so very handsome. Stunning. But even more alluring was the air about him, the way he held himself…

"Tell me of your qualifications, Boy," Master Stephan demands.

My legs are shaking, my cock harder than it's ever been. I can barely believe this is happening, yet nothing has ever felt more real in my life. Thank God.

"Sir, I… Have you not had a chance to review my application, my reference letters?"

He steps closer, his silky movements as threatening as his presence at my side, as the hand going into my hair and pulling my head back until I know deep in my bones never to question this man again—in word or in thought. He is too good. Too deliciously commanding, his touch electric. And I know he will hurt me in all the right ways—hurt me until the core of my pain has been washed away in suffering and servitude.

"Answer me."

Taking a moment to breathe him in — his scent, his authority — I exhale, and answer. "I have been in formal training for only one year, but I've been with a Dominant since I was fifteen. She had me top girls for her pleasure, sometimes. And once, another boy, which I liked. I've been given to other Masters, which I've liked even more. No…I'm sorry. I didn't like it. I loved it. Reveled in it." My head is spinning. What was the question? I scramble to say the right thing. "I am experienced at tea service and boot blacking. I have been thoroughly trained in massage, and can take a great deal of pain, Sir."

"You will call me Master, and nothing else, unless I instruct you otherwise. Is that clear?"

His handsome face holds more authority than I have ever seen in a person — authority and an elegant beauty that reverberates in every cell in my body. It feels like magic, as if my fondest fantasies are about to be fulfilled, and I know with complete certainty they are. I want to go down on my knees for this man. Need to. How have I ever wanted anything but to submit to the kind of total slavehood that's been promised to me at the Training House?

"Please, Master," I whisper, shamefaced at my own stark need, at my twitching cock. But it's always been like this. Shame, in its painful loveliness. I love it all. I love him. Instantly.

And I'm feeling it all again now, on an even larger and more painful, and infinitely more complex, scale.

"Christopher," I whisper urgently, "you know I love you both."

"Yes," he says, "and therefore, I believe you can do this, if you want it enough. Do you?"

Staring at his beautiful face, I see the strength in every line. He is the strongest person I have ever known. Stronger, by far, than my lost Master Stephan ever was. Stronger than any of us. And this may be exactly what I've needed all these years, as loath as I am to admit it. Or it may be the thing that will destroy me.

Do I want it badly enough to take such a risk? I can't answer that without some degree of doubt. I must do this. And it terrifies me. But the "must" fuels the "want".

Fuck.

"Yes. I want it."

Eden Bradley

CHAPTER THREE

That slow, evil and beautiful smile spreads over his face, then in a flash he's out of his chair, his hand gripping the back of my neck and taking me right down to my knees. I don't have time to think about it, to think about anything. I am in absolute shock. But I'm going down, the world blurring before my eyes, chemicals and pleasure and humiliation flooding my brain so quickly I can't possibly process it all.

This is it. This is real. This is where it begins.

I don't know how I can do this. I don't know how I can refuse—or even how I can resist any longer. It's Christopher, after all. Has anyone ever been able to resist him?

He starts stripping my clothes off, and it's all happening so fast—too fast, and yet, in some sense, I know this is the only way I can do it. It has to all be taken from me without giving me a chance to really think about it. It has to be forced on me, now that I've agreed to allow it to be. If I have a moment to pause, I'll change my mind.

Who am I kidding? I am not about to change my mind—not now.

Fear is like a live wire in my body, trying to short out the other sensations, and I'm fighting to wrestle it away even as the rest of me slides almost automatically into accepting his command.

He's rough with me—rough enough that my shirt tears. I don't care. My cock is aching. I need his rough hands on my body, on the raging erection that is all for *him* right now.

Christopher.

Master Christopher.

Fucking Christ. *This* is what it's come to. What I've come to, and I can still hardly believe it.

When he pushes me down onto the rug, mashing my face against the rough fibers, it hits me all over again how damn serious this is, how much more serious it's about to be. It's hard to accept how frightened I am—and I'm as turned on as I've ever been in all my years in kink. Even better knowing that Aimée is watching this happen, which strikes me as odd until I remember what an exhibitionist I once was.

Yes, I love an audience. I want to impress her, want to impress them both. Christopher has talked many times of his ego, but mine may well match his.

He holds me down by the neck with one hand, and presses on the small of my back with the other. My stiff cock grinds as hard into the carpet as my cheek. I force myself to hold very still, not to arch my hips into the rug, which is all I want to do. No... what I want is to make him happy.

God help me.

His face is suddenly next to mine, and he whispers to me the way one would a lover. "I can see your struggle, can see it building. But it's all fucking useless, you know. I'm the one in charge now, and don't think for a minute I don't plan to play that out to full advantage. And oh, yeah, I have a little revenge in mind. Well, not 'revenge', exactly. Think of it as punishment for your transgressions. You know the beauty of punishment, don't you, Damon? As much as you know the agony of it. Expect me to go very hard on you."

I stifle a moan. Or is it a groan of despair?

When he yanks my body over, turning me onto my back, I can't hold it back. I groan aloud—at the manhandling, at his exquisite face above me and the utter command in his expression. At the damn helplessness of my position.

As his gaze rakes over my body, I realize how naked I am. Not that I didn't know it before. God, I don't know what I'm thinking. My brain is in a fog, which I quickly understand is subspace. *Slavespace*. And some distant part of me is furious.

"You are a beautiful Boy, Damon," he says, reaching out to pinch one of my nipples between hard, hurting fingers.

I yelp. I've grown soft over the years. He only grins and leans down to take the same sore nipple between his strong, white teeth, and as he bites into the tender flesh, I have to grit my own teeth against the cry that lodges in my throat. It's fucking awful. It's fucking wonderful. My cock is pulsing, in an agony of need. And as if he can read my mind, he straddles my body and grabs my naked flesh in his hand, squeezing hard at the base. If he weren't squeezing so damn tightly, I might come in a heated burst of spiraling lust. I am totally out of control. But that's what this is about, isn't it? I have no control. He has it all.

Yes.

Fuck.

He begins a vicious pumping motion, his strong hand gripping my cock as he strokes up, ending just beneath the swollen head, then down to grip the base, then back up again. My hips want to pump into his fist. *Need* to.

Biting my lip, I fight for some self-control. But my traitorous hips arch, and he slaps the tip of my cock so hard it leaves me momentarily breathless.

"No, Damon," he says harshly.

"Don't tell me what to do!"

He slaps my face, and it does exactly what it's intended to — it shuts me the hell up, inside and out. It reminds of my place. I can't stand it.

Pressing down on my hip bone with the heel of one hand, he continues his rough and lovely torture of my aching cock. My balls draw up hard, my belly tightens, and pleasure and pain are like some insane dance in my system, melding together. Inextricably bound. I keep my gaze on his face, which is lost in concentration. I have to admit, I love that he's so entirely focused on me. I cannot even think of him as the slave at this moment, and perhaps never again. He is so much the Master.

My Master.

Come gathers in my balls, beginning the pumping pulse that signals my climax.

"No. Hold it back," he demands.

I bite my lip harder, and when my tongue darts out I taste blood. It doesn't help — it only makes it more difficult not to come.

"*I* will make you bleed," he tells me. "Your blood is mine. Your come is mine. Tell me."

"No," I pant. "No."

He slaps me again, leaving my cheek burning. I am ashamed — that I am arguing with him. That another slap was required. That I don't have more self-discipline. That I am in this situation, where I am allowing someone to slap me!

"*Tell* me, Damon, if you know what's good for you, and I think you do."

The problem is, I *do*. God damn him. And damn him even more for making me like it.

"It's...it's all yours," I gasp.

"Is it? Then how dare you start to get off without my permission? How dare you draw your own blood?"

He slaps my face so hard it makes my ears ring. But it also brings some measure of containment, and I breathe through the pleasure and the pain, breathe in the degradation of being hit across the face. And want to beg for more.

I keep my mouth shut.

But he knows what to do—oh, fuck, he knows. Shifting his grip until he's got the base of my balls fisted in his hand, he makes a ring there, drawing them down and tugging hard, which almost makes me spurt all over him. But in a breath he's pulling so damn hard, the pain holds me back, even as it spurs me on. I've forgotten this about the pain/pleasure continuum.

Need to come.

Can't possibly come.

And fuck, it hurts. It hurts like hell, and he's too fucking beautiful, and I know Aimée is watching, and I am absolutely, abjectly humiliated.

I hate knowing it will only get worse. I hate the part of me that revels in that knowledge.

Still gripping my balls, Christopher orders Aimée, "Unzip me. Good girl. Take my dick out."

I see the sway of her silk-covered breasts, smell her perfume, and then Christopher has his thick, golden cock in his hand above me. And it's like some level of punishment I don't quite understand that he's beating himself off, rather than having Aimée or me service him.

His gaze is locked on mine, and though his face goes loose with pleasure, he is obviously maintaining just as much control as he does in everything else. God, he's beautiful. Powerful. His cock gleams with a pearly drop of pre-come, and my cock throbs, jerks in response.

"No!"

He stops handling himself long enough to slap me across

The Training House

the face again.

I am ashamed. In love. Fighting it. Out of my goddamn head.

His fisted hand goes back to work, moving fast and hard on his heavy shaft until the flesh is a blur of hard meat, and I want nothing more than to take him into my mouth and suck.

"Eyes on my face, Damon," he orders.

A groan escapes me, but I do as I'm told, focusing on his face, the lush mouth and the wildcat eyes tightening and shifting as his climax approaches. Then he squeezes my ball sac hard enough to make me yelp as he shoots his hot come all over my face. I want it, love it, hate him a little. And fuck, I need to come... *need* to. But he releases me, stands up, one booted foot on either side of my body.

"Clean yourself up," he tells me with his usual crooked grin.

When I go to get up, his boot comes down hard in the center of my chest.

"Get as much as you can with your tongue. Go on. I'll stay here and make sure you do a good job."

Fuck. Is he serious? But he is, of course.

Fuck!

I don't dare say it. Instead, I do my best to breathe through my inner struggle, and it's like hacking away at an attacking army with nothing but a butter knife. This is supposed to be nothing more than my way to redeem myself with him, with Aimée. But already it's turning into something more. Something real. I can't fucking stand it.

Finally, I have to give in — to him, to my own raging, shameful need — and get to work. My tongue sweeps his come from my lips and I swallow the earthiness of it, give myself over to savoring it, knowing it's *his*.

When I've reached all I can, he removes his foot from my chest. "Very good, Damon. Go get in the shower and clean up while Aimée packs for us. We're leaving. All of us."

I do as I'm told, my old obedience training coming back to me in an endorphin-packed flood that fills my brain — which I'm sure was his intention — until the screaming doubts almost fade away.

Almost.

I turn the shower on without daring to look at my reflection in the bathroom mirror, then step under the hot water. I still have a raging hard-on, but I'm sure that will be the case from now until...when? I don't know. At this moment, it's difficult to care. Except for the small voice still bellowing from somewhere deep within me, telling me I can't possibly be doing this. With what is currently left in me of the Master, I tell it to shut up.

When I get out, Aimée is there in the steamed-filled room, holding a thick white towel for me. Stepping into it, I remain quiet while she rubs me down, but my body, my hard cock, is hyper-aware of her terry-cloth touch, of her femaleness. My heart is aware of how I love her, my brain remembering how I once Mastered her.

When I'm dry, she steps back, and I see she's set out Christopher's grooming kit on the marble vanity. She turns to pick up a bottle of lotion, but before she can squeeze it out onto her hand, I raise mine to stop her.

"Don't."

"Don't? But I've been told to—"

"I know. But if you touch me now..." I shake my head, turning away from her searching green gaze. "I'm too out of practice at being on this end of things. Having you this close to me only makes me want to throw you down on the floor and hurt you, fuck you. It's killing me that I can't."

"Damon," she says on a quiet sob. Taking my hand, she holds it tight, and my heart surges. I squeeze back. It's impossible to stay angry with her.

"Damon," she repeats, "let me help you. This is the way it must be, and from what just happened in there, I am now as certain as Christopher that this is the right thing. For all of us. That was...beautiful, and harsh, and I loved seeing the light in your face as you let go."

And now I am burning with the all too familiar combination of humiliation and pride that comes from having had one's utter submission witnessed and remarked on, but I can't think of a graceful reply—not in the state I'm in.

"I *know* that light, Damon. It's time for you to know it again. For you to serve. For us all to develop trust, a new bond. It has to be unbreakable." Her eyes glisten with tears. "*Unbreakable*," she whispers harshly.

I don't dare stroke her face, which is what I want to do. "I don't know that I can find the balance in all of this, if I can truly let go in the way anything beyond a single experience or two requires."

"You know, perhaps better than anyone that we have to be broken down first. That it hurts. Then the epiphanies will come. Hasn't it started already?"

"Maybe. Yes," I admit.

"He knows what he's doing."

"Lovely Aimée. Do you think if I had any doubt of that I would even be able to try? There is no one else I could do this with, or for."

She smiles, and I feel warmer — and more intimidated than ever at the thought of what happens next.

Christopher has often talked to me of being a walking contradiction, but I think at this moment, I may have him beat.

The Master has fallen. To his knees. Into the humiliation of struggling yet worshipful acceptance of whatever my Master Christopher deems to bestow on me. Pain and come. Pleasure and love.

Oh, yes. This is going to hurt.

The last several hours have gone by in a mad rush. The valet at my hotel packed my things and had them sent over, I've made a call and arranged to have my car picked up and brought back to the House, then a limousine arrived and sped us to the airport, where a small chartered plane waited. It was a quiet flight, while I wondered at how I never knew Christopher had this kind of money. Not that it matters. I care nothing about these things — only that I love him, that he tame me, and that Aimée is with us. All of this is happening — all of this is possible — because it is the only way I can be with them, and because I am aware that I owe them.

Another car picked us up maybe half an hour ago at the tiny Palm Springs airport — I had no idea where we were going until we landed — and now, with the lowering sun making a backdrop of purple and gold outside the car windows, we are being whisked off to…somewhere. Meanwhile, my new Master tortures me by kissing and fondling and pinching Aimée, pulling her full breast from her bra to tweak her succulent nipple, while ignoring me. Which leaves me alone in my head to wonder at my predicament.

Well, my "predicament" that also makes my dick so hard I can barely stand it. And I understand fully the psychology behind what he's doing. I might have done the same myself—in fact, there are times when I have. Ignore a slave and they want you even more. Allow them—fuck, allow *us!*—to wallow in our sense of deprivation and we become even more desperate. The mind fuck is half the game, and he is very, very good at that. Good enough that even as he makes out with Aimée I catch his glance on me often enough to understand I cannot distract myself by looking out the window. He will not have it. The world is nothing more than a blur of soft twilight at the edge of my vision—that and the rampant confusion I'm trying hard to ignore. But the questions keep popping into my head: What the hell am I doing here? How can I possibly leave my responsibilities behind to indulge myself this way? And horribly, excruciatingly, what if this doesn't work?

Perhaps even more excruciating is the idea that perhaps it will.

Eventually, the car slows, then stops. Christopher tucks Aimée's luscious tit back into her silky bra and turns to me as she buttons her blouse.

"Say nothing to the driver, Damon," he instructs as a harsh and delicious mixture of relief and the urge to argue runs like molten silver through my veins. "Go directly to the door, and once it's open I'll expect you to undress in the foyer and get down on your knees."

I swallow hard before nodding.

"Say it," he demands harshly.

I know what he wants. My gut twists, but I have to say the words. "Yes, Master."

It's strangely familiar and unfamiliar on my tongue, and I roll it around, taking in the sensation then swallowing it down, hoping to keep it there, deep inside me.

Master.

Jesus. Fuck no.

I try again.

Master.

Oh, yes.

There is a moment in which I'm certain I'm going to throw up, but I grind my jaw hard until it passes.

The driver pulls open the car door, and Aimée and I wait while Christopher gets out. Then we follow him up a walkway to a modern home with the low, flat roofline common to the desert. The large rocks and scattered plantings are uplit, casting light and shadow onto the white stucco structure. The lines are clean, beautifully done. The house doesn't appear to be overly large, but it really is an exquisite piece of architecture.

He unlocks the front doors — a double door of carved wood, probably from Spain or Morocco or India — and they swing open. He enters, then motions to us, and I wait for Aimée to follow him in before I do.

The lighting is soft, but I quickly take in the elegant expanse of travertine floors, the living area sparsely furnished in sleek white and gray and blue. The opposite wall is all windows, framed in wood, which lends warmth to the room. And beyond is a pool, the lights playing on the turquoise water.

Who would have expected him to have such a place? I would have thought some dark, gothic castle, not this clean space in Palm Springs. But my Christopher has always been full of surprises.

No, not Christopher. Master Christopher, and now I am *his*. I must remember.

"Well, fuck, Damon, if you can't get this one simple goddamn thing right..."

Suddenly his hands are on me as he rips my shirt off so hard the seams bite into my shoulders and the buttons pop, flying onto the pretty floors with a small *tink*. He shoves me up against a wall and in seconds my shoes and pants are off, and I am naked and a little ashamed of myself for getting lost in my musings, rather than my orders. I would never put up with such a thing from a slave. But I must stop thinking of myself as the Master — clearly, I am not.

When he pushes me onto my knees, it hurts, the floor is

so damn hard. But so is my cock, of course. And God, I want nothing more than for him to fuck me right here on the floor of the foyer. Instead, his boot comes down on my neck, pressing my face to the floor, and I remember just in time to keep my ass in the air, hardly believing I'm doing it.

"Aimée," he says.

Her heels click as she comes closer.

"Strip, prettiness," he tells her. "Good girl. Now down on your knees, yeah. Hands behind your back and sit up. Fucking Christ, you're perfect like this. You have the most gorgeous tits I've ever seen."

There's a moment of silence, then her yelp, and despite his booted foot still on my neck, I want desperately to know what he's done to her, but I don't dare try to look.

She groans and my cock twitches. I want to see her. I want to see him. I want him to hurt me, to *force* me into slavehood in a way I know can only happen with real pain, real humiliation. Right now, it's mostly my determination to regain their trust that keeps me here. Or maybe that's the lie I'm still telling myself. I don't know anymore.

He whispers to her, "Get my black bag out of this closet."

There are muffled sounds, then he begins to beat me. The pain is exquisite, stinging like a hive of angry bees on my ass, my thighs, my back… It takes me a moment to ascertain that he's using some sort of long, very narrow, flexible cane. He's hitting me fast and hard, and without any warm-up my body is having trouble converting the pain—it simply fucking hurts.

"What is it, Damon? Don't you remember how to do this? How to move into the pain? To breathe in order to help your brain release all the chemicals that allow us to do this crazy shit? I want you to remember. I want you to be able to take whatever I choose to dish out." He stops the beating long enough to remind me, "Breathe, Damon. Do it. You know how. Your body has the muscle memory. *You* have the memories.

He's right—I do have the memories, and as I follow his instructions, taking in and slowly exhaling one breath after another, they come flowing back to me.

It's summer and I'm sweating in the Carmel Valley sun. The scent of meadow and trees is sharp in my nostrils as a handler drives me down the path toward the arena, my wrists bound tightly at the small of my back with rope that bites into my skin. I am put into a box-like stall, and more rope is used to tie a quick chest harness onto my damp body, then another length is tied around the base of my stiff cock and anchored to the chest harness. Confusion and desire are one and the same, my mind whirling at a hundred miles an hour with a dizzying love for those who abuse me along with the deep, driving need to please.

Another handler leads me from the stall into the arena by a lead attached to the rope around my cock, then one more handler joins them. They all start whipping me at once, so no matter which way I twist or turn, I am faced with another whip. The pain is incredible, and every time I move, the rope pulls hard on my rigid erection. When they wrestle me to the ground, all of them holding me down in the dirt, I almost want to cry. Not because I can't take the pain, but because this is terrifying and beautiful and so utterly degrading, and it's everything I need. The moment is everything.

My legs are kicked roughly apart, and my ass cheeks are spread by hard hands before a plug is shoved into my ass. No lube, of course, and it hurts like hell. I welcome it. It makes me proud — to wear the plug, to take what they're doing to me. I am in heaven.

With the memory come the old feelings, the old conditioning, and just like that, my brain releases all those lovely chemicals as it automatically converts the pain to pleasure, the humiliation to stark wanting fulfilled. Like the muscle memory Christopher mentioned, the conditioned response that has been buried deep inside me. And despite the struggle that always comes with this extreme form of submission, I believe for the first time that I may actually be able to do this. Perhaps even eagerly, gloriously — even as I struggle, as I fight for it, as I fear it down to my bones.

Let my suffering begin in earnest.

Eden Bradley

The Training House
CHAPTER FOUR

Standing back, Christopher holds his instrument of torture in front of my face. "Kiss it."

I obey, my system flooded with adoration I'm striving to comprehend. But along with the bliss comes a wash of emotion that threatens to overtake me, and I can't let it. Can*not* let it.

When was the last time I felt like this—as if I am about to fucking cry? It's not right. Not for me. My mind is doing these crazy tumbles, from sensation to emotion and back, all of it laced with dread and a nameless fear. No, it has a name—it's letting go of all control, and I am powerless against it.

Daniel.

Master Stephan.

It's letting go of everything I have become, and everything feel I must be, for everyone else even more than myself. Is it selfish of me to pursue this? Is it selfish of me not to?

Christopher's warm breath wafts over the back of my neck. "You're fighting it again," he says softly, understanding the power of a lowered tone. "What? Did you think the struggle would be over the first time you gave in? Not even the second, Damon. Not even the tenth, after your years as Master of the House. It wasn't gonna be easy, no matter what, and I've already told you I won't make it easy for you."

Grabbing my hair, he yanks me up until I am sitting up on my knees, his face right next to mine, his low tone now a threatening growl. "Easy is for pussies, Damon, and that word couldn't be used to describe either one of us, could it? Fuck no. You have to suffer. It's the only way, and you know it. Isn't that right? You may answer."

My throat is so tight, I have to swallow not to choke on my own tongue. But a vicious yank on my hair gets my lips moving.

"Yes."

"Yes what?"

"Yes…Master."

Almost painful to say the words aloud. Painful and exhilarating. God, I'm a mess. Blinking, I try to focus, and it's only then I realize there are tears blurring my eyes.

Christopher wipes the corner of my eye with his thumb, then leans in and kisses the wet spot, and oh, it's fucking lovely — his lips pressed to my skin. But when he releases me with a small push. I feel bereft. Angry.

"Aimée, get Damon settled in the first bedroom on the right down that hallway, then come find me in the kitchen. I plan to strap you to the granite counter and see how many spatulas I have on hand to spank you with before I fuck your pretty ass. Oh, and lock the door behind him."

"Yes, Master Christopher," she says.

My heart pounds. I am to be left alone so quickly? God damn him!

But haven't I done the same to him?

I have only an instant to feel sorry for myself before Aimée helps me to my feet, her delicate hands soft on my naked skin. She keeps a steadying palm at the small of my back as we walk down the hall, her heels clicking on the floor. Breathing her in, I can almost tatse the delicious scent of wanton female. It makes me headier than I am already, if that's even possible.

Oh, but I know it is. I know Christopher has plans for me that will make this little welcome scenario seem like a walk in the park. Lust shivers over my skin, like a warm breeze of desire that spirals down to punch me in the gut. In my pulsing, swollen cock. And Jesus, I wish he would punch my cock, take out some of his rage on me. Hurt me enough to stop my mind from screaming. Let me come, from pain or pure bliss or both.

We enter the bedroom and Aimée turns on the light. The room is carpeted in white, furnished with a spanking bench and an interrogation chair, both upholstered in white leather. Steel shackles and chains are set into one white wall, with a pile of white pillows and blankets on the floor beneath it, as well as a mysterious armoire in whitewashed wood. I understand immediately the irony of this entire setup — the innocent white palette, the sparseness of the room. And the back wall is, of course, part of that wide expanse of windows looking out onto the pool, which is, perhaps, all the color this room needs. It's like another world entirely on the other side of the glass.

"Come, lie down," the sweet Aimée says. When I follow her lead and settle onto the pillows, she kneels beside me, her green gaze searching my face. "How are you?" she asks.

I shrug. "Completely mind fucked, but we all know that's the plan. I suppose I didn't quite expect to feel like…this."

Concern furrows her brows as she strokes my cheek, her touch moving through me like warm honey. "Like what?"

"As if I've just come through some horrible ordeal. And I don't mean being beaten or made to strip and kneel on the floor. I mean…fuck it all, I'm not entirely certain."

I pause, flex my hands, trying to get my befuddled brain to work. "It's as if I've been trapped on a deserted island, cut off from all of humanity. Not that I don't love my life, running the House, but it seems alien to me now. I have to wonder if I ever truly belonged there, in that role, if I am even able to comply with Christopher's demands to the extent I have so far. Wielding that kind of power, that much responsibility. Have I been doing the wrong thing all these years? Should I even be here now? I can't begin to figure it out."

"Do you think that life and belonging to him are so mutually exclusive?" she asks. "Because I don't believe it. I've known you as the Master — as *my* Master, *our* Master. And now I see you in this role, and despite your struggle, you wear both so beautifully, I can't imagine you any longer in just one role or the other. I think I am able to see it more clearly than you can, and Master Christopher certainly does. Your slavehood doesn't diminish what you've done, or who you've been."

I sigh. "I'm having a hard time reconciling the two. It seems impossible."

"It's your first day. Give it some time."

I can tell from her expression that she's truly worried. "I'm not going anywhere, if that's what you're thinking. Not yet, anyway. I will give this as fair a shake as I can."

"I…" She pauses, biting down on her lush, pink lip. "Maybe I was thinking that."

"I wasn't. I need to try to see this through. I don't know how I'm going to manage it, or what's at the other end, but I know I have to do this, no matter how at odds I am with who it makes me now."

"You're still you. Your past is still your past. Your kindness and your wickedness are all still there. And we both know there is always power in giving ourselves this way. *Our* choice, yes?"

"Yes." I raise a hand to stroke her silken hair, and for one crazy moment it's almost as if we're back in my quarters at the Training House, with me as her Master. "I love you, Aimée."

Her smile lights up her whole face, easing the crease in her forehead, and I am filled with happiness. Not that my body doesn't hum and pulse with the need to drag her down onto the floor and fuck her senseless, spank her and pinch her and make her cry.

Oh, yes, her tears…

But perhaps it's all right, feeling that way even as I feel the need to have all of these things done to me by Christopher. My new Master.

"This is a fucking mad life," I tell her.

"'We are all mad here'," she says, quoting Lewis Carrol with a sparkle in her eye.

"So we are."

"I have to go now." Leaning down, she brushes a kiss across my cheek.

It's too much—I have to grab her, hold her around her slender waist, tight in my arms. I need to fuck her just as badly, but this will have to do until Christopher gives me permission, if he ever does. Oh, a sharp pain in my belly, in my balls, thinking of the possibility that I might never be allowed inside her beautiful body again.

I'll have to wait, to hope he can forgive me at some point, that he will deem me worthy, which is a strange thought. Until then, there is so much joy simply in being with her, with them both. Until then—the moment I'll hope for, when she is given to me again—I will throb and ache, fight the need to touch myself, to come into my fisted hand thinking of Aimée, of Christopher. I will imagine every wonderful and despicable thing that might happen to me under his command. I will do my best to want it, to accept what this makes me, and everything it could mean in the future.

She turns off the light when she leaves, and I hear the

slide and click of the lock in the silent room. There are rippling shadows everywhere from the pool lights, and it's eerie, yet a strange sort of comfort. I haven't had any time to myself, to simply be in my own head, since this all really started—since I gave myself to him, as much as I'm able to at this point. I'm not sure I could have stood it if it hadn't been for those tender moments with Aimée. Maybe he knows that. She certainly does.

Perhaps I'm more like her than I am like him. It's a new idea, one I would have rejected out of hand just a few weeks ago. A few days ago. But having sustained such a double blow to my heart and my psyche has caused me to reevaluate a lot of things, and this is simply one more. It's not only Christopher that has brought me to my knees, but love. What better—and more horribly painful—way to go down?

Daniel.

Master Stephan.

Oh yes, love and pain always go hand in hand, don't they?

These are the thoughts running through my head until what I imagine is late into the night before I finally, mercifully, fall asleep.

When the door crashes open, I have one moment to think wildly that the sun coming in through the windows should have woken me before Christopher—*Master* Christopher, and when will I get used to that?—stalks in. He's all bluster and good mood this morning, and gloriously golden muscles under his white wife-beater and slouchy gray jeans. God, but he's beautiful.

My morning hard-on is painful with lust and the need to pee, but of course he has no regard for my discomfort. He strides across the room and clamps the steel shackles onto my ankles, then grabs my wrists, pulling me up onto my knees, which he kicks wide apart with his booted feet. Very quickly, he slaps a pair of leather cuffs onto my wrists and, raising my arms over my head, he clips them to the chains behind me with a heavy carabiner. My body is tense, elongated by the pull of the chains, and I love it, the sensation of being elegant, somehow, within this moment of subjugation. But I also hate it, fear it. I fear the part of me that likes what's happening.

I see Aimée standing naked in the doorway, and my poor cock jumps. Oh, I *need*. Need her, need him. Fuck.

Yes, need to fuck, please.

Christopher kneels on the floor, his hand shooting out and grabbing me by the throat.

"Aimée. Come jack him off for me."

My heart leaps, or maybe my erection — or maybe both — as she approaches, as he squeezes tighter. I grow dizzy. My flesh swells even before she touches me. And then she does touch me, closing her hand around the head, and smoothing her palm around it in circles. In a moment pre-come seeps out, making her hand slippery. Fucking divine. I can barely breathe, and it feels so damn good, even with my bladder painfully full, and I know I won't be able to come until I can pee. I am pretty damn certain I will be allowed to do neither.

"Look at me," he orders.

His eyes are lion eyes. Captivating. Intense. He is the most intense human being I've ever known. Isn't that what we look for, we sensation junkies, we high-stim people of kink? The world narrows until there is nothing but his steady gaze, his hand around my throat, and Aimée slowly stroking me.

I begin to choke and he loosens his hold enough for me to cough, then he tightens again.

I'm going to come, despite my bladder.

"Aimée, stop," he orders just in time.

Damn it. And thank you, Master.

He eases his hold once more, allowing me to recover a little breath, to bite back my orgasm. Then he slaps my impossibly hard cock, making it harder still — and yet the pain of it helps me.

"Control yourself, Damon. Don't make me put your dick in a cage."

This makes me swallow hard. I've never been in chastity. I'm sure I would hate it.

When a slow grin spreads over his exquisite face, it makes me panic.

"Ah...I can see your eyes going wide. I've finally found something you're really afraid of," he gloats. "Well, well. So damn tempting."

Fuck. Fuck, fuck, fuck.

He lets me stew on that for a few moments.

"Don't worry," he finally tells me, "I have plans for your fine dick. I'll save that for when you require real punishment. But you'll be good for me, won't you, Damon? You know how. You know what I want from you. And right now, I want to see you fuck our little Aimée. It's partly as a reward for her, and partly because I know how hard this is for you. Yeah, I know — sympathy from me, of all people. Who would have thought it? But you know..." he leans closer, until his luscious mouth is a mere inch from mine, "I only show sympathy for those few I love. And if I didn't love you, you wouldn't be here."

Behind him, Aimée falls to her knees, her head bowed. "Thank you, Master Christopher," she whispers, urgency in her voice.

He turns to grab her face and kisses her hard on the mouth. "Anything for you, prettiness. But this is for me, selfish bastard that I am." Turning back to me he says, "We all have to understand what we're doing here. Yes, I will abuse you, fuck you, humiliate you, Master you, but it's for your own good, and for *our* good. All of us." Reaching out, he strokes my hair from my face. "Do you love me, Damon?"

I am so filled with love for him at this moment, I can barely contain it, can barely believe this is happening.

"You know I do. Yes. *Yes.*" I turn my face into his palm, kissing it.

"Again," he orders, his voice a harsh whisper that vibrates with emotion.

I kiss his palm again, and again, whispering, "I love you, Christopher. I love you. I love Aimée. Madly."

"*Master* Christopher," he insists, squeezing my jaw hard.

"Master Christopher," I repeat, and it's a bit easier this time.

Finally he pulls back and gets to his feet. "Aimée, on your hands and knees in front of him."

She gets down on the floor before me, as docile as ever. She really is spectacular, this girl, presenting the pale curve of her perfect ass, scattershot with teeth marks and a few beautiful bruises.

I look up at him, and he reads my expression. "Cunt now, and no, you don't get to pee first. If you can't come, that's your problem. Ass later, possibly. If you're very, very good. And if I'm in a good mood, which we all know rarely happens, bitter son-of-a-bitch that I am, but I kinda like myself that way. Now take her."

I can't reach her with my hands, bound as they are, but I lean into my chains as I guide my iron-hard cock to her lovely, pink hole. As the tip touches her, she shivers, and so do I. She is gorgeously wet—so wet that I slide in easily.

"Ah!"

I don't even know if the sound was her, or me. I try to begin a slow, even motion, but in moments it's a mad pounding as I grind into her sweet cunt. She rears back, taking all of me in. I need to come too soon, which of course our Master realizes—he bends down and pinches the skin of my ball sac so fucking hard I yelp. There's nothing to either hold back your orgasm or force it from you like the punishing pain of your balls being tortured. It's several seconds before I know which way it will go.

"Pull out," he orders.

I comply, my cock, my balls, aching. My come is a hard pressure in my belly, needing to be released. My full bladder is creating more pressure.

He steps in, straddling Aimée's body, and I have a tempting glance at her wet pussy before he reaches down to grab my cock in his fist. He squeezes until I have to grit my teeth against crying out, and at the same time, he takes one of my nipples between his fingertips, digging his short nails in until I think he'll draw blood.

"Ah!"

"Quiet," he commands, his nails digging deeper, his hand a vice grip around my poor cock.

I groan, trying to bite it back, but it's impossible.

"Just for that, you get to watch me fuck her."

I almost want to cry. But I also want to watch. My victimized dick will have to wait.

He unzips and pulls his thick cock free, the flesh swollen and ready. And God, I want to suck him off, to feel his come shoot down my throat. But his come will not be mine this morning.

"Elbows," he tells her.

She goes down so that her ass is raised high in the air, and he's standing right in front of me, where I can see her cunt as it opens wide. Every cell in my body is pulsing, seeing her like this, and just as much from his utter, easy command of us both.

From my position on the floor, I can see between his spread thighs as he crouches over her and pushes into her waiting hole. She gasps softly, then pants as he begins to fuck her hard. God, he's beautiful to watch, those long, vicious strokes, and at the same time he's spanking her already-marked ass, raking his nails down her sides.

"Bleed for me, pretty girl," he says, his voice rough with desire.

And she does, the wounds from his nails seeping a little. I want to lick it up, to suck those lovely wounds until she is a part of me. My cock is going crazy, and I wonder if I might come simply watching them fuck. But my full bladder may as well be a chastity device, holding my cock hostage.

Fuck me. I am in hell.

No, this is heaven.

How can I tell the difference anymore?

Eden Bradley

CHAPTER FIVE

I am unsure how long we've been here. Five days? A week? More? I've been let out to swim at night, which is standard. My new Master—and I must accept that he *is*, even if temporarily—looks out for my health, as I did for him when the roles were reversed. It's becoming more and more difficult to even comprehend now that I was once his Master. I know his incredible strength, his fight, how fucking bad-ass he is—that it's all part of what makes him so utterly fascinating as a slave, and now as a Master. Still, I am afraid there's not enough to sustain this situation, to sustain me, no matter that I find myself giving in to his command.

Just as mind fucking is being locked up and left alone for long stretches at a time. I never know when he will come to me, when Aimée will be sent to bring me something to eat, when she will be instructed to stay with me for a while. When I will be allowed to come, either by his hand, or hers. Or her mouth, or whatever toy he has buried deep in my ass—whatever the case may be. It almost doesn't matter. Except the one thing he hasn't done to me yet is to fuck me himself, and of course I crave it in a way that's pure torture. No, he would rather fuck our gorgeous Aimée in front of me, or have her give him head, or come all over me. Not that I don't love it all. But when will I *have* him? No, that's not it. When will he fully have me?

I am being broken down at an alarming pace, and in those moments when I am allowed to come up for air, it seems like one of the most frightening experiences of my life. But I also thoroughly understand this process. It's simply what *has* to happen—in order for me to truly submit, yes, but it is also the only way for me to find my way to the two people I love. I give myself because I must, because I can't *not* do this. And—although it's difficult to admit—because I've discovered this is what I need. Or at least, what some part of me needs. How long has this need gone unmet? Has it ever been met so deeply?

I know only now, in going through this, that the answer is

no. *Never.* Because I have never walked this path with someone I loved—not in this wild, nearly desperate way. It will allow me to give in fully, or not—that is still an unknown factor—but I am feeling the *possibility* of it.

The pool's reflection is a rippling glimmer on the ceiling of my room while I ponder all of this. It's become a sort of meditation for me, those ripples of light in the morning. It is something a slave must do—find a way to that quiet space. I know I think too much. And as many times as I've uncovered ways for my own slaves to get out of their heads, I have yet to find a way that works well for me. Still, this is a small comfort. It calms me, distracts me from my ever-hard cock. From the thoughts and memories that torture me in the endless hours alone.

I think too much—more than I have in my entire adult life—of my brother. I remember his face, so very much like my own, except that his eyes were gray. I think of how cheerful he always seemed.

No, not always, if I think hard about it. There were times when Daniel's face would shut down, and he'd lock himself in his room for hours. Days. I'd assumed he was simply being a teenager, maybe playing video games. And perhaps he was, at times, when he wasn't looking into whatever dark void faced him—the one that eventually swallowed him up and took him away from me.

I bite the inside of my cheek, willing the images of my brother away. It's too much to think of him for more than a few minutes at a time. It's the one pain I can't endure.

And as if the universe—or Christopher—has heard my mental plea for distraction the lock on my door clicks and it swings wide. My entire body tightens in anticipation of what might happen, and which of them will enter the room. When I take in the small, feminine figure encased in red leather, my breath stutters in my chest.

Mistress Alexa.

Fucking God! That he would do this to me!

Scrambling to my knees, I have to steel myself, to prevent myself from scooting backward like some terrible coward. I *am* a coward. I can't stand for her to see me like this. And I understand almost instantly that *this* is the game. Total humiliation in front of my peer, one of my closest comrades-in-kink.

She smiles as she moves toward me, a black crop in one hand, slowly slapping the outside of her thigh. Her ice blue eyes are gleaming. With humor. With lust.

"Well, well, if it isn't my dear friend Master Damon. Or *Damon* now, of course. What a pretty Boy you make. I would never have guessed." She pauses, licking her scarlet lips. "But there's always a certain excitement in seeing one of our own being taken down, isn't there? It's the ultimate power exchange, to take a really large degree of power from someone. Oh, I can see why he adores you so. Your cock is beautifully hard." She steps closer, taps my swelling dick with the crop. "And so lusciously long. If I'd known, I would have tried to get you to fuck me before now."

I feel my jaw drop. The very idea that she would call me *Boy*!

Even worse is the knowledge that desire is like a flame licking at my balls.

"What? Did you actually think you were going to fuck me *now*? Today?" She clicks her tongue. "Really, Damon. You, of all people, know better. I'm here to work you over, my dear. I'm here to beat you until you scream."

Fuck. I know damn well she's capable of it, despite her tiny frame. The woman is a powerhouse among the very elite Masters and Mistresses. Even as she raises the damn crop, I can hardly believe this is happening.

"Hands clasped behind your neck," she commands. "*Do it*, Boy."

I find myself following her orders, the slavespace muscle memory working even as my face burns with rage and shame.

She smacks the tip of my dick, and it goes an angry red. Then, moving around me, she begins to hit me all over—my shoulders, my chest, my thighs, then back to my poor, hurting cock. Even the bottoms of my feet. One small implement of torture, but it does the job. It's all happening so fast, the pain building in an excruciating spiral, with no chance to pause, to catch my breath. Nearly instant overload. Pain and desire and utter degradation that *she* should be doing this to me. But I will not scream. I won't give her the pleasure of it.

She pauses a moment, and Aimée appears beside her, handing her a bottle of water. Mistress Alexa drinks a bit down, then pours the rest over me before Aimée hands her a small whip—a single-tail with a double cracker on the end. That on wet flesh...I shiver so damn hard it feels like a muscle spasm moving up my spine. I can't even look at Aimée.

"This is going to hurt rather badly," Alexa says before she draws her arm back, then swings.

And God, the first crack lands on my right nipple, making me yelp. I grind my jaw tighter, my stomach contracting with the pain. She lands another one on my left nipple, and I nearly cry out, my head spinning. When I try to move away from the next blow, she steps closer, kicking one stiletto-booted foot out and digging the heel into my inner thigh.

"You *will* hold still and take it," she says, the cruel scarlet line of her lips tight, only letting up on my tortured thigh when I nod in assent.

The rest quickly becomes a blur. One blow after another, the pain incredible, as it always is with a whip. My body loves it even as it wants to recoil, but somehow I manage to do as I'm told, still resisting the nearly impossible urge to cry out, pride perhaps the only thing allowing me to retain that small shred of control.

She stops and stares at me, her corseted chest heaving a bit with exertion. "You take it well. Better than I thought you would."

Turning, she gives Aimée the whip and opens her palm to receive something that I can't see. Then she stands there with one hand on her hip, staring at me while my body tries to convert the extreme pain of the whip to pleasure. And it succeeds, but only in part. It was too much all at once, and I am left with tiny points of fiery bee stings all over the front of my body, even the shaft of my cock.

"Enter," Mistress Alexa says over her shoulder.

Two male slaves walk into the room, both beautiful and naked, both very strong and muscular, with shaved heads, pierced cocks and nipples, and wearing the brand of her House. I've seen these two before. I know what they can do.

"Boys, put him in the chair."

I blanch a little, hating my helplessness as they carry me by my arms to the interrogation chair. It's a standard piece of torture equipment, on tall legs, the seat split so the thighs are spread wide. I've used them many times myself, but have never been in one.

Until now.

Fuck.

Fuck!

They snap my cuffs and shackles to eyebolts set into the sides of the chair, then use wide thigh straps to bind my legs to the white leather seat. My balls hang down between my spread legs, and I am thoroughly humiliated, utterly vulnerable, and as hard as the steel frame of the damn chair. All of it even worse—or better, depending on my ranging perspective—when she orders Aimée to stand beside her.

"You will watch, Aimée. No, on second thought, you will stand behind the chair and drape your arms around his shoulders. Hold on tight. He's going to need it."

I have a brief moment to savor the sensation of my beautiful Aimée's soft skin as she wraps me up in her arms. Her face beside my ear, she whispers, "I love you. You can do this."

Mistress Alexa grabs my face, and the metal claws she is now wearing on her fingertips bite sharply into my flesh. I know them well—I gave the set to her myself. Filigreed steel, and quite sharp. Evil. They dig into my jaw, and I smell the faint, metallic scent of my own blood.

"You know the joy of my claws, Damon, don't you? Or is it only from a Master's view? How will you handle me drawing your blood? The excruciating pain they can cause? I have to tell you, my heart is pounding at the thought. I'm going to enjoy this." Her tone drops. "And we both know I don't really care whether you do or not."

My stomach goes tight. I don't even have to guess where she'll begin.

Lowering her hands, she keeps her glittering blue gaze on my face, forcing me to look her in the eye. I flinch at the first tiny prick, then another and another as she closes a hand around my balls. And fucking God, it hurts—it hurts like nothing I've ever quite felt before, or perhaps I simply don't remember. She squeezes, and the tips of the damn claws pierce my skin. My warm blood seeps out, damp on my skin, and I hear Aimée's soft gasp next to my ear, feel her tears hot on my shoulder.

"Such a pretty red," Mistress Alexa remarks. "Red *is* my favorite color. But it's also your Master's. Shall we have him come to look? Yes, I think that's an excellent idea. Boys, let Master Christopher know it's time to join us."

Keeping her steady grip on my balls, she waits until heavy booted footsteps behind her indicate Christopher—my Master... *my* Master—has entered the room. Then she squeezes hard, the claws digging into my flesh.

I pant, but I will not scream. I will *not*. Not even when she lifts my balls and uses the other to dig one of the talons into the most tender flesh of my taint.

"Oomph!" Biting back the yell gathering in my throat, tears burn at the back of my eyes. Goddamn tears!

"Does that hurt, Damon? You can tell us. We want it to. No? Then I shall have to try harder."

Fuck. Fuck!

I grit my teeth as the damn claws dig deeper, as she drags them over my flesh, scratching my ball sac. I hear a drop of blood spatter as it hits the floor, and my sweet Aimée lets out a sob.

Master Christopher says, "How generous of you to make one of my slaves bleed and the other cry, Alexa."

"I'm a very giving person," she answers, ice in her voice, in her eyes. "But now I need my Boys to fuck me. You must excuse me, Christopher. All this work makes a woman needy."

She lets me go, giving a farewell flick to the tip of my stiff cock before stepping back. Her Boys remove the claws and clean her hands with steaming cloths, then without another word, she turns and leaves the room, leaving them to trail at a respectful distance behind her.

My world has narrowed once more—there is nothing now but my Master, the quietly sobbing Aimée, and the stinging pain in my balls, in my nipples, in every welt from the evil whip.

He approaches, his gaze on my face. When he is standing before me, he reaches out and strokes a finger over my jaw, then cups my cheek in his hand. Oh, this is going to be very bad, I can tell. It's only when it's bad that he is so tender with me. I love him all the more for it, which he well knows by now, and which is also part of the extreme mind fuck that is ever-present, the one thing I know I can count on. I sink into the certainty of it almost with a kind of relief. There is only one vague corner of my mind which is still capable of pondering how fucked up I am.

When he takes a half step back and slaps my face so hard it leaves my ears ringing, the narrowness of my world contracts even further. Now it is only him, his cruel and loving hand, and my need to please, my need to reject those desires. But I am stuck in the damn chair. Completely powerless.

He once gave it to me, and now he takes it away. Fitting, somehow.

He slaps me again, then a third time, and I am dizzy with love and pain. Love. Yes. I am a sick fuck. I don't care. And Aimée still has her sweet arms around me, holding me tight, crying quietly, her tears all over my neck, my shoulder, sliding down my chest. No one who isn't me—who isn't *us*—can possibly understand the raw beauty of this moment.

And then he kisses me. His lips are hard on mine, his hand going into the back of my hair and pulling tight, holding me in place as his tongue forces its way into my mouth. He tastes of *him*—Christopher, a flavor I can't define—and my body shudders with desire. Pain. Love for him. My heart is bursting. Another piece of my resistance crumbles away, falling like a small pile of dust at my feet. No, at *his* feet.

He pulls back a fraction of an inch, whispers, "Yeah, you are mine, Damon. Mine. Do you know what it does to me to own you? To have you serve me? It's fucking hot as hell, is what it is. To know I can do whatever I want with you. To know you'll take it. To know you want to. Yeah. Fucking hot. And you, my pretty girl…"

He leans over me and pulls Aimée's face to his, kissing her even harder than he did me. She moans softly, then he pulls her to him, dragging her to the center of the room, forcing her onto her knees on the floor. His hands are cupping her breasts, kneading and squeezing and pinching her flesh.

My cock pulses as I watch. *His* hands. *Her* flesh. Jesus.

Then he's pulling his heavy cock from his jeans, and he's down on one knee, forcing Aimée's head to the floor as he plows into her from behind. My entire body twitches as he fucks her, as he leans down to bite her back and shoulders, the back of her neck. As he grabs a fistful of her long, red hair and yanks her body upright, his arm snaking around her. His teeth sink into the back of her neck, and she makes adorable little mewling noises, and in between I can hear his panting breath.

Pre-come drips from my poor cock, and I can smell it in the air, along with Aimée's wetness, and the faint iron-scent of my own blood. Has there ever been a more powerful elixir?

It seems to go on forever—or maybe that's only because I am trapped here, watching, wanting, needing to the point of pain. And just when I'm certain I can't take anymore, my Master pulls from Aimée's sleek little body and gets to his feet, stalking toward me. Very quickly he unbuckles my straps, unclips my cuffs and shackles, and yanks me to my feet.

"Aimée, sit on the side of the spanking bench. Good girl. Now spread your pretty thighs. Damon is going to reward you."

He marches me over to her, and I can't help but stare at her lovely, wet pussy, the pink flesh making my mouth water. And as Master Christopher shoves me forward and onto my knees, I understand it's my mouth he wants me to pleasure her with.

Ah, my poor, throbbing cock! But I can hardly feel sorry for myself as I lean in and taste her. She is all liquid sweetness on my tongue, gently squirming girl as I lick her slit, as I suck on her hard little clit, then slip my tongue down to push it inside her. And the whole time, our Master is grasping the back of my head, shoving my face harder into her soft cunt.

Then he is behind me, parting my ass cheeks with strong hands, and as I bury my face in Aimée's lovely body, he plows into me.

Gasping in pain, in pleasure, I try to relax around his thick cock in my ass. But he's so damn big, loosening my muscles is completely impossible. His solid flesh pushes deeper and I feel myself tearing, but it doesn't matter. Nothing matters except that we are finally joined, he and I and Aimée, and it is perfection. *Perfection.*

Time goes by in a blur of fucking and sucking, hurting and spiraling need. His teeth sink into the back of my neck and his hands dig into Aimée's arching hips until it's her blood I smell—

blood and lust and the scent of her coming as she screams. Then he's coming, pumping so damn hard into me, I would be forced to fall to the floor if it weren't for Aimée's body holding me up.

Christopher coming is a beautiful thing to behold. He growls deep in his throat, the growl becoming more vicious, his cock stabbing into me more savagely, over and over until his hot come spurts inside me.

He whispers harshly, "*Come*, Damon."

And I obey instantly, my lonely cock spilling into the air, untouched.

"Aimée, hold him," he orders.

He starts to smack my ass, my thighs, to rake his nails down my back, to grab my sides in tight, painful fistfuls of flesh. I start to overload right away — as if this entire day hasn't been overload already — and my mind is absolutely empty.

Finally it stops. He's panting hard as he leans over me to kiss Aimée — her lips, her cheeks, her breasts. Then he bends down to brush a kiss across my shoulder before pulling me to my feet and kissing me hard on the mouth. Sinking into him, my body knows only the pleasure of his touch. My heart knows only the bliss of connection. Finally.

Will I never need anything but this again?

Maybe. Don't know. Can't care right now. No, at this moment all I know is this perfection. Purity in a way perhaps no one else could understand.

This is my heaven. This is my hell.

This is fucking heaven. I never want it to end.

Eden Bradley

CHAPTER SIX

It doesn't end until the next night. Until that point, I am well-used, exercised, bathed by Aimée, and shaved by Master Christopher himself with a straight razor, which is terrifying and makes me swoon at the same time. He's nicked my hip, my collarbone, my ribs, and the spot just below my right nipple, which also makes me swoon—something about bleeding for him, as he told Mistress Alexa. For *him*.

It is also he who comes to my room and wakes me from a dead sleep in the dark of night, with nothing but the glimmering pool lights to allow me to see him tossing clothes down beside my pillows on the floor. I see he's just dyed his hair—it's a bit of a shock, from platinum blond to coal black, and he's cut his Mohawk to a short stubble all over his well-shaped head. It looks as good on him—stunning—as everything else does.

"Get dressed, Damon. We're leaving."

"We..." I stop myself just before asking the questions at the tip of my rebellious tongue: Where? Why?

Instead, I simply nod and reach for the clothes as he bends one knee to unlock me from my chains, leaving the cuffs tight around my wrists. But I don't mind. My bonds have become a form of security for me, just as they have for every slave I've ever trained. But I can't think about those days right now. No, if I do, I think I may really lose my mind.

He leaves, and I quickly dress in a pair of nicely tailored slacks and a white shirt—not my own, and I have no idea where they came from. It doesn't matter, though, does it? All I need to know is he wants me to wear it—well, and if this means I haven't done well enough, if he is sending me away, ending our arrangement. But I cannot even deal with that idea right now.

The shoes are mine, and I slide into them. Then Aimée appears, dressed once more, this time in snug-fitting black slacks that hug her hips flawlessly, and a pale green silk blouse, her lovely breasts pushed up and showing a mouth-watering bit of cleavage between the low buttons. She's also wearing a choker-length chain of silver, or probably platinum, around her slender neck—a "day collar", I am certain. I admire the way it lays against her skin. I am filled with envy and a strange sort of dread. Is that what I really want? I realize I do—desperately—and yet I can't even comprehend it, emotion and logic warring in my head, in my chest, making my muscles go tight. Another mind fuck. The story of my life at this point.

Aimée moves gracefully to my side and laces her arms around my waist, bringing me a measure of warmth and calm. Laying her head on my shoulder, she whispers, "How are you, Damon? Are you okay?"

Am I?

"I think so," I tell her. "Wonderful in some ways, completely fucked in others. I'll figure it out. Eventually."

"Are you still so uncertain?"

"My darling girl. So sweet to me. So sweet, always."

"I do try," she says.

Daring for a moment to brush her cheek with my lips, I tell her, "Yes, always. And you? How are you?"

"I'm better than I've ever been in my life. I am honestly living in pure bliss, being exactly what I've always needed to be, where I need to be. And I have you both. For now, at least."

She stays with me for a long, lovely moment, then her arms slip away. "You'd better hurry. Use the bathroom, brush your teeth. He wants us ready in five minutes in the living room."

"Of course."

I go about my tasks, hyper-aware of the loss of her warm embrace, the fragrance of her hair next to my cheek. Trying not to frankly freak the hell out at the idea of being moved again, if he's done with me. He knows how to unsettle, my wicked Master. He does everything with intention, as I once did myself.

No. Don't think about it.

Moving to the unlocked door, I glance around the small, white space I've inhabited these last nine or ten days—I think it's been that long, anyway—and I realize it has become a sort of sanctuary for me, one in which I've been able to discover my submission, to contemplate how my life is changing as I strive to be what I must in order to stay with those I love so deeply. To fear the submission. To hope for it.

I shut the door behind me and go into the living room, where Master Christopher waits. He is spectacular in tight black pants and black dress shirt rolled up at the sleeves. His bad-ass black boots are intimidating. — they make my dick go hard, as does his exquisite face, with his high cheekbones uplit by the dim lamps in the room.

"Aimée," he says.

She steps forward and holds out a heavy wool coat, her green gaze on my face, concern in her eyes. When I take it from her delicate hands, her fingertips brush mine in a subtle offering of comfort and support.

My heart hammers. My cock pulses. For them both. I should be used to this by now, but somehow I'm not. It always comes as another shock, how insanely turned on I am simply being in their presence. Is it my current submissive role that's adding to it? The overall dynamic between the three of us? I'm certain that has something to do with it, as well as the fact that they are truly two of the most enticing human beings ever born.

Our Master moves around me, trailing one hand over my arm and across my chest, before he stops next to me, leaving his arm draped across my shoulders. Leaning in, he takes my earlobe between his sharp, white teeth, and bites down, sending a shock of pain and lust quivering through me.

Then he says quietly, "I suppose you're wondering where I'm taking you, Damon? Ah, but that's the best part." He pauses just long enough to make me squirm inside. "We're going back to San Francisco. I don't believe you know I have a house not too far from The Training House, do you?"

My pulse spikes hard, like a jackhammer in my veins.

No. God, no.

"Oh yeah," he says, as if he is able to hear my thoughts, and at this moment, I'm not entirely certain he can't. "Back in the city, only a few blocks from your home, from the place where you call yourself 'Master'. How fucking delicious is that?"

He kisses my cheek, bites it hard enough to make me flinch. But otherwise I am frozen. How the fuck can he do this to me? And how brilliant that he *is* doing it?

More ultimate mind fuck. He truly is a Master, in every sense of the word. But something in me wants to bolt. *Needs* to, maybe. Sweat breaks out on my forehead.

"What? Afraid of your own home town? Well, you fucking should be." His hand goes into my hair, pulling hard at the base of my skull. "But you can handle it. You will, for me. In case you haven't already understood this down to your bones, that's the only way I'll have things. Which means it's the only way *you'll* have *us*. In case you've forgotten, I am the one in control now—the decisions are mine to make, the shots mine call. So buck the fuck up, Damon. Things could be worse for you. Much worse."

When I tense all over, he seems to relent for a moment. Kissing my cheek again, he brushes his thumb over my jaw, until pleasure and need and the desire to please are surging hard through my veins, through my cock once more.

"It'll be all right," he whispers in my ear. "You can do this."

My system nearly purrs at his tender touch, his kind, bolstering words, and the need to learn to be his blossoms anew in my chest. Kindness and cruelty—what a powerful elixir, and I am no more immune than any other slave.

He snaps his fingers. "Both of you, come."

Oh, my cock jumps, but I am not quite so foolish, regardless of how addled my brain is with lust and his command, to think any relief is in sight. I stand up straighter, as does Aimée, and we follow him out the front door and get into the dark, shining car waiting at the curb.

A few hours and another short chartered flight later and we're in San Francisco, driving north from the airport with Christopher at the wheel of a black Hummer as the rising sun peers through a layer of fog. Aimée sits quietly in the front seat, while I am left alone in the back to simmer in my whirling thoughts. For a while, anyway.

Christopher turns down the heavy, blaring music and says over his shoulder, "Damon, tell me what you're thinking about."

I am startled into silence. What the hell? What does he want to know? What am I to say?

"*Damon*," he repeats, a low threat in his tone, and I find my voice.

"Am I to speak freely?"

"Ha! To a point."

I clear my throat, buying a moment to get my rushing thoughts in some sort of order. It doesn't work terribly well. "This may be pushing the boundaries, but...I'm thinking this is some kind of sick joke, and I know damn well it's supposed to be. It's working, on some levels, at least, which I'm sure you know. Sir. Master Christopher."

"And?"

"And I don't think the fact that I nearly forgot to use your proper title went unnoticed."

He chuckles. "You think not?"

"No, Sir."

"Hmm, 'Sir' is fine, for now, since I don't officially own you. What else?"

"My head is pretty fucked up being back in the City. Thinking about the fact that we're driving toward my House, and how odd it is that it still *is* my House, given my present circumstances."

"And now you know some of the dichotomy that rules my existence."

"I do. I am also beginning to understand that until now—well, until recently—I've never experienced mind fuck in its truest form. And I don't say that to flatter you—it's simply the truth."

He nods, his profile illuminated by the wan early sun, all fine jawline and high cheekbones. He is so beautifully exotic, and I never fail to be affected by him. Not that I'm so entirely shallow that beauty alone is enough for me. No, it's the aura of his power, as either slave or Master, that draws me in. But the exceptional bone structure and lush, cruel mouth don't hurt.

He is quiet again, leaving me in my own head. I try to keep my pulse steady, using breathing techniques taught to me by my first Masters years ago, and used by me on the slaves I've trained.

Don't think about that now.

But it's not easy with Aimée sitting there in the front seat, her hair shining softly in the dim morning light. I can see the lush curve of her breast. I want to touch it. To suck on it. Bite it. I want to remember what it was like to have her in my suite of rooms in the Training House. At my mercy. Under my hands. Under my whip.

No.

I nearly groan aloud. Being here, in this city—*my* city—is already getting to me. How will I bear it? Is this some sort of test, issued not only by Master Christopher, but by the universe? By God? Oh yes, I believe in God, in my own twisted way. It's an element of the taboo part of kink for me. My struggle, whether as Master or slave. Perhaps it is a test on every level, the struggle itself. I am damn well determined to pass it, then. I spend the rest of the ride with my head bowed in contemplation, perhaps in a sort of prayer rather than the subservience I'm supposed to be immersed in.

When the car stops, I look up. We're across the street from the Panhandle end of Golden Gate Park—Fell Street, I believe—in front of a three story stucco home, gray with white trim. There is a garage at street level, with a gated entrance beside it, and the top two floors are all tall shuttered windows. It looks perfectly ordinary. But it's *his* house, and I know already there will be nothing ordinary about it.

We've stopped in the driveway—I can't imagine there is any way a vehicle the size of the small Hummer will fit into the garage of an old San Francisco home—and our Master shuts off the engine.

"Damon, help our girl from the car."

Biting back a flash of annoyance at being told to do something I'd do on my own, I get out and walk around to open Aimée's door. When I offer her my hand, she takes it and gives it a squeeze, smiling at me, but I swear I see a flash of something in her lovely eyes. Fear? Doubt? Or is it nothing more than a reflection of my own?

We follow our Master around the Hummer, and as he unlocks a heavy door next to the garage, it hits me in some impossible new-again way that Christopher is my Master, that I belong to him for whatever term or trial period this is. That my heart wants this as desperately as my mind struggles against it. How did I end up in this strange place that feels so horribly alien to me, and yet so familiar that I'm doing these things—following instruction, taking the beatings—as if I were made for it? I am so afraid that if I allow myself to pause and truly ponder these ideas, I will fall apart, or explode in some fiery blast, like a dying sun.

I am no longer making any sense. Ah, my beautifully wicked Master definitely knows what he's doing.

I give myself an internal shake as we step through and walk up a narrow wood staircase, and finally into a living room filled with morning light. The wood floors are polished to a high sheen. The arched doorways and crown moldings hold the original plaster elements of the 1940's architecture, but nearly everything else is sleek and modern. A pair of large gray suede couches flank a fireplace, facing each other, with a table between them made of an enormous slab of thick glass set on a stone base. Modern art decorates the walls, and I recognize what I believe is an original Dali among the black-and-white photography, along with a few pieces of mounted ancient stone carvings and contemporary abstract paintings.

I am astounded—not that Christopher should have such sophisticated tastes, but by the realization that it simply never occurred to me to wonder how he lived on the outside.

"Sit," he orders.

Aimée and I both obey, settling side by side on one of the sofas like submissive bookends, which amuses me in some small way.

"We're going to talk now," he says. "All of us, I think we're overdue, but I wanted to get you into the necessary headspace, to see if you were able to do it, before we went any further into this. I want you both to put aside the deeper part of the roles of slave and submissive. Do you understand? I want to know where you're both at." He looks directly at me, that searing golden gaze on mine. "Damon. You start."

My skin feels as if it's closing in on me, too tight for my body. Why is the talking more frightening than anything else he does to me? "I…am not exactly certain where I'm at. I'm still in shock, almost constantly questioning myself. I don't know when that will go away, if at all. No, I know it will…if we continue."

"Are you saying you're still not sure you can?"

Now my entire body tightens all over—stomach, chest, even

my fingers—and the words catch for a moment in my throat. "I don't know. To be honest, there's very little I'm sure of at this moment."

He shrugs, muscle rippling beneath the dark shirt. "Fair enough. Go on."

"I'm still fighting it. It makes sense to me that I would, given the complete turnaround in roles. It's a lot to wrap my head around, no matter that it feels good, that it admittedly fills a need. It's still fucking hard. Confusing. I have to question everything I've thought I was all these years."

"It's a small identity crisis, yes?" Aimée interjects, touching the back of my hand.

I glance at our Master, and see him give her a small nod of permission before she takes my hand fully in hers.

"Yes," I agree, lacing my fingers through hers, "except there's nothing small about it. "

He nods. "Of course." Pausing, he rubs a hand over the dark stubble on his scalp, and even this simple motion, in this insanely intense moment, is pure sex to me. "Tell me about Master Stephan, about what your life was like before you became a slave. You've never talked to me about that except in passing."

My fingers tighten on Aimée's. "I've never really talked to anyone but Master Stephan about my life before I came to him, other than my experience in the kink world."

"All the more reason to get into it now, with us. You understand how crucial this is?"

He's right, and I don't like it. But I *have* to do this, to reveal myself, in order to give myself to him in the way I must. I want to fidget, but I resist, and the struggle is a sharp pain in my gut.

"I don't like to discuss these things," I tell him, as if he doesn't already know. Perhaps it's more for my own benefit than his. "But then, we all have our secrets, don't we?"

"Not me," Master Christopher says with one of his glorious little smirks. "I'm a fucking open book. I like to air my dirty laundry. I take a certain pleasure in it."

I smile. "That's true. All right, then—I'll try to take a cue from you."

I fidget a bit, then. I can't help it. The world is closing in on me once more—the world and my tight, tight skin. Attempting to talk about my past feels like a loss, in some weird way, bringing old pain sharply to the surface.

Daniel.

Do not want to do this.

Aimée gives my hand an assuring squeeze, so I take a breath and begin, though dread is coursing through my body. "Well, to start with, there was…my brother."

"What?" our Master demands as Aimée gasps sharply. "I never knew you had a brother.

"No one does. Not anymore. I think even my parents have forgotten Daniel, but I haven't. I keep him tucked away in a safe place, this impenetrable vault inside my mind. Impenetrable until now, I suppose."

I have to stop and take in a deep, gulping breath as goosebumps rise all over my body. I'm surprised at how much it hurts to say his name out loud, and I've only begun to tell the story.

Fuck.

"So…I had a little brother. And God, I hate to say those words—I *had* him—because it makes it even more abundantly clear that I don't anymore." I take another moment to collect myself, rubbing a hand over my jaw, massaging the back of my neck. It's too damn hard to look at either of them now. I simply have to survive this moment. "He was two years younger than me, and we were the best of friends and occasional enemies growing up, as brothers often are. He was…I always thought he was so much like me. My sidekick. But looking back after, I realized I had no idea what his life was like, what went on in his head, how he felt about anything."

"After what?" Aimée dares to ask, her voice soft.

The dread deepens, and I bite the inside of my cheek until there is blood on the edge of my tongue, then swallow some of the silvery-mercury flavor, focusing on the sensation as it slides down my throat. It helps a little. A very little, but I'll take what I can right now.

Just get the words out.

"After he killed himself," I say through numbed lips.

"Oh!"

I catch Aimée's expression from the corner of my eye, but I

can't stand to see it, so I shift my gaze to Master Christopher's stony face. It's easier to look at him—the only change in his expression is a narrowing of his eyes, a slight tightness to his lush mouth. I'm grateful for his controlled demeanor, his lack of reaction. Perhaps he knows I need it. Yes, I'm certain he does.

"He was only thirteen," I continue. "Only thirteen, although I've heard a lot of people say that was the hardest year of their life. It's that in-between space, when you're no longer a child but not yet an adult, the first teen year. It's a transition. I remember it myself, because that's when I first admitted to myself I craved boys as much as girls. But for me, it was more about sexual discovery, and something in me was rebellious enough that I didn't care what my conservative family would think. I *liked* being different from them. But Daniel…"

I shake my head pensively, still so damn clueless after all these years. "I don't actually know what the hell happened with him. Was he bullied? If so, I never saw it. Was he gay? If so, why didn't he come to me? Was he depressed? If he was, he hid it so well I never knew. The mystery of it tortures me. I should have known something was wrong, that he was keeping secrets. I should have fucking known, but I didn't."

In my mind's eye I see his young body hanging from our father's leather belt in the closet in his room. The absolute worst moment of my life. Master Stephan succumbing to cancer in my arms was nothing in comparison. I feel so shallow even thinking it, comparing the two terrible deaths, but it's simply the truth. Perhaps that's why I haven't been able to admit to my love for my former Master? But this moment is about my brother.

"I wasn't the one to discover him—no, that was our maid, who went screaming through the house. But I was the only one home, which happened more often than not, even when we were little. Death is always an ugly thing, and there's nothing uglier than a suicide. Fuck." I have to stop, biting my cheek again to chase away the pain of that awful word. "Just…fuck," I repeat helplessly.

Aimée slips her arm through mine and hangs on, and I lean into her comfort even as my body wants to reject it. I don't deserve it, do I? I am the survivor, after all. It's not fucking fair. I can't even look at Christopher any longer. Instead, I cast my gaze to the floor as I whisper, "He was just a kid. And I was the big brother. I was supposed to protect him. I should have known something, done something, been *more*. I think...I've spent my entire life trying to make up for it."

"And so you took over the House, even though you didn't really want to," my Master says, not unkindly, despite the brutality of that truth.

"Yes," I whisper. My head is pounding, the hot, thready pulse beating in my temples. "Yes," I repeat, perhaps to convince myself of the depth and veracity of this statement. "I've always known losing him—and even more, losing him in that way—has affected me. Profoundly. But until this moment... Well, I don't know that I was ever fully conscious of exactly how it's driven certain things in my life." I have to pause, to think back on what has just come out of my mouth, what Christopher's hit on so squarely. "I've never said the word 'survivor' aloud before. But that's the whole thing, isn't it? Wrapped up in that simple word. Jesus."

There is an opening sensation in my chest, and I understand instantly this admission has freed some part of me, even if it ripped my flesh and my soul on the way out. But is it enough to allow me to go on? To accept finding what I truly want, with my beloved Aimée, with Christopher as our Master? How can I possibly know? All I know is I have torn myself open, exposed the most unsightly, raw, aching part of my being. Is it any easier because I've done so with the people I love?

I don't know. I just don't know.

Eden Bradley

The Training House
CHAPTER SEVEN

When Master Christopher reaches out and wraps his hand around the back of my head, pulling me in to press his lips to mine, I am almost too dazed to respond to the sheer force of his power, his beauty, the primal animal that is *him*. But the response is there behind the daze, along with the sensation of my heart breaking, opening up. My body is numb all over—everywhere but the keen, lancing pain in my chest and where he is touching me. Warm spots, thrumming with heat. Physical sensation that is somehow emotion. I am really falling apart, bursting open in some terrible and glorious fashion. Completely overcome.

I sink into his hard kiss, glorying in the sincerity of it. But a moment later he releases me and steps back to stand in front of me with his arms crossed. He watches me, and I see emotions ranging over his features: empathy, sadness, a resolve I don't quite understand. His jaw clenches, and I wish I knew what was going through his mind. This suddenly seems to be about so much more than the Master/slave dynamic.

No, in truth, it has always been more with us. But the real honesty has begun only now, and I know I've missed out on some key element in the four years prior to this.

Finally, he says, "I'm sorry, Damon."

I nod. What else can I do? There is nothing to say, and I am still too choked with emotion to speak.

"But," he continues, "—and someone else would probably ask you to forgive them for saying this, but you know that's not my style—if you allow this to prevent you from living your life as you need to, then doesn't that make his death all for nothing?"

Painful twisting sensation in my chest, and suddenly I can barely breathe. "I...what?"

"You know I've lost people. A lot of people. My mother, to begin with. Most of the friends I lived with and worked the streets with, back in the day. Overdose, AIDS, violence." He shrugs, but there is nothing casual about it. "I'm not saying my story is any more tragic than yours, because it is and it isn't. But now you have to ask yourself, what the fuck are you gonna do about it? Because if this is what's holding you back, then this is the shit you need to deal with. Isn't that what you've been telling me all the years I've known you?"

The world has narrowed down to a pinpoint of light, with Christopher at the very center, the only thing that exists at this moment.

"But you're a hell of a lot smarter than I am, Damon. I've only been able to do so much. *You* can move further ahead, and you need to, because you're in pain now. Don't think I don't see it. I see everything."

"I know you do." The words come out in a small, strangled whisper. "No one has ever been so honest with me, so brutally frank. I know I need it."

"Glad to hear you know it, because you damn well do need that. I never said this would be easy—just the opposite. So I'm gonna say some hard shit to you right now."

He watches me for a long moment, golden lion eyes narrowed, searing my skin, searching my soul. I feel utterly naked before him. And fucking scared. But needing this—to be so naked and afraid—as much as I've needed anything else with him.

"This is the goddamn truth, Damon," he tells me. "You can't fucking martyr yourself here. Don't do it with me—I have no use for that shit. Either be here authentically and fully immersed, or this isn't going to work. You're the one who's depriving yourself of the experience because you're carrying all this baggage around. You deprive yourself of the joy because you're afraid of losing it again, and because you feel so indebted—but is that a good reason for us to do this crazy shit we do?"

If I didn't know he meant it as a rhetorical question, I'd be tempted to answer, probably incorrectly because it's always worked as a justification for me in the past. And I was happy, or at least content, to go along with that idea. Until *he* turned my world upside down.

"You need to clean up your motives," he insists, his eyes boring into me. "If you're only doing this because I'm making you, then what the fuck are we doing here? It started out that way, but if you can't eventually flow through it, then…fuck it." He makes a vague fluttering motion with his hand, his frustration manifesting in the set of his shoulders. "Yeah, if that's how it's gonna be, then this—*us*—cannot happen. It'll turn to shit for all of us."

My insides turn to ice at the stark reality he's laying out for me. This—us—absolutely *must* happen.

"I want more than that," he says gently, as if he can actually see my rising panic. "I thought you did, too. You said you did. And I'm not saying you're lying, but you need to fucking get it together and decide which way it's gonna go. You work through this—*now*—or it has to be over. Now that I know what the big issue is, I understand that's how it has to work. Do you get what I'm saying?"

I turn away from him, shoving my hands through my hair. "Yes, I understand—I just don't know if I can do it. I don't know. It feels like too much. It feels like everything."

And in this moment, I feel too powerless to be responsible for *anything*, let alone everything.

"Damon," Aimée says softly, "he's right. And I'm here to help you. Tell me what you need."

Dear God, I am overwhelmed—at being faced with the hard truth. At my sweet girl's loving support. At the way Christopher is driving me, pushing me in the way I need to be pushed, which is his way of loving me right now. And I know now I could never have reached this depth with anyone without this blunt honesty between us—all of us. I really have been missing out all these years, which is another painful truth.

"I don't know what I need," I admit. "I don't even know where to begin."

"You already have," she says.

Turning, I smile at her, and her face lights up with warmth. She is so, so lovely. And her encouragement fills my heart with the kind of hope I haven't felt for a very long time.

"I'm giving her to you for the night," our Master announces. "But with this boundary: no kink. Just be together. It'll help you. And if it helps you, it'll help all of us."

For some reason I'm not as surprised as perhaps I should be—maybe because I know, in his own rough way, that he does love me. Loves us. He knows what we need on some instinctual level that is even sharper and more accurate than even my own as a Master.

"Thank you," Aimée says.

I am about to echo her sentiment, but he brushes us off with another wave of his hand.

"Go up to the top floor. You'll find a tray set out in the suite there—I called ahead and left orders for my housekeeper. Be sure you eat something, both of you. I'm leaving the house for the night. I'll be back by noon tomorrow." His features soften as he reaches out to stroke the high curve of Aimée's cheek. "I know you'll comfort him, prettiness." Then he turns to me, his tone hardening once more, he says, "And you—figure it the fuck out, Damon."

I nod. "I will do my best."

Our Master leans down to kiss Aimée's pretty mouth, then brushes my lips too, pausing to nip me gently. Then he takes our hands and folds them together in his, holding on for several long moments as he stares into my eyes. I swear I see a whole world in that steady gaze, all golden light and silver shadow, pain and love and more pain. He's worried, even though he'd never admit it out loud. My heart surges, but I can't say anything about it. He's right—I simply have to figure it out. But is one night enough?

He turns to go, and I can sense Aimée holding her breath, as I am, until the front door closes. I grasp her hand and stand, pulling her up with me. I have to remind myself there is to be no kink, but she is who she is and so am I, and there is still some power dynamic between us. Without Christopher, I must be the one in charge. It automatically steadies the ground beneath my feet—there is safety in the role, even if it's not quite the role of Master, or even Dominant.

"Let's go upstairs," I tell her.

She nods, batting her long lashes at me. In the pale shaft of light coming through a high window, her skin is illuminated, and I can see the pale, gold freckles scattered there. Reaching out, I caress the fine bones of her jawline with my thumb.

"Come on, Aimée. I find I need to take you to bed, to feed you with my own hands."

"Yes, please," she says, her face lighting in one of her precious smiles.

Together we ascend the narrow wooden staircase to the top floor, where the stairs open directly into a room with vaulted ceilings. The walls are painted a pale gray with white trim and the windows and slatted shutters are draped with long, sheer white curtains. The room is dominated by an enormous four-poster bed made of graceful brushed steel, with a canopy of cross-bars overhead and a cage beneath lined with white fur rugs. A bed made for kink. A bed made for royalty. Yet tonight it will simply be Aimée and me, together. How luxurious. How exotic. I feel like an outlaw.

There is a high dresser faced in the same brushed steel to one side, where the tray is set with covered plates, a bottle of wine, and even a bud vase holding a single white rose, which I'm certain he put there simply to amuse me, since he is not the kind of man to keep flowers in his house. Flowers in this bizarre situation? Oh yes, there's a certain irony to it.

"Hungry, lovely girl?" I ask her.

"Yes," she answers simply, standing at the foot of the bed, her arms at her sides. Her posture is almost non-descript, except that I see the tension in every line of her body, and the sensual gleam in her eyes.

My cock goes hard, and in three strides I'm across the room and stripping her down.

No kink.

But this is not kink—it is simply desire. Desire for her body. The desire to be inside her. To feel her all over. To merge.

She gives herself into my embrace with a quiet sigh, and I kiss her even as I undress her. And God, her lips are so soft beneath mine, her mouth so utterly sweet, I don't know how I've lived without this. Soon she is naked, her clothes in a puddle on the floor, and I press my fingers right into her. She is gorgeously wet and tight. Heaven. My cock jumps.

"Hold still," I whisper, and once more it's not about kink, but the need of the moment as I kick my shoes off and get out of my clothes.

Picking her up, I carry her to the side of the bed, lay her down on the crisp gray duvet. She is parting her thighs even as I lean over her to kiss her breasts, her stomach, her smooth thighs. I have to taste her—her skin, her sweet cunt, flushed and swollen already. I leave small bites over her flesh just below her navel, then lower, at the top of her pink clit.

"Ah, God, you are the most succulent creature ever born," I mutter before lowering my mouth and stroking her damp slit with my tongue. "I have to drink you in. To swallow you whole."

"Oh, yes," she murmurs. "Please, yes."

I dive in, licking, sucking hard at her pussy lips, shoving my tongue inside her and fucking her with it. She squirms deliciously while my cock pulses in a hard, rhythmic beat, wanting, wanting, and yet glorying in being denied so I can please my beautiful girl. There is something of both serving and empowerment in doing this for her, *to* her, and I revel in it. This is the balance I crave. This is exactly what I need.

I eat as if I were starving, and some part of me is. She begins to come, and there is nothing more than a tiny voice in the back of my head reminding me I should make her stop, control her orgasm. But that's not the point now, and instead I savor her hot climax as she floods my mouth, her body convulsing, her cries filling the air.

I keep licking her, and she swells once more under my tongue. Pressing a finger inside her, then another, then a third, I find her g-spot, feel it swell under my stroking fingertips before I start fucking her hard with my hand. In moments she is screaming, squirting all over the bed, my face, her thighs. When she's done I sit up to look at her, wiping my chin with the back of one hand. Her eyes are glazed, and she's still sighing and panting, her body squirming with the aftershocks. I'm damn pleased with myself. But now I need her.

Picking her up, I yank back the wet duvet and set her down on the prim white sheets. She is all raw sensuality, her features loose with wanton desire, and she smells deliciously of sex. Her red hair is disheveled—and oh, what a wonderful word that is!—scattered around her face like some marker of pleasure. Her body is all smooth, pale skin, her breasts flawless curves tipped with the most luscious nipples, pink and succulent.

I climb on top of her, my erect flesh poised at the heat of her cunt, and when I look down at her, I am overcome by my love for her, by the keen edge of desire rippling over my skin.

"Aimée, I need to fuck you. I need to be inside your body. But I want you to touch me first."

"Oh! Yes, please." She reaches for my stiff cock, her soft hand tentative at first. When I moan, she moves with more confidence, exploring the length and the shape of the head, with her fingertips, then squeezing the shaft and slipping down to caress my balls. She looks at my cock as if fascinated.

"Damon," she says, without taking her eyes from it, "I have to tell you, it's been so long since I've been with anyone other than in service, it's as if *this* is kink to me now."

"Yes, exactly. I understand," I pant through the pleasure of her touch.

"It's so, so beautiful," she tells me.

"You're beautiful."

She looks up at me. "Damon? *You* are beautiful. *Beautiful.* As beautiful as he is."

"No..."

"Yes," she insists, stroking me, sending shivers of pleasure through my system. "This is beautiful—your lovely cock. Us here together. Every time you touch me. Every time you look at me. Every time you talk to me—*really* talk, revealing yourself."

I want to answer, but she sits up and takes my cock in her mouth, and I am lost in the wet heat. In her searching tongue. In the supremely hot way she swallows me down until she gags, over and over, tears coursing down her cheeks from being choked by my hard flesh.

I fight the urge to hold back, as I normally would. But there is nothing "normal" about this moment—not for people like us. Not in this vanilla sex, which feels like the kinkiest damn thing I've ever done in my life. I take in a quick, gulping breath before pleasure overwhelms me, stinging in my blood coursing at a million miles an hour through my pounding cock.

"Coming into your mouth is...fuck." I bury my fingers in her silky hair. She's still sucking me, licking the come off. "I need it, need to feel every part of you on me. Need to be inside you as soon as I recover. Need to hold you *now*, my girl."

We tumble onto the bed, and I wrap her up in my arms, pulling her close and kissing her.

"I can taste my come on your lovely lips, and I can still taste yours on mine. It's like some divine blend, some powerful intoxicant in itself," I murmur as she presses her cheek harder against my chest. "Maybe I'm a little out of my head, but how can I possibly care? We have the night together. Nothing else really matters right now, does it?"

"No," she agrees. "Only this, for now. We don't need to worry about anything else. We're not meant to, are we? And even though this—the two of us tonight—is not about kink, we are still following his orders. It makes it easier. For me, anyway. Does it for you, as well?"

I take a moment to think about it. "Yes, it does. Maybe that's the only thing that makes this possible."

"Then it's a true gift."

A hard lump forms in my throat, and I pull her in tighter.

We drift for a while. I'm not sure I'm even quite asleep, although I dream of white sheets and her sweet, pink mouth. I dream of the window opening and the white curtains flowing out and over the city, free, yet searching for...something. I wake understanding exactly what the dream means—it's literal enough even for my sleep and sex-fogged brain to comprehend. I am searching for the purity and freedom inherent in the sheer white floating through the sky, the sky of my city. My life. And my sweet love is at the center of it. She is the apex, the key that turned the lock, opening this tightly bound part of myself. Even Christopher could not have done it on his own. We both needed her.

Aimée sleeps beside me, tucked into my side, giving me time to think.

Our Master knew to break me down, knew how necessary that was and still will be for a while—maybe forever. But he also knew when I needed filling up, and he understood exactly how to do it. Which leads me to believe he truly does want me here, truly loves me.

Ours is a complicated situation, more than anyone else could possibly understand. Our standing in the community, our dynamic, all makes this a little insane. But I went into this knowing that part. What I didn't know—what I lacked the foresight to see—was how profoundly letting them go, then coming after them, would impact my life, and theirs, on so many levels. None of us will ever be the same again, regardless of how this turns out.

A small pain lances through my chest at that thought, and I can barely stand it. But the truth is, the outcome is still wildly unpredictable.

"Damon"

Her voice is soft with sleep. Fucking adorable.

"What is it?"

"What are you thinking about? Your heart just began to beat faster. I can feel it."

Kissing her forehead, I whisper against her skin, "Everything. And nothing."

"Tell me about the 'everything'?"

"It's quite a lot."

"'Everything' usually is."

"That sounds exactly like something the Cheshire Cat would have said."

"Or Alice. I like to think of myself as Alice, sometimes. My life is 'through the looking glass', isn't it? In some Wonderland that is surreal in a way Lewis Carrol couldn't imagine, even in his opium dreams."

"Did you read Alice as a little girl?" I ask.

"All the time. And as a big girl. It's one of my comfort books, although sometimes it makes me uncomfortable. It can be frightening."

"But fascinating."

"Yes."

"This does not surprise me, coming from a kinky girl. We pervs love the frightening and fascinating."

"It's complicated, isn't it? But the complication feels like a sort of punishment in itself, so I can't help but glory in even that." She laughs, making my heart expand in my chest. "Am I making any sense?"

I stroke her hair, give her cheek a little pinch. "More than you know, darling girl."

"Damon?" Her tone is more serious now. "Do you think... do you know if we can go through together—through this crazy looking glass that will be our lives with Christopher? Because

I…" a small sob catches in her throat "…I don't want to do it without you."

"I want to. But can I?" I shake my head. "The question is too enormous to be answered in one night. My life would change forever, and even I can't say exactly how. It's been tearing me apart. Not that I don't want to be with you, with him — of course I do — but…I could lose everything."

"Except us," she says, her voice so quiet I can barely hear her.

"Which is why I am so fucked," I mutter quietly.

So fucked, no matter what I do. If I leave them behind, my life is certain: I'll still have the Training House. Slaves to punish. My life as I knew it before. And my heart will be shattered beyond repair. If I stay with them — if he will have me, in the end — what can I expect? There's no way to know without making that leap. It's a common phrase, but it *feels* like a leap, jumping from a high cliff into the unknown, those endless moments hanging suspended in the air. Which way is up? Which way is down?

I had so much less responsibility earlier in my life, so much less to lose.

But no. The truth is, I was braver once. I was willing to give up anything, to let anything go, in the name of experience. Although now, in light of everything that's happened recently, in the aftermath of having finally spoken of Daniel — who is inexplicably linked to everything I do and think and feel — I see the bravery as nothing more than a form of escape. Which means I'm not really very brave after all, doesn't it? Am I, instead, simply used to being this way? Shut down. Surviving. Suffering in fucking silence and pretending to be brave.

Am I so set in my ways, at only thirty-eight, that I haven't been able — or willing — to see myself?

Or, is it possible there's more to it than stubbornness? Perhaps all of the things I've done, in all their kinky glory, have taken a toll on me. Not that I believe, even for one moment, there's anything wrong with what we do. But everything in my life has brought me to this moment of crisis, and I can't discount my experiences, as slave or Master. But, I realize in a blinding flash, it is my time as Master that has aged me. I have taken on too much. Or, at least, more than I ever truly wanted to. Does admitting these things make me inexcusably selfish? I am a sadist through and through, but I am also a submissive, a slave, a physical and emotional masochist, and those desires have gone unmet for far too long. I want this. *Need* it. Christopher has made me see. And yet, there remains my responsibilities.

Aimée reaches up and smooths her hand over my brow, as if she knows my head has begun to ache.

"What is it, Damon?"

"Nothing." I pause, covering her hand with mine. "No. That's a lie. It's everything. *Everything*."

"What can I do?"

Pulling her hand to my lips, I kiss it, then kiss it again. "There is nothing to be done, sweet girl. No one can do anything about this but me."

"I'm sorry," she says, the edge of another sob creeping into her voice.

"I lied again," I tell her. "There is one thing you can do for me."

Rolling on top of her, I kick her legs apart with mine, my cock hard and ready and needing her. Staring into her green, green eyes, I surge into her sweet cunt, losing myself in her eager body in order to keep from losing my mind.

Eden Bradley

CHAPTER EIGHT

It's after four in the morning—that was the time the last time I looked at the small glowing numbers on the clock on the nightstand, and I'm not certain how long I've been lying here since. I haven't slept at all.

I came three times, made Aimée come many more times than that. But that wasn't the goal tonight, was it? There was no goal tonight. Or rather, the goal was me trying to figure my shit out, as Christopher would say. I am no closer than I was when I arrived—perhaps farther away than ever. I've used Aimée for comfort, to lose myself, and it always works. For a while. Nothing ever works for more than "a while". I realize I've spent much of my life trying to fool myself into thinking sex and kink and grand events and luxurious living mean the rest goes away, but it doesn't, does it? It's all simply a cover-up. And my life has been the most spectacular cover-up. Has anyone done a grander job of it? Only a handful, perhaps. I wonder if they're any happier than I am. I wonder if any of them actually know what will make them happy.

I glance at the clock. Nearly five o'clock, and I am not happy. I've lain awake struggling with the inarguable fact that I have no idea how to be.

Peering through the darkness at Aimée's sleeping figure beside me, I reach out, gently pressing my palm to her chest to feel her heartbeat. She sighs quietly, and I think for the thousandth time how very precious she is to me. And yet...

I shake my head, trying to shake away the trembling restlessness in my body, in my fucking soul, God help me. I can't figure it all out—can't figure anything out. I can't think. Can't hold still any longer.

Sighing, I rise and get dressed as silently as possible. I can't bear to even glance at her again, my sweet girl, before I creep from the room, making my way downstairs and out the front door.

Outside, it's eerily quiet, gray fog wrapping the city like a blanket of damp air and mystery. This is something I've always loved about San Francisco, and it fits my mood now. It is as if the air itself protects me from my own whirling thoughts, from the pressure building inside my head that makes me feel as if the top of my skull will blow right off at any moment.

How can I leave her?
How can I stay?
I am fucked, fucked, fucked.

Walking up Fell Street, I wander aimlessly for a while, but it's colder than I anticipated, and so I decide to head toward a small Victorian inn I know of where I might be able to get a room for what's left of the night. I have no idea what my next move should be. I am truly lost, but not in the ways I've sought. No, I am simply *lost*, in every damn sense of the word.

My legs ache by the time I reach the end of the Panhandle—the long, narrow offshoot of Golden Gate Park that runs part of the length of Fell Street—and turn onto Stanyan Street. A few blocks later, at the corner of Stanyan and Haight, groups of homeless kids huddle under tattered sleeping bags with their dogs and their drugs and their empty bottles. They make me think of Christopher, of his time living on these very streets, and my heart hurts so badly I have to suck in a harsh, scraping lungful of cold air to try to clear him from my head. It doesn't work terribly well. Nothing does right now. I am afraid nothing will.

I am afraid.

Another two short blocks and I reach the old Stanyan Park Hotel. There is no doorman this early in the morning, but I ring the bell, and I must be well-dressed enough for the sleepy front desk clerk to assume I'm not there to rob anyone. He buzzes me in.

"Good morning," I say, doing my best to sound normal—whatever that is at this point.

"Good morning, sir."

I try not to cringe at the irony in anyone calling me that right now. "Do you have a room available?"

"We do. One of the nice suites on the top floor. Will that do?"

"Yes. Yes, that will be fine."

But as I reach for my wallet, I realize I have none. No wallet. No cell phone. I am, at this point, a runaway slave, if nothing else, and I am not as well prepared as Christopher has always been. And so, I do what I least want to do.

"My apologies, but I seem to have lost my wallet. May I use your phone to call my assistant?"

"Of course."

He sets the phone on the desk and politely turns away as I dial my House.

Three rings.

"Hallo?"

"Gilby. I need you to pick me up."

The ride back to my House is strange. I can't bear to look at anything but the back of Gilby's stubbled head and massive shoulders as he drives me through the quiet city streets in the black Audi sedan I keep on hand for my staff to use. He is quiet, asking no questions, which is something I know I can depend on, and which is, perhaps, the only way I could have called him—or anyone. But the truth is, Christopher was right—my money and position in our strange world means no one would think to question me. No one but Christopher. But I can't bear to think of him right now. I can't bear to think of anything at the moment.

We pull up in front of the Training House, and Gilby opens my door. I get out without looking at him and my valet, Robert, opens the front door, nodding as I pass into the foyer. They're being very careful with me, their respectful silence going beyond the usual deference with which I am treated by my staff, and I realize they have some sense of my current fragility. I have no idea what they must think is going on with me, but they don't dare ask, which is just as well. I can barely ask that question myself.

I climb the stairs slowly at first, then take them two at a time, my heart hammering with an odd combination of dread, anxiety and relief, until I get to my own quarters. I lock the door, which is a silly move considering no one would dare enter without my permission, and I don't even know why I am doing it. I'm not entirely clear as to why I am doing anything this morning.

After several moments of helpless pacing, I throw myself down on the big bed and close my eyes, trying desperately not to remember the times I had my two loves in this room, in this bed. It's exhausting, all this trying not to think—harder than one might expect—and soon I fall into a deep, dreamless sleep.

By the time I open my eyes, it's dark outside, and I roll onto my side, reaching into the nightstand for the Rolex I keep there—the one that belonged to Master Stephan. It's after eleven o'clock at night. How many hours have I slept? Escapism in its purist form. But no matter how many hours I've lain here, fully dressed and unconscious, nothing has changed. I'm still hurting, fucking aching and undecided.

God damn it.

Getting up, I force myself to turn on the shower, then unlock the door to my suite and call down for a tray before I step under the hot water. But even showering makes me feel too isolated, too alone in my head, and I hurry through it, dry myself off, and slip into a heavy black brocade dressing gown that isn't really me at all. It belonged to my dear Master Stephan, and I've kept it all these years. I can't even remember the last time I wore it, but I need the comfort now.

Back in my room, it seems far too small to contain my frantic energy, but I have no desire to go downstairs. I have no real desire to do anything, including eating the beautifully prepared light meal Robert has delivered for me. Instead, I lift the glass of wine from the tray, then set it back down without taking a sip. My stomach is too much in knots, and I know wine won't help me now unless I drink an entire bottle, which isn't like me. But then, *I* am not like me. My head is a mad rush of thought and emotion, a tangled mess I can't possibly sort out. Not on my own.

I go to the small console table that holds the house phone, pick it up and fidget a moment before putting it back down. Who did I think I was going to call? There are very few people who are truly my friends, people I can confide in. Truthfully, are there any at all? Is this what my life has come to? What I have made of it? Who would even understand, without my having to start at the beginning of this story, something that seems too tiring and painful to contemplate?

Perhaps one person.

I murmur to the empty room, "Fuck".

In less than an hour Robert taps at my door and announces Alexa's arrival. When I open the door, she moves into the room, all red leather, exotic perfume and uncertainty, which is something I've never sensed in her. Of course, she's never seen me in this condition, either, not even as a slave in Christopher's Palm Springs house.

She sits on the small damask sofa, her back straight, elegant as always. But there's a softness in her face I've never seen before.

I sit next to her, and she turns to stare at me, exploring my face. No, *investigating*. I can't blame her.

I rub my jaw. "Christ, Alexa, do I look that awful?"

"Yes," she says simply.

"I thought I might."

She sits quietly, waiting for me to begin, but I don't know how. Finally, she reaches out and lays a hand on my arm—a move that's completely unlike her. God, I really must be in bad shape.

"Damon, tell me what's going on with you."

"All right. Yes, okay." But I need to take several more moments to draw in a breath then exhale, trying to stop the wild tumble going on in my head. "So…I sent them away, you know, to the Primal Ranch. I thought that would be the answer. Or…no, maybe I didn't. Maybe I was fooling myself, and I didn't even do a very good job of that. But it didn't help. It changed nothing. The pain was still there. Still *is* there."

I have to get to my feet and pace off some of the burn the words flare up in my veins, threatening to make me combust, like some urban myth you read about on the Internet.

"Because you love them too much," she says, neatly summing it all up.

"Yes."

"And the question is, what do you do now?"

I pause, run a hand through my hair. "Yes. That's the fucking question."

"Some things only you can answer, Damon. I have no idea

what I would do in your position. I can't even begin to imagine what it must be like. I'm not saying that to judge you, but to tell you how drastically underqualified I feel to help you with this, other than to act as a sounding board."

"That's more than I can trust anyone else with, Alexa."

"All right, then. I'm listening."

I nod, but then again, there is the question of where to start, where to go with this. I decide to simply *go*.

"When I came to this House, it was as a slave, which I believe you now know — I'm certain Christopher explained some of this before bringing you down to the desert." I watch for her nod before continuing. "My relationship with Master Stephan built over time. I was nothing but another slave, at first. But we had a connection. He came to love me, and I came to love him, which is something I've only recently been able to recognize for what it really was. I've always had to deny the extent of my feelings for him, and I still don't fully understand why.

"Well…when he got sick, I felt as if my whole world were collapsing. How could I function without him? Without his guidance, his knowledge, his steady hand? He recognized my struggle, even as he went through chemo, even as he was actively dying. And what a selfish bastard I was for demanding that he still take care of me!"

She shakes her head. "No, Damon. You were a young man whose life was being yanked out from under him. What else could you have done?"

"Been braver. Stronger. *Better*."

"Maybe. But how old were you?"

"I was twenty-eight when he became ill, thirty when he died."

"Well, I can tell you, I'm forty, and it was only five or six years ago that I really matured, and became certain of myself, of exactly what I wanted and needed in my life. For a man of twenty-eight, thirty… That's the time when most young men are discovering themselves, and instead, you had this enormous responsibility. You were living with this enormous strain. And I'll admit something to you I've perhaps never spoken aloud. Even though I adore the lovely, tight flesh of the young slaves, a part of me always has to wonder if we rob them of some of their youth, no matter how badly they might want or need to be slaves. I don't even know that it's a terrible thing, necessarily, but in choosing this path, we gain many insights and experiences, and lose others. But that's true no matter the direction we choose. I don't blame your Master Stephan, and neither do I blame you for taking charge of your own slaves. I'm simply saying that twenty-eight is so young to have to deal with something as all-encompassing as cancer, watching someone you care for dwindle and die. And then, taking on this House. No matter what he did to prepare you, you couldn't have possibly been completely prepared. No one could."

"You don't have to be soft on me because I'm such a damn wreck, Alexa," I say, immediately regretting the bitterness in my tone.

"Come on, Damon, you know me well enough to understand I don't have to blow smoke up anyone's ass, including yours."

That almost makes me smile. "True."

"So, you took on the Training House, and all that goes with it."

"Yes. The privilege and responsibility. The commitment and the luxury."

"And you were very well prepared to do so. This is not a job for just anyone, which I well know from managing my own, smaller house. Why do you judge yourself?"

"How can I not?" I run a hand over my hair, scrubbing hard at my scalp. "And fuck, I can't believe I'm saying all of this to you. That I'm allowing *anyone* to see my doubts. My guilt."

"How much of the guilt is because Master Stephan died and you're still here?"

"I...fuck."

I have to get up and pace again, a million fragmented images flashing through my head.

Stephan lies frail and weak in bed, his face so very pale and ashen. His kidneys have been shutting down, and the plastic bottle that collects his urine via the catheter the home nurse put in him weeks ago is full of dark brown liquid. I want to know if it hurts, but he won't tell me.

"Damon, you can do this. I see it in you — the ability to direct, to

care for the slaves and the staff, to create the intricate scenarios people expect here." He pauses to take a slow, wheezing breath. "I would never ask this of you if I wasn't certain you had it in you."

"I will never be the Master you are."

"No, you will be your own man, your own sort of Master. And it will be more than good enough. You will be spectacular. Oh, I know you don't believe me now, but I promise you, it will become your second nature. It's begun to already."

I am so humbled by his words. Too humbled. Why can't I feel strengthened by the things he's saying to me? Isn't that what a true Master would feel?

"I wish it were me," I tell him quietly.

"No, you don't. And neither do I. You're so young, with your life ahead of you. And don't give me that look. I know damn well fifty-three is too young to die, but I will die shortly. Can you let me leave this world secure in the knowledge that you will carry on for me?"

I lock my gaze with his, fire burning in my veins, in my heart, which is breaking even as I say the word. "Yes. Yes. You can count on it, I swear it."

My heart breaks all over again, remembering. It twists in my chest when I remember an earlier time, a memory I've kept carefully locked away...

I am curled at the foot of my Master's bed as the rising sun lights the windows with golden light. My body may ache from being beaten and fucked, but I am filled with happiness, knowing I served him well last night, and the satiation thrums in my veins like a low, lyrical chord.

He nudges me with his foot. "You're awake, my beautiful boy. Come and kiss me."

I smile as I crawl up the bed and lie next to him, waiting for him. His eyes are a warm, whiskey brown, the lashes long and fair, and it's only in these sleepy morning moments that he allows me to see any softness in them. I treasure these moments, just as I treasure his harshness with me. But it's that stark contrast that makes mornings such bliss. I see the Yin and Yang of it, how there truly cannot be light without the darkness, perhaps even more so for people like us. Contrast is everything.

Shaking my head, I come to sit beside her again. "There was a time when he was everything to me."

"Exactly as it should be. And now?"

I know what she's asking. "And now, *they* are everything to me."

"But there is the question of your identity as a Master?"

I nod. "And there is also the question of what will become of my House, should I go to Christopher, give myself to him."

Alexa bites her lip, ripe with her trademark scarlet lipstick. "What if...what if you give the House to him, too?"

I let out a small, surprised laugh. No, not surprise—shock. "What?"

She leans toward me, her eyes glittering. "It's the perfect solution. He's more than able—we both know that. And you would still be here to help him handle any of the complicated logistics, or duties he'd prefer not to attend to. You can always add more staff as needed, more trained slaves."

I shake my head. "But Alexa, how can I...?"

She lowers her voice. "How can you appear in your own House as a slave yourself? Is that it? There's no shame or weakness in being a slave. You would tell anyone that yourself."

"I know, I know. But this is different, because—"

"Because it's you?" She lets out a short, harsh laugh. "Jesus, Damon. Do you think you're any different from the rest of us? From your darling Christopher himself? How many of us have played both sides of this kinky coin? I have. The best Masters and Mistresses have experienced being a bottom, if not a slave. We come and go through our little community, and yes, there can be a period of adjustment when someone switches, for themselves as well as for others in our circle, but we all live through it. So will you. So will the rest of us. And really, you know as well as I do how we thrive on shock value." She laughs once more, only this time there's real amusement in her tone. "We should have a coming out party for you—our crowd would lose their minds over that!"

"Remind me never to let you be the one to plan anything on my behalf."

But her blue eyes are twinkling. "I believe you're about to have very little control over that."

"I think…" I take a deep, shaky breath. "I think I am about to have control over nothing."

"Not once you call him and see if he'll still take you back. If he'll accept your offer of the House. Except you know quite well that giving yourself over is the ultimate act of power."

"Yes." Nerves suddenly make my body go tight once more. "And if he doesn't accept me, or my offer?"

"Then you go back to your old life, I suppose. If you can."

Impossible to even imagine that now. I don't even know exactly what that was. Who *I* was. No, everything has changed, and there is no going back.

CHAPTER NINE

I lean forward, elbows on my knees to cradle my aching head in my hands. "I know you're right on some level, but given the way my head is spinning right now, I can't seem to sort anything out. Everything feels so completely fucked up."

"You're unused to things being out of your control, that's all," she tells me in a reassuring tone, "but again, if you can move bravely into this new life, you won't have to worry about that, will you? But I believe you can do this. I do. Honestly, I was surprised to see you so deeply in slave space—it wasn't what I expected to find when Christopher called me. It was a little shocking. Delightfully so, but still... And I'm sure you know what that tells me about you."

I look up to meet her searching gaze. "That I'm ready to be his slave? But Alexa, just because my body can respond to that state, because my brain can go there, doesn't necessarily mean it's the right choice for me."

"The right choice as in the right fit for your needs and desires? Or do you mean the one you can live with?"

Her face is expectant as I chew on my lip for several moments, my stomach churning.

"God damn it, Alexa," I finally say in a low tone.

She smiles, the gleam back in her eyes. "I think you have your answer, Damon—the rest is simply logistics. Oh, I know it seems far more complicated than that, but it doesn't have to be. He'll take care of everything, after all. Just as you always have for everyone else."

The truth of what she's saying hits me, and it's a warm, melting relief and a new wave of fear all at once. With it comes a realization, so stark and clear I wonder how I've never completely made the connection before. Briefly, I tell her about my lost brother, Daniel, and having unlocked those gates with Christopher and Aimée, and it's much easier than it was before.

"And then you lost Master Stephan, which only compounded

your survivor's guilt. That pain is a lovely platform to dive from into BDSM, Damon, but it won't serve you well otherwise."

"I never thought it would. I never thought of it at all—or, not from start to finish. I've simply been carrying it around with me, a weight on my back. And even though I've spoken to Christopher and Aimée about it, and now you, the weight is still there."

"A weight that's caused you to reject your own needs. *Needs*, Damon, that go beyond mere wants."

"Yes. But how do I process it all? Accept these things about myself? Accept what those needs are?"

"Come on, Damon. You understand better than most that these things happen over time. You deal with your issues. You make the decision to turn yourself over, and let the rest of it fall into place. Or not. You *decide* to act from a place of strength. But I'm fairly certain none of that will be an issue here. We both know you can do this, if you choose to. Let's not talk ourselves in circles—we've just gone over this."

"But why? *Why* do you think it won't be an issue?" I am desperate to know, to hear her say it out loud—loud enough to get past the screaming in my mind that I can't quite shut off.

"Because of the strength I've seen in you from the first time we met," she says firmly. "Because of what I witnessed in Palm Springs. Your ability to submit, to endure pain and degradation, and to do it all with such love. *So* much love, for both Christopher and Aimée. And because you *will* be accepted back into our world as a slave. Oh, people may talk, but in the end, they will simply accept the shift in roles. It's our way, and you know that as well as I do. We don't allow the judgy ones in our particular circle. We're not amateurs, after all."

"No, we are hardly amateurs."

"And Damon? Do you really believe this is what Master Stephan would have wanted for you? That you deny yourself those things that are the closest to your heart? He was a dying man, as intent on his responsibilities to this House as you are now. But he cared for you, from all accounts. Would he have wanted you to spend the rest of your life doing nothing more than people, or even he, *expected* of you? Oh, I know you love being a Master—that it's a natural aspect of who you are.

Obviously. But it's far from being the only aspect, isn't it?"

I bury my face in my hands once more, letting her words roll through my tortured brain. "You're right—I know it."

"Then stop being so damn stubborn. It's late, darling, and I'm tired. And you've exhausted yourself with all this."

Is she right about that, too? Am I simply being stubborn?

No, it's more than that. I'm afraid. Of so many things. And yet…she's also right that Christopher will take care of everything. He will take care of me. And ah, God, how long has it been since anyone has taken care of me in the way he is capable of? In the way I suddenly realize I yearn for with every cell in my being?

Lifting my head, I reach for her hand and give it a squeeze. "Thank you, Alexa. I've been an idiot. I don't want to be anymore."

"Not an idiot." She shrugs. "You're simply as human as the rest of us. But you don't need to be superhuman any longer—turn that role over to him for a while."

Impatience floods my body. "I have to go to him, talk to him, see if he'll take me back."

"You always took him back. I'm fairly certain you can play that card if necessary, although I don't know that it will be."

"He'll be angry."

"Of course he will, but he is a *Master*. He won't allow himself to be ruled by anger, not even our gorgeously dangerous Christopher. Go to him. I'll let Robert see me out. And Damon? I hope to see you in our circles again soon—perhaps at Christopher's lovely house on Fell Street."

"You know about that place?"

"I know more than you think I do. But I'll let him tell you all about that." Leaning in, she brushes a quick kiss across my cheek. "Be well, my dear Damon."

"I'm trying."

Pulling back, she smiles again as she gets to her feet. "I know you are. He'll know it, too."

I watch her for a moment as she walks gracefully to the door, but the second she closes it I'm tearing through my closet, yanking out dark slacks, a white shirt, shoes. I dress as quickly as I can, then call for Gilby to bring the car around and give a few quick instructions to Robert.

It's after two in the morning, and I'm glad the House is quiet as I make my way downstairs and outside. The fog is heavy, an impenetrable blanket, as it often is at night, since San Francisco is surrounded by water on three sides. It suits my mood, my odd need to move quietly—stealthily—into the night, and my next strange and yet not-so-strange step in this journey.

Gilby remains silent as we glide over the misty streets, and I feel my head sinking a bit into subspace. I fight it, though, if only because I must be able to speak sensibly when we reach Christopher's house. I search for the right words in my mind, hoping to prepare myself somehow, but there don't seem to be any "right" words. Nothing feels right—I'm a mess, to be honest.

Sighing, I give myself over to the sensation of rolling over the pavement, to the pounding of my heart in my chest, the small knot of dread in my stomach telling me this all may go horribly wrong. But I have to try, don't I?

Have to.

We pull up in front of the gray stucco house, and I'm ridiculously relieved to see a dim light shining from behind the shutters on the top floor. They must be up there, Christopher and Aimée. *He* must be up there—the Master of my heart and, now that I've opened myself up enough to see, Master of my soul. How very poetic of me—how romantic. But he always has been, hasn't he? And I've been blind. Foolish.

I don't know how long the car has been idling at the curb before Gilby clears his throat, bringing me back to my senses.

Opening the door, I pause a moment. "You can head back to the House, Gilby. I'll call you if I need you."

"Right. Yes, Sir."

As I get out and close the car door behind me, I realize that all I truly need is up there, in his house. My heart twists in my chest, painful and lovely at the same time, and I cross the sidewalk in a few long, eager strides. Ringing the buzzer, I wait.

Eagerness and anxiety are often one and the same. They are now, as I stand in the dark and the fog, my heart already on my sleeve, as vulnerable as I've ever been in my life. And when he comes to the gate himself, dressed in his worn jeans and nothing else, I sway on my feet.

Please...

He watches me for several long moments, then he reaches out to swing the gate open. When I step forward tentatively, he reaches behind me and slams the gate shut, then gestures with a nod of his finely-sculpted chin for me to follow him up the stairs into the living room. As I obey, I bask in his dark, earthy scent, which is some ethereal essence that is both pure Christopher and pure sex. Pure animal. He is the ultimate primal beast. *My* beast, I hope.

I have no idea what he might be thinking. Oh, there's anger there, and fire. But that's always in him, always visible, even while he's sleeping. The rest is a mystery, one that makes my heart pound and my fingers tighten into fists, nails digging into my palms.

He walks into the living room, where he begins to pace.

"So, you're back," he says finally.

"Yes."

Pausing, he narrows his gaze on me, his eyes gleaming darkly. "Did you have a nice little vacation?"

"I...what?"

"Your vacation," he repeats, "the one in which you took time off from our little arrangement."

"You know I never thought of all this as 'little'."

"Didn't you?" he asks. Accuses.

"You've always left your contracts," I point out.

I immediately regret my words when real anger steals over his face, his mouth going tight. His hand slams down hard on the back of a leather chair, startling me. "This was no bullshit contract, Damon! This isn't just some deal we made. This is our fucking *lives*."

"The contracts aren't bullshit," I say quietly.

"Are you saying you don't see the difference here?"

Oh, he's really fuming. I can't blame him. "Fuck, I'm sorry—of course I do. Of course. If this weren't so important, I would never have left. I'd have never felt the need to. And I'm sorry, truly sorry. I should have left a note, or called—"

"Don't fucking grovel. It's beneath you. I don't like it."

I stop, nod my head in acknowledgement. "Will Aimée be coming down?"

"No."

"But I was hoping to talk to you both—"

"I said *no*. I won't allow it—not until you and I have talked. This is too hard on her, and she's too damn soft when it comes to you. I need to deal with you on my own terms. You and I need to deal with each other."

"Yes. You're right, of course. And this is not groveling. This is me getting a much-needed reality check."

"Then stop all this submissive crap and talk to me, man to man, because we both know if you were my slave, we wouldn't be having this conversation right now."

He's right. And just like that, my brain slams back into my head with a painful thump, and I begin to tell him about my conversation with Alexa. By the time I'm done there's a small grin quirking one corner of his mouth.

"She suggested I take over the Training House? What do you think about that?" he asks.

"Truthfully, I think perhaps it's the only way," I tell him. "I can't turn my back on my responsibilities, and who else can I possibly trust?"

"Don't flatter me, Damon."

"You know damn well it's not flattery. That wouldn't serve my purposes, would it?" My nerves are shot and my hands beginning to ache, feeling the strain of the last day or two. I run my fingers through my hair, trying to calm myself, to focus. "And you know me better than that, Christopher. You *know* me. Jesus."

"Fuck it, you're right," he says. He's at my side in a moment, wrapping his hand around the back of my neck and giving a small, quick squeeze. "I'm still getting over being pissed off, and I'm being an asshole."

I have to smile a little at that. "Yes, you are."

"Nothing new, though," he says with his wickedly crooked grin.

"No, it's nothing new."

My body is surging with the warm tide of relief, and a feeling that we are on the same page, finally—or truly negotiating our possible future together, at any rate.

"Come on. Let's sit." He sinks onto the big sofa, and I take a seat next to him. "So, if I were to do this, what would your role in the House be?"

"I would be yours, if you'll have me."

"And?" he demands without answering my poorly-phrased question.

"And I would be there to guide you or assist you as you became used to running things."

"You don't think you can be mine and Master of the House at the same time?"

I shake my head slowly. "No. And frankly, I need to *not* be—not to be the Master anymore. It's time to turn that job over to someone else. As Alexa so astutely pointed out, I need to give up that role now. I feel as if... This is going to sound stupid, perhaps, but I believe the universe or God, or whatever might be out there, has put you and Aimée and my feelings for you both in front of me now, because it truly is time for me to step down from all I've taken on. I believe this is the only way I'll get back to *myself*. Maybe to discover myself. I don't think I've actually done that yet in my life."

His gaze locked on mine, he reaches out to stroke my chin with his thumb, a move that's both utterly commanding and utterly sweet at the same time. My body goes perfectly still, soaking it in.

"Yeah, you might be right about that," he says. "And it's time for me to morph, too, to take command of my life. Of myself. To stop being so damn impetuous and force myself to focus, force myself to adopt the discipline I've been trained to and rejected mostly out of pure stubbornness." He pauses, blinking at me, his lion eyes gleaming with golden light. "Maybe my adult life really starts now. Because of you."

Love washes over me, my skin going warm, my muscles softening all over. When he pulls my face close and brushes my lips with his, I know we're going to be okay.

Pulling back, he asks, "Tell me what you want, Damon—you know I need to hear the words. Do you want me to take over the House? Do you want to belong to me? To Aimée, too?"

"I want it all, yes. But Christopher..." I need to say the words, but they're going to come out hard, rasping my throat because it feels like a risk. Because I *have* to know. "I can only do this if you love me, as I love you."

He grabs me and pulls me in roughly, pressing his mouth to mine and kissing me so hard he leaves my lips bruised. When he releases me the male taste of him still floods my mouth.

"You know damn well I love you," he says, his voice low and full of heat and gravel, his breath warm on my cheek. "Would I put up with this shit if I didn't? Would I share Aimée with you otherwise?"

I shake my head a little. "No, never."

His hand slides behind my neck once more, and the heat of it seeps immediately into my system. I inhale, breathing him in. Do I dare yet to feel that everything is right with the world?

"Christopher, I have to ask you what *you* want. Do you understand? I need to know, to hear it. Because this is huge — so much bigger than me, or us, even. There are so many other people involved, and I have to consider everything."

"I know you do. Don't think I haven't realized the scope of this situation," he assures me. "Look, it won't be an easy transition, and it's going to last a while. Everyone won't adjust right away, but it'll be easier that so many of them have already seen me as a Master. It might take a little longer for them to accept you as a slave, but as Alexa said, they will. I'll fucking see to it, if nothing else, but I don't think that'll be necessary."

I hope he's right, because relying on him to strong-arm their acceptance of me will make it that much harder for *me* to accept it.

"So, this is what I propose," he says. "No. This is the goddamn way it'll be: I will accept the position as Master of the Training House. You and Aimée will belong to me, and I'll take over ownership of any other current House slaves you have. And I think I *will* have that 'coming out' party Alexa suggested. What an insanely evil idea." He cracks a smile. "Evil and fucking effective as hell. We'll relaunch the Training House under new management. And before then, you'll talk to your staff with me and we'll get the logistics worked out. I'll take over the suite that belongs to you, and you and our girl will stay with me there — our happy little family."

My body is buzzing with love for him, with desire so acute it makes me ache all over.

"What's going on your head?" he demands.

"You always could see right through me." Which is still both comforting and terrifying. Will his perceptiveness ever cease to amaze me?

"Spill, Damon."

I sigh. "It's difficult to believe that…that I can have this."

His golden eyes narrow. "Someday soon, I'm gonna beat this martyr shit out of you."

"I certainly hope so," I tell him with a wry grin.

"We can start right now," he says, reaching for me.

He has me on my feet and stripped bare in mere seconds. Then kicks my legs out from under me, driving me to my knees and leaving me naked and hard and yearning. He moves behind me, and I have one moment to take in the sweet sound of his zipper coming down before he lowers himself to one knee, bending the other at my side.

The pain as he enters my ass is searing, but I welcome the sensation, my body firing on all cylinders as he leans in and bites my shoulders, my back, the back of my neck. I stifle my cries, pride kicking in, but then I realize what I'm doing. I can't hang onto control any longer. That's what this is all about—this dynamic, allowing myself to love. To let go.

Have to let it all go.

He bites me harder, plowing into me and fucking me in long, punishing strokes, probably tearing my ass up, with no lube and his magnificent roughness. And I do let it go, pleasure and pain, love and relief all welling up in my throat as I issue an animal cry that's half growl and half sob.

I'm about to come, barely able to hold it back, when he flips me over onto my back on the floor, and in superb Christopher style, he grabs me by the throat, squeezing the tiniest bit. He chokes me out by allowing the pressure to build a little at a time as he presses his beautiful cock into me once more, and I'm lost in a haze of sweet pleasure and oxygen deprivation that has my mind and my eyes glazed.

He looks into my face, and for the first time ever, his features really let go, loosening and softening as much as I have on the inside. In a mad, lovely rush I realize I am seeing him for the first time, down to the bottom of who he is. He is my beautiful Christopher, my Master. My love. All the exquisite pain and tragedy that has gone into creating him, and he is finally showing me for the first time. I am stunned. Awed. In love.

When Aimée's lovely face appears over his shoulder, he turns and smiles at her, taking her hand and drawing her in. She's wearing nothing but a little silk slip in the same pale green as her eyes, and he slides it over her head with one deft hand, revealing her perfect breasts, the nipples a dark pink, full and luscious. Her sex is a pretty little V between her sleek thighs. But my gaze has to return to her face, to the curve of her pale cheeks, to her sensual lips, and perhaps most of all, to her gorgeously gleaming eyes. An entire world lives in there, deep and dark, sweet and light, all the sides that are her—*our* girl.

I reach for her, as well, and together Christopher and I pull her down onto the floor with us. He guides her to straddle me, his strong arms around her, lifting and lowering her, and then spreading my thighs, still entirely in charge.

And yet there is a certain fluidity to every motion, to each moment of flesh meeting flesh as I thrust into her, as he thrusts into me. He sinks his teeth into the side of her neck, and she sighs, leaning her head back against his shoulder. With his free hand, he digs his nails into my hip, then my waist, and it is that pain and pleasure continuum, where it's impossible to tell where one sensation begins and the other ends. Except that it doesn't have to end. I am *theirs*. And they are mine.

Desire builds, soars, and I fall from that keen edge, into the darkness inside me. But it's a darkness they share with me. What a relief, to know it's true.

Our beautiful Aimée tightens around me, groans, then cries out. "Damon! Ah, Christopher…my Master, yes! Oh, oh…"

Then Christopher is stabbing into me, his gaze on mine, fierce with his peaking pleasure. He drives his cock so hard inside me, the pain rises, spirals, and so does my need to come.

Christopher says, "Yes, do it!"

As I growl out my pleasure, he yells his, pumping into me. "Fuck, yeah!"

We fall into a heap on the floor, the scent of come sharp in the air. Their skin is warm on mine, their panting breaths in my ears like music—that and the knowledge that we are together.

Aimée curls into my side, tucked between Christopher and

me. "I love you, Damon. *We* love you."

Stroking her face, I murmur, "I know you do. I finally know it. And I love you, my beautiful girl, and my beautiful Master. God, what a strange mess this was."

Christopher laughs. "We're a fucking strange bunch, but would we have ended up together any other way? I always say we are the freaks of the world, and that feels more true now than ever."

"Yes, we are," Aimée agrees. "But we are freaks together. We are *together*."

"I just realized…" I start, then have to pause to get a firm hold on the idea forming in my head. "…that despite my position in the kink world, and the brave face I've worn all these years, a part of me has felt, until now, that perhaps I didn't deserve this. That despite my protests about how those in our community are simply expressing their desires and working out conflicts in a healthy manner, maybe I didn't feel I deserved to have this. To have love."

I have to stop once more, to swallow down the emotion clogging my throat. Or maybe it's the heaviness left over from Christopher choking me.

And how apt that I'd think of such a thing in the middle of this discussion. Oh yes, we are the weirdos of the world. It makes me smile. "I've felt entirely deserving of having any luxury, any indulgent fetish or slave or piece of equipment at my disposal, and yet, I didn't feel I deserved to have the two of you."

Christopher gives my face a gentle slap. "I never think I deserve any damn thing in life. It's not even about that."

"But it is," comes Aimée's soft tone, and I'm glad she's said it because Christopher still obviously has lessons to learn too.

"If you say so, prettiness," he says.

"No, please don't," she begs. "It's the truth. What we do, the things we desire—I don't care how odd it must be to other people. It's *us*, and we are the only ones who need to approve. As you would say, Master, fuck them all if they don't like it."

He and I both laugh at that, at our sweet, sophisticated and well-trained Aimée using such profane language.

"Good girl," Christopher says. "Our wise girl."

"Yes," she agrees, "sometimes I am. Being in this life has made me realize my value as much as it has you, Damon. And Master Christopher, you will, too. We'll help you. Oh, I know you don't like to hear that you need help with anything, but isn't that part of our job?"

Christopher kisses her on the cheek, and she squeals when he bites her there. "Your job, little one, is simply to love us."

It hits me like a lightning strike: our job—all of us—is to love each other. That is the ultimate truth. The life I've been living all this time, ever since I lost my brother, and then my Master, has been a sham. I've been protecting my heart from the very thing it craves. *Requires.*

As Aimée said, the rest of it—the kink—doesn't matter. It's *this*. Hearts beating together in between breathless moments of pain, of pleasure.

Reaching for our girl, I hold her soft cheek. "You are wiser than you know. It's you—both of you, but you're the one who started these ideas in my head, Aimée—who's made me see the truth. It's love that is my emancipation, my redemption. I am no longer the Master, but simply Damon, and I can finally accept him for who and what he is. I've found what I require. Who I require. Who I am. And it's you, my lovely girl, and my Master. What else could possibly have pulled me from the stuck place I've been half buried in all these years, busily convincing myself that was a life?" My chest goes tight, swelling with emotion so strong, so deep, it takes my breath away. "Thank you."

Christopher smiles, that crooked grin we all fall in love with, but no one more than Aimée and me.

"Well, you're welcome, of course. But don't worry, you'll repay me. With pain and service, and whatever else I can think up for you."

"I have no doubt that I will. Thank you for that, too. I need it. I need it almost as much as I need you both to love me back."

"We do," Aimée says.

"I know you do. It was myself I doubted. But not anymore. I finally know myself, what I need, what I deserve. I believe it."

It's the truth—a truth I would have thought impossible. I am comfortable in my skin, whether I am slave or Master. It no longer matters. I simply am *me*. And that's good enough. Finally. Because my two loves, and love itself, have shown me the way.

ABOUT EDEN:

New York Times and USA Today Bestselling author Eden Bradley writes dark, edgy erotica and erotic romance for Berkley Heat (as both Eden Bradley and Eve Berlin), Bantam/Delta, Harlequin Spice and HQN, and Samhain Publishing, as well as indie publishing. Two of her books have been Romantic Times Top Picks, and her novel FORBIDDEN FRUIT was profiled in Cosmopolitan Magazine's Red Hot Reads column in 2008. More recently her BDSM book THE DARK GARDEN hit the top paperback fiction charts in the UK. She has received or been nominated for numerous awards, including the Holt Medallion and the Passionate Plume, and several of her books have been RT Book Reviews Top Picks. Her books have been translated into German, French, Romanian, Portuguese, Spanish, Italian, Czech, Polish, Indonesian and Japanese.

As someone who has been involved in BDSM practice for much of her adult life, she relates in particular to her BDSM and kink stories, infusing them with her own truth about kink practice from her life experiences.

Eden has appeared regularly on Playboy Radio's 'Night Calls' and the Hollywood In the Flesh readings. She loves art, shoes, tattoos, her Boston Terrier puppy, reading smutty books, chocolate and sex, of course, not necessarily in that order.

**Sign up for Eden's newsletter and be sure not to miss all her latest book news, special contests, appearances and sneak peeks!

http://tinyurl.com/ncklmhz

Visit Eden online:

Website: www.EdenBradley.com
Group blog: www.Smutketeers.com
Twitter: https://twitter.com/EdenBradley
Facebook: https://www.facebook.com/AuthorEdenBradley.EveBerlin
Eden's Pinterest boards: http://www.pinterest.com/edenandeve /

~~~

More from Eden Bradley

Now Available from Berkley Heat

Dangerous Series
Dangerously Broken
Dangerously Bound

Edge Series
Pleasure's Edge
Desire's Edge
Temptation's Edge

Now Available from Samhain Publishing

Sanctuary

Ink & Iron Series
Obsession

Midnight Playground Series
The Seeking Kiss
BloodsongThe Turning Kiss
Eversong Rogue

Celestial Seductions Series
Winter Solstice
Spring Equinox
Summer Solstice

From The Smutketeers - Eden's novella in the Wasteland Continuity Series
The Breeder

Now Available from Bantam/Delta
The Dark Garden
The Darker Side of Pleasure
Exotica: Seven Days of Kama Sutra, Nine Days of Arabian Nights -
Hot Nights, Dark Desires
Forbidden Fruit
A 21st Century Courtesan
The Beauty of Surrender

Now Available from Harlequin Spice
Naughty Bits (anthology)
Soul Strangers
Night Moves

Also From Eden Bradley

The Training House Series
Book One: Girl
Book Two: Boy
Book Three: Master

Breaking Skye (A San Francisco Doms book)
Pleasure Point (A San Francisco Doms book and part of the Invitation to Eden continuity series)
Dangerously Inked (A Dangerous Romance Series Spin-off)
Ever: The Turning (A Midnight Playground Series spin-off)
Tempt Me Twice
The Lovers
Fallen Angel

Printed in Great Britain
by Amazon